Awake. But why was he already sitting, and why was he ringed by spotlights? Where—?

A voice—speaking in an English accent—asked: "Are the lights too bright? I can dim them, if you wish."

Caine nodded and squinted.

"What is the last thing you remember?"

Caine thought back: he was on the lunar suborbital ferry to Perry City—and then nothing. As though someone had snipped a filmstrip in the middle of a scene.

Abruptly, Caine no longer saw the still-blinding lights: finding no memories to fill that blank space, his awareness exploded inward, like a multitude of rushing hands, scrabbling in a dark closet.

Caine felt a cool hand on his shoulder and suddenly he was seeing again, looking into dark brown eyes in a thin face, skin the color of seared wheat. The eyes were patient, concerned. "Steady now. Tell me: what do you remember?"

"I remember heading to Perry City. But after that—" Caine felt a snap-frost of panic coat his body. "What the hell has happened to me? Have I been in an accident?"

"You were taken into—let's call it protective custody."

"Protective custody? Why? And what kind of protective custody would cause me to black out, or—" *Or lose my muscle tone,* Caine suddenly realized, seeing his wrists and arms for the first time.

Long-face-brown-eyes nodded at Caine's sudden fixation with his limbs. "In your case, Mr. Riordan, protective custody meant being placed in cryogenic suspension."

BAEN BOOKS by
CHARLES E. GANNON

The Starfire Series
Extremis (with Steve White)

The Ring of Fire Series
1635: Papal Stakes (with Eric Flint)

Fire with Fire
Trial by Fire (forthcoming)

FIRE WITH FIRE

CHARLES E. GANNON

WITHDRAWN

FIRE WITH FIRE

This is a work of fiction. All the characters and events portrayed in this book are fictional, and any resemblance to real people or incidents is purely coincidental.

A Baen Books Original

Baen Publishing Enterprises
P.O. Box 1403
Riverdale, NY 10471
www.baen.com

ISBN: 978-1-4767-3632-7

Cover art by Sam Kennedy

First paperback printing, March 2014

Library of Congress Control Number: 2012051562

Distributed by Simon & Schuster
1230 Avenue of the Americas
New York, NY 10020

Pages by Joy Freeman (www.pagesbyjoy.com)
Printed in the United States of America

ACKNOWLEDGMENTS:

My profound thanks go to—

— my loyal legion of advance readers, but particularly Tom MacCarrol;

— Ian Tregillis, PhD, high-energy physicist at Los Alamos, who vetted the theoretical logic of the Wasserman Drive;

— my late mother, who believed that I could and should pursue the calling and life of an author;

— and my late father, who imbued me with his own interest in the future and the limitless possibilities of space.

But above all, this book is . . .

DEDICATED TO:

My wife Andrea Trisciuzzi,
without whom it would
never have been written.

CONTENTS

Interstellar shift links operative as of July 2118
(max shift range: 8.35 ly)

(Biogenic worlds are labeled in **BOLD FACE**)

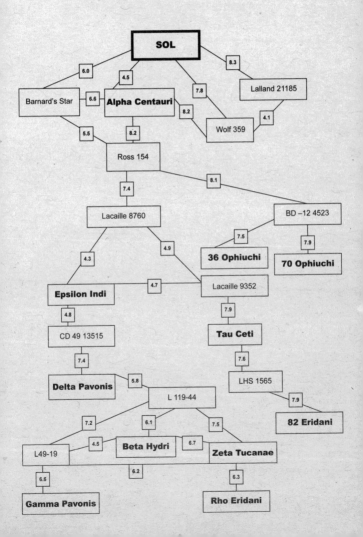

FIRE WITH FIRE

BOOK ONE

CONTACT

Prologue

Perry City, Luna
September, 2105

The Taiwanese captain bowed quickly when his temporary commander—USSF Admiral Nolan Corcoran—rounded the corner. "Admiral Corcoran, I—"

Corcoran, a tall, broad-shouldered man whose sharp blue eyes and trim physique belied his advancing age, raised a silencing hand. He ignored the captain's waiting covert ops team, and moved instead to the cryogenic suspension unit resting on a gurney just behind them. "Is that the intruder?"

"Yes, Admiral. We found him right outside the door to your quarters. I'm sure you have the report by now."

"We do, Captain Chen," answered a second man who came around the same corner that Corcoran had. "But the details are sketchy."

Chen did not recognize the man, who spoke with an English accent. "Apologies, sir: I relayed what I had at the time."

The tall, thin Englishman looked up from his dataslate. "So you weren't present at the incident?"

Chen stood even straighter. "Nonetheless, I am the team leader, sirs."

Corcoran canted his head toward the Englishman. "Mr. Downing is not implying you were at fault, Captain Chen. We know it's your job to take responsibility for what happens on your watch. Even if you weren't there yourself. Now, what more have you learned since alerting us?"

"The subject—Mr. Riordan—was detected near your quarters at 2020 hours GMT, Admiral. He was behaving in a suspicious manner, apparently attempting to force entry. Since you had shared classified information with him earlier today, we feared that he intended to steal additional, sensitive data from your suite."

Downing stared at the cryogenic suspension unit. "And he resisted so strongly that you had to render him unconscious and stick him in a cold cell?"

Chen felt sweat rising on his upper lip. "That was, in hindsight, an excessive response. However, when accosted, Riordan turned sharply and his hand was concealed in a bag. Our operative had originally conjectured it might hold tools, but then feared that it might conceal a weapon. So the subject was—subdued."

Corcoran nodded, but, Chen noted, without the peripheral signs of reassurance that were common among Western commanders. "That explains why he's unconscious. Why did you put him in a cold cell?"

Chen's upper lip was now thoroughly wet with perspiration. "Sirs, you were on the Far Side. I had no way of knowing if you had received our communications. And we had to act quickly."

Downing folded his arms. "Why?"

"I reasoned that Mr. Riordan's books might have

made him too well-known for us to detain until you returned. And if the local authorities had discovered him in our custody, that would have necessitated explaining why my team is here at all, thereby attracting more attenti—"

"Yes, you had a difficult situation," Corcoran said. And Chen saw that he meant it, but was also disappointed. Now that Caine Riordan was in cold sleep, there was no way to awaken him without calling attention to the covert activities being undertaken on Luna. Which meant that—

"Have you informed our contacts that we will need to initiate a 'missing, presumed dead' scenario to cover up Mr. Riordan's disappearance?"

"Yes, sir."

"Very good. Mr. Downing will need access to the corridor security footage. We'll overwrite the recording of the incident with 'neutral view' footage. See to that quickly, Rich."

The Englishman grumbled. "Let's just hope somebody hasn't reviewed the video logs already." He moved off to establish communication with their operative inside Perry City's security force. Corcoran turned back to Chen. "And what were the contents of the bag Mr. Riordan was carrying?"

The Taiwanese captain handed it to the admiral, who looked inside as Downing called over, "We're clear; no one's screened the security footage, yet."

The retired admiral stared down into the bag for several seconds before handing it back to Chen. "Keep the contents with Mr. Riordan for now. I'll have need of them later."

Chen did not allow himself to look puzzled. "Yes, sir."

Downing had returned. He looked at Caine Riordan's deathly white face, made blue by the glass of the cryocell's lid. "You know, I believed Riordan when he said he wouldn't reveal our work here." He shook his head, ran a hand rearwards over his prominent widow's peak. "Somehow, I still believe him."

Corcoran's response was quiet. "Well, that's a moot point now."

Downing shrugged. "No tools for breaking and entering, then?" He scanned the area. "So what was in the bag?"

"Nothing," answered Corcoran. "Nothing of importance, at any rate."

Chen almost started in surprise, managed not to glance down at the bag he was holding.

Downing shook his head again. "I'll make arrangements to have Riordan's cold cell shipped to our holding facility in—"

"No, Rich. The Taiwanese will have to transfer Caine from their cryogenic system to ours, first. We can't take receipt of a foreign cryocell: too likely that someone will ask an awkward question."

Downing nodded. "Right," he said. "I'll set up the exchange paperwork now." He moved off to send the necessary orders.

When Downing was well out of earshot, Corcoran looked down at the cold cell again and spoke to Chen in a very low tone. "Because your cryogenic technology is so different from ours, I imagine Mr. Riordan will experience a difficult reanimation."

"Oh no, Admiral," Chen corrected in a voice that was both deferential and enthusiastic. "This cryocell utilizes Taiwan's improved pre-toxification system. It is vastly superior to our current models. Memory loss has been reduced to the same level as your 'slow freeze' technology. Indeed, recent studies—"

Corcoran looked up from the cold cell, his eyes unblinking. "I said, Mr. Chen, that this will be a difficult reanimation. In fact, it will be very difficult, and I'm sure the memory loss will be even worse than with your older models." Corcoran still did not blink. "Do I make myself clear?"

Chen had come to the conclusion that Western commanders were not particularly good at fixing underlings with stern, even terrifying, stares. Now, looking into Nolan Corcoran's blue eyes, he suddenly found himself revising his opinion. "Y-yes, Admiral. Mr. Riordan's reanimation will be most difficult. Singularly difficult."

But Corcoran was staring down at the cryocell again. The look on his face puzzled Chen: was it guilt, regret, resolve—or all three?

Chen turned to his security detachment. "Flag Mr. Riordan for 'augmented' reanimation prior to transfer back to the US authorities."

"What kind of augmentation?" asked Chen's adjutant, taking Riordan's bag when his superior held it out toward him.

"Short term memory suppression. Chemical and electroconvulsive."

"How intensive?"

Chen fixed his underling with a baleful stare of his own. "Do you really have to ask?"

PART ONE

Approaching heliopause,
Junction system (Lacaille 8760)

March–April, 2118

Chapter One .

Caine Riordan felt himself floating back up to awareness through fragments of many dreams. It seemed as though, in the midst of this waking, he had eaten, gone back to sleep, had conversations, other dreams, more meals, then finally...

Awake. But why was he already sitting, and why was he ringed by spotlights? Where—?

A voice—speaking in an English accent—asked: "Are the lights too bright? I can dim them, if you wish."

Caine nodded, squinted, seeking the source of the voice.

"What is the last thing you remember?"

Odd question. Caine thought back: he was on the lunar suborbital ferry to Perry City—and then nothing. As though someone had snipped a filmstrip in the middle of a scene. First he was there, and then he was here. And between the two—nothing.

Abruptly, Caine no longer saw the still-blinding lights: finding no memories to fill that blank space, his awareness exploded inward, like a multitude of

11

rushing hands, scrabbling in a dark closet. But instead of touching something tangible, they only encountered more yawning darkness, into which he was falling, falling, falling...

Caine felt a cool hand on his shoulder and suddenly he was seeing again, looking into dark brown eyes in a thin face, skin the color of seared wheat. Male, early middle-aged but lean, and seamed enough to look older, brown hair receding from either side of a widow's peak. The eyes were patient, concerned. "Steady now. Tell me: what do you remember?"

"I remember heading to Perry City. But after that—" Caine felt a snap-frost of panic coat his body. "What the hell has happened to me? Have I been in an accident?"

Downing retrieved a folder from a black, wire-frame table that Caine only now distinguished against the darkness. "You were taken into—let's call it protective custody."

"Protective custody? Why? And what kind of protective custody would cause me to black out, or—" *Or lose my muscle tone,* Caine suddenly realized, seeing his wrists and arms for the first time: *my God, I must have lost five kilos. More. How long have I—?*

Long-face-brown-eyes nodded at Caine's sudden fixation with his limbs. "In your case, Mr. Riordan, protective custody meant being placed in cryogenic suspension."

Terror pulsed from the rear of Caine's skull, across his back, and out into his arms and legs. "How long have I been in cold sleep?"

The crow's feet bracketing the dark brown eyes bunched in a wince. "Thirteen years: it is now 2118."

Caine felt a trembling in his limbs, was unsure

whether it was a muscular spasm, or a fear reaction. Waking up after thirteen years felt like a surreal reversal of learning that you had only a dozen years or so left to live. This way, it was not he who was going to die sooner than expected, it was everyone else. There was also a sharp, sudden fear of personal obsolescence: *will I even have a place in this world?*

Caine shook off that doubt, willed himself not to shudder again, wasn't entirely successful. "Why was I cryogenically suspended? That's a risky process—or it was thirteen years ago."

"By comparison to today, yes. But the risk to you was a great deal less serious than the threat you posed to us."

"I posed a threat to you?"

"Your investigations for the Independent Interplanetary News Network jeopardized crucial national interests."

That's right: I was on my way to Luna to conduct research. Aloud: "And so you decided to 'sedate' me before I could step off the shuttle?"

"Oh, no. You debarked safely on Luna and were quite active for just under one hundred hours."

"Then why don't I remember any of those one hundred hours?"

Mr. Long-face-brown-eyes tilted his head apologetically. "Side effect of the cold sleep, I'm afraid."

"Hold on. Cold sleep only disrupts memories that haven't been fixed in the brain by a natural sleep cycle. So at most, I should have lost twenty-four hours. But I've lost more than four days. What caused the extra memory loss? And what happened during that time?"

"I wish I knew, but my superiors didn't share that

information with me. I'll look into it when I get access to the full records, back on Earth."

But for now, how utterly convenient for you. With no memories of those one hundred crucial hours, Caine had no way of knowing if Long-face-brown-eyes was telling the truth or not. *So did I give them grounds to put me on ice? Or is that just a shrewd lie, an attempt to make me feel responsible for my own condition?* A hot wave of resentment shriveled Caine's uncertainties: either way, he was the one who had lost thirteen years, not his captors. "And *you* are...?"

Caine was gratified to see the other man blink, but Long-face-brown-eyes recovered quickly: "I am Richard Downing."

"And who do you work for? Why are *you* here?"

"I handle special projects for the government."

"Which government? That accent doesn't come from Mobile, Maine, or the Midwest."

"Quite right, but I do work for the American government, and I'm here to help you get reoriented. And to prepare you."

Caine didn't like the sound of that. "Prepare me for what?"

"Let's just say I'm here to prepare you to investigate the biggest story of your life."

"Then you've got the wrong guy. I'm an analyst, not a reporter."

Downing shrugged. "That's not how it appeared to us when you came to Perry with your IINN credentials."

"Look: that was a one-time deal so I could get to the Moon and finish my research on lunar budget cover-ups. IINN read about my suspicions in *Time*, asked me to write an exclusive feature on whatever I found—and I could hardly say 'no' to top rates and all expenses paid. Hell, I just wish I could remember *what* I found."

Downing smiled. "You found that the visible Commonwealth development on Luna barely accounted for half of the new expenditures."

"I already knew that. My guess was that a lot of government craft weren't actually completing their listed Luna-Earth runs—"

"But, instead, were going from Tycho up to Perry City at the north pole, and then to the Far Side." Downing nodded. "So you went on a little walk-about and discovered that our cometary ice-mining cover story was a sham."

"So it *was* a cover-up for some other operation."

"Yes. As you also guessed, we were manufacturing antimatter, using the twenty-four/seven solar power available at Perry."

"So once I got some solid evidence, you cryoed me: surest way of keeping me silent."

"Logical, but no; we approached you and explained the situation. And you agreed to sit on the story."

"Then why the hell *did* you coldcell me?"

"You were not put in suspension by us, but by Taiwanese security operatives that were—well, 'loaned' to us. They saw you preparing to enter my superior's suite, surmised that you had lied when you agreed to sit on the story, and were instead attempting to steal evidentiary documents. They stunned you, tried to contact us directly, couldn't."

"Why?"

Downing sighed. "Security blackout; we were on the Far Side. Only communiqués of national urgency."

"So they didn't know what to do with me."

"Well, we learned later that some wanted to kill you."

"*Kill* me?"

"Yes."

"Christ sakes—kill me over an antimatter plant?"

"No. Over what it was built to enable, which you had started hypothesizing shortly after your arrival."

Which put those hypotheses in Caine's one-hundred-hour dead zone, along with the other lost memories of his time on the Moon. But a vague recollection—perhaps a wild guess from his prelunar investigations—teased a conjecture into existence. *Antimatter: gram for gram the most potent energy source known. Not good for weapons, since its containment requirements make it much harder to work with than radioactives. So why would anyone need all that antimatter in one place, at one time—?*

Caine blurted it out before he confirmed his thinking. "Interstellar travel: you were creating the power supply for a starship."

Downing smiled. "Yes."

"And did it work?"

Downing leaned back, considered the windowless walls. "Rather. We are currently in the Junction system. Technically, it's still listed as Lacaille 8760. But only astrographers use that label, now."

Caine had to focus—hard—in order to stay on track: "Okay: so now that interstellar travel is public knowledge, I'm free to go, right?" But even as he asked it, Caine knew there had to be a catch: otherwise, why take him light-years away from Earth before waking him up?

Downing shifted uncomfortably in his chair. "Ultimately, it was not the interstellar travel we had to keep

a secret. It was the mere fact that you were coldcelled
at all. Even after interstellar travel—and colonies—
became commonplace, we still couldn't reanimate you."

Caine understood. "Because then people would
want to know who had the authority to put me in a
deep freeze and get everyone to think I was missing,
presumed dead, for thirteen years."

Downing nodded.

"Well, since you woke me up, you're obviously ready
to answer the question if it comes from me: so, on
whose authority did you coldcell me?"

Downing seemed to retract into himself for a
moment: whatever was about to come out was apparently kept deep within. "I am—call it the executive
officer—for the Institute of Reconnaissance, Intelligence, and Security. IRIS, for short. Officially, it is a
civilian think tank housed at the Naval War College."

"And unofficially?"

Downing resisted the same retractile reflex he'd
combated a moment earlier. "The Institute covertly
coordinates the actions of, and analyzes data gathered
by, the world's various intelligence services."

Caine stared, then shook his head. "No, I don't buy
that: intelligence organizations would never cooperate
that closely."

"Not knowingly. Which is why IRIS exists: to provide
an invisible intelligence locus that is aware of, and
able to coordinate responses to, our new global crisis."

"How can something be a 'global' crisis if only your
handful of analysts are even aware of it?"

"If something endangers the whole world, then
it's a global crisis—regardless of whether one or one
million persons are aware of the danger."

"Okay, so what the hell caused this secret global crisis?"

Downing frowned. "Our first interstellar missions were extremely circumspect. And so we asked ourselves: if there's anyone else out here, wouldn't they explore the same way? Accordingly, we started watching for subtle signs—"

"And now you've found something. Out here. And that's your new secret."

"Yes. We've received reports that point to the possibility of past exosapience on Delta Pavonis Three. But we can't investigate it with any of our contacts in the military or intelligence services, not without drawing attention to both the site and the Institute. So we need you to go there—on your own—and report back on what you find."

Caine considered this rather surreal scheme and quickly arrived at three possible alternatives. Firstly, he might be hallucinating—in which case he had nothing to lose if he agreed to go looking for exosapients.

If, on the other hand, he was not hallucinating, Downing could be either lying or telling the truth—but whichever it was, he and whoever he worked for were serious enough to abduct and coldcell Caine for a very long time. So if Caine refused to cooperate, Downing might decide he was a liability that had to be eliminated. Meaning that Caine had to appear to cooperate, if only to buy enough time to escape.

Or, lastly, it was possible that Downing *was* telling the truth—in which case there was so much at stake that Caine could not, in good conscience, refuse. So all logical roads seemed to lead to cooperation, albeit by very different paths.

But damn it, Caine didn't like being impressed labor, and he didn't have to make Downing's job easy. So his answer took the form of a grudging mutter: "I'll think about it."

However, that attempt at gruff defiance came out pathetically slurred: "Althinka bowt."

Caine started, stared at Downing—and discovered the tall Englishman was becoming a dark gray silhouette, shrinking against the burgeoning, burning lights. "Whu—wuzhapn me?" Caine mumbled.

And then the world contracted, sank, and he plummeted down into the black hole that it became.

MENTOR

Downing checked the monitors attached to Caine's chair as two orderlies eased the tall, unconscious American into a gurney.

"How is he?" asked Nolan Corcoran's voice from speakers hidden behind baffles in the debriefing chamber's matte black walls.

Downing nodded toward the concealed observation booth. "Passed out. Again. But he's doing better than yesterday. Pupil dilation and contraction rates are back to normal. So are his EEG and the levels of his acetylcholine, serotonin, potassium, and endorphins. I daresay he'll remember most of today's conversation."

"Did he recall any of yesterday's session?"

"No, nor of the two days before that. Riordan's brain chemistries were too imbalanced to form true memories. Until now, that is. Huzzah and hooray."

"All good news, so why the bitter tone, Richard?"

Downing dismissed the orderlies with a wave.

"I'm bitter because there's simply no indication that he had any intention of leaking the story on the Far Side anti-matter plant." Downing stalked back into the spartan observation room"So whatever Riordan was doing outside your suite thirteen years ago, Nolan, it wasn't to break in and steal secrets."

"No," Nolan said quietly, "probably not."

"So essentially, we're now sending a perfectly innocent man on a clandestine mission to the far reaches of interstellar space." Downing sat and crossed his arms. "Besides, Riordan's not suited for covert operations. And I do not mean his skills: I mean his character."

Corcoran, avoiding Downing's eyes, scanned the day's bio data. "What's wrong with Caine's character?"

"There's nothing wrong with it—and that's the problem. He made a career out of speaking truth to power—and getting fired for doing so. In short, he's *too* straight an arrow for this line of work. And we can't change that." *And damn it, we shouldn't even try. It's bad enough that we have to lie for a living; we've no right to corrupt Riordan, too.*

But Nolan was shaking his head. "You're wrong, Rich; he'll get the job done. Besides, there are two shifts left before you reach Delta Pavonis: seventy days, almost. That is plenty of training time."

"With all due respect, Admiral, that is hogwash. That might be a lot of training time for an operative who already has the right background: military, counterintelligence, even police work. But an author and analyst?"

Nolan nodded. "Yes, he's an author—and a big part of his success was that when he analyzed military or space policy, he got his hands dirty. He went and learned the ropes himself. He's gone through Basic and part of ROTC, and was on site in some pretty dangerous situations, like the Pretoria Quarantine. And as for dealing with shady characters—well, he's had an arm's-length relationship with the press for ten years, so we know he can think on his feet and smell hidden agendas a mile off." Nolan glanced out the observation panel at the limp body lying on the gurney; Riordan's auburn hair was lank with sweat, his half-lidded green eyes as inert as those of a corpse. "Caine will do just fine."

Downing grunted, picked up his dataslate from the booth's control panel. "Nolan, there's one last thing you might want to consider: a straight arrow like Riordan might veer from his initial trajectory if he begins to doubt the integrity of the bowmen who launched him."

Corcoran nodded. "I've considered it. Anything else?"

Downing shrugged. "No. I'll be heading off to dinner, then. Coming, Nolan?"

The retired admiral did not look away from Riordan when he replied. "Thanks, Rich. I'm not hungry yet. I'll see you tomorrow."

Downing nodded. "Bright and early." He entered the security code for the debriefing chamber's exit. It hissed open.

But as Downing stepped into the corridor beyond, he heard a faint sound behind him: Corcoran had left the observer's booth, was already next to Riordan's gurney. And, just as the security door closed, Downing noticed that Nolan had abandoned his customary military bearing. He looked more like a troubled father standing beside the bed of a desperately ill child.

Chapter Two

ODYSSEUS

Annoyed, Caine glanced up at the training area's control booth. "Do you have to keep distracting me while I try to memorize this circuitry?" He had frayed another wire end.

Downing nodded down at him. "It's part of the training. If you ever need to jury-rig a command override, or cut a control circuit, you will probably be in a loud, chaotic, and dangerous environment."

Caine looked around as buzzers shrieked and lights flashed erratically. "At least you left out the dangerous parts."

"In this scenario, the hatch just to your left—the one you're trying to bypass now—opens directly to space. And you are not wearing a spacesuit."

"Well, that's not a big deal, since the vacuum is just make-believe."

"That's a dangerous assumption, Caine."

"But this is just training. You wouldn't—"

"I suggest you work while we talk. A tight schedule such as ours means we have to train you using the fastest form of operant conditioning: negative reinforcement. So failures *will* have unpleasant consequences."

Caine found that the hatchway seemed slightly ominous, now. He started stripping the next wire more vigorously. "Yeah, but this is a training exercise—"

"And, as I said, part of it is to train you to perform tasks while being distracted. So, as you work, I will continue answering the questions you asked about IRIS. To resume, the Institute's primary mandate is to reduce our home system's vulnerability to exosapient invasion."

Caine twisted the exposed wires. "If the exosapients have a technological edge, you'd be winning a victory just to get them to *land* on Earth itself."

Downing paused. "And how would that be a victory?"

"Hell, it's better than having them exterminate us from orbit." Caine looked for the green lead, found it snugged behind the red one: *good thing I'm not color blind.* "Look: if alien invaders beat us in space, they could stay in Earth orbit and play 'drop the rock' until they've battered us back into the Stone Age. Of course, if they're genocidal, they'll do that anyway—and none of this matters."

"Wouldn't mass landings be as bad as bombardment?"

"You won't be facing mass landings." Caine fumbled the multitool: it grazed across two leads, imparted a mild shock. "From what you told me earlier, FTL craft will almost certainly remain big, expensive, and therefore, rare. That means our adversary should have limited forces."

"Very well—but I still don't see how having them establish a beachhead is a victory for us."

Caine looked up at the control booth. "Are you familiar with the Vietnam War?"

Downing stared down: there was a split second of uncertainty in his responding nod.

Caine shrugged. "The Vietnamese were utter underdogs: inferior tech, lack of air supremacy, unable to strike at their opponent's homeland. But they won the war, despite losing every major battle." Caine twisted two wires together, realized he had only half the job done but had used almost three-quarters of his available time. "They understood that when your enemy is large and technologically superior, you *want* him in your territory, because—if you are still the true master of your own countryside—his invasion force will become your hostage."

"Not if their orbital fire reduces our cities to rubble first."

Caine shook his head. "If they intend to rule us rather than exterminate us, they'll want to avoid a 'final solution.' So you dangle the prospect of capitulation—or even collaboration—under their noses while preparing to strike at them."

"And with their superior technology, how do you propose to get close enough to strike at them?"

Caine glanced up. "By getting—or prepositioning—forces inside their beachhead. And don't give me that doubting-Thomas look: there are always methods of infiltrating forces through 'secure perimeters' or 'impassable' borders."

Caine quickly stripped the insulation off the last two wires. "Even the old ploy of the Trojan Horse still has merit; it just needs some clever updating. Hey, I'm almost done here."

"Yes. But unfortunately, you have just run out of time."

Red lights flashed and spun; a klaxon howled next to Caine's ear. The hatchway beside him wrenched open with a high-speed hiss. But instead of finding himself sucked out into space, Caine was slammed backwards by a lateral geyser of water.

And, as the roaring flume bounced him off the mock-up bulkheads—which Caine discovered were just as hard as real ones—he thought: *Well, shit.*

MENTOR

Nolan edged into the control room as the orderlies were helping a bruised and waterlogged Caine limp out of the test chamber. "How'd it go?"

Downing snatched up his dataslate. "A brilliant success and a dismal failure. Riordan effortlessly spewed out a number of completely novel—and potentially game-changing—strategic insights, but botched the main task: a simple circuitry bypass job that many of our average trainees learn in half the time." Downing shook his head. "I'm afraid Caine's genius must be of a very narrow sort."

"Oh, Riordan isn't a genius. I mean, he is, but that's not what makes him useful to us. And that's not why he excelled at one task while botching another."

Downing looked up. "Then what was the cause?"

"Interest versus boredom."

"I beg your pardon?"

"Caine was interested in your strategic brainstorming but bored by the circuitry test."

Downing reared back in his seat. "Well, isn't that

simply awful for him. Next time, I will create an amusing vignette involving the circuitry."

Nolan smiled. "It can be challenging working with a true polymath. We don't see many in our line of work, mostly because they lack either the depth of interest to become world-class experts at any one thing, or the ability to maintain a brutally narrow field of focus. Or both."

"Hmm. That doesn't sound like a polymath; that sounds like a dilettante. Or a spoiled brat."

Nolan shrugged. "In some cases, they are both. But for most polymaths, that's just how they're wired. The intensive detail work that intrigues most field-specific geniuses is usually suffocating for them."

"So that's why Riordan can't memorize the circuitry?"

"Maybe. Or maybe he's just bad at it. Or maybe he's subconsciously responding to the inconsistency between what we've been telling him about the mission versus what we've been training him for. We assure him that he's being sent to Delta Pavonis Three just to look around, ask some questions, gather some evidence: nothing dangerous at all. But then we spend most of our time teaching him how to hotwire bulkheads, crack security codes, recognize counterintelligence agents, and a dozen other field craft skills that you only need when the work gets risky."

Downing folded his arms. "I see: he must be trained in a 'special way.' Most edifying. Except you've never answered the more important question."

"Which is?"

"Which is: why in bloody hell is a polymath any good for us?"

Nolan smiled. "Because, if sufficiently interested or

motivated, a true polymath can learn almost anything. They don't see the world as a big pile of discrete facts and figures. They see it as a matrix of paradigms and interrelated data. Hell, sometimes they find a solution to a problem in one field of knowledge by applying the established principles of another field."

"Ah," exhaled Downing with mock reverence, "a Renaissance man."

Nolan shrugged. "That term may be increasingly accurate."

"Why?"

"Because in the Renaissance, broadly integrative thought was at a premium; empirical method was in its infancy. Now, with the tools of measurement so highly refined, we produce lots of narrow specialists but fewer expansive thinkers."

"Well, I doubt expansive thought is going to help Mr. Riordan when he gets into the field." Downing rose. "And that time is approaching all too quickly. With our luck, Caine's op could come apart before it's started, probably before he even debarks from the shuttle down to Dee Pee Three...."

ODYSSEUS

Caine squinted through the gloom of the generic shuttle's cargo bay. On its far side, he could see the partial silhouettes of the two terrorists who would surely resume their attack soon.

Why the terrorists had been on the shuttle, and what they were after, was not clear and probably never would be. Their attempt to hold the bridge crew hostage had apparently devolved into a firefight which ended up blasting out the flight deck windows and exposing friend and foe alike to hard vacuum.

Caine had heard that much over the comm system before the carnage had spiraled out into the small ship's passageways. As one of the last persons out of the portside passenger compartment, he moved away from the general rush toward the escape pods, since that was also the route to the bridge. Shortly afterward, a sudden increase in gunfire and screams from the bow confirmed his instincts against heading forward. Continuing aft toward the cargo bay, he hoped to find something there that might serve as a weapon.

Finding the bay access doors closed, he had presumed he was the first to enter, but as he stepped inside and hit the reseal button, he caught sight of hurried movement to his left. He dove to the right, behind a cargo-heaped plat, just before a flurry of handgun shots spattered it and the bulkhead behind him.

And so here he was, pinned down by the very terrorists he had been hoping to elude. He had no time to wonder what the terrorists were doing in the cargo bay, or why the overhead lume panels suddenly failed, leaving only the red glow of the emergency lights. Whether or not the battle for control of the shuttle continued was equally unknown. But, at the moment, it was also wholly extraneous: he was in a cavernous hold, alone and unarmed, facing two very armed and dangerous enemies.

Scanning, he saw nothing but the freight and tools common to a cargo bay. *Wait: common tools.* Caine scuttled over to a power tool bench-box, found a pneumatic wrench. It was typically used for unbolting containers, or affixing modular cargoes to plats like the one he was sheltering behind. But with a slightly undersized bolt snugged into its socket—

Caine inserted an undersized bolt, adjusted the wrench's torque and pressure settings to maximum, and popped up. Before the two terrorists could react, he snapped the trigger of the wrench sharply: it emitted a curt blast and sent the puny bolt caroming off boxes well to the left of the terrorists. However, the bolt made a sound passably akin to a ricochet.

Caine ducked down a moment before his enemies' return fire sent two rounds thumping into his cover. *Well, since they're not charging at me yet, they at least think it* possible *that I have a real gun. And until they decide to test that possibility, I can look around.*

Unfortunately, there wasn't much to see, and almost none of it was useful. There were numerous spools of reinforced cargo netting on the floor and affixed to the bulkheads, most of it made of variable-elastic polymers: tough as nails yet lots of give. There was also a liberal scattering of containers, boxes, packing materials, lashings, c-clamps, carabineer clips, spare parts, and just plain rubbish. But Caine detected one notable detail: a circuitry-access panel was hanging askew at the near side of the door. The terrorists had obviously cracked it open to bypass the lock-outs that restricted access to the doors into and out of the cargo bay—including the bay doors themselves. That was probably why they had come down here: their job was to secure key cargos and get local control over the bay doors for off-loading.

Studying the locations of the nearby containers and boxes more carefully, Caine also realized that he had a mostly covered route back to that panel. There was a single, exposed gap, but it was only half a meter wide. The two terrorists wouldn't be able to react fast enough to hit him if he rolled, low and fast, across that open space. And once at the door's control keypad, Caine could open the main entry back into the shuttle, open the bay doors on his way out, and reseal the entry behind him. *Heh. Let's see how those two bastards like getting sucked out into hard vacuum . . .*

Caine flinched as the main entry opened. A young boy—no more than nine—ran in, shouting as he did, "Hello? Anyone? We need help! We've almost taken back the bridge but we—"

"Get down!" shouted Caine at the same moment that one of the pirates' guns spat.

The boy fell forward sharply, as if someone had swung a bat into his kneecaps. He shouted in pain, then terror as dark blood began leaking out of a through-and-through wound in his left thigh. "Help me!" he screamed in Caine's general direction. A moment later, the two terrorists rose up slightly, training their guns carefully on the approaches to the boy.

Caine felt his molars grind together: he could sneak over to the controls using the boxes as cover, trigger the bay doors, and then help retake the shuttle. But that would kill the boy, too. Or he could run to help the boy and get shot to pieces.

Or maybe there was a third option—

Caine quickly scanned the lashings on the plat in front of him and snatched off the biggest carabineer clip he could find. "I'm coming!" he shouted at the boy, tossed up a piece of trash—and was then moving across the open gap toward the control panel even

as two shots barked at the fluttering piece of paper
he had lofted.

More shots whined off the containers that covered
his route to the hanging access panel. Once there, he
reached out for a spool of cargo netting affixed to the
bulkhead. He uncoiled it, opened the carabineer clip,
snagged a section of netting with it, and snapped the
clip closed around his own belt. As the two thugs
started to move and the boy started to whimper,
Caine sucked in a deep breath and jumped over to
the control pad: he punched the button that opened
the cargo bay doors and sprinted toward the child.

At the other end of the hold, a small wedge of stars
and a sliver of blue—Delta Pavonis Three—appeared,
widening rapidly. Shots were already barking after
Caine's heels: startled by his unexpected charge, the
terrorists didn't have him in their sights—yet. But
Riordan's attention remained fixed on the boy, whose
round, terrified eyes had turned away from the yawning spacescape and outrushing debris and were now
fixed upon his own. Pleading.

Caine finished his short sprint to the boy just as the
outbound hurricane intensified into the full, ferocious
suction of hard vacuum. He dove, caught the boy by
the arm as they were swept off the deck and pulled
out toward space.

The two terrorists, screaming, shot past them,
arms flailing to grab something—anything—to arrest
their fatal tumble outward. Caine closed his nostrils
tightly, slapped his hand over the boy's face, pinching
his nose shut. They too were almost through the bay
doors and into the void—

—when the cargo netting snapped straight out to

its limit, humming like an immense, just-fired bow-string. Caine jackknifed at the waist, but held on to the child. He felt as though his own belt might cut him in two—

But then the netting's inevitable return flex began, pulling them away from the widening panorama of airless death even as the cyclone diminished, the bay's air almost fully spent. Caine looked over his shoulder: when they had retracted all the way to the bulkhead, he would have to quickly close the bay and cycle the interior access doors so that—

—the world faded to gray. Its sounds ended more sharply, as if someone had turned them off. The temperature and pressure extremes faded back to norm within seconds as Caine reoriented himself, wondering what had caused the simulation to terminate so abruptly.

Around him, the sensory suit sagged with uncommon suddenness: the sensa-gel in which it was immersed was being speed-purged from the simchamber. *What the hell is goi—?*

The hatch behind Caine opened with a breathy hiss and Downing's voice—sharp, unpleasant—was audible even through the full-enclosure headphones. "Riordan, get out here. Now."

Caine complied, but without any particular rush: *you may be my trainer and handler, Downing, but you don't own me.*

But before Caine had his second leg all the way out of the simulation pod, Downing was acting very much like he did own his impressed recruit. "Mr. Riordan, would you care to tell me what the hell you were doing at the end of the simulation?"

"Uh—completing the mission."

"'Completing the mission'? Do you even know what your mission was?"

"To retake the shuttle and get down to Delta Pavonis Three."

"Yes. And you jeopardized that by stopping to rescue the boy."

"Look, I'm not going to ignore an opportunity to save a kid, even if it means adding a little more risk."

"'A little more risk'? Is that how you'd characterize the harebrained stunt you pulled in the cargo bay? The objective here was to retake the shuttle so you could continue the mission. Period. Saving the boy was an *unnecessary* risk. Even saving the other passengers would simply have been a happy byproduct. You have failed, Mr. Riordan—failed to learn that the mission always comes first. *That* was the test."

"Huh. I thought the test was to do the best job possible."

"'Doing the best job' means minimizing risk. This time, it meant sacrificing innocents."

"But I didn't have to: I found a way to save both the boy and the mission."

"That's a sim. In the field, those instincts will get you killed."

Caine yanked off his virtual reality helmet. "Fine. So I flunk. Go get some other student. Please."

MENTOR

Downing pushed down his annoyance. "Caine," he said calmly, "you know you can't just walk away from this job. You're too much of a security risk, given everything we've told you."

Caine folded his arms. "So how will you ensure my continued cooperation? Threaten to withhold information about my one hundred missing hours?"

Downing shook his head. "That would not be effective enough."

Caine's eyes widened, then became very narrow. "Oh. I get it. If I don't shape up, then you stick me back into the freezer?"

Downing shrugged. "Let's not let it get to that point, shall we?"

Caine stared at him, yanked the leads off the sensory suit and stalked out of the sim chamber.

A moment later, Nolan entered from the sim operator's booth. "Well, that went well."

Downing pulled off the virtual gloves with which he had controlled the actions of one of the two terrorists in the cargo bay. "Caine won't be a safe operative, Nolan. He refuses to learn."

"Is that what's bothering you—or that he not only won, but pretty much broke your sim?"

Downing thought about it. "Both, probably. He certainly made me feel a right dolt: I designed a sim to force him to choose between his mission and his conscience. Instead, he turns it around so that the outcome winds up reinforcing his belief that he can always stop to save orphans and stray kittens. Mark my words, Nolan: that attitude is going to get him killed. Besides, he's too damned smart for his own good."

"Look, Caine's clever and he's got a lot of breadth, but he lacks expertise and real field experience. And he's not a genius at everything, you know. Hell, taken separately, no one of his abilities is really that jaw-dropping."

Downing looked at Nolan, having heard the hanging tone. "Except...?"

Nolan shrugged. "Except that, because he tends to avoid preconceptions, he can constantly integrate almost everything he knows to solve problems. You and I see a screwdriver; Caine not only sees a screwdriver, but a weapon, and a lever, and a straight-edge, and a counterweight, and ad infinitum. Polymaths don't *try* to do that; it's just how their brains work."

Downing returned his virtual reality goggles to their protective case. "So when we included the netting in the sim, we gave him a tool we weren't aware of."

"Right. And that couldn't have happened with the old sims, where there was a lot of restriction regarding how many items in the environment were manipulable. But now, everything in the environment is available. So Caine didn't break your sim: he just saw a solution none of the programmers—including you—anticipated."

Downing grabbed his dataslate, started making notes. "I still say he's not right for the mission."

"You mean, you're still pissed he got the better of your sim."

Downing rounded on Nolan. "No, I'm pissed that he's got a better soul than he should. He's too decent a bloke for this shite, and you know it."

"'Too decent'?"

"Of course. You saw the end of the sim: sooner or later, Caine's fine moral sensibilities are going to get him killed."

Corcoran leaned back, his eyes assessing. "Rich, I can't tell if you resent him or admire him."

Downing stared at his superior. "Nolan, I not only admire Riordan; I envy him. He isn't up to his neck

in the lies that we peddle, that we *live*. And that's
why he can't be trusted: because he won't jump into
the cesspool with the rest of us."

Nolan smiled. "Well, he can be trusted to do the
right thing, can't he?"

"Yes."

"Then he's predictable. You can work with that."

Nolan smiled and left Downing sitting speechless,
mouth open—partly at his superior's easy sagacity,
and partly at his ruthless pragmatism.

When they arrived at Epsilon Indi five days later,
Downing accompanied Nolan to the pinnace that
would ferry him to the Earth-bound shift-carrier
Commonwealth. The retired admiral put out his hand.
"So long, Rich. Have you settled on a code name for
Riordan, yet?"

Downing shook Corcoran's wide, strong hand. "Yes.
He's 'Odysseus'—who wound up getting lost and not
coming home, you might recall. Not exactly an auspicious code name. Although it could well be prophetic."

Nolan smiled. "Odysseus was a proto-polymath,
though. How does *The Odyssey* begin? 'This is the
story of a man who was never at a loss.' We could
do worse, I think."

Downing frowned. "It would still be better if we
sent a professional operative."

"I would if I could, Rich. But that won't work on
Delta Pavonis Three. If, as we suspect, the megacorporations are trying to conceal the evidence of sentients
there, they'll be alert for interference. They probably
have dossiers on all our professional operatives, or
could sniff out a new one. Either way, they'd clean

up their act before our agent gets to see what's really going on. But they won't know that Caine is a covert operator, or foresee his intents, for quite a while."

"So we hope."

Nolan's smile widened as he waved. "I'll miss your sunny optimism, Rich. Don't waste any time getting back to Earth."

Downing returned the wave and wondered when Caine Riordan might be able to make such a return trip himself.

If ever.

PART TWO

Delta Pavonis and Junction systems

June–October, 2118

Chapter Three

ODYSSEUS

A humid wind snapped at Caine's pants as he started down the mobile airway-stairs toward the tarmac. But even the tinted plexiglass roof-tube was unable to defeat the thick yellow heat of Delta Pavonis: it almost smote him back into the spaceplane—which was where he wanted to go, anyway.

His shirt started to stick as the humidity rose to meet him, and Caine suddenly realized that covert operatives—even those as new and unprepared as he—didn't stop, dumbstruck, as they debarked on a new planet. Which meant that at this particular moment, he certainly didn't look like a covert operative—and that was good. But, if he stood there any longer, he'd start to attract undue attention—and that was bad. So Caine breathed in the thick, musky air, and began a loose-jointed descent of the stairs: *first rule of tropical weather—don't fight against it; go with it.*

A stubby, sunburned man with a flattop of bristly hair was waiting for him on the tarmac, hand extended. "You Riordan, Caine Riordan?"

"That's me," replied Caine. "Pleased to meet you."

A full head shorter than Caine, the other man smiled and pumped his hand with the excessive vigor of a membership officer for a failing Shriner's lodge. "I'm Brinkley. Downport Ops Manager."

Caine nodded. "Thanks for coming to pick me up."

Brinkley snorted. "I should be thanking you: anything to get me away from my damned desk." Brinkley extracted his hand from Caine's, swept it at the buildings in the distance, then around at the tropical foliage hemming them in on all sides. "Welcome to Downport, Mr. Riordan."

At first, Caine couldn't tell if the grandiose gesture was ironic or genuine. But then Brinkley began gathering himself for another grand pronouncement—

There was a splintering blast behind Caine's right ear. A spatter of microscopic lances cut into that side of his neck: needle-fragments from the plexiglass roofing, which had been holed by a single bullet.

Caine dove into a prone position, his sternum thumping against the sun-softened tarmac, his heart thumping behind it. *Goddamnit: a sniper? Here? Already?* For a moment Caine couldn't think—and then he heard Downing reciting one of the mantras of his recent training: "If you're too scared to think, get to cover. *Then* think."

So—cover. Find cover. Caine scanned his surroundings: two klicks of cleared ground in all directions. No cover except the spaceplane. That meant there was only one option: a double-fast low crawl behind the air-stairs and then—

But Brinkley was laughing, rising from his casual crouch. "Don't let the yokels spook you: it's nothing personal."

Caine remained prone, looked up at him, and then at the bullet hole in the plexiglass. "Seems pretty personal to me." Caine's teeth chattered once; he gritted them into immobility and regained enough control to speak. "Who are these 'yokels'?"

"Outbackers. Neo-Luddites, mostly. Want to discourage further colonization. Every week or so, one of 'em wanders down here, takes a potshot at a spaceplane or a new colonist. Then they fade back into the hills to hunt whatever critters they're hunting up there." Brinkley's smile was a little less amused as he nodded toward the blood Caine could feel trickling down toward his collar. "Gotta say that they put this round a little closer than usual. They must really like you."

Caine tried to smile back, thought: *You have no idea how much they like me—since you have no idea who just shot at me. That was not a hunter's rifle. There was no report. And at more than a mile's range, it put a perfect four-millimeter hole in the plexiglass. Meaning that this was the work of an assassin with a silenced high-velocity weapon, not some backwoods renegade with an antique bolt-action rifle.*

As Caine rose up, so did a tiltrotor from the small, squat skyline to the north of the spaceport. The tiltrotor's lazy movements matched Brinkley's bored drawl. "They won't find the shooter. Never do. Stupid game, if you ask me."

Except this time it's not a game. But you're right about the tiltrotor not finding anything. By now, a professional will have moved well away from the firing position. And will then go to ground for hours, maybe days. That's the SOP. Or so Downing told me.

Brinkley gestured toward the edge of the tarmac:

through the heat-shimmer, Caine could make out a boxy, dull-green silhouette. "It ain't a limo, but it'll do. Say, are you going to be all right? Do you need anything?"

Yes. I need to know whether that shot was meant to drop me or warn me. But either way, a little more cross-wind and that bullet would have gone straight through my right eye.

Brinkley droned on. "Listen, I've got a medkit in the car. We'll put a compress on those nicks. They're not too deep. Day or two and you won't even feel 'em—"

True—because I might be dead by then, without ever knowing who pulled the trigger. Probably somebody working for the Colonial Development Combine's planet-rapers, but Downing said there could be other players in this game. But they—whoever "they" are— shouldn't know I'm on Delta Pavonis, or even who I am. Instead, I step straight off the spaceplane and into someone's waiting crosshairs.

And Brinkley still droned on. "Yep; we'll have you fixed up good as new. And we'll make sure it doesn't happen again. To the extent that's possible, of course. Sure don't want folks like yourself taking home bad reports. Hey, who'd you say you work for?"

"I didn't."

Brinkley had walked a step ahead, was trying to catch Caine's eye. "Of course, I understand if you can't say who you work for. We get that all the time. A lot of covert ops passing through. Every once in a while, our pilots have to ferry super spooks into or out of the bush. Incognito commandos, I call 'em." Brinkley smiled wider, seemed to be expecting a sign that Caine appreciated his clever nomenclature.

Caine just kept walking, kept his eyes on the low skyline of the settlement, and kept hoping it was big enough to get lost in for a while. Long enough, at least, to decide his next move. From all appearances, the mission had been compromised—so what should he do? Call it busted and catch a shuttle to the next outbound shift-carrier?

No: not acceptable. Even if there hadn't been any lives depending on the success of his mission, retreat was simply not an option. The next shift-carrier wasn't due to leave for at least three weeks. And even if he could hop on one this very second, what would stop an assassin from following him? So retreating only made him an easier target.

Meaning, by process of elimination, that he had to drop out of sight until he could come up with a better strategy. And if he couldn't "get lost" in the colony itself, then in the jungle—which, ironically was the source of the reports he'd been sent to investigate.

Brinkley nudged his elbow. "C'mon, you can tell me. They sent you here to find *them*, right?"

Caine forced his face to remain unsurprised as he echoed, "What do you mean, 'find *them*'?"

Brinkley looked over his shoulder furtively—even though the closest person was still over a hundred meters away. He lowered his voice to a stage whisper. "You know; *them*. The xeno-chimps. The 'locals.'"

Caine smiled, but thought: *this just gets better and better. I step off the shuttle and—after a quick little welcome bullet—the first guy I meet asks me if I'm here to conduct a secret investigation into reports of xenointelligence. Aren't secret missions supposed to remain—well, secret?*

Brinkley was still looking expectantly at Caine. Who stumbled over the requisite lie he should have told readily: "I'm—I'm here to investigate reports that the Colonial Development Combine has been breaking the local resource exploitation laws." It wasn't a complete lie, but it had sounded—and felt—awful.

Oblivious, Brinkley was pouting. "Well, I guess it's more important to investigate CoDevCo than a bunch of fool rumors about xeno-chimps. Hell, it's about time the Commonwealth did something about the Euros' high-handed corporate partners. You out here from the States?"

Again, Caine couldn't utter the easy lie, the easy "yes." Instead, he muttered, "Not directly."

"Have a good trip?"

"Sure. A bit long, though." *Yeah, thanks to being stuck in cold sleep, about thirteen years too long. But who's counting?*

Brinkley nodded. "Yeah, a six-month trip from Earth is a long haul. Seems a shame, too. You look up in the sky at night and you think, 'that should be a fast, straight run.'"

"I beg your pardon?"

"Look at the night sky while you're here. Locate Alpha Centauri—you'll find it crowding Omicron Ursa Major, like a bright new eye in the head of the bear. Sol is there, too—right behind Alpha Centauri. So, as seen from this system, all the major green worlds are pretty much on a straight line: here, Alpha Centauri, Earth. It could be two hops—ten weeks—to Earth, if the Wasserman drive only had a little more shift range."

Yeah, and if pigs could fly— But Caine only nodded: "A damned shame."

Brinkley nodded back, then jerked his head toward the hydrogen-burning Rover now only ten meters away. "C'mon; let's get out of the heat."

And off of this shooting range. But Caine only said: "Fine by me."

Downport had the look of a well-established paramilitary compound: a lot of high-quality prefab; about a dozen permanent buildings; twice that number in various phases of construction. Neatly stacked rows of modular containers radiated out from several cruciform warehouses. Vehicles were plentiful, worn but well maintained, a smattering of new ones mixed in. The people had the same look: a bit worn, but fit and active, always on the move, dressed in practical, loose-fitting tan and khaki trail clothes, all wearing hats—sombreros, ten-gallons, panamas, outbacks— according to taste or cultural origin. Always in pairs or larger groups, always talking, always immersed in their purpose. Rapid expansion, American style. But it still wasn't a city, or even a town: certainly nothing which could swallow you up and conceal you. So this was not a place in which Caine could elude an assassin for more than a few hours.

Brinkley resumed his stream-of-conscious narration, nodding proudly around him as he drove. "We've got about eighty-nine thousand settlers on Dee Pee Three, now. Mostly from Earth. A lot of Amexicans. Good workers. Hey: I don't mean anything by that. They're just good workers, y'know? Lot of new buildings going up, lot of new settlers coming in. A lot heading into the frontier, though. Some pretty feisty animals out there. Some of them are good eating. I mean, that's what they say. But you never heard that from me. I'll tell you, though, it can get pretty tiresome, eating the same old prepackaged meals."

Caine glanced at the outré foliage that was peeking over the surrounding roofs. "So the wildlife here is edible?"

"Some, but it's hard to know which animals are safe to eat, or rather, which parts of them. Easy to make a mistake. Some of the bigger animals make the same mistake with us. But they'll try just about anything once."

Just great. The jungle didn't sound like a very good hiding place either.

Brinkley hadn't paused for breath. "So it's pretty dangerous in the brush. Hey: if you're going in there, you'll want a gun. Nothing too fancy, mind you. But I can lend you something better than the museum pieces the Neo-Luddites use."

"Thanks: I'd appreciate that." But Caine didn't hear his own words; he was busy confronting a grim deduction. *So: no way to run, no place to hide. And, if the last update on CoDevCo was right, any further delay puts lives—exosapient or otherwise—at risk. Meaning I've got to stick with an already busted mission. Great.*

And, paradoxically, that meant his only remaining option was to head directly towards his enemies. Downing had provided him with the means of exerting considerable political leverage over the Colonial Development Combine, more commonly referred to as CoDevCo. So if they had sent this morning's sniper, Caine could probably compel them to back off—but only if he could get close enough to talk privately with

CoDevCo's local leadership, to strike an unspoken bargain that would give him the safety of an equally unspoken cease-fire.

Caine felt himself sink into—and then past—the odd calm that arises after accepting a course of action that might end in one's own death. "Mr. Brinkley, have any of your personnel catalogued the wildlife, examined their physiology, anatomy?"

The silence that ensued was not promising.

"You have a staff xenozoologist, right?"

"Uh—we have a xenobiologist: same thing?"

"Not exactly. Listen: didn't you have a zoologist by the name of"—Caine scanned down his palmtop—"by the name of Janel Bisacquino on your staff?"

"Oh, yeah, sure—but she shipped out four months ago. Science guys from further down the Big Green Main pulled rank and got her transferred to Zeta Tucanae."

Great. And since Bisacquino's transfer wasn't mentioned in Caine's mission packet, it meant that his briefing materials were so outdated as to be almost useless. But Brinkley—garrulous and incautious—showed every sign of being precisely the sort of unwitting intelligence asset who would fill in all the relevant blanks—if given the chance to talk. So Caine urged him to continue: "Do you know if they have any zoologists where I'm going?"

"Up there? Don't know. Doubt it. The Euros have left most of the science and infrastructure to us, I'm afraid."

"I thought you had a good relationship with the European Union settlement."

"We did. Well, I guess we still do. But they grabbed a second site that the international survey posted as off-limits. Prime real estate, too: big island, nice sheltered valley with a deep river opening out into a long ocean inlet. Great weather up there in the northern archipelago: more moderate than down here. That island was our first choice, you know, but the Colonial Authority put us here, instead."

"And then the European Union just grabbed the island?"

"Yeah—well, no, not exactly. Their first settlement is just a few dozen klicks south of us here. Nice facility they were building there."

"*Were* building?"

"Yeah. I mean, it's still there, but then CoDevCo got involved. When they arrived, they were already partnered with a new EU administrator, and ran their own survey. After that, it was like the EU forgot those poor folks down in Little Leyden even existed. All the Euro supplies are earmarked for Shangri-La, now."

"Where?"

"That's the name—well, the nickname—they gave to the island that they claim-jumped. Our pilot should have you up there by nightfall—and you can depend on him: he's had 'special passengers' like you before." Brinkley actually winked. "Hey: you'll also be the first person from here to see their new airstrip, expanded for spaceplanes. I tell you, CoDevCo's going to out-build us one day, despite our—"

"Mr. Brinkley."

"—uh, yes?"

"Why have we stopped?"

"Oh. Right. We're here. Let me show you around. Hey, you're going to need a hat. Do you have a hat? I've got an extra. You can even borrow it for your trip."

"Thanks, but—"

"Don't mention it. My pleasure. Now, before you go, let me show you around Downport. It's not your average colony town—and do you know why?"

Caine did not know why. But he was quite sure he was about to find out.

In agonizing detail.

Chapter Four

ODYSSEUS

Rocking in unison with the wind-shear chop, Caine's borrowed slouch hat flopped up and down against his upper back, the rawhide chinstrap tugging at his throat in time with the drumming downdrafts.

"Sorry about this, Mr. Riordan," the pilot called over his shoulder into the payload bay. "We're over the coast and hitting some thermals. We should be out of it soon."

"Not a problem. How long to Shangri-La?"

"Instruments are telling me five minutes, maybe a few more."

"What does human experience tell you?"

"Nothing, sir: only made this run once before, about a year ago. Then, no more."

"What happened a year ago?"

The vertibird shuddered, pitched down and sideways, righted. "CoDevCo came in, took over all the runs to and from the downport. Not real friendly about it, either. This is the first time they've let one of our planes into their airspace in six months."

"That's a violation of the colonial 'equal-use' policy, isn't it?"

"I'm no lawyer, but it sure seems that way to me. If you're done checking your gear, I'd recommend you strap in. We've got a few more—"

The deck dove away from Caine's feet at the same instant that the ceiling struck a quick downward blow: the impact against the top of his head made a sound like an iron hammer hitting an anvil. Felt like it, too.

"Shit. Sir, are you—?"

"I'm fine," Caine lied, staying on hands and knees as he moved forward into the cockpit, letting the pulsing spots—and the dull hum between his ears—subside. He half-slid, half-crawled, into the copilot's chair.

The pilot stole a sideways look at him. "You sure you're—?"

"I'm fine."

"I really am sorry, sir. I should have warned you that—"

"Listen: it's my fault. Wasn't like I needed to check the lashings on my gear a fourth time."

"What is all that stuff, anyway?"

"Research materials."

Another sideways look from the pilot, skeptical this time. "Really? What kind of research do you do with a trail kit and a rifle?"

Caine smiled. "Field research." Caine wondered if the pilot had noticed any of the other unusual items. Besides the predictable collection of rations, salt pills, water purification tabs, and personal medkit, there were the less standard items: thermal imaging goggles, a multi-spectrum sensor kit, high-end photographic gear, a binary-propellant NeoCoBro machine pistol with heterogeneous clips that alternated between discarding sabot and expanding rounds, and a sealed gray-green canister covered with indecipherable abbreviations and acronyms—all stenciled in the dusty yellow block letters favored by the USSF. Well, if the pilot had seen the last two, it meant he had X-ray vision: they were buried under the mundane gear in the A-frame backpack.

The pilot was still considering Caine's explanation. "Field research, huh? Well, I hope you find what you're looking for—before it finds you." He looked away with a small, tight smile.

Me, too. Hell, I just wish I really knew what I was looking for. "Is that the valley?"

The pilot craned his neck to look further. "Yup. It's pretty wide here; gets narrower, the further up you go."

The chop had subsided and the pilot banked to angle onto the valley's southwest-to-northeast center-line, following a glittering blue ribbon that preceded them. Thick swaths of green hemmed it in its course, worked away from the river and up the sheltering slopes. Which grew steeper as they flew. Caine checked his watch; they were right on time. "Nice country."

The pilot nodded. "Seems so—but I've never had a chance to get out and see for myself." He glanced at the dense jungle canopy scudding beneath them. "Not too safe on your own, even if you're well armed. We can digest the flora and fauna here, so it only makes sense that they can return the favor. And from what I hear, some critters are pretty enthusiastic about doing so. The ones here in Shangri-La haven't learned to fear guns yet, so shoot to kill: they won't run away."

"Thanks. That's good to know."

"You shoot much?"

Caine shook his head, thought he saw a hint of right angles distressing the landscape up ahead. "Some. Not too often."

"Well, you might want to get in a little time at the range before you go into the bush. Adjust the sights, get a feel for the—"

"Already did it, before we took off from Downport."

"Oh. I thought you said you don't shoot much."

"I didn't—until this afternoon."

The pilot smiled. "Yeah, I heard about your welcoming committee this morning. So now you're ready to return the sentiments?"

"Something like that." Caine pointed at the horizon, now clearly sprouting low rectangular silhouettes in the middle of wide, squared clearings. "Is that—what do they call their base anyway?"

"Site One: how's that for an imaginative name? Typical bureaucrats. Yeah, that's it up ahead."

"Looks like they've cleared a lot of the forest at that wide point."

The pilot was stretching to get a.better look. "A whole hell of a lot more than I've seen—or heard about."

Well off to the north, nestled up against the skirts of the low hills on that side, were what appeared to be a cluster of towers. "Know anything about those?"

The pilot shook his head. "Not a clue."

"How long until we land?"

"They'll be talking me toward a vertipad any second now."

Caine thought for a moment. Then: "You've made a mistake; you need to come around for another pass."

"Sir, we're right on—"

"I know what the instruments say. But I'm telling you: we've made a mistake; you need to circle around for another landing approach."

The pilot's frown became a study in strained patience. "Sir, even if I knew what the hell you're talking about, please remember that this is a vertibird: we don't make 'approach runs,' so I would never need to circle around for another landing attempt."

"Today you need to."

The beginning of the comchatter from Site One's ground control was on general speaker. "Commonwealth Zero-Tango-Niner; you are correctly vectored for transition to vertical landing at Pad Two, coming to a range of ten kilometers on my mark. And...mark."

"Site One ATC, this is Commonwealth flight 0T9. I roger your telemetry, and am requesting confirmation for—"

Caine made a throat-cutting gesture with his right hand. The pilot sighed, snapped off the transmitter. "Sir, what now?"

"Tell him you don't trust the gimballing servos on your thrusters; you want to make a runway landing, not vertical."

"Look, sir—"

Caine pulled out the magic ID card that Downing had given him: this might be the one chance he'd get for close aerial reconnaissance of the site.

The pilot looked over at the card—bored and a little annoyed—and had started to look away when his eyes grew wide, and he looked back. Quickly. As his eyes went through a high-speed back-and-forth scan of the ID and clearance card, his lips slowly dilated and contracted through the cycle of a soundless "Wow."

"Charlie Whiskey Zero-Tango-Niner: please say again. Your last transmission broke up."

The pilot turned the transmitter back on. "Site One ATC, I'm having problems reading you. Am also showing orange lights on the thrust vectoring panel: I'll need to skip transition to vertical. Requesting emergency access to runway one."

"Negative, CW 0T9—you do not have authorization for—"

"Site One ATC, your commo is breaking up. Please say again." He let the increasingly anxious ground controller get about half way through his denial for the runway landing request before speaking right over the top: "Site One ATC, I am no longer reading you. Please be advised: I am coming about bearing 235 true for approach to Runway One. Please signal 'all clear' by setting runway approach lights to strobe mode. CW 0T9 out." The pilot snapped off the transmitter, banked the plane into a long, left-sweeping curve toward the towers, which now showed themselves as a cluster of girder frameworks. "Do you think they'll buy it?"

Caine leaned forward to get a better look at what appeared to be a quarry at Site One's extreme northern perimeter. "Can't say that I care."

Within five minutes of landing, Caine was being ushered into a room of uncompromising opulence. As he set his A-frame down next to the auto-closing door, he was careful not to scratch the wood-paneling. *Is it ebony? No, apparently not.* High overhead, descending from a vaulted ceiling reminiscent of Louis 14th enameled and gold-leafed grandeur, were two immense chandeliers. At the far end of the room was a dark

wood desk large enough to pass as a small mesa. The
man behind it—spare, trimly mustachioed, adjusting
a data-link viewing monocle—waited: no motion suggested that he was prepared to close the distance to
Caine, nor that he was even going to come around the
end of his desk. *So that's the way it's going to be*—

Caine took his time walking the length of the
salon, studying its various appointments. By the time
he reached the desk, the man behind it seemed less
composed. Maybe he wasn't used to waiting for his
guests to approach, or maybe he had hoped that
this guest would be indefinitely detained by a prior
engagement with a bullet.

"Welcome to Site One, Mr. Riordan."

"Thank you, Mr.—?"

"Helger, Louis Helger. I am the Co-Administrative
Manager of this joint facility."

"A 'joint facility'?" That was another new—and
worrisome—terminological twist: in another half year,
CoDevCo would probably push out the EU altogether.

Helger shrugged. "Very well: technically, Site One
is a European Union colony with a full partnership
extended to the Colonial Development Combine. However, we consolidated administrative operations when
I arrived eight months ago. Too much duplication of
effort, other inefficiencies. That is all behind us."

"I see. But which of the partners do *you* work for,
Mr. Helger?"

"I am an EU employee, Mr. Riordan, but I also
have a history of employment with CoDevCo."

"Oh? What kind of history?"

"Not that it is any business of yours, but I retired
as the Regional Manager for Nordic operations, after

having served as an Associate Product Manager for the prior eight years."

"Impressive."

Helger's shrug seemed less genuine than his small, satisfied smile. "It was thought that as we moved toward joint operations here on Delta Pavonis Three, it would be best to appoint a person who also had extensive experience with CoDevCo project management."

"Well, that was clearly achieved. And the other half of your credentials are, I'm sure, equally impressive."

Helger's face went protectively blank. "What other credentials are you referring to?"

"Your prior experience as an EU administrator, of course."

Helger's face did not change. "Mr. Riordan, I regret that I do not have time for a casual chat—"

You mean you don't want to admit that the first day you worked for the EU was the day you stepped onto the tarmac at the Dee Pee Three Downport.

"—so I must ask that we constrain our discussion to official matters. Firstly, I have now received your dossier—"

Obviously. If you hadn't, you wouldn't have let me set foot in your little fiefdom.

"—and I must say I am somewhat puzzled: who, exactly, do you represent?"

"Officially? No one."

Helger was clearly not prepared for such a frank admission. "Then how did you get this rather sweeping writ of cooperation from the European Union?"

"That was a courtesy, provided at the request of Senator Tarasenko, head of the United States Congressional Committee on Strategic Space Initiatives."

"So you are an official representative of the US government? And not the Commonwealth *in toto*?"

"Neither. I am not a representative of any one government, which is why the other Commonwealth nations—as well as the EU—were willing to accept me as a general observer."

"And your credentials are—?"

"I am an analyst and a writer, Mr. Helger."

"So I see. But without any particular experience in xenobiology or—"

"Mr. Helger, unless a large delegation was to be sent, there was no way to address all the specializations required for this investigation: xenobiology, xenozoology, evolutionary biology, anthropology, archeology, corporate and international law—"

"Law? I'm not sure I understand."

"Mr. Helger, since you arrived here, there have been a number of legal irregularities which have caused friction back home. You've imposed airspace restrictions in direct contravention of international interstellar colonization accords, have constructed a separate downport which only serves your own carriers—another international violation—and conducted an independent regional survey that contradicted and dismissed the original planetary assessment. You then began resource exploitation in a zone which had been interdicted by the first survey—this zone that you now call the Shangri-La Valley. Clearly, these are matters that would ideally be handled by official representatives of, and legal counsel for, the various parties."

Helger sat; he did not invite Caine to do so. "I am afraid that is where your analysis is already flawed, Mr. Riordan. The survey was conducted by CoDevCo, not by the EU. Similarly, many of the restrictions and actions undertaken here at Site One have been according to orders sent from Earth by higher CoDevCo authorities. According to the co-administrative agreement with the EU, I must act upon those orders until the contradictions between our corporate prerogatives and national commitments are resolved through arbitration, back on Earth. Therefore, while I would be happy to lift the ban on access to our facilities, I cannot legally do so at this time."

Caine sat. "Mr. Helger, the wording of your joint agreement—of which I have a copy—quite explicitly states that the EU's existing agreements with other parties take precedence over the authority of the co-administration. In short, the European Union's commitment to the international colonization covenant comes first—no exceptions, no special clauses."

"I'm sorry we have such a difference of interpretation, Mr. Riordan, but I am not about to change my operations based on your reading of this contract."

"It is not my reading, Mr. Helger: I am following an explication from lawyers at The Hague."

"Regardless, I do not recognize your authority here."

"Then I'm sorry to say that I must immediately suspend your downport's interface operations with the highport."

Helger laughed, leaned back. "Mr. Riordan, do you really expect me to pick up the phone and ground my spaceplanes? Just because you tell me to do so?"

"No, Mr. Helger. I know you won't take any directives from me. But the system Port Authority will."

Helger was no longer smiling or leaning back in his chair. "You cannot do this. Port facilities—no matter who owns them—must be kept freely available to all nations—"

"That's true. It's part of the international colonization covenant. But then again, you've decided to ignore that covenant. Now, as I understand contract law, Mr. Helger, when one side defaults on a contract, the other party is freed from its obligations under that same contract. Which means that the system Port Authority—which is wholly a Commonwealth entity—is now free to deny you docking access, may impound any cargoes currently held, refuse to accept or relay communications of any kind—"

"This is outrageous: it is blackmail."

"It seems more like blackjack to me, Mr. Helger. You bet that you held the better cards and were willing to reject recognizing my authority. But now it seems that I hold the better cards. Of course, that doesn't necessarily mean I am eager to play them...."

C'mon, Helger: take the bait.

Helger did. "What exactly do you mean by that, Mr. Riordan?"

"I mean that it would be best if we could avoid a showdown, Mr. Helger. Yes, I'd win—but at what cost? I can do a better job here if I have your cooperation. And I'm willing to make sure that cooperating with me is worth your while."

"I'm listening."

"I'd be happy not to suspend your Port Authority rights. And—for now—you can keep your airspace and regional exclusivity. But I need to be able to go wherever I want, whenever I want, without obstruction. Agreed?"

Come on, take the step—

Helger's lower teeth sought, and chewed lightly at, his neat moustache. "Agreed."

Caine managed to effect boredom as he looked out the window. That had been close: *if Helger had pushed, he'd have found out that I only have the authority to shut down his outbound traffic, not the inbound. Which means that he would have been able to maintain operations—and kill me with near-impunity.*

"Of course, I will want to confirm this with your superiors."

Trying to see if I flinch, if I've overplayed my hand. Without looking away from the window, Caine shrugged. "Suit yourself. But I think you'll find that the Navy brass upstairs are not merely ready, but eager, to find an excuse to shut you down. If you make me show them what I've shown you—that *I* have the authority to shut you down—they might exert pressure on me to do so, and I need their cooperation even more than I need yours. So if I'm forced to choose between them and you, I'm sure you see where that might lead. On the other hand, I'd be delighted to have you confirm my authority: then we won't have to do this dance every time I make a polite request."

Helger did not say anything, but stared at his commplex for three full seconds. Then he rose: "It is a shame we got off to such a bad start. Here, allow me to show you around our facilities—but then again, you've already seen them. You had an aerial tour on the way in, if I'm not mistaken."

Caine rose also, ignoring the bait. "I'd like to stow my gear first, Mr. Helger."

"Certainly. Best that you should find your room before trying to find anything else."

Caine did not return Helger's knowing smile. The issue of *what* he'd find on Delta Pavonis Three had suddenly become secondary. The far more urgent question was whether CoDevCo would let Caine find it—or let him live to report, if he did.

Chapter Five

ODYSSEUS

Caine's guide, Ms. Rakir, drove the Rover as hard and fast as an adolescent male overdosing on testosterone, but her voice and the movements of her head were as smooth and unhurried as those of a pampered contessa. "How was your flight yesterday, Mr. Riordan?"

"Pretty much like this drive."

She laughed, throwing back her head while swerving to avoid a stump of rock protruding from the unfinished roadbed. "You don't like my driving?"

"It's—exhilarating."

"Or is it that you don't trust women as drivers?" Her voice had modulated into a lower register, became as sinuous as she. "It's not unusual. Many men still don't like to surrender control to women." She glanced sideways out of catlike eyes. "Are you like that?"

Caine smiled and looked away. He had seen this coming the moment she had come to pick him up for his driving tour of Site One's operations. Everything about her was suggestive curves: her body, her lips, her eyes, her face. And the motif was curves in motion, motion that pressed at the limits of physics—and clothing—as she had walked toward him, hand extending and swaying slightly with the rest of her. Her shirt was open two buttons down from the collar; her shorts ended two hands-widths above the knee: provocative without being outrageous.

"I'm sorry; did my question make you— uncomfortable?" Her voice had become a little more formal: she had overplayed her hand and she knew it. *She's used to men who allow the orders they get from below their belt to veto those that originate between their ears.* And looking at her again, he could see why. It wasn't just her physical attributes; it was how they seemed an external expression—and promise—of what was within her: a sensual mix of feline poise and feral energy. Judging from his own physical reactions, Caine realized he'd better start thinking about something else: he had been dead for thirteen years, and his body—at least one particular part of it—was evidently eager to prove that it had very much come back to life.

"You never told me where we're going first, Ms. Rakir."

"Please, call me Consuela. Well, I thought we'd start with a drive around the main compound, but Mr. Helger evidently showed that to you yesterday afternoon."

"Yes, but it was a pretty brief tour. Night comes on pretty quickly, here. As did morning: I'm still a little earth-lagged, I'm afraid."

"Yes, Dee Pee Three's seventeen-hour day takes a little getting used to. Not so bad for me, though: I grew up with midday siestas and late-night tapas.

The rules for day and night are less rigid, that way. Less restrictive."

He decided not to look over at her again: he heard the insinuation in her voice. The modulation was far fainter, the suggestion was a fading grace note instead of a major chord, but it was still there. *Persistent and adaptive—in all aspects of seduction, I'm sure.* Aloud: "And where are you from?"

"All over. Caracas, Corpus Christi, Lagos, Amsterdam. We moved a lot."

"That accent sounds more Cambridge than Corpus Christi."

"Millfield and Oxford, actually. I only lived in Corpus Christi for two years. What about you?"

"Me?"

"Yes; where are you from?"

Caine felt a sudden disorientation: *where do I say I'm from, now? An unlisted refrigerator?* He gargled out an awkward laugh. "The stars. I'm from the stars."

He could feel her looking at him. She laughed along, a second too late. *Have to change the topic: I'm weak here.* "Bad joke. D.C. area, most recently. Lots of places before that. Sounds a bit like you."

"Yes—we have that gypsy background in common, then." Consuela's voice made him think of her fingers working their way between his: wiggling in, sliding and writhing around index and middle fingers, the occasional graze of a well-sharpened nail reminding that half of the excitement was in the peril.

And she was indeed peril. Caine couldn't be sure whether Helger had sent her as a spy, a distraction, or a peace—*or should that be "piece"?*—offering, but it was plain that she had been hand-picked for the job of escorting him. She was too striking to be a spy, so she was either intended as baffling bait or as a bribe. Or both. Yes. That was the way Helger would work. She was a gift that was meant to divert not merely his senses, but his attention—and she was too clever to be an ignorant cat's-paw: she had to be a knowing accomplice. *Good: now I'm thinking straight again.*

He looked up, seeing the foliage for the first time. They were speeding under a canopy of—well, not exactly trees: more like oversized ferns and sponge-sheathed goldenrod of gargantuan proportions. Oddly angular vines wound around and hung between them, speckling the shadows with impulsive constellations of small fuchsia and indigo flowers. Amazing that any world could be so habitable and look so different. Amazing that anything could be so biologically compatible with species that evolved 19.9 light-years away.

"Beautiful, no?"

Caine wondered if Consuela were talking about the flowers or herself—and thought: *that's exactly the way she wants me to think. She doesn't want me to like her: she wants me to be mystified, intrigued, aroused, maybe even a little resentful of the titillation—anything to keep my mind off my job.*

"The flowers are unlike anything I've seen before. All of it is. How long have you been here?"

"About a year. It's been—"

"And what do you do? What is your job?"

She almost stuttered. *You'd decided I was a gentleman—wouldn't interrupt, sure to be susceptible to a slow seductive dance, out of good manners, if nothing else. But here's where the game changes.*

"I'm assistant director for new product marketing."

"What new products?"

"Well,"—sweeping around a corner and out from under the foliage, they came to a dusty stop in front of a lightly-built oil rig—"petroleum."

The action of the sudden halt sent the inevitable reactive shock waves undulating through the upper part of Consuela's torso. Caine did his best not to notice. Instead, he smiled: "Venezuela, Corpus Christi, Amsterdam: Exxon?"

She smiled: it was a predatory leer, but honest, and—he intuited—a species of grudging congratulations on his deduction. "So you must be an investigative reporter, then. Yes, Exxon. Daddy, his dad before him, now me: crude runs in the family."

And in your veins, I'll bet. "So, that's the part of CoDevCo that you hail from."

"Guilty as charged. I am one of the she-wolves of energy corporation notoriety. The despised of the earth."

Because you create the wretched of the earth, you supercilious bitch. You'll be telling them to eat cake, next. It was becoming rapidly easier to find her less captivating. *But I can't show that. This is my opportunity.*

He swung his legs over the side of the Rover, shaded his eyes, looked to either side: dozens of light-framed derricks in both directions. A thin, steady stream of black-smeared workers—most silent, a few muttering in Farsi, others in what might have been Uzbek—straggled toward the access road. Caine noted a profusion of unmended tears in their clothing, and the dull-eyed stares of the perpetually exhausted. "I suppose you're aware that I flew over this area yesterday?"

"Did you? I didn't know."

Liar. "Yep—but I didn't spot these as oil rigs. They looked—well, too flimsy. I thought they were construction frames for towers of some kind."

"It's a new derrick design made possible by lighter, stronger materials." Consuela had come to stand alongside him—very close. That was either her arm brushing his elbow, or—

"And so this is why Site One became off-limits? You wanted to establish exclusive production?"

She nodded. "That's what I guess: the Board doesn't consult with little fish such as me."

Caine stared up along the black-gray girders: *Too easy. They're showing me this without effort, so they're hiding something else. But for now, play it out. If you jump topic too fast, she'll sense that you know there's more. Play the part of the triumphant—and successfully decoyed—investigator.*

He had to wait before speaking; a high speed VTOL approached, transitioned into level flight just about directly overhead, and arrowed up and over the steep green slope of the nearest mountain. "Why show me?"

She shrugged. "Louis didn't tell me much—"

So, Consuela: Helger is "Louis," despite being four tiers above you on the chain of command? What is he: a friend you made back home, or a friend you made on your back?

"—but I gather he didn't have much choice left, in your case. So here it is: our deep, dark secret."

"It'll be dark enough when the Commonwealth and the Union learn about it."

She shrugged. "Possession is nine-tenths, Mr. Riordan. And what are they going to do: impound the site?

It will be months before they can get new work crews out here. Besides, no one's going to stop us, anyway."

"Why?"

She smiled, not entirely suppressing the condescension.

Go ahead, Consuela, believe I'm not quick enough to see it all for myself. If you decide I'm a little dim now, you'll let your guard down later—

"Mr. Riordan, surely you know the value of oil."

"Of course. Even after it was phased out as a fuel, it remains essential."

"That's right: plastics, lubricants, fertilizers, chemicals. It is priceless."

Caine shrugged. "But at six shifts from Earth, the transport cost of oil from Dee Pee Three will eat the profits to nothing. Oil futures are still no more than one hundred c-dollars a barrel, and since we stopped burning it, the remaining supply is deemed sufficient for any foreseeable future."

She nodded patiently. "Yes, it is. That is the state of the petroleum market on Earth. But there's something you're overlooking."

No, there isn't—but I'm glad you think so. "And what's that?"

"New worlds, Mr. Riordan. CoDevCo has moved beyond terracentric marketing assumptions. We are thinking in interstellar terms: our new oil industry on Delta Pavonis Three is a prime example of that."

"How?"

"Well, let's do the math, Mr. Riordan. How much does it cost to move a one-liter volume of cargo from one solar system to another? Not freight charges: break-even cost, only."

"Uh—about three c-dollars a liter, per shift."

She seemed surprised that he knew. "Right. And how many shifts from Earth to Delta Pavonis?"

"Six."

"Correct. So, in terms of interstellar transportation alone, it costs eighteen dollars to ship a liter of petroleum from Earth, the only known source of substantial fossil fuel deposits. Now, at one hundred dollars a barrel, that means that the market price for oil on Earth is about two dollars a gallon, or fifty cents a liter. Add in one c-dollar per liter for surcharges and transportation fees, and it costs the distributor about a dollar and fifty cents just to purchase every liter. You see now?"

"If Delta Pavonis wanted oil from Earth, the cost would be immense: a base price of a dollar-fifty per liter, plus eighteen dollars more for six interstellar shifts. Add another six dollars for initial lift to orbit at fully subsidized bulk costs. That's twenty-five dollars and fifty cents of cost to the provider, which will be passed along to the user, plus markup. At that rate, no one out here could afford to buy oil. But, if you can pump your own oil on Dee Pee Three, you'll be able to sell it here for about the same as Earth rates: that means a higher profit margin, and plenty of ready consumers."

"Yes, but that's only part of it. Right now, all the products that require fossil fuels must be made on Earth. That means that all those products also entail immense shipping costs: the further out they must go, the worse it gets. So—"

"So you plan on building all those industries here on Dee Pee Three."

"Exactly. Plastics manufacturing, pharmaceuticals, lubricant refineries—"

Over her shoulder, Caine saw a collage of the fuchsia and indigo blooms. *She's foretelling your extinction.* "*Beautiful, aren't they?*" *commented the robber-baroness as she burned the flowers to ashes and soot . . .*

"Now do you see?"

"Sure: Dee Pee Three becomes a new industrial hub. Perfectly placed, too: most of our colonies would be within three shifts of your products."

"Precisely. Call it corporate greed if you like, Mr. Riordan, but the more quickly we can develop the oil reserves here, the faster and further humanity can expand into interstellar space."

Oh, so this is your selfless contribution to the glorious future of homo sapiens? I mustn't laugh . . . so change topic: "Look, I also need to ask about these reports of a possibly intelligent species. Navy thermal imaging detected nocturnal activity, which is highly suggestive of coherent group movement. Significantly, the movement suggests bipedal physiology. There are also reports that dressed stone has been found."

"And what does that have to do with anything?"

"There are those who feel that CoDevCo replaced the Navy survey with one of their own in an attempt to cover up possible environmental obstacles to just this kind of resource exploitation."

"Oh, so even on other planets, the energy companies are still suspected of ruining habitats, exterminating indigenous species—even intelligent ones?"

"Well, why else would you ignore the Navy survey? That was pretty much a slap in the face to both the Commonwealth and the original EU policy-makers, who assessed the thoroughness of the survey, and voted to accept it. Personally, I'm guessing that the stakes here on Dee Pee Three must be pretty high if CoDevCo is willing to risk that kind of political friction and insult."

"Well, the stakes certainly are high. However, our operations here haven't involved any environmental abuse—but you won't believe me until you've seen the evidence with your own eyes." She crooked a finger. "Follow me."

And watching her from behind, Caine locked his teeth gently, acknowledging that, despite whom and what she was, a large and libidinal part of him was quite willing to follow her anywhere.

She stopped where the valley floor began its transition into a steep-sided mountain. As Caine approached, she pointed along the leeward base of a granite outcropping. A five-meter line of regular stones—almost invisible in the mossy ground—paralleled the stony tendril of the mountain at a distance of one meter. She smiled. "There's what we were hiding."

He looked. "That?"

She smiled more widely. "That, and about three or four others we've found like it. Is it an artifact of intelligent life? Unquestionably. But that's all we've got. We haven't seen any current evidence of a sapient species that could build this. In fact, these are the only such signs we've found whatsoever."

"Have you dated the stones?"

"Not exactly the kind of equipment we carry, and if we had asked for it, there was always the chance that someone would ask why we wanted it. I understand it's a find of some significance—"

Some significance? Could balance sheets really blind her—or anyone—to the immense implications of it?

"—but we're being careful not to disturb the sites, and it's not as though they're going to disappear. I realize the research they will stimulate is important, but how *urgent* can it be?" She smiled. "Judging from ruins I saw when I was growing up, I'd say we're at least ten thousand years too late for the matter to be 'urgent' in any practical sense."

He knew she was watching him carefully behind her vaguely coquettish stare. So Caine made sure that he appeared to be trying to keep his face expressionless—as if he were attempting to suppress disappointment. After a moment, she looked away, evidently satisfied with what she thought she had seen. "Ready to go?"

He nodded, turned without a word, heard her fall in behind him.

As they got near the Rover, he swayed forward slightly, stretched out an arm, caught and steadied himself against the hood.

She was at his side—surprisingly swift—and did not miss the opportunity to put a solicitous hand on his left bicep. "Are you quite well?"

"Yeah. I just feel—a bit faint. The heat—I think."

"Well, we can always do this another time."

"No—no, I'll be okay."

She looked at him closely. "Very well, but I think we should end early today. Finish up with a visit to the executive pool. It's wonderfully cool. Soothing."

Caine looked at her. "That sounds—appealing."

She nodded slowly, her eyes constantly on his. "It's a great way to relax, to release the stress."

"I suppose it is." He straightened up. "But that's for later: what's next on our agenda?"

"Our own downport—and thanks for reminding me." She reached into the Rover for the radio, sharply informed whoever answered that she'd be there with the V.I.P. in about twenty minutes, and signed off without a goodbye. She turned a sweeter-than-candy smile on Caine and resumed her review of their schedule: "After the downport, we'll see the workers' compound, including the fee-free clinic; our survey command center; and one of our weather-monitoring stations. And then, a quick dip. Before drinks and dinner."

Caine smiled, nodded, thought: *That agenda is one item short of what Helger promised—and one item short of what I really want to see.* "Great, but what happened to my visit with the EU's Deputy Administrator, Ms. Fireau?" *Who might not be very happy with the current state of affairs here.* Fireau had been in charge before Helger—and the consequent deluge of CoDevCo money, personnel, and influence.

Consuela leaned her arms on the Rover's hood, adopting a posture that provided a half-obstructed view of her cleavage. She pouted and smiled at the same time: "I'm sorry, I thought Louis sent you word: Ms. Fireau had to fly back to Little Leyden today. Business emergency, I'm afraid."

Naturally. "When did she leave?"

"Just a few minutes ago. That must have been her vertibird that went over us earlier: we don't send out a lot of VTOL traffic."

Okay, so there it was: Helger's ploy of using Consuela as a subtly salacious species of flypaper had already impeded him and his investigation. It was a shame to miss Fireau, but Caine hadn't expected Helger to permit a meeting with her. He elected to look surprised, then sound annoyed: "When will Ms. Fireau return?"

"I'm sorry, Mr. Riordan. I don't know."

Shall I tell you? Just as soon as I'm airborne back for Downport, Ms. Fireau will be on a plane back here. That way, I can't interview her back in Little Leyden, either.

"And that's it? That's our day-trip?"

"That's it. Why? Was there something else you wanted to see?"

He didn't hear a probe, but he was sure it was there. *She called ahead right before we came here, and she just called ahead to our next stop. She's calling ahead with a warning everyplace we go. I'll never get an honest look at anything, particularly what I want to see the most: that big dig to the north. That doesn't look like oil wells to me. But I can't let her take me there, can't even let her know I'm interested in it, or that I noticed. So here's a bone for you to chase later on, Consuela:* "I was hoping to see the river, further downstream: I hear you've got some aquaculture experiments going on there?"

"Why, yes, we do. Sure: we can fit that in."

Caine smiled—then staggered during his attempt to get into the Rover. He half sat down, half fell down, into the front passenger seat.

She came around quickly. "Mr. Riordan, are you quite sure you're—?"

"I'm okay. But I think—I think I need some water. Do we have some?"

"No—"

I know that.

"—but I can go to the break shed and get you a bottle. Will you be all right here?"

"Sure. Thanks. Sorry about—this."

She smiled, turned to assume her newest role as his loyal Gunga Dinette—and, from the corner of his eye, he saw that, as she turned, her reassuring smile became tight and contemptuous.

He watched her stride away: this was a woman who didn't like weakness. Except, of course, when she stood to benefit by it. Right now, she was probably thinking: *Outstanding. I get to control him without having to get laid by him.*

Caine smiled as she disappeared around the corner: *So you don't like weakness. I hope you like surprises.* He swung his legs up into the Rover, scooted over to the driver's seat, turned the key, and upshifted, turning the vehicle in a slow, dustless arc back onto the road that plunged into the shadows of the not-trees.

Chapter Six

ODYSSEUS

The low buildings of the open quarry—or whatever it was—barely rose above the ferns and clusters of helical, bone-white tubers that seemed frozen in the midst of a delicate, upward-spiraling dance. Caine drove past thickets of them, wondered what they were called, reflected on the utter lack of poetry in the meretricious souls that had come to command the fate of this valley. They probably hadn't even bothered to name any of the plants they had seen. To them, it would all simply be categorized as "obstructive vegetation—removal pending."

He eased off the accelerator as he approached: *Don't want to look like I'm in a rush.* He heard and ignored yet another page on the radio, thought a moment, then reached under the dashboard and disconnected the unit.

He emerged into the clearing and, as he heard the spatter of loose rock under his tires once again, he realized that the road to this site was more worn, and smoother, than the one to the oil rigs. It either got more use, more attention, or both. Yet it led to the one location that was left off Caine's itinerary. Whatever Helger didn't want him to see was here.

He slowed as he came amidst the cluster of prefab buildings: newer and better maintained than the ones out at the oil field. More vehicles, also. But it was the small groups of workers—two lounging against a truck, three more under the awning of an administrative prefab, another two walking slowly past a pile of white and dusty dig spoor—who were the most strikingly different. It took a moment for Caine to see what the difference was, as they looked up briefly over the rims of their coffee cups before resuming their casual chats. It wasn't their crisply clean clothes, or their neatly groomed hair, or even their alert faces and scanning eyes: it was their postures of relaxed self-assurance.

One or two looked up from their coffee again, matching Caine's gaze. *Christ: don't stare. Get moving.*

He swung his legs out the door port that had been scalloped low into the chassis of the Rover, settled his hat on his head as he looked up at the sun, and then at his watch. He peripherally saw the watching eyes withdraw as he walked with a casual surety that was pure bluff; he only knew that he needed to get to the excavations.

Caine hadn't been sure what to expect in the way of challenges, but was utterly surprised by what he did encounter: nothing. Slowing to a stroll, he passed compact excavating equipment: caterpillar-tracked backhoes, drills, one small articulated hoist jury-rigged on the back of a large truck. One hard-hatted mechanic emerged from the truck's cab, stared at him without nodding, went on his way.

And that was it: no Cerberus guarding the gate

to whatever buried secret CoDevCo had found here. Caine suppressed the urge to laugh at the anticlimax of the moment, kept walking forward—

—into a litter of chalky white rock. Oval pits dug here and there, one of which was long and narrow. Beyond that was a high berm of loose dirt. *Well, might as well start looking—*

"Hello there."

Caine managed not to flinch, turned to face the voice. A middle-aged man, half-a-head shorter than Caine's six feet, was approaching. He looked more like a librarian than a machine operator: it wasn't just his clothes—appropriate for a company picnic—but his soft, almost delicate face and bookish glasses. "Yes?"

"Hello," the man repeated. "Can I help you?"

"You in charge here?"

"Well, I—I have final authority over dig priorities and scheduling, so I suppose—"

"Fine, then I can talk to you. I've got to check drainage and pump placement. We don't have any details on it and the weather stations are confirming a possible hurricane. So I need to see a schematic of your flood-management systems."

Bookworm blinked several times. "I—but I don't know about this. I mean, no one told me—"

"It's okay, I'll take care of it. No one's fault, really. Not the responsibility of the excavation crews, and the research teams wouldn't know to ask about it if someone didn't mention it. So here I am. Do you have any sump pumps in place?"

"A few down in the main site, near the base of the columns—"

Columns?

"—but only one, just to handle regular rainwater accumulations. This hurricane: could it damage—?"

Caine waved a dismissive hand. "Look: you don't have anything tall exposed above ground level, right?"

"Right."

"Then the worst that could happen is that things will get wet."

"But there might be seepage. The soil we've removed was a barrier, prevented any water from getting as far down as the foundation. If there are sealed chambers, then—"

"Okay, I get the picture. We'll get the necessary machinery out here to take care of it."

"Thank you. Thank you, Mr.—"

But Caine had already turned, and walking away, acknowledged Bookworm's hand-wringing gratitude with a lazy wave. He also resisted the choking urge to race ahead, to run everywhere the ground had been torn up, looking, looking, looking. Columns. Foundations. Possible sealed chambers. A little bit more than just a line of rocks in the ground.

In the small dig pits, he saw what had caught the attention of the CoDevCo surveyors, and what one naval officer—a j.g. who had minored in forensic archeology—had noted in his analysis of close aerial imagery: right angles. Throughout this area, the ground rose up in low, flat, elbowed humps that looked like barrows for carpenter's squares. CoDevCo had obviously read and heeded the j.g.'s report, and sent archeologists—not construction workers—to unearth the underlying mysteries: every hole had the carefully graded sides and the strange yet irregular precision of historical dig sites. The archeologists had evidently started by exhuming these old bones of isodomic wall junctures: moored upon large cornerstones, quoined blocks were stacked two, occasionally three, courses above that fundament.

Caine sidestepped up the final embankment of dirt, backsliding slightly, finally digging in with a quick sprint to get him over the lip—

—and which nearly propelled him into a pit where something vaguely like a partial floor plan of a half-sized Greek temple lay exposed to the sun. After several seconds, Caine realized his mouth was open, closed it. The half-buried stones at the oilfield and the nearby wall-fragments had whispered that a millennium of humanocentrism might need reconsideration. But this bone-white expanse of quasi-Classical architecture decisively rebutted any arrogant assumptions that humanity might be the center of all things, the origin of all causes, the denouement of all purposes.

Caine sidestepped down to the base of the embankment, stretched his foot out onto the marble esplanade, thinking ridiculously, "One small step for a man—" Ridiculous because dozens of humans—hundreds maybe—had walked here before him. But he felt a narrow shiver arc up his spine, nonetheless.

Starting at the extreme left hand of the facing colonnade, four one-meter-high remains of columns were the only vertical objects protruding up beyond the lateral plane of the stylobate. Lighter circular shadows completed the peristyle sequence that the extant columns predicted, all the way out to the far right hand corner. Leading up to them were steps— cracked, disintegrated in many places, but unquestionably steps—which spanned the entire frontage of the structure's crepidoma, or base. Caine raised his foot, knowing he should not tread upon them, but drawn by an urge far stronger—and far more important—than the one which Consuela had inspired in him half an hour earlier.

Movement to the left, from around the corner. Caine pulled his foot back, put his hands in his pockets. An unusually short man of late middle age seemed to emerge from the ground behind the left hand corner of the crepidoma. Tubby, hirsute, bespectacled, making smacking noises with his lips, the gnomish creature stopped when he saw Caine. "Oh. Hello," said the Gnome. "It's something, isn't it?"

"Yeah. Something. Look. There might be a hurricane coming. I've gotta do an assessment for flood control: drainage, sump placement—"

"Good, good," said the Gnome, "glad to hear they're taking the value of the find seriously. Although,"—he stopped, eyes dim through his round, dust-smeared glasses—"I suppose I'm being overly optimistic again. They don't care about the history of this, or its significance. They just want to protect what *they're* hoping to find—and the hell with the rest."

"And what is it that they hope to find?"

Gnome—who had been standing arms akimbo, admiring the structure—turned to look at Caine again, eyebrows raised, "What else? Artifacts."

"Why? For sale on the black market? Alien antiquities, that kind of angle?"

"No, no, no." Gnome shifted into a professorial head-wagging remonstration; he was doing his best to be patient with a slow student. "Not primitive artifacts. Advanced artifacture. Devices. They didn't tell you?"

Caine shook his head. At first, he couldn't speak;

he was simply glad he wasn't gaping. Then, hoarsely: "So, how long—?"

"How long has it been here? Can't be sure; we're still waiting for the radioisotope dating equipment. But I'm guessing—judging from the depth of overhead sediments, the speed with which they seem to accumulate here, the erosion—ten thousand years, at the very least. Instinct and experience tells me it's twice that. I doubt it's more than forty thousand."

"And you found their machines?"

"Not yet. Frankly, I don't think there's anything to find. Stone weathers better than almost anything else. Intricate machines and objects—well, they are the first things to go. And given the priority list Mr. Helger gave us, I don't think he's particularly interested in museum pieces."

Caine had recovered enough to actively steer the conversation. "CoDevCo wants toys that work, huh?"

"Yes, indeed. Weapons applications, I suspect—the blackguards. But I accept their pay, so I suppose I should remain a bit more philosophical about it all."

"They're looking for weapons?"

"Oh, no—not directly. But there are plenty of indications that—" Gnome stopped himself, mouth open in mid-syllable, as if he had checked his didactic enthusiasm at the last possible moment: he was concealing something. When Gnome resumed, his tone was more controlled, careful: "There are indications—historical indications on Earth, that is—showing that there's a close relationship between new weapons and new technologies." He hurried onward from that lame generality: "Personally, I think their hope to find advanced technology at this site is a pipe dream, and I wish they'd wake up from it. Until they do, we're going to be isolated in this damn valley—leaves suspended, contract extension clauses invoked—until God knows when."

"Yep: it's tough." Caine wondered what Gnome had almost revealed, but a deep animal instinct told him not to exert any pressure.

Gnome had evidently forgotten his near-misstep. "It is not merely 'tough': it is crippling. I am not permitted to submit reports, articles, or get proper equipment. And my old university would come back to me on hands and knees with the offer of an endowed chair if they knew half—"

"Thanks," said Caine. He turned and walked back the way he had come, bypassed the embankment, continued up out of the far side of the dig site and kept walking until he reached the edge of the forest. Fifty meters to his right, a trail wound up the slight incline that led into the alien foliage, sparsely peppered with startling red-purples and subtler mauves. Somewhere—in there—were creatures, presumed bipedal, who traveled in groups. Heat signature, speed, and inferred length of gait suggested something roughly man-sized. Who were being pushed out of their natural habitat. Or worse.

But that jungle was, for all intents and purposes, still *terra incognita*: a heart of alien darkness. He stared into it, trying to see further, thought: *And perhaps they are staring out at me.* He thought he saw something move—sweep from the trees down to the ground, a blurred shadow—but it was too quick to be an animal of any kind, he realized. He laughed at himself, part of a fruitless attempt to displace the fear that rose up as he looked into the underbrush and thought: *I must go in there.*

Alone.

Chapter Seven

ODYSSEUS

Consuela didn't meet him at the pool. Didn't join him for drinks. Was not in sight when he entered the executive refectory—which appeared comparable to a three-star restaurant—and asked for dinner.

"Very well—oh, you are Mr. Riordan, are you not?"

"I am."

"I have a private alcove reserved for you. Courtesy of Mr. Helger. Would you please follow me?"

The alcove was paneled in the same faux-ebony as Helger's office. It felt like wood—but with a faint hint of increased surface flexibility. The *maître-d´* smiled efficiently. "Your waiter will be with you momentarily. Is there anything I can do in the meantime?"

Cheerful subservience accompanies all entrees. The house special both within and beyond the refectory. "Nothing, thank you." He reached for a chair himself, forestalling the *maître-d´*'s incipient lunge to help. He had his palmtop out before he sat, reopening the survey files that he was now ready to reassess.

He ran the real-time aerial surveys collected by the

USSF. The best of the thermal imaging scans—from a recon VTOL's FLIR—was partially degraded by the foliage, but the results were still clear: a dozen, maybe fifteen vertically oblong signatures, holding together in pack movement. They had the long, rolling gait of bipeds, not the reach-and-pull movement of quadrupeds at high speed. Mass was indeterminate, but the sensors estimated maximum height to be just under two meters: the right size.

The Navy had landed, looked around, found nothing definitive. In the hollow of a dense thicket of helical tubers, a rating—apparently seeking privacy for a moment of personal relief—discovered some spoor which suggested possible tool use: sharpened sticks, unusually smooth rocks that seemed about hand-sized. There were no anthropologists among that shore party, so they could only guess. The Navy marked the area for subsequent detailed study, posted it as off-limits to the first wave of Commonwealth colonists, and kept an eye out for similar signs in the other regions of Dee Pee Three.

The results of that haphazard monitoring effort were not encouraging. There were one or two possible contacts, but they were recorded by automated sensors: by the time anyone saw the results and dispatched a manned survey unit, the site was cold. Had there been hundreds, even thousands, of the creatures, Dee Pee Three was a big enough world that they could remain unencountered for years, maybe decades.

Dee Pee Three's size wasn't the only variable that complicated the search. Despite being farther from its star than Earth was from the Sun—1.14 AU—Dee Pee Three was a hotter world. Although fractionally smaller than Earth, greater density gave it greater gravity, which in turn had led to a more dense atmosphere. Along with a slightly greater greenhouse effect, it also had less liquid water: sixty percent surface coverage, and those oceans were not very deep. Only a tiny spot on each pole failed to reach summertime highs above zero degrees Celsius, meaning that the ice-caps "migrated" with the seasons, just as they did on Mars. The net result was a planetary mean of about twenty-four degrees Celsius, almost ten degrees higher than Earth. And much of the deviation from an Earthlike baseline was relatively recent: spectral analysis and other indicators suggested that Delta Pavonis had undergone a small but steady increase in stellar luminosity over the last five to ten thousand years. With the sun lamp set a bit higher, Dee Pee Three's thermic equilibrium had teetered a bit: there was plentiful evidence of a recent past in which the weather patterns had been milder, the poles had been small but permanent features, and the heat of the tropic zones had been merely punishing, not lethal. Erosion patterns indicated that in the relatively recent geological past there had been a far greater profusion of ground plants in the equatorial plains, which had held the soils in place: now there were deserts of superheated dust, often carried aloft by the cyclones that followed the changes of the seasons.

Caine read this story of a planet wobbling at the edge of meteorological stability and wondered: is this why the local civilization collapsed, why they almost (or completely) died out? Dee Pee Three had achieved a new equilibrium now, but had there been a period of cataclysmic weather effects? Had an epoch of floods, tornadoes, hurricanes driven a fragile young civilization back over the edge of progress, propelled the survivors back into preintelligent primitivism?

The Navy had expressed similar uncertainty about the climate, but not from the standpoint of forensic anthropology: they were concerned with long-term habitability. Therefore, after the early days of the survey—when the first tantalizing hints of unseen bipeds were trickling in—the official emphasis was shifted to meteorological data gathering. The combination of higher average temperature and lower hydrographics still created some ferocious—but fairly localized—weather anomalies. So, in order to avoid colonizing such areas, the assessment and measurement of regional weather and environment got first priority.

Later travelers' tales had been appended to the official Navy reports. Ruins (but it failed to say which) were first reported by a mixed group of Canadians and Irish who decided to go on a lark and see the off-limits Shangri-La valley for themselves. The apocryphal tale—retold in the clipped, unimaginative diction of Navy reportage—was that the group had started gathering rocks to build a windbreak for a campfire when they realized they were picking up chunks of dressed stone. Caine smiled: what a moment that must have been...

"Did you find your independent excursion illuminating, Mr. Riordan? I'm sure you would have found it more informative—and enjoyable—had you remained with your guide."

Caine looked up: Helger and a companion. "The guide left the final, very illuminating site off my itinerary."

"An unfortunate oversight." Helger sat, signaled for wine, looked to Caine, who shook his head. Helger did not extend the offer to his companion: an immense, square-shouldered man with pale blond hair and pale blue eyes, who sat immobile in trail clothes. He was the only male in the refectory wearing shorts, and who was not recently shaven. He either did not notice, or did not mind, Helger's failure to offer him wine.

Helger continued his unapologetic apology. "Had you so wanted to see that site, you could have simply requested it."

"So Ms. Rakir could call ahead and confabulate a closure, or flood the dig site, or report a quarantine? Thanks, no: I felt I was more likely to get a good look if I went on my own."

"Your suspicions are hardly flattering to me, Mr. Riordan—or consistent with the agreement we made yesterday. Cooperation is a two-way proposition, and one that can only work if we are being open with each other."

"Oh—you must mean the kind of openness that Ms. Rakir exhibited when she assured me that a couple of half-buried wall remains at the oil field were the *only* evidence of intelligent habitation."

"*Prior* habitation," Helger corrected. "And I think you must have misunderstood Ms. Rakir—or she was unclear. We would never have claimed such a thing."

"No? Then why did you leave the main ruins off my itinerary? You presumed that I'd be *un*interested? Strange presumption, considering that this is just the kind of violation I was sent to investigate—and which only makes your dismissal of the USSF survey that much more suspect. I think 'suspect' is a very charitable term, don't you?"

Helger was silent as his wine arrived. He sampled it and then dabbed his lips. "We discovered the ruins after our independent survey. But we were quite aware of how it would look. We saw no reason to attract the inevitable accusations and condemnation any earlier than necessary."

"That's another strange statement, since the group that inadvertently found the first sign of ruins did so five months *before* CoDevCo conducted its survey. And, according to their report"—*okay, just one lie to see if I've guessed correctly*—"they didn't stumble across the rocks near the oilfields first; my report indicates the group was 'relatively near the river' when they came across the 'remains.' That means that they discovered the main site first."

Helger sipped his wine. "I fail to see the relevance of these rather insignificant details."

So the main ruins were the first ones discovered. Hell, the others might just be decoys—for dupes like me. "These insignificant details will interest the Hague, the EU Investigatory Commission, and the Commonwealth, Mr. Helger. They indicate that you knew—before your surveyors arrived—what you really wanted to extract from Dee Pee Three. The survey was a sham to cover up your attempt to prospect for alien artifacts."

"So you are reneging on your offer of cooperation so soon? My, it didn't even last one day."

"Mr. Helger, it didn't even last one morning, because while Ms. Rakir made sure I was discovering your supposed company secret—the oil wells—you were hustling Ms. Fireau into a VTOL for Downport. So much for my meeting with her—which you yourself scheduled for me."

"Mr. Riordan, you flatter me with your presumption that I am God, for you seem to assume that I can foresee and prevent any event which would intrude upon the plans we made in good faith. In the case of Ms. Fireau, there was a business emergency in Little Leyden that was best attended to by the manager who had the longest tenure there. So what you are characterizing as conspiracy is merely an unfortunate coincidence."

"Unfortunate for me—suspiciously convenient for you. I wonder if she will return before I depart, just as I wonder if I will find her in Little Leyden once I've returned to Downport."

Helger's mouth didn't smile, but his eyes were crinkled and smug. "Who can say?"

"Who indeed. Besides, when I get back to Downport, I expect to be too busy to look her up."

"Oh? And why is that?"

"I'll be too busy filing reports that will retroactively justify the instructions I am going to relay immediately after dinner tonight."

Helger seemed amused. "Instructions? What instructions? And to whom?"

"To the Navy—which, if CoDevCo doesn't immediately cease archeological excavation, will compel the Port Authority to suspend *all* inbound and outbound movement of cargos, personnel, and communiqués."

Helger got pale, but then his color returned along with an unpleasant smile. "Mr. Riordan, this bluff is beneath your dignity. No messages get in or out of Shangri-La without my express permission: all external contact is routed through our Office of Communications. And I am not about to authorize any such transmissions."

"Actually, I think you are."

Helger's smile widened and he studied his blood-red wine. "Mr. Riordan, in a place such as this, it is not wise to presume that you know what will happen next. This is a frontier world: anything can happen. And often, the most unusual events go unobserved or unreported. For instance, were you to fail to stroll out the front door of the refectory this evening, who would notice—or miss you?"

There it was: the thinly veiled threat—and with it, the opportunity to riposte. "Actually, some people *would* miss me—and would be asking you where I was, shortly after I failed to walk out that door."

Helger was evidently disappointed that his threat had not jarred Caine's composure. His tone was more brusque: "I don't think you realize how very alone you are, Mr. Riordan. No one here is obsessed with your whereabouts, or your moment-to-moment safety."

Caine sipped his water. "I have friends in high places."

"I know all about your clearance—"

"No, I don't mean 'high places' figuratively; I mean it literally. 'High' as in 'orbital.'" Caine checked his watch. "In fourteen minutes, I'm due to contact Admiral Eli Silverstein on the USS *Roosevelt:* my daily call-in. He last heard from me when I landed here yesterday, just over sixteen-and-a-half hours ago—and Dee Pee Three's seventeen-hour day rolls around mighty fast. So if he doesn't hear from me very soon, twenty Marines are going to be landing, thrusters and rifles hot, in your courtyard. All told, that would be about twenty-nine minutes from now. And the Marines will be—pointedly—interested in whether or not I ever emerged from this refectory."

Helger had become pale, was no longer smiling.

"You are bluffing. You—the Commonwealth—would not dare—"

"Let's not waste time and words on hypotheticals, Mr. Helger. Why don't we just sit here for twenty-nine minutes and see what happens next? I'm sure you can wait that long to put a bullet in me."

Helger's eyes wavered; had they been equipped with nictating lids, Caine was sure they would have slowly shut at that moment. "Mr. Riordan, you are becoming overly dramatic. I never said anything so overtly threatening."

Caine forced himself to smile. "Of course not."

Helger's smile was no less manufactured. "Perhaps I might be present when you make your call to the admiral, so that I might extend my compliments?"

And to make sure I'm not bluffing. "I would welcome that, Mr. Helger. That way, if you have any questions about my status here—and his prerogatives—you may ask him yourself."

"Very well. Now, surely you were exaggerating when you threatened to have even our routine landings and launches suspended."

"Surely, I was not."

"Preposterous: you haven't the authority to initiate such an action."

"Be assured, Mr. Helger: I have the authority, and I will use it. Today, if I must."

Helger's hand stopped short of his glass. "Again, you are bluffing."

"Again, you are wrong. I have no naval rank, but I have access to classified codes which can activate a variety of local contingency orders. I submitted one such code to the admiral the moment I arrived in-system."

"Odd: the Commonwealth naval routine seems unaltered."

"And it will remain so—until and unless a certain activating condition is met."

"And what is the activating condition?"

Caine smiled. "My disappearance or demise."

"I see." Helger waved the waiter away restively. "So, if I shut down the dig site, I can keep my oil operation running."

"For now, yes." *Of course, once I'm no longer in your crosshairs, I'll recommend the Navy shuts that down, too. But if I take away the oil now, then you've got nothing left to lose—and you might once again decide that there's no reason* not *to get rid of me—permanently.*

"What guarantee do I have that I will be allowed to keep my wells in operation after you leave?"

"Mr. Helger, I do not have the power to make such guarantees. I will assure you of this: if I find no further violations, I will not make any negative recommendations regarding your oil operations." *Not that the Navy's going to listen to my recommendations, anyway: I already know how Eli Silverstein is going to react. When I leave, and I give him the code authorizing his use of full discretionary powers, Silverstein is going to demand that site control is restored to the legitimate European Union administrators, or he'll impose a full shutdown.*

Helger's lower lip protruded a bit; he pulled at it. "Very well: it seems I have little choice. Does this mean you are done here?"

"I'm afraid not. I have something else that I need to investigate, although it's nothing that should concern you directly."

Helger relaxed a bit; he curved a finger in the direction of the waiter, gestured toward the wine. The waiter dutifully disappeared to fetch and do as he was bid. "And this final investigation is...what?"

"Reports of possibly intelligent creatures in this valley. Would you happen to know anything about that?"

Helger maintained the same nerveless pose, but his face was less relaxed. "I hear the same wild stories that everyone else hears. Local apes, forest men, spirits of the wood: relatives of sasquatch and the yeti, I will wager."

"You have no evidence of local wildlife that travels in groups, shows any tendency toward tool use?"

"Me? No—but you could consult Mr. Bendixen, here. I brought him along because he is our best field expert and woodsman, and I suspected that you were planning on conducting a search for these fabled creatures. Why else would you have arrived with a backpack instead of luggage, and a rifle instead of golf clubs?"

"Thanks. I might indeed ask Mr. Bendixen a few questions."

"I suggest you make better use of him than that. He is an excellent guide."

"Again, thanks—but I had planned on working alone."

"You might wish to reconsider that plan, Mr. Riordan. You may not be aware of it, but we have our share of dangerous animals here in the valley. One in particular—we call it Pavonosaurus rex—is quite aggressive. More akin to an undersized allosaurus, I am told, but then again, paleontology has never been my strong suit. So do take Mr. Bendixen along: he has had experience with them. Personally."

Caine looked over at Bendixen: square-banged, square-jawed, square-headed, and sleepy-eyed—but very watchful. Throughout the conversation with Helger, Caine could not recall having seen Bendixen blink or smile or even move. Prominently featured in the front-strap bandoleers that were part of Bendixen's web-gear were two different kinds of old-fashioned brass cartridges: one kind for shotguns, the other an immense round with a sharply-tapering—or *spitzen*—bullet. He had a magazine bag that Caine recognized as being for an H&K G-81 assault rifle: caseless ammo, bullpup configuration, extremely high rate of fire. The more primitive tools of his apparently less-than-pacifistic trade included a machete, and a knife: no, two—no, *three* knives. One of the knives was a very old—almost antique—Spetsnaz all-tool utility blade, another was balanced for throwing, and the third was a kukri: the combat blade made famous by the Gurkhas, who swore that its design made it the optimal weapon for close-quarters combat.

Helger's second glass of wine had arrived. "Mr. Bendixen is ready to go tomorrow."

Caine looked at Bendixen again—who looked back without blinking. "No thanks." Caine was relatively certain that Pavonosaurus rex represented far less threat to his continued existence than did Mr. Bendixen.

"A pity. He is so routinely in the bush—surveying—that I'm sure he would have been of immense help as a guide, as well."

"I'm sure." Of course, not bringing Bendixen didn't neutralize the threat: "accidents" were always possible. "Mr. Helger, actually I would like to make a request of Mr. Bendixen."

"Which is?"

"Which is that he suspend his field activities for a few days—at least until I'm done with mine."

Helger feigned perplexity: Bendixen just stared.

"Well, if we were both out in the bush at the same time, we could be a risk to each other. As strange as it sounds, I am particularly worried about being a risk to him."

Helger laughed. "Really?"

"Well, yes. If our paths were to cross—by accident—I might only see the movement and shoot preemptively, thinking to kill a predator." *Which is what I'd be doing in either case.* "So, please follow this directive, Mr. Helger: until I return, I'm requesting—politely—that you suspend sending any personnel into my search area. Which is here." Caine picked up his palmtop, pulled up the Navy Survey map again, drew a box on it with his stylus: the red rectangle began at the north edge of the main ruins and extended all the way up the floor of the valley. "I'll be relaying those grid coordinates—and the fact that I should be the only human in that area—to Admiral Silverstein's ops officer in five minutes. That way, if I go missing for any reason, they'll know where to look for me. And they'll know that there couldn't be any chance of Mr. Bendixen having mistaken *me* for a pavonosaurus."

Helger had not laughed again; he was no longer even smiling. "I see. You seem to fear the errors of humans more than the appetites of large animals."

"Perhaps I fear the many dangerous appetites of humans more than anything else, Mr. Helger. At any rate, I thank you for seeing to it that I will be working in isolation."

Now Helger smiled. "Be assured: you will be working in complete isolation. Do be sure to bring enough batteries for your radio."

Caine nodded: in addition to testing his conventional radio, the time had come to unpack his special equipment from the Navy and give it a trial run. The uplink beacon/communicator—currently folded down into the yellow-stenciled olive-drab canister at the bottom of his A-frame—had been a gift from one Lieutenant Mike Brill, communications officer for the high port naval detachment. Caine had protested the weight and the awkwardness. Brill had insisted that Caine take the system planetside: "You can save your life with a direct link to orbit; remember that every time you're tempted to bitch about the extra weight." At that time, Caine had thought Brill's precautionary insistence to be absurdly melodramatic.

It did not seem so anymore.

Chapter Eight

ODYSSEUS

Two weeks later, the treetop chittering of what Caine had dubbed squirrel-spiders was almost drowning out the bored commo operator back at Site One: "We have CINCPAV COMCENT on the line for another check-in, Mr. Riordan; your signals are being relayed directly through our transceiver. You may proceed."

"Lieutenant Brill?"

"Negative: this is Eli Silverstein. How was day one of your extended walkabout, Caine?"

"Admiral Silverstein. I'm, uh, honored—and surprised."

The answering laugh was gruff, honest. "You're not Navy, so I'm not 'Admiral.' Just Eli—unless you've taken a dislike to me."

"No, no—Eli." *And thanks for answering yourself today: it will help keep Helger's head down, keep him from hatching any bright new schemes about "accidents" I might have. He won't risk pissing off the USSF's system CO.* "Good to hear from you. The new walkabout is going just fine."

"No more trouble with your equipment?"

"No more troubles." A week ago, just before his second day-trip further north into the valley, Caine had decided to inspect his ammunition. The rifle rounds—dependable, old-fashioned 7.62 x 51 mm— were fine, but he had discovered a potentially fatal flaw in the propellant receptacle of his NeoCoBro machine pistol. The receptacle seal had a deep and recent nick in its gasket: had Caine even test-fired the weapon before checking it, excessive amounts of the exothermic liquid in the propellant canister would have been injected into the catalytic ignition chamber. The resulting explosion would have been dangerous, even deadly. It was a suspicious flaw—particularly since Caine had checked the gasket himself after Brinkley had issued him the weapon as a close-range defense against pavonosaurs and their ilk. He had not bothered to mention—for everyone implicitly understood the significance—that the only time the weapon had been out of his immediate possession was when he had gone for his drive with Consuela. Helger's symbolic fingerprints were manifest upon the gasket.

"Caine, I chose to be here when you checked in today because I want you to reconsider your change in plans. Frankly, I'm not sure how good an idea it is for you to start camping out in the bush at night, rather than always returning to Site One. You've got no backup."

Caine looked up at the rapidly setting yellow disk of Delta Pavonis, sliced into segments by the palmate leaves adorning the tops of the giant ferns. *Silverstein's worried about both the human and indigenous predators. So am I.* "I copy that, Eli. But it can't be helped.

There's no road access to the northern reaches of the valley, and there's no place to put down a vertibird: we conducted a close aerial recon for landing sites all of yesterday. No luck. Do you have maps that show otherwise?"

The pause gave him the answer before Silverstein spoke. "Negative. The few areas that are flat enough are all covered by jungle canopy."

"That's what we saw from the air. But I've got to get further in, Eli: round trip in and out doesn't allow me to push more than about twenty klicks beyond the ruins. And that doesn't give me any time to look around. I'm just humping my ruck blind through the bush. No recon value."

"I copy that, Caine. Listen, do you have enough batteries?"

"I'm fine, and will check in frequently with Site One."

"Who will patch me through every time."

A command given for the benefit of Helger, who had not indicated that he was listening to their communiqué. But again, everyone knew better.

"Okay, Eli. I should be fine. As it is, I'm now about thirty klicks in. First new ground I've seen in nine days."

"Well, good luck. Keep us in the loop and don't be shy about calling in. Brill's giving me all sorts of hell for not sending you out with more equipment." That was a backhanded reference to the equipment he *did* have: specifically, the uplink beacon/communicator. It was also a reference that Helger wouldn't understand: Caine had hidden the uplink/communicator before leaving his room that first morning: its tamper-proof case had never been disturbed.

"It was good chatting with you, Eli. I'll keep you posted. Out."

"Out."

Caine folded in the antenna on his smaller, conventional radio and watched Delta Pavonis wink out behind the sheltering peaks: fronds waved in front of it, their silhouettes coyly assisting the setting star with its farewell fan-dance. The largest of the weed-bushes resisted the dying of that light: the mauve spines of their great, spatulate leaves began to glow faintly. Floral bioluminescence.

Caine unwrapped a condensed protein chew-stick, gnawed at the exposed end while he unpacked the perimeter motion sensors he had borrowed from Helger's equipment cache. He hopped down from the broad rocky shelf upon which he planned to sleep: according to most accounts, the pavonosaurs and their smaller relatives did not like moving across rock. Their heavily taloned, four-toed feet were evolved for maximum traction and turning speed in the thick loams and dense underbrush of heavily vegetated areas. Upon unyielding rocks, their talons were like iron spikes, always at risk of skittering out of control.

Caine moved fifteen meters away from his little sleeping-mesa, starting walking its perimeter at that range, placing the sensors as he went. It was already deep dusk when he finished his protein stick, placed the last sensor—and heard a noise in the brush behind him.

Recent practice paid off: he had the shoulder-slung Valmet semiautomatic down and in his hands in a single motion, snapping the safety off as he brought it against his hip. Nothing—yet. *Use the seconds you have.* Holding the venerable assault rifle steady—his right hand tucking the pistol grip into his body—he reached up with his left and pulled the night vision goggles down sharply from their perch on his forehead. His left hand never stopped moving: leaving the goggles, he brought it down to the rifle's forestock, then brought the weapon up to his shoulder as he scanned the brush.

The bioluminescent leaves stuck out like the skeletons of burning green-white trees, courtesy of the light-amplification lenses. The integrated thermal-imaging system showed the body heat of a fading contact—either very small or very distant—receding up the slope, directly away from Caine's camp. Intriguing, but first things first: he turned slowly, weapon up, scanning the entire perimeter. Nothing else. He swung back to the first contact: gone. As though it had never been there. Very small—or very fast—indeed. Here, as on Earth, and probably on every world where predators had ears, the night sounds reasserted once the rapid motions and urgent activity had passed.

Caine tilted the goggles back up on his head, felt the darkness wash in around him like a tidal surge of enigma. He hopped back up on the irregular rock platform that was his campsite, stared at his sleeping roll. Before, at the end of a day's hiking, it had always been a mute promise of sleep.

Tonight, it looked like a body bag.

Caine looked up at the sun: almost midday. He finished rolling up the sleeping bag, felt himself smile. Three days ago—his first alone in the bush—he had hardly been able to sleep. This morning, he had slept until noon. Part of that was exhaustion: he had pushed hard the last two days, criss-crossing the land from the western bank of the river to the foot of the mountains as he pressed further north. But mostly, he owed his sound sleep to acclimatization. The nights were quiet here—or had been so far. Dawn and dusk were periods of frenetic activity for the smaller animals, the most plentiful of which were small burrowing lizard-toads (or so they appeared) and arboreal opossum-koalas that were ugly enough to make him wince. He had heard some large animals during the day, but had never seen them. Because he was stalking immobile objects—spoor, further ruins, anything that might signify the past or current presence of an intelligent creature—he made no special attempt to remain silent or unseen. Consequently, the larger animals—whatever they were—obviously saw and/or heard him coming from far away, and elected to maintain their distance. Having slept late, he wondered if any of the larger creatures might have strayed a little closer to him: maybe he would get a glimpse—

A shuddering crash in the underbrush—not more than one hundred meters further up the valley—triggered an immediate repentance of his curiosity. He snatched the Valmet, snapped the large safety lever down, dropped to one knee, sighted in the direction of the sound.

Which reprised itself, coming closer. Something was pounding through the bush: a dense *thump, thump, thump* was punctuating the other intermittent sounds—ferns being smashed aside, tuber-trees squealing out sharp bursts of the air that they held within their hollow trunks, bladderlike. He saw movement—a rustle in the ferntops—at two o'clock, swung about slowly to face in that direction, iron sights raised to his right eye.

A blackish-brown shape burst out of the brush, well in advance of the approaching thumps. Caine almost fired, then flinched his finger off the trigger—just before he realized it was going too fast for him to hit, anyhow: the creature had already swerved to one side, evidently either avoiding Caine or taking evasive action. *Probably evasive action*—because the heavy pounding sound was now right behind it.

The sound seemed to break free of the same dense thicket in a dusty burst of tubers, shoots, and fronds, all erupting away from the pavonosaur that churned to a stop in the midst of the savaged foliage. The predator searched right and left—and then snapped erect as it noticed something it had evidently never seen before.

A human.

Caine stared back at the monster. The pavonosaur's body had a narrow cross section, tapering into a long, sharp, paddlelike tail that might have belonged to a monstrous tadpole. Its head completed the suggestion that this creature was built for speed both on land and in the water: the long, thin snout—more reminiscent of a crocodile than a dinosaur—was not scaled, but was the tip of a seamless carapace that swept back around and over the eye-and-ear sensor cluster, ending in a small, bone-finned crest that covered the rear of the skull. The mouth cycled through a panting open-closed motion, revealing not teeth, but a set of serrated ridges, threatening like three serried ranks of wood saws.

Caine swallowed, held as still as he could, cheated

the barrel down a little lower. *It's a young one. Three meters toe to top, at most. Aim low and shoot steady. Twenty rounds in the box, staggered between dum-dums and tungsten-cored discarding sabot. He can't take more than four or five hits. Can he? Can he? Jesus, let's get this over with: start your charge, you ugly bast—*

The pavonosaur's head swung back in the direction his prey had fled, and with a hissing rattle, he leaped along that course—

Because the black-brown biped was still there.

Caine—maniacally focused upon the pavonosaur—only now noticed that the first creature had not made good its escape. Or, if it had, it had returned. *What the hell—?*

It's trying to help. No other possible reason.

Caine had swung the gun, tracking the pavonosaur, before he was aware of doing so. He squeezed the trigger twice, shouted "Hey, HEY!" in the intervals between the recoil of the rounds.

Neither hit. But the pavonosaur swiveled its head in his direction so quickly that Caine wasn't sure he saw the motion: one moment its head was lowered in pursuit of the biped, the next it was staring at Caine.

Staring back, leaning forward into a challenge posture, wondering if this meant he was suicidal, brave, or both, Caine shouted: "HEEYYY! SHIT-HEAD!"

The pavonosaur answered with a painfully high-pitched screech and came streaming over the ground, bent low and forward as it sprinted toward him.

Caine leaned low into the sights and fired one, two, three rounds—

The third clipped the pavonosaur in the shoulder.

It came more quickly, if that were possible, without a single waver in its stride.

Caine was about to start hammering out the rest of the clip but saw a change in the creature's gait. It was slowing—but not because it was hurt, or reconsidering its charge: it was preparing to gather its legs under it to jump up on the rock that Caine had slept upon.

Wait: right before it jumps—was an instinct more than a thought. Fortunate, because the pavonosaur was quicker than human cognition. Even as Caine was realizing that the creature was going to give him a split-second opportunity to fire at a stationary target, the monster had half-contracted into its preparatory crouch.

Caine saw the torso rise into his sights; he fired three fast rounds. He rode the recoil of the last back down and kept firing, steady and sustained, about one round every second.

At least two of the first three hit: the pavonosaur stopped just as it was about to uncoil upwards into its leap, tried to recover, caught another round square in the center of its chest. That produced a dark coppery-purple stain and a screech that was equal parts shock, pain, and indignation. It tried to reset for its jump, but Caine's steady volume of fire kept the monster from regaining the initiative. Two rounds went wide or high: two more hit its torso—and the animal staggered back, either unaccustomed, or completely unadapted, to a flight reflex.

That moment of delay was the fateful—and fatal—moment in its attack. Caine's bullets now hit regularly. More purple spattered outward, this time lower in the belly. Then a thin, pulsing spray—brighter and more coppery—at the base of the neck. Two more hits and the pavonosaur slumped over with a crash that Caine could feel through the rock under his knees.

Caine breathed, was ready to indulge in a relieved forward sag—and realized that he had, at most, three rounds left in the clip. *And if they hunt in pairs—*

He was on his feet, right index finger pushing forward against the magazine release as his left hand tore open the cover of an ammo pouch and tugged out a fresh magazine. As the expended clip clattered at his feet, he brought the other up into the receiver, wrestled briefly to get it seated correctly, and then gave its bottom a sharp upwards slap. A crisp snap announced it was ready. Caine retrained the rifle on the bush that had vomited out the pavonosaur: nothing.

Movement to the left—slow, silent—caught his attention: the biped? Still there?

He turned his head, careful not to have the barrel of the gun track along with his gaze.

The biped was still there—possibly staring back at him. Caine couldn't tell because he couldn't see anything that looked like eyes. A smallish and tightly-furred head—shaped like an edge-on tetrahedron—topped an improbably long neck that swayed slightly back and forth like that of an ostrich: that had been the motion Caine had noticed. The body, also closely furred, was akin to a wasp-waisted gibbon with comically long limbs and oddly-flanged hip joints. A knee-length, bifurcated tail flexed once, restively—and then each half pursued its own, independent prehensile coilings and unfurlings.

Now what? Want a nice banana, monkey? Take me to your leader? Let's pretend this never happened?

Caine decided not to move, not to speak. Anything could be misunderstood—except what he was doing now. With all animals—whether intelligent or not—the best outcome for any first encounter is not a breakthrough in communication, or peace-offerings, or an exchange of phone numbers: it can simply be measured by duration. The longer it is, the better it is—and the more likely that neither party will consider a second contact aversive.

So Caine stood and looked at the biped, which was evidently doing something similar in return. Caine started counting: *one-one-thousand, two-one-thousand, three-one-thousand . . .*

At "thirty," the gangly gibbon-with-double-coati-tail was still there, scratching at one—thigh?—with half of his tail. Evidently, this degree of relief was insufficient; he/she/it reached out a hand—or paw, or something—that seemed to writhe at, rather than scratch, the troublesome spot.

Oh, well, if we've become comfortable enough for actual movement—Caine shifted the gun, looked down to check the time—and noted rapid motion from the corner of his eye.

The biped seemed to speed sideways into the bush, as though it had turned its hips without turning its torso, or had somehow rotated its legs at the hip. Either way, it was gone before Caine could blink.

Evidently, the biped's prior decision to engage in unconstrained movement had not indicated a willingness to tolerate the same from Caine. Instead, the creature had reserved the exclusive right to run like hell at the faintest hint of action from the newcomer. Which was a perfectly reasonable choice, Caine reflected: had anyone taken a picture of him during his motionless half minute, they might well have titled

the image, "Still Life of Human with Assault Rifle."
After what the local had seen that weapon do to a
pavonosaur, he/she/it had every reason to err on the
side of extreme caution.

*Local. I'm calling it a "local." The assumption of
intelligence—that's a big step.*

But was it? Bipedal posture, opposable manipulatory
digits, a voluntary return to danger in the hope of—
what?—luring the pavonosaur away from the hapless
stranger? Or was it all on a par with African mountain
gorillas—behaviors that mimicked, yet were not really
indicative of, intelligence? *One way to find out.*

Caine moved off the rock slowly—both watchful
for other predators and determined not to make any
sudden motions that an unseen observer might find
unsettling—and walked over to where the biped had
stood. A quick scan revealed nothing. Caine followed
the creature's exit trajectory into the bush and again
saw nothing—except a large, recently snapped frond
stem. Caine frowned: odd. The creature seemed so
adept at moving in the forests, it was hard to believe
that it would have been so clumsy as to break—

No. That wasn't what had happened.

Caine darted into the bush, scanning quickly—and
five meters further on, found another freshly snapped
tuber. No other damage to the foliage was evident: not
a leaf turned back, not a weed crumpled underfoot.
Nothing except the freshly exposed pith of the tuber,
gleaming like a white trail-blaze. Which is exactly what
the local was doing: leaving a trail.

Caine looked into the forest: yes, they were *locals*.

Chapter Nine

ODYSSEUS

Caine shifted the A-frame, ran a wet forearm across his more-wet brow, checked his watch: three hours until sunset and he was still playing follow-the-leader with the local. *How long is this going to go on?*

Caine could have spat at himself: *as long as it takes, asshole. This is first contact: not something you fit into a convenient slot on your busy day-planner.* He pushed on—

—and emerged onto a trail. An actual, groomed foot path, a little wide, by human standards. It would have been invisible had he not been looking for it: no visible damage to the surrounding vegetation, yet no growth in the harder-packed dirt, or starting up from the sides of stones worn smooth and flat. Weeds never got a chance to grow here.

Caine pulled out his palmtop, patched into the rudimentary GPS net, synced it to the survey maps, and as he waited for the machine to orient itself, he looked up and down the trail.

About ten meters to the left—roughly to the

113

south—there was a broken vine: snapped clean, the two dusty-rose-colored cross sections stared at him like a pair of bright, pupilless eyes. *Okay, that way then.*

The palmtop flashed readiness: the broken vine was, in fact, due south. Just a kilometer further west— although he couldn't see it through the canopy—was the foot of the nearest mountain. The local had been pushing in that direction until he reached this north-south trail. Caine zoomed out from the map, tapped the stylus on his current location, then again on the main ruins at the extreme southern edge of the screen, made a range inquiry. 102.4 kilometers. He turned the palmtop off to save the batteries, looked south. *Okay, so you want me to follow you south. Back the way I came. Are you trying to get me to go away, to return to my start point? Or do you think I'm lost and you're trying to help me find my way back home? Or do you have something else in mind?*

Caine slipped the palmtop back into his chest pocket, hefted the A-frame higher up onto his shoulders: *only one way to find out.* He started south.

Less than a kilometer further on, the footpath split. The main trail, marked by a broken tuber, was still visible, although somewhat less distinct; it angled gently to the right, up into the hills. The other path was new, almost invisible: it was the faintest hint of parted foliage—barely a game trail. It veered sharply to the left, back east toward the river. Five meters down that trail, through two layers of overhanging mosses, Caine caught a glimpse of yet another cleanly-snapped tuber.

I'm to follow both paths. Hmm. A tour of the local highlights.

He pulled out the palmtop, marked the position on the GPS map overlay, moved up the main trail to the right.

He had covered about a kilometer—could see the steep, green sheltering slope through the gaps in the canopy—when the path widened and then disappeared around an outthrust spur of the mountain. Caine followed in that direction—and stopped as he turned the corner of the moss-mottled stone ridge.

The structure—cut out of the natural rock—would have been invisible to scans. Its density and smooth outlines were consistent with, and blended directly into, the skirts of the mountain. Steps radiated out and down from a broad, out-curving esplanade. Tiers cut into either side of the rocky shoulders hemmed it in: an amphitheater of some kind.

Caine looked behind: nothing was following him—at least nothing he could see. He turned back toward the structure, noting the squat obelisks that followed the curved lip of the esplanade like low, roofless pillars. He approached slowly, resisted an impulse to unsling his rifle, saw hints of galleries in the shadows at the rear of the raised floor of the arena, cut back into the mountain itself.

He stopped at the base of the stairs, uncertain, noted that the hair along his brow had become more damp. *Why so anxious? Look: nothing lives here, nothing has for thousands of years. And if the local wanted you dead, you'd have been led into a deadfall pit or some other trap an hour ago. You're supposed to see this, which means you're probably safer now than any time since you landed in this valley. So why the jitters?* Caine looked at the outthrust arc of the broad stairs, each riser almost half a meter in width, and then up at the squat obelisks. *Because it's strange, alien-looking: not like the mini-Acropolis back at Site One. And because*—he looked around again—*because there are no weeds. None of the stones have fallen—or, if they have, they've been removed. Maybe the locals—*caretake *this place...?*

The locals provisionally rose higher on Caine's *ad hoc* scale of cultural complexity. Did they remember that these were the creations of their ancestors? Did they have a sense of history that strove to reach back into such a distant past? If they did, they were not so very different from some of the more remote tribes of Earth, only a century ago.

Caine took out his photographic equipment slowly, as if a sudden movement would startle the stones, would scare the—*well, what do I call this? The ruins? No; not the right word. The memorial? The historical preserve?* Whatever it was, "ruin" was not the correct label: that term suggested the wear of ages and of neglect. This structure was, admittedly, time-worn—but there was no sign of neglect.

He measured the steps, so strangely broad and low; each one was between fifty and fifty-one centimeters wide, but only ten centimeters high. And they were not "built": like everything except the ring of low obelisks, they had been hewn from the native stone. Caine traversed the floor of the arena, hearing the whisper of his boots bounce back from the rock that rose up on either side, stopped in front of the rear galleries. Again, a strange architecture: the walls that faced out into the arena had been cut through, converted into openworks of intricate filigree patterns. The two doorways that led into the cavelike chamber beyond were ovate, narrowing up into a peak.

Caine recorded and measured and inspected the site for ten minutes, checked his watch, and discovered his perceptual error: he had been here for almost an hour. He had ninety minutes—at most—before the sun started to set, and he still had the second, smaller trail to explore. He hastily stuffed his sensors and photographic gear into the top of his backpack and jogged away from the structure.

Having been in all its chambers, he knew there was no one in the structure watching him as he left. But that didn't diminish the sense that timeless eyes were fixed upon his spine as he disappeared back into the jungle.

After reaching the narrow, newer trail, he followed it for five hundred meters and then stopped: up ahead, there was a break in the canopy, large enough to let in a considerable volume of Delta Pavonis' fading honey-colored rays. Caine took another dozen steps, glad for the opportunity to enjoy standing in some bright, unobstructed light. His day-end fantasies concocted a convenient shelf of rock, handy kindling, a campfire: all so real he could almost smell it—

He could. He could smell it. Burned wood, or plants—like a grass fire.

He unshouldered the rifle and moved off the trail, but kept it in sight, ten meters to his left. He edged forward, paralleling it as the canopy thinned and the light grew—and revealed a broad, open circle of dirt. *What the hell—?*

Hell. Yes, hell would smell like that. It wasn't just the odor of burnt grass: it was meat, too. But not cooked: incinerated. He did not sweat, but felt his temples pulsing hard and fast: it was a different species of terror than he had felt while facing down a charging pavonosaur. This was a sharp, cold wariness—because any bush could hide death, and any thicket could conceal the worst foe of all:

Humans. They had been here. This was their— his—work, Caine realized as he crept to the edge of the circle of dirt, and pushed at it with his boot. Scorched rock underneath. He rose, rifle muzzle tracking along the brush-line as he moved into the center of the ring, the charnel smell rising around him. He probed with his boot; more burnt rock underfoot, but at the far edge, another smell: gasoline. Thick and pungent, like avgas.

And something else, at the very edge of the circle: a footprint. But not human. Splay-footed, with the heel-print deeper than the front, it looked like a cross between a duck's and a human's foot. Four front toes—long and without any evidence of a strong metatarsal bridge—angled back into a wide, flat sole that flared out again where the heel erupted into a bifurcated back toe. But that rear digit had not left the kind of deep, crisp-edged imprint consistent with a sharp rear talon: it, too, was soft, flexible.

He followed the footprint out of the circle—and stopped: three freshly broken tubers. Just five meters in front of him. All in a row. What could it mean?

Then he looked down and he knew what it meant. End of the trail.

To the right and the left were oval cocoons—or

would that be coffin-garlands?—of the fuchsia and indigo flowers, propped up into tented arches by their jointed, stick-like vines. Inside each colorful shell was a single, usually charred, bone. More footprints were here—dozens, some older, some recent.

He counted: there were thirty-seven of the memorials, stretching away into the brush in either direction. The northernmost end of the burial line was marked by a cluster of snapped tubers, and, looking down as the sun's light faded from honey to amber, he saw a metallic glint. He knew what it was before he picked it up: a spent shotgun casing. The brass collar was twice as high as a commercial round, and its side was stamped with a single "0": single-aught buckshot. A favorite with mass murderers of innocents—and a match for what Caine had seen winking at him from Bendixen's bandoliers. Using a lens-wipe from his photo kit, he picked up the shell casing, wrapped it, put it in his other chest pocket. *Bastards.*

As he emerged back into the small clearing, he saw movement in the bush, crouched, but knew—from the strange sideways rush and then stillness—that it wasn't human. The local had followed—or waited for—him here.

More motion on the other side, and a rush of air in the trees behind him. *Scratch that: the locals are here. All around me.*

Caine held the gun away, knew what he had to do even while several million years of carefully-evolved self-preservation instincts roared negations so loud that he couldn't think. So he acted.

He crouched down, reached far forward, laid the rifle in the direct sunlight. Then he frog-walked a step back, waited another moment, and kneeled. He bowed his head.

The only thing he heard was the blood pounding in his ears—and he listened to it for what seemed like a very long time. Then, from the left, came a shuddering whistle that slowly turned into what was clearly recognizable as a thin keening. Two more "voices" rose up from the right, then many from the higher branches of the canopy behind him. He lost count, knowing only that there were many—dozens, probably.

And then nothing. As if someone had found the off-switch for their grieving, it was over. He looked up, heard a single, dwindling swooping noise in the trees behind him. And that was all. He was alone again.

He rose slowly, picked up his weapon, looked at the sun. *Where to sleep tonight? I need to find some flat rock, a good clear area*—and he suddenly knew that he had seen only one suitable place since leaving the camp where he had killed the pavonosaur twenty years ago this morning. The mountainside amphitheater. He expected to feel fear, but didn't. Not because he had become brave—he knew he hadn't—but because he was too tired by the many successive shocks, fears, and enigmas of the day. He headed back up the trail.

So when he arrived at the head of the trail—where it met the western extension which led to the amphitheater, and the broad northern trail which led back toward the site of his encounter with the pavonosaur—he was beyond being surprised to discover the local waiting there for him. Caine stopped, realized he was still carrying his gun in his hands, shouldered it. The local made a low noise—something like a buzzing purr—and set off on the northern trail. Caine, shrugging to no one but himself, followed without a word.

Following behind the local, Caine noticed what he had not before: that the creature's—*no, the being's*—legs had a "reverse knee," like a dog or a cat, but that it stood and walked in a plantigrade fashion: its full foot in contact with the ground. However, when the local used a bit more speed, he leaned forward into the motion and came up onto his toes, shifting into a typical digitigrade stance. Which produced the distinctive loping gait that Caine had seen in the thermal-imaging footage from the Navy recon VTOL.

Four times within the first five or six kilometers, Mr. Local turned aside, led them into the brush for a few hundred yards. Each time their detour ended at another—albeit smaller—burnt dirt clearing. Caine was beyond outrage or even pity: that was for later, for a time and a place at which the responsible parties could be made—somehow—to pay for their deeds.

The fifth time, Mr. Local did not even bother with a detour. He stopped, turned, pointed off into the bush, huddled down and drew a circle with his finger—which was actually one of four radially-arranged, prehensile digits. He pointed into the bush again. Caine just nodded and followed when Mr. Local resumed their northward course.

The next time, Mr. Local just pointed off to one side of the trail and kept moving. After half a dozen such indications, Caine stopped counting.

Night was falling when Mr. Local veered onto a small path to the left. It plunged into a narrow defile between the shoulders of two foothills which crowded against the trail from the west. Caine checked his watch: in thirty minutes, he was due to contact Site One so that they could relay his daily check-in call to CINCPAV COMCEN—but flanked by these steep granite escarpments, there was no way he was going to get that signal through. And then he realized that, tonight, he would not be checking in with Site One at all. He would be using Brill's portable transmitter to send a three-digit recall code directly to Admiral Silverstein. Establishing contact with Mr. Local meant that Caine's mission was over. It also meant that he had to be extracted posthaste, because now he was in a race to reach Earth before CoDevCo—and possibly others—could stop him from delivering the news of what he had found on Dee Pee Three.

Mr. Local seemed to pick up the pace a bit when the defile opened out into another valley: much smaller, but—for all practical intents and purposes—inaccessible, except through the narrow passage they had just come. *A refuge? Mr. Local's hidden home?*

But Caine saw he was not to learn the answer to that, for Mr. Local selected yet another new trail. This one was a narrow switchback that ascended the rear of the hills, which sheltered this glen from the main valley. It was an easy climb and was mostly carpeted by the spongy weeds and low fronds that were Dee Pee Three's equivalent of meadow grass.

It was dark when they reached the summit of the hill and stood looking out across the valley and up toward the stars. Caine hazarded a closer approach to Mr. Local, who made no move away when the human came to stand beside him. Caine wondered if he would be so brave in the Pavonian's place—and doubted it.

For a long moment they looked at the stars together

in silence. Then the Pavonian crouched down and patted the ground. Then he patted his own chest. He repeated the combination: he patted the ground and patted his chest.

Yes. Your place. Your planet. I wish I could tell you how sorry—

But then Mr. Local stood again, and pointed at Caine, the tendril-finger unfolding with slow, deliberate precision at the center of his chest. Then Mr. Local turned and pointed up, back across the valley.

At the stars.

Caine felt his scalp jump back reflexively. *My God, he knows. He knows we're from space. Good Christ—* "Yes. Yes, yes. That's right. We're from there, from the stars—"

The Pavonian made a rumbling noise in his chest—which was where his mouth seemed to be—and moved back a step. He pointed at Caine again.

Who nodded. *Okay. Me.*

Then Mr. Local slowly, cautiously, moved behind Caine, before extending his arm, then his hand, and then one tendril at the stars—again.

Caine followed along the sightline of the alien arm, hand, finger—and noted, with surprise, that he was looking at something very familiar. Although appearing flattened, the Big Dipper was clearly visible about one-third of the way above the center of the western horizon. The cup of the dipper was a square box here, the handle now a straight bar with one kink in it.

The surrounding stellar patterns similarly reprised those found in Earth's own night sky. The Big Dipper was still discernibly part of the larger constellation of Ursa Majoris, which had retained much of its shape.

However, here the Great Bear was somewhat thinner, leaner—more like a wolverine. Except, this one had grown bull's horns—and had a very bright yellow eye.

Caine stood silently for several long seconds, waiting. *Okay: so I'm looking.* He turned; Mr. Local was very close, and Caine finally saw his eyes—a triangle of lusterless mauve circles on each angled "side" of his face.

Mr. Local withdrew his arm and waited a moment. Then with great, deliberate slowness—as if educating a child of unpromising perspicacity—he pointed at Caine. His finger recurled into his palm. He moved so that he was directly behind Caine and his arm stretched out above Caine's shoulder. Once again the finger uncoiled—but this time, so sharply that it snapped out like a whip and quivered.

Okay—I get it. Right—there: and Caine noted that the finger was pointing at Ursa Majoris' new eye—or to the horn just above it: he couldn't quite tell.

Caine frowned: what was so important about this bright new star in Ursa Majoris? *A new star*—which meant it had to be a star that was between Delta Pavonis and Sol itself, a star that would therefore *not* appear in the constellation as seen from Earth. Indeed, back home, that new star would have to be on the opposite side of the sky from the Ursa Majoris constellation. And come to think of it, someone had mentioned Ursa Majoris when he arrived, someone at Downport—

Brinkley. Brinkley had mentioned that, from Delta Pavonis, you could locate Alpha Centauri by finding it crowded into the head of Ursa Major. So the big yellow eye, just to the right of Epsilon Ursa Major, that was Alpha Centauri. But the more Caine looked, the more he realized that no, Mr. Local's finger was stabbing urgently—almost trembling—at the tip of the wolverine's most prominent horn. Located just a finger's width above the new eye, the horn was capped by a smaller, dimmer yellow star that was also a newcomer to the constellation. That put the new star on an almost straight line that started at Delta Pavonis, went through Alpha Centauri, and then on toward—

Caine felt his skin freeze and the hair on the back of his neck rise up. Trembling, he turned slowly to look at Mr. Local, who leaned back a little and emitted a long, low purr. He pointed outward yet again, clearly indicating the tip of Ursa Majoris' horn.

Caine turned back, his legs shaking, saw nothing but the little yellow star, heard nothing but Brinkley's inane introductory chatter: *". . . as seen from this system, all the major green worlds are pretty much on a straight line: here, Alpha Centauri, Earth—"*

Earth. He's pointing at Earth. He knows I'm from—

Caine spun around: Mr. Local was gone. As if he had never been there. Caine swallowed, heard the great mechanical gulping noise it made in his throat, and turned back. Earth. Of course: Earth.

And then, all the pieces started to fall into place—

Chapter Ten

ODYSSEUS

Caine, alone on the observation deck of the interface liner *Tyne*, had to admit that there wasn't any concrete evidence that the new second engineer was actually an assassin.

Indeed, the image on Caine's bug-linked palmtop showed the bridge crewman merely carrying out the same routine duties he had been performing for five days now. If anything, he sat his post more easily than ever, pitched back in a casual slouch, checking monitors, occasionally glancing toward the starboard viewport.

Caine stole a starboard glance of his own: the *Tyne*'s gallery window framed a craft shaped like a cubist kraken of deep space. She was the shift carrier *Commonwealth*, her mile-long keel capped by a boxy sleeve that resembled the mantle of a giant squid. However, this mantle was rotating and comprised of four long panels: habitat nacelles. Less than fifty meters aft of the slowly spinning mantle, hundreds of cold-sleep modules—or "cryopods"—were clustered as tightly as the facets of an insect's compound eye, staring at him with bone-white pupils: the pod doors.

He forced himself to return their stare, and thought: *there's no way I'm going to use a cryopod again. Not now; not ever.* Common sense countered: *You may have to. If there is an assassin on this ship, a cryopod may be your only chance. So, you choose: pseudo-death—or the real thing?*

The rotation of the *Commonwealth*'s habitation nacelles was slowing: that meant the end of spin-gravity and the start of docking preparations. Soon Caine's hab module would be transferred to the shift carrier and he'd be another step closer to Earth. *Which is probably why I'm so nervous: because I'm almost home. So not only am I starting to see danger everywhere, but beginner's paranoia is adding to the problem, spawning false threats. So calm down: the second engineer is just a second engineer. You can go back to your module, strap in, relax—*

The negation was swift: *no, you can't—not until you're sure.* And if Caine couldn't be sure, then he might have to initiate an escape plan that bordered on lunacy, and depended entirely upon the contents of his shoulder-bag.

He zipped open the bag: a big-handled aluminum Thermos, a multi-tool, a bottle of antidiarrheic tablets, and his shipboard transponder. He dug out the transponder: the silver-gray face of the metal card flashed at him, and he thought: *If you bail out, you have to leave the transponder behind.* If he didn't, the second engineer would certainly use its signal to locate him, track him down. *So don't take any chances; drop it here, now.*

But Caine held the silver card tight. Dropping

the transponder was the final step. It meant he was committed—at least symbolically—to executing an escape plan that had to—*had* to—conclude with him reentering a cryopod. *Except this time will be even worse. Because—unlike thirteen-and-a-half years ago—you won't be cold-celled by someone else. This time, you'll have to do it to yourself.*

The speakers toned twice. "All passengers: please return immediately to your staterooms. Counterthrust will end in fifteen minutes." On his palmtop, Caine saw the XO snap off the shipwide, nod to the junior flight officer: "Prepare to rig for zero-gee operations."

Caine watched the second engineer closely: the end of thrust meant the end of pseudo-gravity on the *Tyne.* If the new second engineer *was* an assassin, he would have to start after Caine soon: movement about the ship was "at need only" during weightlessness.

But the second engineer's only movement was a hand raised to cover a yawn.

Caine checked his watch. *He doesn't have enough time to get to me anymore—not before my hab module and I are transferred to the* Commonwealth. *Whether he's an assassin or not, I'm safe now*—but Caine felt his stomach rise up: *no; something's still wrong.*

As he left the observation lounge, a quick double-tone signaled another general announcement. "Attention. Counterthrust will terminate in thirteen minutes. All personnel and passengers must be secured in acceleration couches." A brief pause, then: "Passenger Riordan, please proceed immediately to hab module DPV 6, or report your location to a steward if you are in need of assistance." Caine swallowed, checked his palmtop yet again. If the second engineer was an assassin, that *had* to get him moving: in addition to killing Caine, he'd now have to find him first.

Smiling slightly, the second engineer snapped a toggle with his left forefinger. Clearly, the only possible reason that the engineer did not move to pursue Caine was because he had no intention, and therefore no reason, to do so.

Riordan felt himself lean toward that comforting thought, but fought back. *No: the answer you like the most is the one you should trust the least. Go over the evidence one more time: be sure you haven't missed something.*

Downing had warned Caine to be watchful when he started back to Earth, and had provided special tools to help him watch: six near-microscopic AV bugs and the palmtop that also served as a receiver for the bugs' signals. However, as on Dee Pee Three, what Caine found the most useful was his official security classification—the highest level of clearance among the nations of the New World Commonwealth bloc. Perhaps because Caine had never been conditioned to obey the unwritten rules of the intelligence community, he discovered a novel use for his access: locating and tapping dozens of covert operating funds. On every ship, the ample cash quickly made him a favorite with the bartenders, waiters, and restaurateurs in each hull's ubiquitous core concourse, which was the only place where passengers from different hab mods were permitted to mingle. It also made the concourse the most logical site for an assassin to access a target— and therefore, a site that Caine had to watch closely.

So, furnished with all the friends that government monies could buy, Caine had made daily circuits around each ship's concourse. After surreptitiously planting a micro-bug at each compass point of the main promenade, he slowed his pace, checking the palmtop's screen for a figure that moved with him. Caine acquired no such shadow during the first shift to CD-49, nor at Epsilon Indi. Even upon arrival in Junction, Caine saw no suspicious repetition in the churn of new eyes, faces, profiles. He had begun to dismiss Downing's warning—that Junction was the most likely point of intercept—when he sensed the first shadows of a threat stretch toward him.

A week before they were scheduled to transfer to the *Commonwealth,* the *Tyne*'s captain—an amiable Scot named Burnham—got on the shipwide at 0400 hours, apologized for waking everyone up, and then ordered everyone to strap in. Minutes later, acceleration cut out; the ship did a 180-degree tumble and initiated a day of unscheduled counterthrust in order to rendezvous with the Euro clipper *Schnellwind,* which was already stern-chasing the *Tyne,* sometimes at a punishing five gees. But the clipper's passengers turned out to be a meager group of very shaken and very junior executives—whose jobs clearly did not warrant such high-speed transport—and a second engineer whose dossier was still "in transit" from his last posting. That last bit of information sent a cool fingernail of warning down Caine's spine.

As if to confirm Caine's worst fears, the second engineer appeared in the *Tyne*'s concourse soon after. Using the pre-positioned bugs, Caine watched the new bridge crewman trail him through two complete circuits of the crowded promenade, never closer than fifteen meters, never further than thirty.

Caine countered with a few calls to his fellow passengers on DPV 6. Ten minutes later, a convivial group had gathered at Le Café Viennese. The endless stream of champagne overcame (as Caine knew it would) one of his more susceptible neighbors: a jovial, undersized accountant returning to Earth from Zeta Tucanae. A ship's steward was called to escort the revelers back to their hab mod, along with one member of the security watch, a Gold Coast Aussie by the name of Digger Mack. Caine remained at the center of this knot of unknowing rescuers until he was safely back in his suite. The next day, he bought a tour of Captain Burnham's bridge with carefully underplayed flattery and complimentary bottles of Bollinger, and left behind another of his spy-eyes/ears, wedged in a crevice between two access panels. Then he holed up in DPV 6 and watched the second engineer cycle through his daily duties. And saw nothing even vaguely suspicious for five dull days.

Nothing even vaguely *suspicious*, Caine recited to himself as he entered the module access tube. Forty meters away, the watch officer manning the security checkpoint into hab mod DPV 6 waved for Caine to hurry. A closer look revealed the officer to be none other than the ever-affable Digger Mack. Caine took a final look at his palmtop. On the bridge, the second engineer continued in the casual execution of his tedious duties. The only unusual feature was his faint, unnervingly persistent smile. But what did that prove? *Nothing. And besides, he can't reach me anymore. So just accept that you are not going to see any danger signs—because there are none to be seen.* Caine fished the transponder out of his shoulder bag.

He slipped it back into his pocket, slightly horrified as he reflected upon the plot he had been prepared to carry out: how utterly bizarre, to save yourself by being ready to virtually kill yourself—

He froze. *Kill himself? Kill* himself? *What if the second engineer is on a suicide mission?* Logic rebutted quickly: *Another human being ready to die just to kill me? Me? Besides, how can he do it? He's bridge crew; he doesn't have access to the fuel tanks or the power plants or the drives*—

The drives. During docking. That was it. As they prepared to dock with the *Commonwealth*, Burnham would give a shut-down order, requiring the engineer to access the *Tyne's* drive-control programming. *And what if there is an "error" when the engineer shuts down the pulse fusion engines? What if, say, the magnetic containment cuts out a split second before the fusion ignition system does? If the interlock safeguards are rigged for simultaneous deactivation, orchestrating that mishap is simplicity itself: a brief stutter in one of the ultraconductor coils and*... The explosion would vaporize the *Tyne*—and anything else nearby.

But the *Tyne* would not shut down her engines until she had come right alongside the *Commonwealth*. And at that range—

Caine discovered that he had stopped breathing: the two ships, including crew, were carrying almost seven thousand people. Caine glanced at the bridge feed on the palmtop, then at his transponder, trying to think the way Downing had taught him. *If the second engineer is on a suicide mission, then the only way I can be certain of surviving is to drop the transponder here. As long as my transponder is aboard this hull, he'll think I am, too—so he'll just wait for the* Tyne *to come alongside the* Commonwealth, *sabotage the engine shut-down, destroy both ships. And miss me, because I'll be long gone.*

Caine shuddered. *Yes, he'll miss me—but no one else on the* Tyne *or the* Commonwealth *will survive.* Unless, that is, Caine took the transponder with him when he bailed out. The second engineer would hear Security report that Caine—his transponder fading—was clearly abandoning ship. That would compel the assassin to act immediately, prematurely. With luck, Burnham would notice and intervene, but regardless, the second engineer would have to attempt to blow the engines early—meaning that the *Tyne* would not be close enough to the *Commonwealth* to catch her in the explosion. But the *Tyne* itself—

The other options were scant and unpromising. Caine could attempt to convince Burnham to relieve the second engineer—but how, with only a few minutes left and no evidence? And if Burnham didn't listen, or didn't believe...

And then, the memory of Downing's measured voice and somber face intruded: "*You must not, under any circumstances, reveal your mission. You may have to make decisions which cause others—many others—to die, so that you can get the information back to us and keep it secret.*" Downing would tell him that he should leave the transponder. That the *Tyne*, the *Commonwealth*, even seven thousand lives were all "acceptable losses." That Caine must not risk himself or the data. That he must choose the safe, the smart option: to drop the transponder. Right now. Yes, that's what Downing would want.

Fuck that. Caine jammed the transponder back down into his bag, clenched his teeth so they wouldn't chatter, and reactivated the insane escape plan he had just abandoned.

He retrieved the bottle of pills from the carry-all, popped the cap, tumbled a few into his palm. Ten meters to go, and Digger Mack was shifting impatiently from foot to foot. Caine smiled what he hoped was a sickly grin, ground his molars behind it: *poor, trusting Digger.* Raising one weak hand in greeting, Caine began his carefully orchestrated performance with a cool self-detachment: *what a son of a bitch I am.*

Digger was frowning. "Here, mate, where've you been? Look worse for wear, you do."

Caine inhaled: point of no return. He held up the tablets, swayed a little. "Got some bad food. Or somethin'. Went to the dispensary."

Digger's sympathetic tone contrasted sharply with his hurried movements. "'Kay then, Caine. Let's get through the check and then into the couches. You know the drill; bag on the scanner."

Caine laid the bag down, fumbled to put the pills back in the bottle, failed, juggling unsuccessfully as they fell and skittered in every direction.

"Ah—" began Digger, and then, apparently suppressing a string of expletives, he bent over to help scoop up the pills.

Caine straightened, reached into the carry-all, got the Thermos by the handle. He brought it out and up in a single arc, and then swung down. Hard.

Caine felt the shock of the blow from his wrist to his pectoral, restrained a sudden urge to retch as he heard the dull impact of the lead-lined Thermos against the base of Digger's skull. Digger went down with a choking groan. Caine dropped the Thermos, yanked the stun baton from Digger's belt, brought it down against Digger's left jaw hinge and thumbed the activation button.

Digger made a shuddering *hnnnhhhh* sound, back arching—but he was not unconscious. Caine felt for the selector switch, snapped it to max, laid the baton across Digger's twitching cheek, closed his eyes and held down the button.

Digger made two quick gagging sounds and then was silent, his body quaking spasmodically. Caine cast the baton aside, stowed the Thermos, and pulled out the multitool, peripherally noting that Digger was still alive. *And will hopefully live to hate my guts.*

Caine backtracked down the corridor, stopped at a ceiling-to-floor panel outlined in yellow-and-black caution striping, located the release bolts.

"Five minutes to zero-gee. Mr. Riordan is to report his whereabouts immediately by any means possible." The intercom went silent, but Caine heard Captain Burnham's follow-on orders over the palmtop: "Damn it, where is he? Harris, I say three times, breach the privacy protocol and locate Mr. Riordan's transponder. This has gone far enough."

"Breaching privacy protocol on your order, sir."

Caine undid the last bolt: the panel swung down.

And revealed a white door. Caine swallowed, so loud he could hear it. A cryopod—or, more accurately, a lifepod: the newest means of abandoning ship in a hurry, and in deep space. Once inside, you surrendered control. The machine's expert system would make all the decisions. Would do away with his clothes, his consciousness, and maybe his life, with cool impersonal efficiency.

He knelt down before the white door and began—inexpertly, and with the aid of a "how-to" program—to override the control protocols. *And if I'm really lucky, I won't cut the wrong wire and pre-launch the pod—and myself—into hard vacuum.* As Caine started clipping wires—and dripping sweat—he heard the predictable exchange begin on the bridge:

"Captain?"

"Yes, Trilling?"

"Sir, I have a red light on portside escape pod aught-five. Systems indicate that the pod is no longer in the command loop."

"Damn; as if we didn't have enough problems. Run a diagnostic."

"Sir, we can't. The pod is entirely nonresponsive."

"Bloody hell. Have security check it, then. Have them pull the damn thing's plug if they must."

Caine stared at the recessed handle in the center of the white door. *You have to do it. You have to do it to yourself. And you have to do it now.*

"Sir, no response from security in that sector."

"What the—? What sector, man?"

"Section B3: portside module pylon, just near hab mod DPV 6."

A long pause, then Burnham's voice—firm, decided—rapping out orders: the chance events—Caine's truancy from his suite in DPV 6, the pod's malfunction, security's failure to respond in that same area—were all coming together. "Security, all available personnel to section B3, portside pylon. Detain Mr. Riordan on sight. Engineering, prepare for new orders—"

Caine saw the second engineer glance up sharply at that command, then look uncertainly toward his control panel.

Time to leave. Caine pulled the handle in the center of the white door. The oval hatch opened with a pop and a sigh; the emergency klaxon shrilled at him. He made sure the transponder was in his bag, then jumped into the closet-like interior of the life pod.

From there on, everything happened with unnatural speed. The door slammed shut behind him with a breathy squeal: hermetically sealed. Straps closed down around him and pulled him tight into an acceleration harness. There was a deafening yet hoarse blast and a sudden full-body sledgehammer of five gee acceleration: the jettisoning charge was kicking the lifepod free of the *Tyne*.

The sound and image on the palmtop were starting to break up. One of the bridge officers—Sensor Ops, probably—called out: "Sir, secondary array indicates we have a pod away."

"Engineering, confirm."

"Unable to confirm, sir. It's either away or no longer drawing power."

That was when the pod's real rockets kicked in: a less intense, but steady pressure on his chest pinned him down. Using the armrest controls, Caine snapped on the pod's small external viewscreen while watching the last seconds of clear transmission from his bug aboard the *Tyne*'s bridge.

"Sir,"—the sensor officer, again—"we've located Mr. Riordan's transponder signal—but we're losing it."

"Losing it?"

"Yes sir; best guess is that he's—"

"Aboard the pod. Yes, of course. Engineering, clear your board for an emergency counterboost. Communications, hail the *Commonwealth* and—"

But Caine didn't hear the rest: over the captain's shoulder, he saw the second engineer frown and pull a microdisk out of his breast-pocket. He slipped it into his station's dataport and grazed his index finger across the control panel before anyone even noticed.

Still visible in the pod's viewscreen, the *Tyne*'s massive engine decks flickered unevenly, flashed, then erupted into a burgeoning sphere of blue-white plasma that whited out the screen.

The buffeting hit as the image of space came back; Caine tried to resist a sudden wave of nausea, most of which was not due to the rough ride. He hadn't saved the *Tyne* or its eight hundred passengers and crew. He himself wasn't going to be in much better shape: even now there were enough rads sleeting through him to cost some hair, and the pod was tumbling out of the Junction system's ecliptic. But Caine's burgeoning pangs of guilt and misgiving froze, paralyzed by the ominous hum of cryogenic suspension machinery coming to life all around him: the gurgling of the blood exchange system, the slow hum of the unfolding catheters and colonic cleansing waldos, the snipping of the disrobing shears, the sigh of the approaching hypodermic. His body would be subjected to a gruesome variety of IV violations, but only after an initial dose of synthetic morphine had drifted him off into a dreamless sleep.

The needle slid efficiently but sharply into his left forearm. As Caine felt the opiating warmth leap along his veins, he let himself look outward and flow into the stars, carried along by a sudden, drugged impulse toward the poetic: *From our small green island in the heavens, we steer our ships into black depths. And as we veer and tack from one star to the next, we have chased a question as old, as fundamental, as our fascination with the night skies: "Are we alone?"*

And he, Caine, homeward bound to his island in the archipelago of systems now navigated by humans, was returning with the answer to that question.

Unfortunately, Downing and IRIS might never have the opportunity to extract that answer from Caine, or from the data crystals in his shielded Thermos. It was, after all, entirely possible that the assassin's allies would be the first to reach his tumbling lifepod. If anyone ever did.

Which was, Caine conceded as he slipped deeper into the unnatural calm of a morphine haze, a most unsettling prospect.

PART THREE

Earth

March–April, 2119

Chapter Eleven

MENTOR

Richard Downing took his customary seat on the west end of the conference table, which afforded the best view of the white dome of the Capitol building. It was only the first day of spring, so the light was fading fast, sliding down the spectrum from yellow to a tired amber that glowed weakly off the wind-rippled surface of the Reflecting Pool. No sign of the cherry blossoms yet: it had been a cold winter. Twice, snow had shut down the city, to the predictable delight of the children.

Before Downing had finished settling in, the door opened, knob banging into the precisely dented wood paneling behind it: Nolan Corcoran's usual entrance. Crossing the room, he tossed his deck-coat into a chair, kept moving in a broad arc around the table and toward Richard, smile growing as he came.

His "Good to have you back, Rich" was accompanied by the usual hearty handshake—but there was a subtle thread of tension in the greeting.

Downing smiled. "It's good to be back. I presume you've already read the reports."

143

"Scanned them on the suborbital from Jakarta. Lucky thing you reached Junction in time to handle Riordan's retrieval personally." Corcoran moved toward his seat at the east end of the table. From there, he could look out at the Lincoln Memorial, now a gold-rimmed box of black shadow. "So, Caine's going to be okay?"

"Physically, yes. Psychologically—well, Riordan is less resilient this time."

Corcoran frowned. "Less resilient? To what?"

"To the neural and mental traumas of being rapidly processed—again—out of long duration cryo-suspension. His recent experience of time is not as a steady flow, but as a disjointed set of abrupt, often painful changes. For instance, he enters coldsleep in 2105 with his two parents still alive; he comes out in 2118, and they're both dead."

Corcoran avoided Downing's gaze: he looked at the floor, then out at the Lincoln monument. Downing had the distinct impression that Nolan would not have been able to look full into the statue's solemn marble face.

Downing continued. "Clinically, Riordan's reorientation was normative, but one thing puzzled me: do you have any idea why the psychologists inserted so many probes of Caine's first short-term memory loss into the initial sessions?"

Nolan glanced up from under his hand. "What? No, no idea; frankly, I didn't notice."

And indeed, maybe Nolan hadn't noticed—but then again, maybe he had. It was as if the measurements of Caine's memory had been designed to surreptitiously assess where his earlier, lunar memory loss began and ended, with an *a priori* presumption of about one hundred hours. So, had Nolan *expected* a one-hundred-hour memory loss from the outset? If so, had Nolan instructed his Taiwanese contacts to do more than just ship Caine back to the US after they had swapped him out of their cryocell and into an American model, fourteen years ago? Had they taken "therapeutic" steps to ensure this greater memory loss?

Downing stopped: *steady, old boy. Look very carefully at where these inquiries are taking you: toward the notion that Nolan not only took premeditated steps to deny Caine information about what happened during his last one hundred hours on Luna, but that he kept me in the dark about doing so. But what would possibly—?*

Nolan's voice severed that troubling line of thought: "While we're on the topic of Caine's cold sleep, I've been wondering if his memory loss might have been caused by the kind of cryo-suspension the Taiwanese used. Or maybe it was the rapid shift between their system and ours."

Downing managed not to flinch: *so has Nolan started reading my mind, now?* "That shift—is that why they held Caine for about a month after cold-sleeping him on Luna?"

Nolan nodded. "The pharmacology of the pre-toxification approach is radically different from ours. They had to purge their chemicals out of him before ours could go in. It took about two weeks between partial rethaw and full resleep."

"Ah." Nolan's comments about Taiwan's controversial pre-toxification cryotechnology were accurate, and Caine might very well have spent two weeks having his fluids exchanged. Or Caine might just as easily have spent two weeks in a drugged stupor, inhabiting a twilit land where the mental fogs induced by serotonin derivatives were intermittently pierced by lightning strokes of electro-convulsive "therapy" sessions.

Nolan leaned forward, his smile a little wider but less relaxed. Downing knew what that signified; the admiral wanted to get off the topic of Caine's memory loss: "Any other concerns regarding Mr. Riordan?"

Downing folded his hands. "Riordan has every reason to hate us—and to distrust us. I'm uncomfortable with our decision to let him present his own findings at the Parthenon Dialogs. He could decide that an international summit is exactly the right forum in which to expose IRIS, its manipulation of foreign governments, and his displeasure with it."

Nolan smiled. "We anticipated this risk from the first day we reanimated Riordan. Face it, Richard: the part of him that is a polymath is impossible to predict. They never do just one thing, or follow just one path, for very long. It's not in their nature. Unless they become authors. Or troublemakers. Or both."

"You mean like Caine."

"You said it, not me."

"So how do we make sure he stays in line?"

"By appealing to the part of him that is the Boy Scout, the straight arrow. By reminding him what's at stake and then bringing him inside—all the way inside."

"Nolan, if we do that—"

"If we don't, he'll only resent us more. And it's the least we can do. Besides, as a purely cultural operative, he'd be invaluable. Once the publicity surrounding Caine dies down, he'll have a dim, but permanent, halo of historical fame, which will get him through just about any door, into any party, onto any invite list."

Downing shrugged: there was no arguing that point. Riordan had a future—if he wanted it—on the lecture and book-signing circuit. He'd be sought after, but not a star, and his deeds would be much better known than his face: all advantageous for the kind of operative Nolan was envisioning. He frowned. "Very well—and he probably won't want to make a scandal out of himself along with us. He's got the pluck to do it, but is prudent enough to know it's simply not the best move for him, or for the planet."

Nolan smiled broadly. "You named him pretty well."

"Pardon?"

"*Odysseus*—the code name you hung on Riordan. Odysseus was no coward, but he always looked before he leaped."

"Yes, I suppose, but that has nothing to do with how Riordan got his code name. It came from a play on words—on names, actually."

And suddenly, Downing was reliving the moment now one year past. . . .

Caine was recovering from drowning himself during the circuitry training exercise: Richard brought him a towel and sat down.

Caine shook his head. "This whole scheme of yours is nuts, you know. I've only written about the military and intelligence work—and now you think you can teach me to be a field operative in just a few weeks?"

Downing made sure his nod was relaxed. "We're simply asking you to collect information, just as if you were researching another book. And don't think of me as a teacher; think of me as your mentor."

"Mentor, huh? And that makes me who? Odysseus?"

Downing smiled at the Homeric pun. "If you like."

He leaned back. "We need a code name for you, anyway. Would 'Odysseus' suit you?"

Caine shrugged. "Sure: I'm 'Odysseus.'"

Nolan's voice startled Downing out of the recollection. "Anything else on Riordan?"

"Just this footnote from the psychologists: this time, his recovery may also be complicated by feelings of guilt."

Nolan frowned, turned his face back toward the darkening windows. "How so?"

"Over the loss of the *Tyne*."

"Has he *said* anything about feeling guilty?"

"No, but he does seem a bit distracted . . ."

ODYSSEUS

Caine took another sip of water to rinse out the faint fish-and-glycol aftertaste that followed reanimation. It was no good: the foreign tastes and smells kept seeping out of him, making Caine feel alien in his own skin.

Downing laid his dataslate down on the black wireframe table. "I think that's enough for today. You're doing very well."

What a lovely lie. "Great. So when do *I* get to ask a few questions?"

Downing shrugged. "You may do so now, if you wish."

"When am I going to get my short-term memories back?"

"So far as I can tell, your short-term memories from the *Tyne* are quite complete. In fact—"

"Cut the bullshit: you know what I mean, Richard. I'm talking about the memories from fourteen years ago, on Luna: when am I going to get those one hundred hours back?"

"Difficult to say. The loss may be permanent. The doctors speculate it was the duration of your suspension. Some speculate that the particulars of your deanimation may have played a role, also."

"What do you mean, 'the particulars'?"

"In 2105, the Taiwanese were still using a pre-toxification system."

"You mean where they almost kill you with poisons before they begin the cryo-suspension?"

"Yes."

"So the toxins retroactively scrambled more of my memories than our slow-freeze method?"

"That's one hypothesis. Problem is, there simply aren't any precedent cases: no one has spent thirteen years in suspension after starting with the pre-toxification method."

"I'd have been happy to skip the honor of being the first. And while we're on the topic of oversleeping, why the hell didn't you revive me as soon as you retrieved my lifepod from Junction last December?"

"An unacceptable risk. You had to remain 'lost, presumed dead' until we conducted a full debriefing and arranged for a summit at Parthenon. And until that meeting is over, we can't let you go out on your own. But after that, you're a free man. And you will have your career back. Better than ever."

"Yes, but you'll still have me under your thumb. Because when I agreed to carry out your mission, I became complicit in your schemes. So I can't indict IRIS without also indicting myself."

"Well—yes."

Caine resisted an urge to retch: whether at the returning fish-and-glycol taste or at IRIS's partial ownership of him, he wasn't sure. "So my job is to stay alive long enough to speak at the summit."

"That's it."

"Well, if I can't be allowed out into the world, then I want a little of the world piped in here. You've got me cooped up in a room without a window, without a phone, without net access, without hard-copy newspapers."

Downing nodded back. "Fair enough. I'll need until morning to arrange your net access. Acceptable?"

But things were not acceptable. Someone was in the room with them. The figure hadn't suddenly materialized; it was just standing patiently, as though it had been there all along, waiting to be noticed. Caine pushed away from it, back into his chair. His brow was suddenly wet, cold. The figure remained in the shadows, unmoving.

Downing looked up, one eyebrow raised. "Something wrong?"

Caine swallowed to make sure that his voice did not crack when he spoke. "Who's that behind you?"

Downing turned, gestured into the shadows. "That? Why, that's Digger Mack."

Caine felt his damp hairline tug backwards. "What?"

"Not what; *who*. It's Digger Mack. You remember him."

The indistinct silhouette edged forward. "S'right. You remember me, mate—don't you?" It wasn't a question: it was an accusation.

It was indeed Digger Mack—security officer Douglas Mackenzie, late of the transfer liner *Tyne*—his clothes scorched and tattered, his torso seared and blackened, three fingers gone from the left hand, slowly dripping half-clear plasma. His face—where Caine had pressed the stun baton—was half gone, an open gash splitting his cheekbone in two like a glacial crevasse, ending in the oozing hole that was his ruined left eye-socket. The remaining eye—a bright and cheerful cornflower blue—winked at him.

Two other figures emerged from the darkness. The first was Captain Burnham, whose face was incongruously intact while the rest of his body was charred to an almost skeletal parody of human form. And lastly, the tippler from Zeta Tucanae, both arms missing at the shoulder, splintered shards of clavicle protruding out of his upper chest like bloody horn gibbets. Capering unsteadily, eyes no longer focusing on the same place, he stooped and searched in time with a giggling whine: "Want a drink? Need a drink. Want a drink? Need a drink. Want—"

Caine's lungs would not work. Could not breathe. He tried to jump up. Away from the haunts. Couldn't. Could only jerk upright. But that must have chased them off: they were gone. Everyone was gone. Only darkness. Where—?

He heard himself panting, felt the soaked pajama top clinging across the breadth of his forward-hunched back. *Dream.*

Or was it? He held his breath, waiting to find out. It had seemed real, largely because of the part with Downing, which was a genuine memory from earlier today. Or was that "genuine memory," and even this moment, just part of a bigger dream—?

Or was this—finally—what it seemed to be; the

mundane reality of a small, dark room, reminiscent
of shipboard staterooms? Low bunk with built-in
drawers overhead, full bathroom just to the left of
the entrance, the room opening up to a kitchenette
on the right, a commplex against the far wall. From
the control panel of the stove, a dim blue nightlight
stared at him like Digger Mack's one remaining eye.

This, this was reality.

Probably.

Caine shook off a shiver, swung his feet to the
floor: time to put reality to the test. He crossed the
room to the commplex, snapped it on, slid into the
chair in front of the workstation. Rubbing his biceps
against the chill, he glanced up to see if the system
was ready—and saw a dim, spectral face staring out
at him from the screen.

He lurched backward reflexively—and then noticed
that the spectre had reacted similarly. Distant and
small in the still inert screen, the ghostly visage was
now just a vague silhouette, without any discernible
features. A closer look and he recognized it: it was
his own reflection.

The computer toned once. "Ready," it said, as the
same word scrolled into existence on the screen. Caine
stared at it: so, he decided, was he. Ready to start
searching for any thread of information about what
had occurred during his one hundred lost lunar hours.

MENTOR

Nolan pushed back from the mahogany tabletop, started
rummaging around in the lower drawers of the small
credenza behind him.

Downing cleared his throat. "If Riordan is to be a long-term asset, he will need long-term security. And not an entourage: it has to be a single person, one who isn't associated with the Institute. Tricky."

Nolan lifted a decanter and two glasses out of the credenza, poured a finger of Delamain into one of the snifters. "Actually, I think I've found an excellent guardian angel for our Odysseus."

"I wasn't aware you had started reviewing dossiers."

"Only did it yesterday. It was a pretty short list."

Downing let the first sip of the long-legged cognac burn away the sting of being left out of the process: after twenty-three years, there were still times when he absolutely hated this business.

Like right now.

ODYSSEUS

Caine leaned away from the glowing computer screen: if, fourteen years ago, he had entertained secret hopes of leaving a discernible, enduring mark on the legacy of humankind, he was now fully disabused of them. After his disappearance at Perry City, there was no further mention of Caine Riordan. And certainly nothing that helped detail the events of the lost one hundred hours that preceded his first, fateful cryosuspension.

But that didn't mean that Caine had to sit on his hands. He knew there would have been at least two independent attempts to reconstruct his time and activities on the Moon. Firstly, Caine's father would have continued to search for him long after he was declared missing, and those inquiries would necessarily have focused on retroactively establishing Caine's movements while at Perry City. Also, once they hit a dead end, IINN would have made inquiries of its own, and would probably have run an article that was half-obituary, half exposé. Logically, those two leads formed the nexus from which Caine could expand his own investigation.

Caine entered the necessary search parameters—

—And the touchscreen went dark, followed by a shrill klaxon—two strident hootings—which stopped abruptly. Just as all the lights went out.

Shit: did I cause that? Caine dismissed the thought as quickly as it came. That klaxon wasn't in his room; it was down the hall. And it wasn't just the lights that had gone off: he could hear the data-access heads spinning down, heard the hum of the refrigerator fading. It was a power outage—but in a secure intelligence facility? Then the two wall lights came back on, but were dim red: emergency lights.

Not good. A government facility wouldn't usually be part of the local power grid, and if it was, it would certainly have its own generator, running low as a constant ready backup. Which meant—

The reflexes he had learned from his hypervigilant months aboard hab module DPV-6 came back along with the cool spine-and-outward rush of an adrenal surge. Time seemed to move more slowly as he snatched the biggest knife in the kitchen. Then he grabbed a towel and ran it under the tap for a second, in the event he'd have to move through smoke or gas. Next, he'd want—

Quick steps, just outside the door. Not the drumlike pounding of charging rescue personnel: a fast, gliding patter. He looked around: no time to find anything better than the knife. He flipped it over on the move,

flapped the towel out like a flag to cover one of the
wall lights. He brought the flat of the knife handle
down firmly against the towel; the light within made
a sound like a Christmas ornament dropped on a flag-
stone floor: a thin tinkling. The footsteps had stopped
by the time he eliminated the second light. Without
stopping, Caine swung around into the kitchenette,
his back flat against the cabinets. Knife hand back,
he crouched down, and heard the door's lock snap
over: opened.

Chapter Twelve

MENTOR

Downing feigned intense interest in the cognac. "I'm sure you had a host of suitable volunteers already standing in line to become Riordan's full-time guardian angel."

"Well, strictly speaking, we do have one 'volunteer'— but not standing in line. In fact, standing is something our volunteer hasn't done for a very long time."

Downing frowned. "I'm sure that's quite witty, but I have no idea what you mean."

Half of Nolan's face was hidden behind his raised glass: "Our 'volunteer' is another long-duration sleeper."

"You can't be serious."

"Think about it, Richard. Another sleeper will be in the same boat as Riordan. If we choose a person with the right temperament and attitude, the two of them will probably become close as a result of their common experience—and losses."

Downing had to nod. "Yes, *if* we create the right kind of bonding events, the odds are good that they'd develop a strong affinity for each other." He lifted his snifter. "I must say, it's an inspired bit of madness, Nolan. It might even work. So tell me about our 'volunteer': who is he?"

"It's not 'he,' Richard; it's 'she'—"

CALYPSO

The first thing she was aware of was nausea and the overpowering smell of chemicals: sharp, artificial, astringent. And the smell was not just around her; it was coming from her, too.

Hard on the heels of that realization came the sense of cold: deep, numbing, down-to-the-bone cold. And she was tired, so tired.

Hours of repetitive drill worked even though her mind refused to. Altered senses, deep cold, drowsiness: onset of hypothermia. *I'm freezing, blacking out. Gotta move.*

And then she was wide awake, as though someone had slapped her with an electric cattle prod—but the source of her sudden alertness seemed to be the hypodermic that was now sliding stiffly out of her left forearm. That was when she heard the oddly brief klaxon—two shrills and then off—and opened her eyes.

She was in a bed—a hospital? No, there was a panel above her, hinged like the lid of a tanning bed or a—

Coffin? She sat up quickly, looking around. A surge of nausea almost knocked her back down, blurred her vision. All she could see were angular shapes in the darkness of this large room in which she had awakened. Shapes in the darkness—

Shapes and voices in the darkness. Cold and wet. Sudden light in the eyes. Then gone. More voices,

most American, some British, a few translating rapidly
into—what was it? Spanish? Portuguese?

The light came back. And sound. "Captain? Captain?" The light was so bright. Seemed so far and so
close all at the same time.

"Nonresponsive. I say we triage and move on."

"Excuse me, Major, but that's my CO. You are not
'triaging' her."

Shapes with shoulders, with hides of brown and
green mottling, swam above her and between eddies
of light and dark.

"Corporal, I'm in charge here—"

"Doctor, you are in charge here. But this assault
rifle has a special veto power, if you get my drift."

The voices stopped. No, no; bring the nice voices
back.

"Son, I know about her—she's a good officer, but
we can't save her. Look."

She felt waves with fingers move her body, roll
her to the left. There was pressure—unpleasant—
behind her.

"Christ."

—then the tide of fingers receded, lowering her,
and she was flat and level and comfortable again.

"She won't make it through surgery. And how long
ago did she get hit?"

"About forty minutes now."

"Evacced how long ago?"

"Twelve, maybe fifteen minutes."

"Okay, then here's the rest of the bad news: she's
been in her shredded MOPP for at least twenty-five
minutes. And those weren't all fragmentation devices
you waded through. There were chemical rounds

mixed in. Viral agent; that's all we know so far, but I don't like what I'm seeing around the wounds. If it had been anything other than the liver—"

"Doc, what about the cold cells?"

"I haven't...we...How do you know—?"

"Major, I know you're really a civilian, but understand: this is the Army. There's no way to keep a secret in the field."

The voices stopped, but she could tell they would start soon again.

"Okay, she's as good a first candidate as any. She signed the release?"

"Must have. Bitched no end to get us all to sign ours."

"Okay. But, son—"

"Yes, Major?"

"You do know you're never going to see her again?"

"Yes, sir. But it's not about whether I see her again, is it?"

"No, I guess not."

"You take good care of her."

"The best."

The best best best feeling was the warm blackness that came next. All warm and all black black black...

The room was not entirely black: but then this room was not *that* room—or had that been a tent?

No time to think about it now. Something was wrong in this new room: only dim red emergency lights, nobody around. Just a row-and-column array of long, dark boxes, most of which had small red and green lights of their own. Her eyes adjusting to the darkness, she looked over the edge of her bed/coffin:

it confirmed her first impression. She was in some high-tech equivalent of a tanning cell. Except it was clearly not a tanning cell: an IV line tugged at her bicep, another at the inside of her thigh—and she was catheterized.

Okay, some form of medical life support. A phalanx of similar cells stretched away before her, into the dark, all closed. Definitely not a hospital; more like some kind of—her mind flailed for an appropriate term—a parking garage for sarcophagi. But it didn't look like long-term parking: the cells were all on wheels—heavy-duty hospital gurneys—and if they had once been in a neat checkerboard arrangement, they were somewhat scattered now. There were gaps in the grid—whole rectangles were missing—and her own might have previously occupied one of those gaps, for she was not a part of the checkerboard pattern. Her cell was near the room's one open door, pushed close to the wall, where a cluster of cables and hoses ran from sockets directly into the side of her cell.

She became aware of a growing ache at the midpoint of the right side of her back, then of distant noises: faint chaotic cries, stifled by fainter stutterings—automatic weapons with sound suppressors. *Okay, that clinches it: time to leave.*

MENTOR

Downing wasn't sure whether he was mostly indignant or stunned. "Nolan, just how are we going to get a woman to furnish long-term, twenty-four/seven undercover security coverage for Riordan? Have her become his personal valet?"

Nolan twirled the compupad stylus slowly between his fingers. "No, his partner."

For a long moment, Downing did not comprehend. Then: "You're not serious."

"I am—dead serious."

"Nolan, this is immoral—compelling people to become intimate."

Nolan put down his glass. "Rich, you and I have given orders that got other people—innocents as well as enemies—killed. Quite frankly, I have far greater moral qualms over those decisions than this one."

"We had no choice in those cases; it was—either overtly or covertly—war."

"We don't have any choice in this case, either. No one else fits the bill—or do you think Riordan will tolerate us assigning him an overt, round-the-clock bodyguard?"

Downing didn't bother to answer with the obvious "no." "So we protect him by procuring a romantic involvement with a woman who also happens to be—unbeknownst to him—his guardian angel. But what if they fail to find each other—erm . . . 'compelling'?"

"Then we'll invent a love potion. Hell, Rich; I don't know. But here's what I think will happen: we take two healthy, attractive, intelligent people who have—according to the Psych folks—compatible personality profiles. We put them together, and they share a commonality that almost no one else in the entire world can boast: they are time travelers. They have made a one-way trip into the future and are now orphans here: no family, no children, no circle of friends, nothing. All they've got is each other."

Downing nodded, thinking. "If we could add an

intense, shared crisis of some kind, that intimacy might easily become romantic, sexual. But once they get over—well, 'needing'—each other, what then?"

Nolan sighed. "Then nature will take whatever course it's determined to take. But by then, with any luck, Riordan won't need round-the-clock protection anymore."

"And what of the woman? What becomes of her?"

"She will have had a relatively gentle—and well-funded—reintroduction into the world."

Downing sighed. "So should we be optimistic when we assign her a code name?"

Nolan frowned. "What do you mean?"

"Well, if we were being optimistic, and if we stick with your pattern of Homeric sobriquets, we should assign her the code name 'Penelope.'"

"And if we're not so optimistic?"

"'Calypso,' of course."

Nolan's eyes seemed very tired, then he turned away. "We name her Calypso. Of course."

CALYPSO

She tore out the tubes and the catheter, tried vaulting the side of the cell: she half fell, half collapsed onto the floor. *Damn: legs wobbly as a boiled chicken neck, everything else stiff and too cold to move or even feel things reliably.* Her fingers were particularly bad: almost no strength or sensation.

More shouting, again abruptly terminated by the weapons fire: closer now. Tactical training kicked in: since the hallway beyond the open door was as dark as this room, how were the gunmen moving, aiming?

Had to be equipped with night-vision gear. That and suppressed weapons added up to covert ops or special forces. Yes, time to leave.

But how? Frozen, weak, apparently still wounded, and lost in the dark of an unfamiliar facility, she was as good as already dead.

But not if they couldn't see her: that was the key tactical variable. Night vision—how could she defeat that? And then she knew.

Using the rim of the cell to hoist herself up, she hastily inspected its exterior. Yes, as expected: hard-copy status reports clipped to its side. Would have been interesting to read them, but she had far more important plans for the paper.

She tore off the sheets, rolled them into a long, composite taper, scanned the room for heating vents. She found one, scuttled feebly over to it, fumbled for the cover-release as the sounds came closer—which now included curt, muted exchanges she could not make out, occasionally broken by a few seconds of silence. But she knew what those exchanges were, just by the cadence of them: commo chatter on a tactical command net. Staccato-paced sitreps as the search-and-destroy team went room to room, objective to objective.

She bloodied her fingers getting the cover off the vent, discovered the dim reddish glow she had expected to find: battery-driven electric backup heaters that would take over for a few hours in the event of general power loss. She shoved one end of the crumpled rod of papers against the heating elements, waited for several interminable seconds.

A wisp of smoke, a glowing ember, and then a

sudden yellow flare: they were burning. She crawled back to her tanning cell, holding the paper upright to extend the burn time, looked overhead: there was a smoke and heat sensor, just a foot behind her unit. She pushed the leg of the gurney: it resisted, then rolled half a meter. She locked the wheels, grabbed the edge of the cell with her free hand, took a deep breath, and pulled with her arm as she pushed with her legs.

Her muscles were obviously reawakening, because hoisting herself into the cell was not as difficult a task as she anticipated. But evidently her nervous system was becoming more responsive as well: the ache in her back became a knot of searing pain—so sharp and sudden that her lungs froze in mid-inhale.

Can't yell, can't even gasp: they're too close. And it's going to get worse—right now. She doubled her legs under her so that she was crouched and then stood slowly.

She might have blacked out for an instant—from the persistent dizziness or the crushing pain, she wasn't sure. But there was no time to wonder. As she lifted the half-burned taper up to the smoke sensor, she heard distant footfalls—the sliding, sibilant gait of trained killers advancing in a double-time leapfrog pattern along the corridor. She looked up: the taper was burning directly under the sensor. *Damnit, why don't you work? Why don't you—*

The sudden downpour of water blinded her, soaked her, re-froze her—but it meant a fighting chance. Neither infrared nor light-amplification goggles liked precipitation much—and she had just called up a non-stop monsoon. She looked down, hesitated, daunted by the probable pain, but had no time to waste: she jumped down to the floor. She fell awkwardly, too nauseous and agonized to breathe, but she kept moving, hobbling to the door. She heard a break in the commo chatter and a muttered curse off to the left. Staying low, she tucked around the corner into the hallway, heading to the right. A 12-and-6-o'clock snap check: the corridor—what little she could see of it through the deluge of spraying water—was all clear. Clutching the sodden, flapping hospital smock close to her with one arm, she continued to the right at the fastest lope that she could sustain.

Chapter Thirteen

ODYSSEUS

The knob turned; the door swung inward. Caine was surprised by the casual confidence of the intruder: no low dodge to either side of the door. He came straight in, the muzzle of his assault rifle poking ahead. Caine waited a split second—until the intruder's black-sleeved arms cleared the door jamb—before grabbing the muzzle with his left hand and yanking, hard.

As he had hoped, this good soldier reflexively hung on to his gun—which brought him spinning around the corner, blind. Caine planted his left leg across the intruder's path, still pulling the barrel of the assault rifle while holding its muzzle wide of his own body. The soldier, struggling to keep balance, tried a skittering sidestep and tripped over Caine's left leg. Caine followed him down, and—shocked at how calm he was—cocked back his knife hand to finish the job with a single overhand attack—

That he never completed. Strong fingers locked around Caine's right wrist, one of them digging expertly into the nerve cluster just south of the base of his thumb. A sudden numbing spasm and his thumb popped away from the handle of the knife, which was immediately knocked out of his hand. Caine tried to spin out of the grip, found his arm already twisted behind him, then a knee in his back, pushing him forward and down. Caine belly-flopped on the floor of the kitchenette, the second assailant's knee like a pile driver in his back: the air went out of Caine with a noise like a full bellows suddenly squashed flat. He was dimly aware of the first intruder scrambling back to his feet: "Son of a bitch! Who—?"

"It's him," said a voice behind Caine. "Livelier than we were told. Mr. Riordan, don't give us any more trouble: we're here to help you."

Caine's first response was flat disbelief—*it's just a ploy*—but then he reconsidered: if they had wanted him dead, they wouldn't be talking with him now. And it would also explain their casual entry. "Okay—but it's customary for guests to knock before they come in. Particularly when they're uninvited, the door is locked, and they arrive in the middle of the night. With big guns."

"Fair enough," said the voice as the knee came out of the small of Caine's back and the hand came away from his wrist. Rolling over, Caine found the same hand now extended to help him up: at the other end of that arm was a surprisingly small, wiry man in black-and-gray urban camos. "Sorry about all this. We thought you'd be asleep; never expected you'd be up and"—he looked at the knife on the floor—"ready."

"Yeah, well, I was. Now what the hell is—?"

"No time for questions. We're here to get you out. Put on these goggles: they'll help you see in the dark. Stay between us and follow our orders exactly. Meyerson, check the hall."

Caine adjusted the goggles—light amplification augmented by thermal imaging—and let the larger one lead him out into the corridor after he had given it a quick duck-around check. "How'd you guys get here so quickly?"

"We were already here."

"You're site security?"

"No."

"Then—?"

"This is special duty for us. We were assigned to stay here round the clock as dedicated protection. For you. In case something like this happened."

Downing had remarked that someone might still want Caine dead. Obviously, he had been correct. "Okay, so what do we—?"

"'We' don't do anything," muttered the small man as they moved into a slow trot. "Meyerson and I have one job: to get you to the roof."

"The roof?"

"For VTOL extraction. Contingency orders in the event the facility is compromised. And, sir?"

"Yes?"

"Unnecessary talking will get us killed."

Caine closed his mouth tightly, nodded, and followed.

MENTOR

"So who is our Calypso?"

Nolan tapped his compupad. "Opal Marie Patrone, born May 14, 2035, Knoxville, Tennessee. Grew up all over the place: an Army brat. Father was stationed in

Cleveland, San Antonio, Buffalo, Fort Bragg. Five-foot-five, a hundred twenty-five pounds, all fitness indices in the ninetieth percentiles. Got a full ride for her first two years at Vanderbilt, then had to go ROTC to finish her degree: biology, specializing in zoology, magna cum laude. Exemplary soldier, well-liked by those who served under her. Qualified as a medic and sharpshooter. She was severely wounded during a counterterrorist joint op with the Royal Marines, September 16, 2066, British Guyana. Hers was the third successful field application of cryogenic reduction."

"Sounds like she was going career military."

"Doesn't say. We don't have a lot of time to get her ready, though."

"I beg your pardon?"

"The virus that compromised her is a garden-variety terrorist construct that we can now eliminate with several different therapies. But her liver is a mess."

"Reparable?"

"No way. She was surgically stabilized before they put her in cryogenic suspension; she can function for a day or so, but then she's going to need regrowth therapy and a two-stage—"

The commplex buzzed. Nolan tapped his collarcom: "Corcoran."

Downing had just raised the snifter when he heard Nolan's tone change. "They what? When? How many—no, forget it. Response code X-Ray Alpha. Yes—all of them. I'll be on the roof for pick-up in three minutes. Sitreps every two."

Downing was already on his feet, coat on. "Sidearm?"

"If you've got it."

"What—?"

Nolan shrugged into his overcoat. "The safehouse in Alexandria. It's being hit. Right now."

"Bloody hell," breathed Downing.

ODYSSEUS

They moved using a modified version of a leapfrog advance: after the rear man moved forward, Caine swerved out of cover to follow him at a distance of about five meters, staying close and low against the same wall. They were nearing a bank of elevators when Little Guy, who was in the lead, dropped to one knee, fist raised.

Caine heard it too. Gunshots. Full automatic— breathy and extremely rapid. Almost like someone tearing a paperback in half: the individual reports were so quick that they bled into one smooth patter of sound. Meyerson had come off the tail position, kneeled next to Caine.

"Damn."

Little Guy looked back, harpooned Meyerson with his eyes. "Until it's your turn to advance, you watch our six."

Meyerson looked to the rear—but his head spun back forward as the sounds resumed, closer this time, apparently rising up through the stairwell that was co-located with the elevators. Caine listened, heard a buzz of sharp, thin snaps mixed seamlessly into the reports.

"Machine pistols. Silenced," Meyerson commented.

Before Caine could think the better of it, he was voicing his own assessment. "Maybe not. Each of those little snaps is a round going supersonic. But that high rate of fire and smooth suppression—I think they're using liquid propellant assault rifles. No ejection ports, so only the muzzle blast to suppress. And only full-bore rifle rounds have that crisp supersonic snap."

Meyerson looked incredulously at Caine, then smirked. "Anything else?"

Caine shrugged, looked forward. "Probably bullpup weapons; they'll want something short and handy for close-quarters combat."

Meyerson grinned forward toward the back of Little Guy. "You believe this? He's a real—"

"He's right. And this is the last time I'm going to tell you to watch our six, Meyerson. We're heading for the roof, now. Let's go."

They rose, Little Guy's weapon up and ready. Caine edged closer to him. "Those guns—doesn't seem like amateur hour."

"No, sir. I think you're right about that."

Six meters from the elevator gallery.

"Probably had to come in on the ground."

"That's certain: we've got the airspace locked up tight. Sensors all over. Verticals on two-minute standby."

Two meters.

"Which they'd probably anticipate."

One meter. Little Guy paused. "What are you saying?"

"Even if they don't dare go to the roof themselves, wouldn't they try to prevent us from getting there? Send someone ahead?"

Little Guy turned to look at Caine. "A blocking force."

"Wouldn't you?"

Little Guy nodded, moved forward at the double-quick, waving for Meyerson to catch up. Meyerson did, went for the stairs: Little Guy waved him off.

Meyerson's eyes were surprised, his voice quizzical: "We're taking the elevator? It's a death trap."

Little Guy shook his head. "Cover me." When Meyerson had set himself up, Little Guy took out a palmtop. Looking over his shoulder, Caine saw a building schematic on the small screen. Little Guy scrolled through it, selected, enlarged, selected again—too fast for Caine to follow. Then he was turning off the palmtop, slipping it back into his shoulder pocket, and pulling a master key/wrench combination from a pouch on his web-gear.

"Can I give you a hand?"

Little Guy nodded at Caine, who followed him over to a panel between the staircase and the leftmost of the elevators. Jerking his head at the wall panel, he told Caine, "Keep it from falling. No noise." He already had the first of the restraining bolts out of the panel.

About twenty seconds later, the last bolt came out and the panel sagged forward toward Caine—who lugged it away from the wall and lowered it to the floor. A half-size access door was embedded in the wall.

"Meyerson." Little Guy had the key in the lock; the access door swung open with a stiff squeal.

"Yeah?"

"Give us ten seconds, then follow us up. Close the door after you and keep watching below as we climb."

Little Guy stuck his head in the maintenance shaft, did a quick up-down check. Popped back out, looked at Caine. "Here's the drill. I go in first. Give me five seconds, then you start up. It's not a self-contained chute; it's a recessed ladder in an access channel that runs the length of the elevator shaft. Keep your rump and your shoulders within that channel and you'll be invisible.

Stay about five feet lower than I am and don't come out on to the roof until I give you an all-clear. We're on the second floor; the roof is only three above us, so you shouldn't need to pace yourself on the climb. Got it?"

"Got it."

"Okay. And good thinking about that blocking force."

Little Guy ducked under the top edge of the doorway and was gone. Caine counted to five and swung himself in.

Little Guy was already far above him. Down below was nothing but blackness, except for what sounded like a distant rush of falling water, the sound one hears when nearing a waterfall. Caine looked down. Far below—was that a hint of movement? He listened for a second he couldn't spare: only liquid susurrations. No time to check again. He aimed his eyes at the disappearing soles of Little Guy's boots and started to climb.

CALYPSO

Just ahead, through the torrents of water, Opal could see two elevators at a T intersection, flanking a large letter "B." So she was in the basement. Great.

And she wasn't alone. Approaching the elevators from the opposite direction were three figures. Running. In white coats. Workers.

She was about to wave, then ducked back as far as she could into the doorway, which was her cover: one of the workers kept looking back over his shoulder, panicked. The first of the three—a woman—reached the elevators, evidently found them inoperable, jumped over to the stairway fire door, hand upon the knob—

The center of her white lab coat exploded outward

into a red smear, followed quickly by another bloody eruption from where her appendix would be, and a third misty blast that shattered her right knee, almost severing the lower leg. The growling hiss of suppressed weapons-fire grew: the other two bodies tumbled, one losing an arm. Stray rounds streaked past Opal's shallow shelter, emitting vicious cracks as they did: projectiles sharply breaking the sound barrier. What the hell kind of guns were these?

Then, silence, except for the dull thunder of the water spraying down. She waited. Through the water, she barely heard footsteps approach, then stop about fifteen, maybe twenty feet away: right about where the kill zone had been. Muttered reports, a pause, a response, then footsteps again—receding, but the sound took longer to die away. They were not returning the way they had come: they were going down the corridor that branched off from the intersection, down the leg of the T.

So she had to wait. If she went to the elevators now, and they turned around, they'd have her. *So move as close to the elevators as possible, listen, maybe steal a quick peek.*

Which she did, keeping her bare feet in gliding contact with the wet floor: anything else and she would sound like a kid playing in a puddle. She reached the corner of the T intersection, went low, did a quick out-and-back check: three distant figures disappearing into the artificial downpour, then pausing, preparing to make an assault entry to another room. Timing was everything now: she took the risk of looking again, saw one of the strikers fire a round into the lock, just before another shouldered the door open. *Now.*

Using the cover of their noise, she limp-sprinted to the elevator, wedged her arm through the partially open door, braced her legs and pushed one direction with her arms, the other direction with the shoulder-blade she had squirmed into the gap. A moment of resistance—and breath-stopping pain—and the door opened enough for her to slide through sideways.

Inside the elevator, she found what she had been hoping to find at a medical facility: handrail/bumpers lining the interior at about waist height. And at the rear left corner of the ceiling, an overhead panel.

One last agony, now. Facing into the left rear corner, she raised her shaking left leg up onto one of the handrails and wedged her left hand into the crevice between the left and rear wall panels. Trembling with the effort and pain, she hoisted herself off the floor, got her other foot up onto the rear wall handrail. Once she was steady, she pushed upward against the overhead access panel with her free hand. Stuck or locked. But flimsy. No choice. She hammered upwards with her fist, thinking: *any second, they'll hear it.*

But after three blows, the panel popped up, the sheared head of a single restraining screw dropping past her. *Now, both arms through the access panel, palms to either side, and lift.* Slowly, she rose into the darkness of the elevator shaft, choking on the dust— and then began shaking convulsively. She couldn't tell if it was from relief, exhaustion, pain, or noradrenal aftermath—or all of them.

Guiding the access panel back with careful fingers, she snugged it in place, thought: *I just might make it—*

She heard a faint metallic squeak overhead, threw herself to the side of the elevator car's roof, almost tumbling into the gap between it and the wall. She was still, silent. So too was whatever had made the noise overhead. Where, looking up, she saw a faint hint of something other than absolute darkness. Not a light, per se: more like a reflection of twilight? And were those voices she heard? A hint of a whisper and then nothing?

Alongside her, disappearing up into the near shadows, was a ladder in a recessed channel. It was a pathway to salvation—or to death. The all-important variable was this: whose voices had she—maybe—heard up there? Was it the intruders? Had they come in that way?

She leaned back against the ladder: *wondering won't do any good. You have to think, and then you have to act.* So she thought: this might be a secure facility, but she doubted it was top secret. It had the sprawling look of a complex built for, and worked by, civilians. That meant it would have high security, but was unlikely to be some remote subterranean warren that was dozens of klicks from human habitation. So the building was probably situated in a typical civilian environment. If that was the case, would the bad guys have come in through the roof?

Probably not. Aerial insertion would be risky if they were in a developed area—and aerial extraction would be suicide. Local forces would be on the way in, and the first thing they'd be able to assess and control was the surrounding airspace.

Unless this was a black op—where the "intruders" were actually the "men in black" from the government—in which case there was no hope either way. Local law enforcement would be countermanded or delayed long enough to give the hunter-killer teams plenty of time to finish their sweeps.

So it was either men in black and certain death, or honest-to-god intruders—which meant that the cavalry was probably be on the way, and they would almost certainly come by air and secure the roof first.

She turned slowly, reached out for the rungs of the ladder and hoped her legs would hold her for what looked like—judging from the distance of that little bit of grayness above her—a five story climb.

ODYSSEUS

Little Guy's hand appeared in the shaft above him, waving sharply. All clear.

Caine yanked himself up the last five rungs, but, despite his eagerness to be outside, kept low as he came out. Little Guy, watching from a crouch, gave a nod of approval, then stared meaningfully off into the night. Caine followed his gaze.

A green and red light, blinking, about three kilometers away, and coming closer—rapidly. The roar of VTOL jets crescendoed: the approaching craft was swiveling them into more of a vertical lift attitude.

"Our ride?"

Little Guy nodded, scuttled crablike to a spot a few meters away, where he set and adjusted a black disk about the size of a hockey puck.

"What is it?"

He didn't look up. "Multiphase UV beacon: can't see it without special goggles, set to see the right frequencies at the right intervals."

Meyerson burst out of the doorway, somewhat crouched, but ready to stand. Caine reached up, grabbed the front of his web-gear, tugged him down.

"Son of a—"

Little Guy interrupted. "Meyerson."

Meyerson looked away. "Okay. I just wanted to get the hell out of there."

"You'll get dead if you do it standing up. Stay low."

The VTOL roared closer, looming larger and on what seemed like a collision course.

"Hey—" began Caine.

"No worries," commented Little Guy. "Standard operating procedure for a hot extraction. They'll keep pouring on the speed until the last second, then they'll swivel into vertical hard and fast: can shake your teeth loose, but minimizes the amount of time that you're a sitting duck for hostiles."

Caine tried hard to believe Little Guy's explanation as the twelve-meter attack sled cleared the far end of the roof—and then, like a bristly mechanical wasp, came to a sudden, shuddering midair halt, vertical thrusters slamming forward with a high-RPM scream.

Meyerson was coiled to go, Caine—for once—ready to follow his lead, when Little Guy's hand came down on his left bicep. "No, we wait for the signal."

"Which is?"

But Little Guy was watching the vertibird through narrowed eyes. The craft seemed to roll lazily toward the left side of the roof, turning slightly as it did so. A ready door gunner rotated into view; the chin-mounted autocannon swiveled in the opposite direction.

Meyerson fidgeted. "What's taking—?"

Little Guy made a harsh noise. "Something's wrong."

The VTOL stopped for a second, then danced quickly to the right, thrusters swiveling sharply into lateral flight mode. It started picking up speed, swinging back out over the street—

From somewhere off to the left, a sharp, growling cough gave birth to another sound—that of a severed pressure hose, which up-dopplered sharply. A flash of motion from behind them—and then the object was past, the sound down-dopplering. Caine identified it as a missile just before it hit the VTOL a meter behind the cockpit.

The explosion was ferocious: the sudden blast of flame and heat whited out his goggles' thermal imaging circuits, blinding Caine just as the shockwave knocked him back several feet. Something heavy and hot—he couldn't tell what—went crashing past him.

The goggles faded back in: burning wreckage, a madman's arabesque of twisted metal.

"Jesus Christ!" shouted Meyerson.

"Stow that, or I'll kick your ass when—if—we get back to the shack." Little Guy scanned to the left, took off his goggles, stared intently, then put them back on and signaled to Meyerson.

"What's up, Petty?"

"Target, adjoining rooftop. Wearing a cold suit— probably running a chill can, so no IR signature: that's why the bird didn't see him at first. He won't be alone."

"I'm on it." Meyerson went past, running a jack from his goggles into the scope of his gun.

Caine felt himself being tugged in the other direction: Little Guy was moving low and fast to the center of the roof, into a cluster of fan cowlings, ventilators, and elevator access sheds. The master key appeared

in his hand as they drew abreast of a waist-high tool
and materials locker. He opened it, raised the lid.
"In you go."

"In there?"

"Now. No time for arguments."

"Wait a minute; I can help you wi—"

The stunning blow—a palm heel strike to Caine's
chin—was so fast and unexpected that he didn't even
see Little Guy unleash it. Didn't even feel himself fall
into the locker backwards. Caine was dimly aware of
Little Guy's voice. "You're a stand-up guy, but you're a
newb—and *you're* the package we're here to protect."

As Caine started swimming up out of his unsteady
fog, he heard Meyerson's rifle stutter off into the night.
The lid of the locker banged shut over him and the
key turned in the lock. *Damn it . . .*

Meyerson's fire went on—a sustained raucous rip-
ping sound that lasted three or four seconds: he had
emptied his magazine in one long blast of fire. A
moment of silence, another—and then, even through
the metal sides of the locker, Caine heard a roaring
response that sounded like a horrible mix between
a calliope and an immense, high-speed chainsaw.
A rotary machine gun of some kind: good Christ.
After a brief pause, it roared again—but was swiftly
counterpointed by a whispering rush that ended in a
sharp blast. The rotary gun abruptly fell silent, did
not speak again.

Caine couldn't follow much after that, as sporadic
bursts of fire alternated with long stretches of silence.
Eventually, the thin metal walls of the locker started
to hum with the approach of something airborne and
powerful—just before the lid lifted up and a hand

came in to help him out. Again, Little Guy. Caine clambered out, saw another VTOL swing past, firing single rounds down at a nearby roof, although not the one from which the missile had been launched. He turned to Little Guy. "Where's Meyerson?"

Little Guy shook his head. "He didn't make it. Come on." Yet another VTOL—a troop carrier—was skimming across the rooftops, approaching swiftly. Little Guy led the way back toward the elevator access doorway, put down another UV beacon. Again, the sudden shrill blast of thrusters as the VTOL rotated them into the vertical mode—so loud that the pair almost didn't hear the faint scrabbling in the doorway behind them.

Caine rolled to the side; Little Guy spun, gun up so fast that it didn't look like a human action at all. It was as though he went from cradling the weapon to having it ready and aimed without any intervening motion of his arms or body.

A gasped "Hold . . . your fire!" stayed his trigger finger long enough to reveal that it wasn't an assassin emerging from the shaft behind them. Not unless one of the assassins had disguised herself as a young woman in a drenched and clinging hospital gown, with blood staining the back.

Caine, doubled over to run low, reached her and helped her out onto the roof. The blood was not just a stain on the back of her shift: a steady trickle ran down the back of her right leg.

He uttered what he knew to be an idiocy: "You're hurt."

Her eyes followed his to the blood, and she smiled. "Hell, I think I was dead."

She was going to add something, but just then the VTOL came down—loud, massive, ominous. Her almond-shaped eyes grew large and round. Little Guy whistled: Caine looked over. "You're clear. And sorry about clipping you earlier."

Caine grinned. "No problem. I'm probably alive because you did." He started helping the young woman over to the VTOL, looked back at Little Guy. "What about you?"

"I stay here, mind the store. See you safely on your way. We don't want any more surprises. Go."

Caine nodded and obeyed, helping the shivering woman up toward the hands reaching down from the passenger section of the vertibird.

As he climbed in next to her, finding and securing her belt, then his, he noticed that she was looking around, dazed and uncertain.

"Where are we?"

Good question, Caine thought. The thrusters roared: they swooped off the roof and swung upwards into the night sky. They could see more clearly now; off to their right were the unmistakable moonlit coils and windings of the Potomac. In a town always making news, Caine had the strange feeling that this just might make the morning edition.

"We're near DC," he said.

The young woman nodded, eyes now locked on a distant and immense white cubist finger that was accusing the sky, brightly lit by floodlights: the Washington Monument. Then, her pecan-brown eyes slid sideways, seeking Caine's. "And when?"

Caine, not sure he had heard her, leaned closer, shouted over the thrusters, "I'm sorry: say again?"

She closed her eyes; when they opened, they were bright with tears. He felt his chest constrict as she repeated: "I asked you 'when': *when* are we?"

Unable to speak—silenced by seeing his own loss in her eyes—Caine reached out without thinking, placed his palm gently along her left cheek.

She smiled, eyes brighter and more liquid still, and held his hand there. Tightly.

Chapter Fourteen

ODYSSEUS

The perfect blue of it, Caine thought, watching the flawless surface of the Mediterranean dapple beneath the approaching security delta. It banked hard right until it came about, then its jets burned bright cobalt. The delta powered back out over deeper water, its small weapons blister rotating away from the Doric columns, which partitioned Caine's view into a succession of eight tall, sequential seascapes.

In the center of the fourth seascape, framed between two columns, was a silver-haired man facing away from him. He was still in good shape, but there was a telltale thickening of the body, loss of muscle mass in the shoulders and neck. His posture—straight-backed and vital—almost concealed the physical changes, inviting an observer's eye to remain fixed upon the distinctive military bearing. In all probability, he was older than he looked.

Well, that cinches it, Caine decided as he passed through the shadow of the temple's still-intact entablature. According to five weeks of research while he was confined to a stateroom on the attack sub *Nevada*, only one man over sixty could both be the head of IRIS and boast that trim a physique.

Caine emerged back into the beating glare of the Aegean sun, drew abreast of the man, and stole a sideways glance: patient blue eyes were tracking the delta's speedy disappearance into the horizon.

"Admiral Corcoran?"

Nolan Corcoran, unmistakable from the many photographs and film clips Caine had seen—first as a teen and then over the past five weeks—turned and smiled. "Hello, Mr. Riordan. I'd thank you for joining me, but under the circumstances that wouldn't be a courtesy: it would be an insult to your intelligence."

"True enough."

"I do wonder if you might call me Nolan, however— and if I might call you Caine."

Riordan shrugged.

Nolan looked back out to sea. "I don't blame you for being angry—not one damned bit. If I was in your shoes, I wouldn't trust anyone right now. I'd hate a few, though. Above all, I'd hate the person who'd been responsible for playing god with my life. Which means, in your case, hating me."

Well, at least Corcoran wasn't a bullshitter—and he seemed far more direct than Downing. Of course, maybe that was just a polished act. "Hate might be too strong a word. But I'm not a happy guy."

Nolan's response was a wry bend at the right side of his mouth. "A sense of humor—bitter or otherwise— is the hallmark of a survivor." He turned, looked at Caine frankly—a casual, head-to-toe inspection. *Checking the condition of the merchandise?* But as Caine thought it, he also noted an oddly paternal nuance in Corcoran's demeanor. "I'm glad to see that you are no worse for the wear."

"How could I be? Not much was going to happen to me once you stuck me down at the bottom of the sea. And without so much as briefing: straight from the vertibird to a ship to a sub."

Nolan nodded, made a motion to start walking; Caine angled to trail alongside. "Sorry about that, but after the attack in Alexandria—well, we were in a bind. We couldn't figure out how the opposing team found you there in the first place. So we had to get you off the playing field right away. No time for explanations which, truth be told, would only have undermined our efforts to compartmentalize information as much as possible."

"Well, you could have at least provided me with more entertaining company. The SEAL team that brought me on board and babysat me—they were a pretty taciturn bunch."

"They had to be. Orders. Not all of them are always so quiet."

"Oh? Their dossiers indicate if they're sparkling conversationalists?"

"No: their CO was my son. And he's never been shy or retiring."

"Oh. Sorry."

"Why? Because you were a little snide? We've earned your spite—and more—and it's bound to bubble up now and again." They walked on a few steps. "You didn't seem very surprised to see me, just now," Nolan observed dryly.

"Well, Admiral—"

"Nolan."

"Okay—Nolan. I simply built a timeline of who Downing was associated with when he showed up in the news. The pivotal clue was Senator Tarasenko's Near Earth-approaching Asteroid Response subcommittee, which tasked you to intercept the Doomsday Rock in 2083."

"And how was that so pivotal?"

Caine looked at Nolan out of the corner of his eye. "Sir, don't be coy: it's incongruous in an eighty-five-year-old man."

Nolan exhaled a small laugh. "Touché."

"The NEAR subcommittee was where all three of IRIS's major players—and my prime suspects—overlapped. Tarasenko was an old crony from your midshipman days at Annapolis. Shortly after he sent you to deflect the Doomsday Rock with a nuke, he hired a strategic space analyst named Richard Downing—an Oxbridge import who was also, incongruously, ex-SAS. I couldn't find any more details on that connection, but I'm betting it was actually you who did the reach-out to Downing."

"Correct."

"You and Downing were often 'coincidentally' on the same blue-ribbon committees and think tanks until you began cutting back in 2101. Rumors of fragile coronary health provided the context—or should I say pretext?—for your retirement. At the same time, Downing took a low-profile job running a fusty little think tank in Newport. Which was the embryo of IRIS."

"For a couple of supposed spymasters, Richard and I sound a bit far from the center of things."

"Well, sure. That's what you'd want: perfect misdirection and plausible deniability, all in one. Nosy journalists or counterintelligence analysts would presume that

Tarasenko would be *giving* orders, not *taking* them. So if they watch him, they find nothing. They might look at Downing, but they'll conclude—rightly—that he's too junior to be controlling a major intelligence operation.

"But you've got the perfect credentials *and* cover-story for the job. Having retired from all official posts, you're now just a private citizen. You also happen to be a war hero who travels a lot, consulting for defense and aerospace contractors. But instead of becoming a typical spymaster, you have Downing construct a black-box organization: the Institute. Which you control from afar."

Nolan raised one eyebrow. "To run the kind of operation you're envisioning, you need plenty of contacts in the military, government, industry. Downing doesn't have those contacts, Tarasenko does but is always being watched, and I'm still living too public a life."

"Oh, I don't know about that," Caine objected. "When you consider it with a properly jaded eye, your public life is not so public after all. You've always been a closed-door consultant, so I can't help but wonder: during your visits, were you advising on policy—or were you dictating it? And if so, you'd also be able to use *their* secure channels to confer with Downing, Tarasenko, and the various section heads of IRIS's widely distributed net of covert overseers."

"'Covert overseers'?"

"Of course. Practically speaking, IRIS is an invisible organization because it exists—in small, completely firewalled packages—within other organizations."

"A very impressive hypothesis, but why all the charades, the false fronts, and—quite frankly—the subversion of public institutions?"

"Downing gave me that answer when he reanimated

me last year. The *raison d'être* for IRIS is exosapient threats. Right after you intercepted the Doomsday Rock, we started creating the kind of space technology that would protect us from subsequent planet-killer asteroids. But what if the threat was so big that there was nothing we could do to stop it? We had to be able to get out of the way, maybe leave the Solar System—which was why you started Project Prometheus. And as you did, you thought: 'If humans can learn to travel faster than light, other species can too.' That's why you created IRIS: to ensure that humanity can survive both inanimate and *animate* threats from space."

Nolan reversed direction, chin raising into the direction of their stroll. "You don't miss much."

"I had two unfair advantages: knowing about IRIS and Downing, and then five weeks in which I had nothing to do but gather the facts and think. But I couldn't get answers to the really important questions."

"Which questions are those?"

"Nolan, if you had no memory of the most pivotal four days of your life, wouldn't it be your top priority to ask questions about them, to get them back? Hell, Downing told me your agents grabbed me outside the door of your suite, and that I was behaving in a 'suspicious manner.' Accepting for the moment that this was true, what was I doing there? Why did I go to a place—a place I can't even remember—that was so sensitive that it got me stuck into cold sleep for thirteen years?"

Nolan nodded. "Those are important questions, I agree. I just hope I'll be able to provide the information you need. Our conversation a day and a half before you were cold-celled was the first, last, and only contact Richard or I had with you."

"Then you shouldn't have any problem sharing the records of that conversation. Or a list of my financial transactions while on the Moon. Or any of the several other dozen data trails that any visitor to Perry City can't help leaving."

Nolan stopped walking, faced him with a small smile that was unlike any of those Caine had seen in the media: it was gentle, maybe a bit sad. "I'm sorry, Caine, I really am—but I have to ask you to wait one more day. We can't risk having you dig around for those records now: there's no way of knowing where they might lead you, or how pursuing any given line of inquiry might somehow compromise all the work we've done to bring together the Parthenon Dialogs. But tomorrow, when the Dialogs are over—well, then it will be safe for you to seek your answers."

"C'mon, Admiral: if I wait another day, am I really going to be that much safer?"

"Yes, absolutely."

"What? Why?"

"Because Parthenon has already started: we met in Athens for Day One this morning." Corcoran started strolling back to where they had begun. "Tomorrow— Day Two—is the wrap-up, here at the Temple of Poseidon."

Caine looked sideways. "I expected that I'd be at the first day's proceedings, since the main item on the agenda was what I found on Delta Pavonis."

"Most of which has already been presented. But the details you'll share tomorrow are the capstones of the Dialogs. And will change everyone's perspective yet again."

"You know, that's something I've never understood: after you had thoroughly debriefed me, what the hell did anyone have to gain by killing me? Would it have really have made such a difference?"

Corcoran shrugged. "You know how it is: it's not just *what* is said; there's the matter of *how* it's said, and by *whom*. You are not just an eyewitness; you are an investigator whose writing makes the facts seem real. You breathe the life of human experience into lifeless data—and some people are scared of that."

"So if I'm still at risk, why the hell did you bring me out here? Like the real Odysseus, I'm not a risk-taker if I don't have to be."

Nolan laughed. "Relax: all the Circes, sirens, and other monsters are far away from here. First, the tip of this headland is well beyond sniper range. Secondly, the slopes and crags around you are bristling with active intercept and denial systems: together, they can knock down anything from an incoming bullet to a missile salvo. But most importantly, no one could know that you're in Greece—yet." Nolan waved back toward the mainland. "So go use your freedom now, because you'll be losing it again tomorrow. The world will want to know—and will find out quickly enough—who first brought them news of exosapients."

Caine looked over at the serried ranks of low, white buildings that started four kilometers back from the base of the headland. His glance must have imparted his dubious opinion of an excursion there. Nolan urged, "Look, don't waste this day: go do a little sightseeing. The view from the bluffs"—he waved in a vague northwesterly direction—"is spectacular."

"And how am I supposed to get around?"

"The car you came in is still down at the bottom of the slope."

"I think my driver's license expired about fourteen years ago."

"We've already taken care of that. Besides, cars are automated now—well, in most places. Should be here, although I think they may still be expanding the road sensor nets."

"Guards?"

"Not needed—and they'd only draw attention."

Caine looked up at the craggy, arid highlands Nolan had indicated. *Well, maybe a quick drive would be fun—*

"Oh, and on the way up, drop in on Richard and tell him his collarcom has apparently died."

"Sure. Where is he?"

"At the Herakles Olympic training stadium, just a few kilometers out on the western coast road, near Legonia. The car will have it in memory."

"The keys?"

"In the car. Tell Richard I'll meet him at the villa, and will brief him at 1900. It's where you're staying also, so the car knows the way back home."

Caine nodded, put up a hand in farewell.

Nolan returned the wave, smiled, and went back to inspecting the sea and the sky, framed between the same two columns.

Chapter Fifteen

ODYSSEUS

The car clearly knew where to go: at a word, it started itself and sped out of the Kapo Sounio national park, swerving briskly to the right as it came to the coast road. It plunged down into the town/hotel zone. Half of the buildings were faux reproductions of the ubiquitous whitewashed cottages of the Aegean, and all somewhat worse for the wear: clearly, this area had gone through the full cycle of boom and bust in the past few decades.

The vehicle, conspicuously large among the prevalent two-seater fuel cell econoboxes, weaved expertly through the streets, giving wide berths to the terrifyingly fearless pedestrians, who pushed their food carts and baby carriages within inches of the roadway. In an Irish accent, the vehicle started asking Caine if he wanted music, news, sport, weather—

And then bucked and screeched to a halt in the middle of the road, a red light pulsing urgently at the center of the dash.

Caine searched for a problem, found none, wasn't

even sure what all the gauges meant. "What the hell is wrong?" he asked, and then realized, *Jesus Christ, I'm talking to a car.*

Stranger still, it answered. "Road sensors inoperative in this region; please assume manual control."

"But which way do I—?"

"All automated functions suspended. Road sensors inoperative in this region: please assume—"

"Oh, all right"—and, foot on the brake, he fumbled for the shifter. Expecting more resistance—it was a digital sliding switch now, not a mechanical gear selector—he over-shifted into low gear: the car jumped forward, then banged down into a crawl.

Horns—from behind and in the cross-street he had just blocked—registered local reactions to his driving abilities. As Caine eased into the next gear—the car shuddering forward against the still-locked brakes— locals turned to look. They were joined by a few tourists, distinctive in their sundresses, sports jackets, sunglasses. One man, very tall, smiled a little.

Caine grimaced a smile back at him, advanced the gear switch, realized he still had his foot on the brake, and lifted it. The car seemed to hop forward, rushing him swiftly away from the scene of embarrassment.

In the rearview mirror, the tall tourist with the sunglasses was still looking after him. And was still smiling...

CIRCE

Still smiling, the tall man turned to resume his journey, found his way blocked by a squat and rather hirsute local who was shaking a half-hearted fist after the fleeing

vehicle. "Tourist," the local snorted, and then, noticing
the attention of the tall—and obviously foreign—man,
looked up with apologetic eyes.

The tall man kept looking, kept smiling, the wraparound sunglasses a bar of black opacity. The local
smiled, shrugged an apology, and moved off, with one
backward glance at the tall man—who had not moved,
but who kept watching him. The squat local disappeared quickly into a cluster of oncoming pedestrians.

Turning on his heel, the tall man resumed his
measured walk to the corner, turning into the narrow side street. Genuine cobblestones—older than the
mostly repro buildings that flanked them—wobbled
down toward the sea, some buildings tilting inward
over them, some away. He shifted the bag of grocer-
ies he was carrying to his left arm, reached into his
right pocket, produced a keyring festooned with real
keys: toothed, mechanical, archaic keys.

Three young boys blocked his path, playing something akin to street hockey with makeshift boards
and a small child's ball, stamped with the outline of
a Mickey Mouse head, the face erased by sun and
time. He slowed as he approached; the boys looked up,
stopped playing. He walked on, down the cobblestone
street and up the small rise at its end, from which
one could enjoy a commanding view of the ocean and
the high angles of the Temple of Poseidon, poised on
the tip of the south-pointing headland to the west.

The tall man carefully selected one of the keys as
he approached the only two-story building at the end
of the street: a dilapidated duplex with a distinct lack
of local charm. He opened the door, looked back. Up
the street, the boys turned away quickly as if to deny

that they had been watching him the whole time, and hastily resumed their game. The man smiled, shut the door behind him and mounted the stairs with long, even steps.

Entering the sea-facing apartment, he put the keys back in his pocket as he crossed into the kitchenette: cockroaches scurried away to refuges under the cupboards, alarmed at the intrusion. He dumped the bag's uppermost contents—the bread, the oranges, soda cans and other unnecessary items—into the rust-stained sink as he walked past, not breaking his stride.

He pushed open the balcony door, still cradling the bag carefully, and scanned north. Halfway to the hills which flattened down into the coast, a small rim of concrete rose above the low roofs: the Herakles stadium. He scanned south: the sea. One security delta was slowly angling back in. He noted the vehicle, checked his watch.

Then he scanned west. A clear view of the Sounion headland and the Temple of Poseidon, just over six kilometers away. He reached down into the grocery bag, pulled out a canned ham and a large ceramic bell jar, crookedly adorned with the label of a grinning, buxom farm girl carrying a cornucopia of agricultural riches. He opened the lid; from the dark, glass-lined interior, there rose a sharp tang of high-molarity acid. He replaced the cap, resealed the jar, put it down to his right, behind the balcony's chest-high weather wall.

He pried back the seal on the canned ham, pulled the covering façade of meat aside, removed the plastic-sealed wide-lens binoculars, the jar of Vaseline, and a small, separately wrapped tripod. Throwing the wrappings aside, he snugged the binoculars into the tripod,

which he mounted on the corner of the weather wall.
He leaned over, swiveled the binoculars in the direction of the Temple of Poseidon, adjusted the lenses.
Beyond the columns, occluded from the waist down,
Corcoran's silhouette swam into focus. He counted
the number of columns to Nolan's left, to his right,
checked his watch, pulled out a paper pad, hastily
scribbled additions to a growing set of notes.

He began to lean away from the binoculars, halted,
then rotated them in the other direction, slowing
and adjusting the focus as the roof-topping lip of the
Herakles stadium slid sideways into view...

MENTOR

As she sprinted out of view to the right, Downing noted
the way Opal pumped her arms from the shoulders,
and he thought, *she runs like a man.*

He advanced until he could see the entirety of the
track, but remained in the shadows of the entry. As
she crossed what would normally be the finish line, she
picked up the pace to a near sprint: the last lap, probably.

*She heals quickly. Tans nicely too; gold-bronze,
despite the fair skin and light brown hair. Feet and
hands so small that you could almost call them dainty.
Torso proportionally long and flowing: shapely but lean.*

But her shoulders and her pelvis were square and
strong, her legs well-muscled, and she moved with
a slight, forward-leaning tension: she was a spring
coiled in readiness. It would be easy to miss those
hints of an incongruous, even unexpected strength.
Her dossier indicated that more than one adversary
had underestimated her—either on a battlefield or in

a briefing room—and she had been quick to capitalize on those mistakes. Good: that was part of what made her perfect for this assignment.

If only she embraced it. That, so far, had been the sticking point.

As Opal entered the last turn, her sandy bangs were wet at the fringes, her chin tucked down. Still pumping her arms, she leaned into the turn until she emerged onto the straight again, huffing through the last few meters and over her self-imposed finish line. Downing emerged from the archway—

But she had already turned around. "Do you approve of my training, Mr. Downing?"

He had watched her eyes as she ran; she had never looked over in his direction. Impressive peripheral vision. "Captain, I'm sorry if I surprised you—"

"You didn't." She was walking toward a towel hung over the spectator railing. "I've come to expect your scrutiny. Tell me: do you enjoy watching women exercise?"

"Captain—"

Rubbing her hair briskly, she laughed through the towel. "You fluster pretty easily. Must make it easy for your wife to keep you in line."

He didn't like her insolence; he liked the stinging accuracy of her insight even less. "I assume you're finished with today's PT."

"Yep. About twenty minutes ago. Just putting in a little extra work: I need it. And I've got nothing better to do, since you won't give me any reading materials."

"That changes today."

"So you've said."

"It's true."

"That'll be a first."

Downing felt a thin line of heat along his brow. "I have not told you one lie about this assignment. Not one."

"Okay. You haven't lied about this assignment. But you've evaded. Declined to comment. Makes me feel real welcome here in the fabulous future."

"I'm sorry its been such a—a disappointing beginning for you, Captain."

"Yeah, I'm sure your heart is just bleeding for me." She stopped adjusting her shoes, turned quickly. "I apologize: that was uncalled for."

"No need for regrets, Captain. May I call you Opal?"

She thought for a second, looking off into the green scrub hills to the north. "No, I don't think so. Not yet. Maybe never. We'll have to see."

"About what?"

She looked directly at him. "About whether you turn out to be someone I can trust. Downing, I might one day come to tolerate, even like you, but I'll never like what you do. Oh, I know it's necessary: I'm no idiot. There's no way to get rid of the need for covert agencies and operatives: I've seen enough bad shit to know that well enough. And you might even be one of the good guys, the way you say you are. But you lie for a living. And now you want—you're ordering—me to do the same."

"I'm sorry you see it that way. You may find that it's something you'd want to do anyway."

"Yes, but I'm not free to find that out for myself."

"True. You were also not free to choose which of your combat assignments you felt were justified and which weren't."

"Look: I volunteered to serve my country as a combat soldier, not a courtesan."

"But it seemed as though you liked Caine—"

"So you tell me, but now I can't even remember him. That whole first week is pretty much gone."

"I'm not surprised. Emergency wake-ups are very hard on the nervous system, on brain chemistries. You can lose a lot—"

"Or it can be taken from me, as well."

Oh, bloody hell. "I beg your pardon?"

Her eyes were an unblinking challenge. "I mean, if the wake-up memories are fragile, it must be particularly easy to erase them—if you wanted to. Maybe with drugs, or maybe that's why I seem to recall shock therapy—"

She's right: I lie for a living. Lie number one: "There were no drugs." *Lie number two:* "As for electroconvulsive therapy, you might be misremembering cardiac stimulation: your heart stopped twice during the first surgery."

She had not stopped looking at him. "Could be. But I seem to recall something a lot less benign than a few zaps with the paddles." She broke the accusing stare, picked up her gym bag: "Anyway, I'll never know if you're telling me the truth or not, so I might as well let it go—but that's the problem, isn't it, Mr. Downing? I never know if you're telling me the truth."

He couldn't bring himself to contradict her: that would be just one more lie. "You can be sure of this: today you're free."

"Free to do what? To become a commando-courtesan for a man I don't even know? You've got a mighty strange definition of 'freedom,' Mr. Downing."

"Captain, you're not a civilian—and nor am I. For us, freedom isn't a blank check: it's a limited, occasional luxury—that we buy for millions of others at the expense of our own."

She looked up: he hadn't realized that the tone of his voice had become so sharp. Then she nodded: "Okay, you're a true believer. I wasn't sure until right now, when you got pissed off at me. Took two weeks to find out, but better late than never." She rose, walked over to him, put her hands on her hips and looked up into his face from only a foot away. "Nothing else could make what you do excusable. I still don't like you; I still don't trust you. But I can accept a person who feels he is performing a necessary duty." She extended her hand.

Downing looked at it, smiled, was grateful, but also thought: *I should find out how good she is.*

He extended his hand toward hers, but at the last possible moment, reached past it and grabbed her wrist—

—but she had seen, or felt, it coming. She let him pull her in—he had the advantage of height and weight—but stepped outside and past him. With surprising—fearsome—speed, she had her right leg snugged behind his right knee. He felt her trapped hand recoil sharply, tugging him toward a forward fall—but the instant that he leaned back to pull away, her left hand came up, grabbed a fistful of his right shoulder and shirt, and added a sharp push to his backward reflex.

Flat on his back, Downing looked up at her. "Textbook," he grunted. "Well done."

"Wish I could say the same for you, Scarecrow. That was pretty predictable."

He rose to his spare elbows. "Just a basic check;

sometimes, after extended time in cryosleep, reflexes go along with short-term memories."

"Not in my case. Here." She extended a hand to help him up.

He smiled crookedly, reached across with his own right hand—and again, snapped it down sharply on her wrist.

But she rolled her wrist around and out of his grab, even as she once again allowed herself to be pulled forward by him, this time into a trajectory that carried her across his body. But as her right wrist finished rotating, the outer edge of her hand came up around his own wrist, clasped hard. She landed on the far side of his body, breaking her fall with her right knee, and using her left hand to secure a double grip on his wrist. She tugged towards herself sharply with both hands. Downing felt his elbow snap straight and then strain uncomfortably: his upper arm was tucked unyielding against her right tibia. Four or five more foot-pounds of backward pressure on his forearm from the combined pull of her arms and his elbow would snap.

"Ow," he said.

Her eyes—the color of pecans, the shape of almonds—did not blink or smile. "Do I pass the audition or do we dance some more?"

"That will be quite enough, Captain: I'm done."

Her eyes flicked down at his pilloried elbow. "Yes, I'd say you are." She pushed his arm away in the same motion that she used to stand up. "Like I said, Downing, you never give me reason to do anything except distrust—"

And she stopped. Her eyes were looking beyond

him, her mouth still open a little, but the words abandoned. He rolled his head around, back in the direction of the shadowed archway.

A man was walking out of its black maw: Caine. "Am I interrupting—something?" he asked, looking from Opal to Downing.

"No, no, not at all, Caine. I just had a tumble trying to get in a little exercise of my own. Can't keep up with this young lady. She's too fit for me, I'm afraid."

Opal offered Downing a helpful hand, tried to smile at him, failed. Caine stepped in, extended his hand as soon as she had finished helping Richard. "Hello. I don't think we really had a chance to meet, other than a few minutes in the back of that vertibird five weeks ago. I'm Caine Riordan."

She seemed to think about that for a moment—and then Downing realized why she was pausing: *she's attracted to him. No surprise: he's handsome enough and fit. An excellent start.* "Nice to meet you," she was saying. "I'm Opal—Opal Patrone. Can't say I remember you—or really anything about that night, really. They tell me that you lose memories if they jump-start you out of coldsleep."

Caine looked sidelong at Downing. "Supposedly, if they put you under or wake you up too quickly, memories get lost. Something about trauma to the chemical encoding of memories, with the more recent ones being the most vulnerable. Although I seem to have been particularly susceptible."

"What do you mean?" Which was theater, since she had been briefed about Riordan's memory loss. *So, she also lies passably well.*

He broke eye contact, looked off at nothing in

the stands: "I seem to have lost a bit more memory than usual."

"I'm sorry."

Caine looked at her with a sharp yet sympathetic intensity. "From what I hear, some people have it far worse than I do."

Opal started. "You mean me? Oh, I don't know: a fresh start on life sounds good. Particularly since I was pretty much dying when they put me in the freezer."

Caine didn't say anything; but his lips crinkled upward at the edges, as if the two of them had shared a rueful private joke. She smiled back—and Downing sensed that she was about to move closer to him. *No, too soon. She's so damned frank, she'll chase him off.* Downing preemptively edged closer to Caine, blocking her. "When did you get in?"

"About an hour ago. Nolan also wanted me to tell you that your collarcom is dead, and that you have a briefing at 1900 hours." He turned to Opal. "Ms. Patrone, can I offer you a lift, or—?"

Downing strolled toward the track. "Actually, that's *Captain* Patrone. I'd be grateful if you could give her a ride back: I was late coming to collect her, and I'd like to get in a quick jog. Be a good chap and take her on back to the villa—or better yet, why not take a quick sightseeing tour?"

"Sightseeing?" Opal repeated incredulously.

Damnit, woman: do you have any subtle court-ship instincts whatsoever? Downing provided a more specific prompt: "You certainly have enough time to drive up to the Legonia overlook. The ocean views are breathtaking. Or so I'm told."

That seemed to get Opal back on track. She smiled

at Caine. "After being cooped up for almost six weeks, I could do with a change of scenery. It's also just what the doctors ordered. Literally."

Caine's eyes had not left hers, although his eyebrows had risen a notch when Downing had indicated that she was an officer. "Well, Captain Patrone? Shall we see the sights?"

Opal smiled back. "Oh, just call me Opal—and yes, I'd love a look around. But, fair warning: you might want to rethink your offer. I've been working out for almost ninety minutes in this heat." She used thumbs and forefingers to pull her sweat-soaked shirt away from her torso; when she let it go, it fell back and clung to her closely. Unplanned, but a nice effect, Downing had to admit.

Caine managed not to glance down at her shirt-sculpted breasts, but his smile may have broadened a bit: "No matter her condition, it's always a privilege to help a lady in need—or to squire her about."

She laughed out loud—quite genuinely, Downing thought. "My, how gallant!" she exclaimed. "Lead on."

Chapter Sixteen

ODYSSEUS

Once in the car, Caine turned to Opal. "You sure you want to drive up a mountain?"

"Anything without security guards is fine by me."

He smiled at her for a moment before telling the car, "Legonia overlook, please."

"Yes, sir." The engine whined into activity and they reversed toward the exit. Opal started to clutch the sides of her seat when the car started moving without human control, then she fumbled for the seatbelts.

Caine smiled again. "First time in one of these?"

Opal both smiled back and glared at him. "Look, in my day, the people drove the cars—not the other way around."

He nodded, looked out the windshield as they glided smoothly into the sparse traffic passing the stadium. "And when exactly was your day?"

Opal's chin came up, almost defiantly. "They made me an ice-pop in 2066. Couple of bad coincidences during a counterterrorist operation. But only the good die young, so I'm destined to be immortal, I guess."

He looked over at her with a raised eyebrow. "I envy your confidence in your own immortality."

"What do you mean?"

"I guess you could say I've become painfully aware of just how mortal I am. Being on someone's death list tends to do that to you. Yet here I am anyhow, ready to do my master's bidding." He turned to her. "And what about you?"

Her response bordered on truculence. "What do you mean?"

"I mean, why has Downing brought *you* here?"

"Convenience, according to Downing."

"'Convenience'?"

"Yeah, in terms of security, anyway. Yesterday he arrives at my rehab facility far too early—0500, I think it was—and tells me, 'we're moving you.' He also chooses that moment to tell me that I was the only sleeper who survived the attack in Alexandria, and that they can't be sure of security at the base anymore. An hour later, I'm getting on a plane with him, flanked by a pair of suit-and-sunglasses types who apparently never learned how to talk. We land somewhere, Downing gets off: that's the last I see of him. I wait in the back of the plane with the mute musclemen for I don't know how long—better part of a day, I guess. Then we take off and after an hour or two, we're in Athens—0400, I'm guessing. That was this morning. And here I am. Still don't know what the hell Downing plans to do with me."

Caine looked over at her. "Why 'what Downing plans to do' with you? Don't you have a say in what comes next?"

"Not much; officially, I'm still a soldier for Uncle

Sam. But apparently I'm on loan to Mr. Downing, who hasn't filled me in on where we're going, or what I'm supposed to do when we get there. Of course, since Downing himself is the one who told me all this, I suppose all—or a lot—of it could be a lie."

Caine nodded, but said, "Downing walks a pretty narrow tightrope, I think."

"Yeah, maybe—but that doesn't mean I'm ever going to trust him. Do you? Trust him, I mean?"

"I don't trust what he says, but I trust his intentions—I think."

Opal raised one eyebrow. "You 'think' you trust him?"

Caine shrugged. "He tells lies, but somehow, he doesn't feel like a liar. I don't think he likes that part of his job."

Opal leaned back. "Well, Caine, you're a much more understanding person than I am. I know we have to have people in intelligence who lie for a living, but I don't trust them. And now he's taking my choices away from me. Hell, today's run is the first real freedom I've had in—well, I guess about fifty-three years."

"You like running?"

"Me? God, no—but I've got to work hard if I'm going to get back into shape after spending half a century frozen." She glanced over at him. "So what's *your* secret? If you were in cold storage for a few years, then how did you keep fit? Just naturally gifted?"

"I was worse off than you were when they woke me up the first time. But we can talk about that later: right now, there are far more important things for you to learn about."

"Such as?"

"The state of the world. This car does have a radio."

The prospect seemed to excite her. "Where are the controls?"

"Just ask."

"I just did."

Caine grinned. "No. Ask the car. To turn it on."

She looked at him with wide eyes. "Too creepy." Then she leaned tentatively toward the dashboard. "Car, please turn on the radio."

The Irish-accented radio greeted her, then asked her to choose a channel. She asked for World News.

"Thank you. Connecting to World News..."

"This is weird," she said.

Caine smiled. "That's nothing; wait 'til you *hear* the news."

Which cut directly in on the strident voice of a career newscaster: "—which leads observers to ask: has the UK now decided to confirm its membership in the New World Commonwealth? If so, this would also represent a final abandonment of the long-standing bilateral—and increasingly unproductive—efforts to integrate with the European Union. Prime Minister Hadley-Singh announced that his government's commission on assessing membership in the Commonwealth cited more benefits than detriments, despite the opposition's repeated warnings of the United States' preponderant influence within the NWCW. Moderates in Commons observed that accepting membership might be made contingent upon nomenclature change, with Speaker Reginald Kendrick suggesting that a more accurate name for this expanded international bloc would be the United Commonwealths and Aligned States."

Opal looked over at him. "'International bloc'?"

He nodded, answered in the short space between

news items. "Five blocs. More important than nations, now."

The same newscaster pressed on. "In interstellar news,—"

Her eyes widened. "Whoa."

"—the sharp debates over the co-dominium of Delta Pavonis Three now seem to be abating. Observers attribute the restoration of normative relations between the planet's Commonwealth and European Union communities to the universal threat posed by the D-Pav virus, or 'Pavirus' as it has been dubbed by the WHO's Office of Xenobiology and Epidemiology. Mounting pressure by megacorporations, particularly the Colonial Development Combine, to restore commercial access to Delta Pavonis have been denied. CoDevCo spokesperson Theresa Farkhan asserted that the bloc-imposed quarantine of Delta Pavonis Three was unnecessary and might be, quote, 'Yet another ploy by nation-states to undermine the legitimate interests and rights of transnational corporations.'"

Opal frowned. "Those sound like fighting words."

Caine just nodded and waited for the next item.

"In other business headlines, CoDevCo continues to deny allegations that hundreds of outsystem-worker deaths were caused by transport in unsafe or outdated cryocells. CoDevCo Public Affairs Director Robin Astor-Smath claimed that the Combine had not violated any of its contractual obligations, and that its semi-skilled outbound employees willingly accepted greater hazards in order to secure better pay. Astor-Smath went on to assert that the international blocs were to blame for the disproportionate risks borne by contract laborers from the Undeveloped World:

'The blocs would not have green world colonies if it wasn't for the inexpensive labor that we hire to extract needed resources from inhospitable worlds.'"

"And that—" Caine said, manually switching off the radio, "—is the end of the news." The car had ceased moving. "Seems like we've hit a snag," he observed. They were stopped before a yellow-and-black-striped roadblock sawhorse. Just beyond it, a woman in a hard hat was inspecting small silver disks embedded in the margins of the roadway.

"I'll see what the problem is," Opal volunteered, and fumbled at the door for a moment before remembering to unfasten her seat belt.

As he watched her exit the vehicle, he heard the air conditioning increase, felt the engine race to keep up with the sudden power drain. "Stop," he instructed the car.

"This car is stopped."

"Uh . . . 'off.'"

"Shutting down." The fuel-cell engine diminuendoed into a bass hum and then nothing.

Watching Opal saunter toward the road worker was a pleasant distraction. But after an exchange of smiles and nods, she seemed to hit a language snag. As her arm and head gestures became more expansive, the rest of her body exhibited a clipped sinuousness. She certainly did move like a woman who had worked around men—soldiers—almost all of her life. There were other signs of that background, too: she was capable and direct, but a little unsure of herself when it came to the subtler social banter of civilians.

Caine wondered what Downing had in mind for her: almost certainly something involving her military training. Her movements also suggested that if she had missed having the opportunity to learn the minuet, she hadn't missed any of her martial arts classes. That, in conjunction with not being on any intelligence agency's radar, were her greatest assets—at least right now. So what was she here for? To work as a bodyguard, maybe?

He considered her empty seat: *a bodyguard... for me?* Possible. And a bodyguard could also work as a watchdog, an informant. Caine frowned: that would certainly be Downing's style, but it was hard to see Opal in such a role. Her dislike of Downing was genuine, palpable, and she seemed too socially awkward to be a very proficient actress or a reliable—

The door opened; Opal was almost in her seat by the time he turned. Reaching for the safety belt, she frowned and smiled at the same time. "You know how to drive this thing—I mean, the old-fashioned way?"

"I've had a few instructive misadventures trying to learn: why?"

She looked ahead, nodded at a road marker two hundred meters further on. "We're going to have to take the 'old road' up to a different lookout. And from what I was just told—if I understood the Engreek correctly—the locals still call it the 'goat path.'"

"Will we have to dodge the animals?"

She smiled. "Just a figure of speech, but a few parts are still single lane gravel. I got the whole sad story: seems they were in the process of modernizing it last year when the funding dried up."

"And what's wrong with the road to the main site?"

She looked over her shoulder at the woman in the hard hat, who had resumed her fixated roadside crouch.

"Apparently, the sensors steered someone right over an embankment earlier today. So they have to keep the grid active—but empty—while they run their diagnostics and fix the problem."

"Uh . . . Opal, I've got to confess: I'm still getting the hang of these quasi-cars. I might not be the safest driver."

Her smile was back. "We'd be in a hell of a lot more trouble with me behind the wheel. So drive on: I have every confidence in your manly automotive abilities. Besides, like I told you, I'm immortal—so you'll be safe as long as you're with me."

Her radiant confidence was gratifying, but not particularly reassuring. Caine forced himself to return her smile, restarted the car in manual, turned off the computer, eased slowly into gear. *Driving like a maiden aunt on her way to church.* "So we take that turn up ahead?"

"Yup. Let me see; the woman back there said that most rentals have maps in the glove compartment." She opened it and rummaged through the various manuals and registration papers.

As he moved off the shoulder of the road and back into the northbound lane, Caine checked the rearview mirror: no traffic—and the hard-hatted road worker had apparently finished her chores, coming to stand at the side of the road, walkie-talkie in hand.

Opal was muttering and still rummaging: "Every damn promotional brochure known to man, but if you need to find a map—" Caine stole a quick sideways glance; she was bent over, face almost in the glove compartment. A hint of the elfin in the faintly retroussé nose, the delicate, almost pointed chin, the bright, wide, vaguely feline eyes. Since being reawakened six weeks ago, he'd occasionally wondered if his libido had followed his lunar memories into limbo: it was reassuring to discover—as he did now—that this was not the case.

"You turn here." Her head had swiveled toward him, and, smiling, she cocked it in the direction of the oncoming white concrete marker.

Caught staring. Damn. "Um . . . yes, right."

He checked the rearview mirror before turning. Still no traffic, although the road technician seemed to be looking after them. *Wondering if the tourists understood the directions,* he surmised, turning in at the marker, kicking up dust from the unused roadbed. Evidently satisfied, the technician removed her hard hat, opened the door to her own car, and got in.

Chapter Seventeen

MENTOR

Downing checked his watch. This was taking too long. And besides, it was madness.

The old-fashioned hand radio on the passenger seat paged once. There was no subsequent sound of a channel opening—and there wasn't supposed to be: coded signals only.

He looked at the radio, looked up at the rough-hewn slopes two kilometers to the north. There had to be a better way, a safer way. But he hadn't been able to think of one—and now it was too late. *The Fox is in the woods— let's just hope there are no Hounds around to chase it ...*

ODYSSEUS

As the car bounced over a rock and down into a pothole, Opal's hand flinched to support her recovering liver. "Damn, this really is a goat trail."

"Sorry," Caine apologized through gritted teeth.

"Not your fault," she said through a slow, measured exhalation.

They entered a short, straight stretch of road, refreshingly dark under the glowering brows of a steep upslope overhang. Spoor of the prior year's abandoned construction efforts—piles of gravel, a half-completed drainage ditch, a flatbed with a load of PVC pipe sagging against weathered downslope straps, a forlorn shovel twinned with an equally forlorn pickaxe—seemed to huddle in the shade as they went past, and the incline increased.

The car skittered on some of the gravel; Opal bounced against the door again, briefly went pale. Caine winced in sympathetic pain: "We could go back."

She shook her head, checked the map. "Naw, we don't have much further to go." The car's engine began wailing unsteadily as the incline became even steeper, the bone-dry dust swirling up around. "Assuming this car can get us there, that is."

Caine nodded, looked at the gauges. "It's overheating. Too much engine strain." He reached over, snapped a switch. The air conditioning sighed and died. The engine immediately ceased its high-pitched, surging struggles, eased back into a consistent and steady hum. "With the AC off, the engine should be able to handle the slope. But you might want to open your window."

Opal smiled her assent, sought the window controls, pushed the button with two downward pointing arrows—just a moment after Caine noticed that there was another button alongside it which had only one such arrow. "Wait—!" he said.

The window, responding to the "fast-retract" control, snapped down as they came out of the shadow of the overhang. An abrupt rush of air scalloped into the car and out again, fiercely snatching the map right out of Opal's hand. "Shit!" she cried.

In the rearview mirror, Caine saw it flutter down into the shadows behind them.

He also noticed, now three hundred meters below, with four kilometers of treacherous switchback roadway between them, two vehicles exiting the main highway onto the same turnoff they had used. *More sightseers turned away from the main overlook.* He hoped their vehicles were up to the strain of the climb. Probably were: they were large-wheeled, boxy, off-road machines—apparently of matching make and model. Tourists straight from the rental agency, from the look of it.

MENTOR

The radio paged twice, quickly. Then a single signal, a long pause, and another single signal. Hounds had arrived—and there were two of them. *Bloody hell; Nolan was right.*

Downing started the car. Not that he needed to: there was no cause for alarm, and he had no role other than to await the results—and to clean up any mess left behind when his SEAL snipers were done "protecting" Caine and Opal.

But twenty-five years in covert operations had taught him one lesson above all others:

When a perfect plan meets imperfect, unpredictable reality, things go wrong. And sometimes, the greatest damage can be done by the smallest unforeseen detail—

ODYSSEUS

Opal turned back toward Caine with a sheepish smile. "Sorry about the map. But we'd better go back and get it."

He matched her smile. "You're proving to be nothing but trouble."

Her eyes did not waver, but her smile changed slightly. "That is my mission in life."

He heard the muted insinuation in her tone, felt his body begin to respond—and doused himself with a cold shower of reason: *Okay, Caine, let's not accompany her too quickly down the flirtation flume-ride.* "Well, you have accomplished your mission, Captain."

"For now." Her voice was still playful, still subtly provocative. Caine decided that he was starting to like Greece a great deal.

As he swung the car through a tight 180-degree turn, he saw two approaching plumes of dust on the roadway below: the approaching sightseers. He hit the accelerator; better to retrieve the map before the new arrivals reached the area they had to search. No reason to create a traffic jam on a cliffside stretch of road that was officially two-lane, but sure didn't look or feel that way.

They plunged back into the sharply delimited shadow of the overhang.

MENTOR

The radio paged once, twice—and then the fateful third time. *Bollocks: something's awry. Murphy's Law strikes again.*

Downing waited for his collarcom to chirrup—but instead, the handset toned another three times.

He snatched up the radio as he shifted out of neutral. "This is not a secure line. Reroute to command channel alpha—"

"Game Warden, this is Huntsman. We do not have time—repeat, do not have time—to wait for secure com clearance and switching."

Crikey, the op is going pear-shaped. "Understood. Sitrep, Huntsman."

"Fox doubled back into our blindspot—"

"Your *what*?"

"Our blindspot: a forty-meter stretch of road where we have no line of sight."

Just fucking brilliant. "Huntsman, advance Dogcatcher One to the nearest fire enabled position immediately."

"Game Warden, that is a negative. Our OpOrd requires we stay under aerial cover at all—"

"Huntsman, I *wrote* your operation orders. I say three times; move Dogcatcher One to a fire-enabled overlook on the blind spot *now*. Fox must be protected at all costs, even if you compromise your OP. Game Warden out."

"Out."

Downing rolled out of the convenience store's parking lot, and northward into the heat shimmers of the two-lane macadam. As he accelerated—steadily, but not abruptly—he reached over and popped open the briefcase that was resting on the passenger seat...

ODYSSEUS

"Do you see the map?"

Opal squinted forward into the dust that was still hanging in the air from their uphill passage of half a minute ago. "No, I—"

The car lurched slightly to the right and Caine realized that, in scanning for the map himself, he had taken his eyes off the road. He snapped his attention forward again, but too late: he had veered toward the edge of the road and put the passenger side front wheel into the gravel of the partially completed drainage ditch.

He swung the wheel hard to the left—and immediately regretted it: the digital controls were too sensitive for performance driving. He felt the rear tires shudder, struggle, then lose traction—and suddenly they were speeding downhill sideways in a gradual spin.

He tried to countersteer, but the tires didn't bite; driving on the slick macadam was like driving on a sheet of water. They skitter-screeched forward at an angle, heading straight for the flatbed. Opal snapped forward at the waist, hands over her head: he felt a flash of envy for the speed of her reflex, started into the same position—

He slammed into, then bounced back from, the dashboard. The shattering of glass and squeals of twisted metal were loud in his ears. The car continued to move, but no longer forward; it slung him sideways as it completed its 180-degree counter-clockwise spin with a crunch against the side of flatbed, its nose pointed uphill. The PVC pipes rattled hollowly, shifted slightly toward the roof of the car; angry, drifting spirits of agitated dust swirled around them.

"You okay?" Caine dabbed a finger at his forehead; his knuckle came away shining dark red.

Opal nodded, hand tucked down against her right side. "Jesus, you really *are* a bad driver."

"Sorry. Can I help—?"

"No, I'm fine. And I wasn't serious about your driving. Lighten up: this road is a death trap."

"Can you move?"

"I said I was fine—but this door's mashed in and pinched against the flatbed. I'll have to get out the driver's side."

Caine opened his door, assessed the damage as Opal clambered out: the car wasn't going anywhere soon. Its sideways spin had, fortunately, brought it across the road and away from the precipitous ledge, but had also sent it straight into the protruding corner of the low-slung flatbed. The right front wheel had received the full brunt of the edge-on impact: the flatbed's corner had crumpled the car's front quarter panel and struts, sliced clean through the tire, and had half-bisected the wheel itself.

"Well, at least we've got company coming." Opal stepped around to the rear of the car. "Maybe they'll give us a lift." As the two off-road vehicles rose into view over a hump in the road six hundred meters downslope, she started waving her arms in a slow cycle: wide arms to crossed arms and back again.

The reaction of the vehicles was peculiar; whereas most motorists confronted with an accident slow down, these sped up, the second vehicle moving out of line and taking up a flanking position in the other lane. Caine, who was moving toward the trunk, stopped: *Something's wrong—*

—and his world slammed into slow motion, the way it did when he felt, more than saw, a threat approaching. The vehicles were moving in concert; their actions were sure, swift, coordinated. And their passengers, although he could barely make out silhouettes, were all dark, broad-shouldered masses: not a rabble of variously-aged, -dressed, and -shaped tourists. *Not tourists*—

"Get behind the flatbed—now." He moved past Opal to the trunk.

"What are you talki—?"

"Just do it." He popped the trunk, pulled up the liner.

Opal frowned at him, mouth open to object, then heard the revving engines of the closing vehicles, looked over in their direction: her eyes widened. She turned and sprinted around the corner of the truck.

Caine had found the small toolkit for changing flats, followed around after Opal—and found her crouched low, looking out under the long expanse of carrier bed by peering around the tires. She glanced up at him: he held out the toolkit, proffering the half-sized crowbar-wrench combination. She shook her head. "Would only slow me down."

Caine looked at the flatbed, the pipes, the shovel, the weathered straps, fraying where their fabric attached to the buckles. *Yeah, that might work.*

Opal was still looking at him. "Now what?"

The engines were coming markedly closer. Twenty-five seconds, maybe thirty—

"Can you fight?"

"Better than you can breathe."

Well, always time for a little bravado. He picked

up the shovel, tested the heft. "I think I can take out the first car—at least long enough for us to close in and have a fighting chance."

"To do what?"

"Take some down and get their guns." He cocked the shovel back like a baseball bat, angled for an edge-on swing. "Tell me when they're within one hundred meters."

"Uh—now!"

He swung: the edge of the shovel bit into the fraying uphill strap, just below the buckle, sliced through about half of it. *Shit*—and he cocked the shovel back, swung again.

The tattered fibers were already groaning—the PVC pipes pulling against them—when the shovel hit and sheared the rest of the strap. Pipes started cascading off the other, downhill side of the flatbed. Caine jammed the point of the shovel under the bottom-most pipe and levered upward, throwing his whole weight down upon the tool's handle. The spatter of falling pipes became a hollow-sounding avalanche.

Turning toward Opal, he shouted "Go—"

—but she was no longer there. Having evidently scooted under the flatbed as the first pipes came down, she was now sprinting downhill in the immediate, dust-roiling wake of the storm crest of tumbling, sometimes high-bouncing plastic tubes. Caine picked up the small crowbar, ran back around the corner of the flatbed, heading for the first car.

The first vehicle tried braking but the pipes were under its wheels, whanging off the windshield as it lost control and skittered into the drainage ditch. Caine stretched his legs and body toward it—and, through the dust, saw a smallish figure sprinting straight toward the side of the listing vehicle. The front passenger-side door started to open. Without breaking stride, the smallish figure launched into a long, sideways leap. Just as a head and shoulders started to emerge from the car, the silhouette crashed into the door like a pile driver, feet first. The door slammed back; a sickening crunch was audible over the tumult of tumbling pipes. The door rebounded from crushing the passenger, became a springboard which launched the silhouette back in the direction from which she had come. And gone: into the dust.

But, now almost at the car and looking for any weapon that the crushed man might have dropped, Caine saw the rear passenger door opening. Still running, he flung the crowbar overhand, went into a long leaping dive—

—saw the spinning, shining tool hit the door's window, glass shattering inward—

—and then he landed just in front of the vehicle. He immediately snap-rolled under it.

There were sounds of blows, blocks, and grunts over on the driver's side: Opal going after the wheelman, probably. And now, the rear passenger door resumed opening, crashing back on its hinges, unleashing curses and a pair of feet in cheap leather shoes.

Five feet to the left side of those shoes—lying on the ground just beyond the rim of the right wheel well—was what Caine had been hoping to find: the pistol formerly carried by the man Opal had crushed in the door. Caine grabbed the weapon, realizing that, if he were seen doing so, he was now probably living the last few seconds of his life.

But the man in the cheap shoes was exiting the rear passenger door more cautiously, had evidently not yet moved to a point where he could see around his own door to the ground near the front of the vehicle.

Caine wasn't sure of the make of the weapon—maybe an older Sig Sauer—but it was clearly chambered for caseless ammunition: there was no ejection port.

The man's feet moved swiftly forward alongside the vehicle, drew abreast of the wheel well, crept more cautiously as they neared the front bumper. One more step and he'd discover that the dim figure that had thrown the crowbar at him was no longer hidden there. An explosion—muffled by distance—made him pause a moment.

Caine checked the safety: off. The weapon was cocked. Steadying it with two hands, he aimed the pistol at a point just beyond the front right tire.

The man's cheap shoes tensed, flexed—and then he jumped around the front fender of the vehicle, evidently in a crouch. This move put his feet and ankles in the pistol's gunsights: Caine squeezed the trigger and kept squeezing.

Other than the expected roar of the gun, the first split second was utterly surreal: there was a misty blast of blood from the ankle only three feet in front of Caine, flying specks of flesh and bone—and no other sound or movement. Then, as the pistol barked and jumped again, a stunned animal howl harmonized with it, and the ankle and foot buckled. More of the man appeared, falling into the gunsights. Caine kept firing, one part of him stunned by what he was doing, the other part coolly wondering how many rounds were in the weapon. The bullets made a nasty, meat-ripping sound:

the man struggled to rise—another bullet hit him. He flinched—another bullet—then quaked—another bullet—and collapsed into stillness. One last bullet.

A thump to the left; Caine rolled to face in that direction, and found a sunglassed man—the driver?—staring straight at him, right cheek flush against the cracked macadam. However, he was also lying with the back of his jacket facing Caine—meaning that his head was apparently on backwards. His neck bulged hideously, twisted: Opal's handiwork.

Link up with her, gather weapons, look for radios. Then, suppress—or take out—the next carload of them.

Caine rolled toward the man with the rear-facing head, squirmed out over him and a clutch of tangled PVC pipes. No sign of Opal. *Damn. Maybe she's already moved on to engage—*

Caine heard motion behind him, turned, saw his death in the black hole of a gun muzzle that was coming around the front of the vehicle, almost trained on him. He began bringing his own weapon around toward the new gunman, who had evidently exited the back of the car from the same side as the one with the cheap shoes. And Caine knew: *I won't make it; he's going to get me.*

The unwinking black pupil of the pistol's barrel was staring straight through Caine's retina into his brain—when the gunman's head snapped over suddenly. A slight puff of red vapor next to his uphill temple seemed to push his entire head in the downslope direction—and a lateral jet of blood erupted from that side. The pistol twisted up and away with his fall, firing into the air, responding to a death reflex in the trigger finger.

Who saved me? Was it—?

"Opal?"

Footsteps—too heavy—came around the front of the vehicle: Downing, at a crouch, gun in hand.

"Wha—?"

"Are you hurt?"

Footsteps, softer, behind: "He'd better not be."

Caine turned, smiled to see Opal's smile—and noted the wide, worried eyes that quickly recovered—and cut into Downing. "What the hell is going on here?"

"As if I know?" Downing helped Caine to his feet. "What I do know is that we have to leave here—now."

Caine shook him off, gun in both hands again. "There was a second vehicle—"

Downing jerked his head back downslope. "They went over the edge—courtesy of your landslide of tubing, from what I saw."

Opal snorted. "Yeah? And what the hell are *you* doing here anyway?"

"Oh, well, I beg your pardon, Captain: I thought my timing and arrival were both rather serendipitous."

"Yeah—maybe a little *too* serendipitous?"

"Are they? Have you stopped to think that you both left the stadium without one of these?" He yanked off a collarcom. "And that was my fault, damn it, because I was supposed to give one to each of you, just in case you got into any trouble and needed to call."

"So you followed us."

"Yes, of course: is that a crime? So I ran into the roadblock to the main overlook. Closer scrutiny, and a quick call to our local contacts, revealed that it was a sham. From that point, it became obvious where you must have been sent, and what was going to happen when you got here. I'm just sorry I didn't arrive sooner."

"Yeah, well—we did all right on our own." Hands on hips as she moved toward the front of the first vehicle, Opal blew sweaty bangs out of her eyes and stalked past Downing.

Caine smiled at her as she passed. "'We' weren't so great, but *she* was outstanding."

Opal looked back over her shoulder—face smudged, hair awry, primal, compelling—and then stared down at the much-shot body in front of the car and the tangle of tubing all around them. "Oh, I don't know: seems like you held up your end."

Downing looked from her to Caine and back again. "Well, you are both very welcome: how gracious of you to thank me for my help."

Caine kept his voice low, controlled. "Downing, we're only here because of your agenda and actions, so don't expect any gratitude. Far as I can tell, you were just protecting valuable merchandise. Now, if you say we've got to get out of here—"

Downing, stiff-lipped, nodded. "We do. Captain, you police up their weapons and keep watch." He tossed her his pistol; she caught it—the grip in her palm, finger just outside the guard—with lazy ease. Downing moved around to the rear of the stricken vehicle. "Caine, help me get their bodies back in the car; then go to mine, and bring back the cigarette lighter as soon as it's hot."

Caine had never moved a dead body. It was not only as heavy as several sacks of potatoes, but equally unwieldy; grab the torso, and the legs and arms splay and flop around, dragging you off balance. Cinch in the limbs, and you lose leverage on the torso. And always, the loose, bouncing head, the eyes staring, accusing . . .

As Caine finished shoving a second corpse into the vehicle, Richard—who evinced a surprising facility for the same job—dropped to the ground, scuttled under its rear bumper. Caine trotted back to Downing's car, opened the door, noting the thick curlicue of black smoke that marked the final resting place of the assassins' second vehicle. He pushed in the lighter, waited for it to pop out, arrived with it just as Downing was scrabbling back out.

Opal sneered. "Field repairs, Mr. Downing?"

"Preparing to destroy evidence, Captain Patrone. Had to uncap the engine oil pan."

"Why not just cut the fuel lines and light 'er up?"

"Captain, these are fuel-cell vehicles. So the best accelerant we have is the oil that lubricates the transmission and turbine. Now please step back. Caine, the lighter."

Caine turned it over to Downing, who leaned forward, tossed it into the thickest part of the oil slick that was spreading from underneath the vehicle in a downhill swath.

As the fire caught and raced back up under the car, Opal frowned. "Shouldn't we report this to—?"

Caine, backing away, shook his head. "No, we can't. Not without compromising, maybe scuttling, the Parthenon Dialogs. That's why we're setting the fire and removing the weapons."

Downing was at his car, holding the door for Opal. "That's right: we have to make this look—at least for the first twenty-four hours of investigation—as though it might be a comparatively normal road accident. If the delegates learn that there was an attempt on the life of an expert witness the day before he testifies, it might scare them all off. These were supposed to be secret proceedings, after all."

"Then what about the evidence in the second car?" She paused, hand on the door frame, looking down at the flaming wreckage.

"Hopefully, that fire is intense enough to incinerate the bodies and weapons."

"So why is that one burning so well?"

Downing shrugged, closed her door. "Probably because they were carrying a few liters of petrol to burn *your* bodies and car once they had finished their job."

Caine held in a shudder, felt as though he might vomit. "Let's just get the hell out of here."

Chapter Eighteen

ODYSSEUS

At the villa—a burnt-ochre mission-style home with a tiled roof and innumerable perimeter cameras—Downing held the door for Opal while two guards stood at either flank of the broad entry. Caine, awaiting the conclusion of the chivalric ritual, saw himself in the glass doors, his image cut into irregular pieces by the black wrought-iron framing. The tinted glass muted the colors of whatever it reflected, so the bloodstains on his shirt and pants and forehead were rendered as brown-mauve patches and spatterings. The three seconds he waited, staring at the stains and himself, seemed unusually long, as though minutes, even hours, were passing—

"Christ, Caine—come in. Come on in."

Nolan's voice, then his face, were coming out of the now-vacated doorway at him. Caine nodded, entered as bid.

The interior, he noticed calmly, was quite beautiful: beyond the high-ceilinged entry hall, dark wood raftering lent a stately antiquity to the wide, bright interior. He was also aware that Nolan was studying him with a frown, the jocularity of his first exhortation quite gone.

But that convivial demeanor returned—with astonishing, almost disgusting rapidity—as the retired admiral turned quickly to Opal. He scooped a glass from a waiting tray, and stuck a drink in her hand. Caine noted, with a queasy irony, that it was a Bloody Mary.

Caine heard Nolan's voice grow loud behind him, as though the rising volume were trying to fill up an empty space, or trying to push everything else out: "Captain, it's a pleasure to finally meet you. I just wish it was under happier circumstances. But you are intact and in a safe place, so let's drink to that. You know, this whole thing was my fault, really. I shouldn't have cleared Caine—and you—for unescorted travel. I am becoming an optimistic old man, I guess. Now you just enjoy your drink; I've got to hijack Caine for a few minutes. Some unfinished business. Excuse us?"

Her mouth puckering, full of drink, she nodded them out, waving them on with her free hand.

Nolan crinkled his avuncular eyes at her, waved for Caine to follow him.

Which Caine did at a measured pace: *If I was a betting man, I'd lay odds we'll wind up in a windowless conference room.*

Nolan led Caine into the room he'd envisioned. Downing closed the door behind them. Caine remained on his feet.

Nolan looked at him. "Caine, will you have a seat?"

"No, not until I get some answers."

Nolan stared. "Very well: what do you want to know?"

"What the hell happened out there? I thought you said—"

Nolan held up a hand. "Caine, as I was telling Captain Patrone, that was my fault, all of it. I got lazy, overconfident, and jeopardized not only you, but also a crucial opportunity for international cooperation. There is no excuse for my laxity; I can only ask your forgiveness and forbearance."

Nolan, and the apology, seemed sincere—but still, it seemed to come too easy, was too facile. *Of course, he's probably been in this position a dozen times, so he's had ample opportunities to rehearse this little scene of genuine self-abnegation.* "I'll assume that's true—for now. But who the hell is trying to kill me? Do you have any better idea now than when you retrieved my lifepod in Junction?"

Downing shook his head. "'Fraid not. There's a long list of possible suspects, but we have no way of knowing which one—or several—might be responsible. On the *Tyne*, the only lead was the second engineer, and his identity, and prior assignment at Epsilon Indi, were fabrications. The assassins at Alexandria either escaped or were vaporized by personal failsafe devices—"

"By what?"

"The five strikers we neutralized on adjacent rooftops were burned beyond analysis. Our after-action forensics indicate that each one was equipped with a biomonitor deadman switch rigged to a medley of thermite and white phosphorous charges. If the heart stops—poof: the body and most of the equipment are vaporized by warheads that explode and then burn at twenty-two hundred to twenty-eight hundred degrees Celsius."

Caine stared at the tabletop. "Wonderful."

"Almost as wonderful as the cleanup you and I had to perform less than an hour ago. But here, we had to abandon and burn the evidence ourselves because we have only limited influence over the local authorities."

Nolan shrugged. "I don't think we'd have learned much from the bodies, anyway."

Caine looked hard at Corcoran. "Why not?"

"Because they were amateurs, local freelancers. They came after you without any backup plan, their equipment was second-rate, and they were already here."

"Waiting for me?"

"No: if our adversaries had had any lead time, if they *knew* you'd be arriving here, they'd have shipped in an A-team. Real professionals. They'd have done the job right: sure, clean, and with absolute plausible deniability. This bunch—they were local muscle, quickly rustled together with phone calls and a few hundred thousand euros, because someone saw you in this area and got the word back to whoever wants you dead. Our opponents probably had only an hour or two to set something up—and by ambushing you with amateurs and failing, they've revealed that they don't yet have an A-team on site. Meaning that they won't get another shot at you, because by this time tomorrow, you will have told the last of your secrets. After that, there will be no reason left to kill you. Now: will you sit and join us?"

Caine felt the instinct to remain standing: sitting implied a trust, or acceptance, that he did not feel. But to remain standing was to signal hostility. *No middle course.* So he sat.

Downing hunched forward. "So—what's the news from Day One, Nolan?"

"Bottom line: there's general agreement to create

a global confederation. When the five blocs were presented with irrefutable evidence of exosapience, there was a unanimous decision to create a central organization with practical political, economic, and military authority."

Caine cleared his throat; Nolan paused, nodded. "Just cut in whenever you want. No Robert's Rules, here."

"What you're talking about—sounds to me like it makes the U.N. redundant."

Downing nodded. "Hardly a surprise: the U.N. was never able to put into practice more than a handful of the edicts that it promulgated or the ideals that it espoused. It's little more than a symbolic memorial."

"Whereas now the big powers really *want* to work together?"

Nolan waved away that notion. "Oh, 'want' has never achieved anything. But the threat of exosapience means that they *need* to work together. Of course, that didn't keep some of the bigger bulls from locking horns for a while."

Downing looked up from scribbling on his dataslate. "Beijing and Moscow?"

Nolan nodded. "The predictable axes were ground."

"But they're going to play nice?"

"So they say."

Caine frowned. "This all sounds surprisingly civilized."

"We knew that there would be a baseline of sanity from some of the blocs. Of course, there were still a few cranky gadflies in the ointment—even from the EU."

Downing grunted. "Oh? Who?"

"Well . . . Gaspard."

"But of course. Parisian diplomat of the old school. Wanker."

"C'mon, Rich, cut him some slack. He's fighting to maintain some shred of France's past preeminence—"

Downing tapped his pencil. "Well, he—and the rest of his ilk—will just have to bloody well get used to the fact that France hasn't been an empire since Napoleon left Moscow."

"That's a hard thing for a country to accept."

"Rot. Look at England: we've faced facts and moved on."

Nolan's left eyebrow arched. "Oh? Really?" Downing's mouth was open to begin a rebuttal, but Nolan held up his hand. "For now, let's just get through the day's news. Which boils down to this: the Confederation government will be a council of five blocs, two voting members per bloc, and one proconsul with a two-year term."

Downing tapped his stylus on his slate. "Military authority?"

"Separate forces and R&D within each bloc. However, each bloc structures its forces and production to meet the defense responsibilities assigned to it by the Confederation Council."

Downing seemed pensive. "And—what about intelligence operations?"

"The same model; separate national agencies, coordinated at the bloc level. Each bloc then contributes some assets to a centralized Confederation bureau."

"With which IRIS can augment its own data gathering and spread its influence."

Caine looked from Downing to Nolan and back to Downing: the same shrewd, satisfied smile on both faces. "You're not going to tell them about IRIS? I mean, isn't this the logical moment?"

Downing studied his fingers. "No: revealing IRIS now would destroy this infant Confederation in its crib."

"Why?"

"For twenty years, strings have been pulled, policies have been massaged—mostly by agents of the Commonwealth bloc—to bring delegates of the major nations to this very place. If they were to learn that they are here because they have been played like puppets, they would utterly renounce this summit. But if we wait until the Confederation is a *fait accompli*, then we'll be able to stand down safely and quietly."

Caine shook his head. "I wonder how many times a misguided international involvement has been prolonged with that kind of rhetoric: 'We will leave once the situation has been stabilized.'"

Nolan shrugged. "Historical precedent is on your side, so I won't argue. I can only say that the alternative seems worse to me."

Caine silently conceded that Nolan also had a good—maybe superior—point. "So, what now?"

Nolan produced a bottle from the credenza, glanced at Richard. "Metaxa?"

"A double, if you please."

Nolan turned to Caine. "Want to join us? Just our little evening ritual."

"Thanks, I'll pass. I've got a big day tomorrow."

Nolan nodded. "We all do. But I could use some exercise to clear my head: want to take a walk up to the temple before dinner?"

Already halfway out, Caine turned. *Not really.* But he said: "Sure. I'll come along."

Chapter Nineteen

MENTOR

On his way out the door, Caine added, "Find me when you're done here."

"I will." Nolan pushed a glass of Metaxa toward Richard.

Caine nodded, closed the door behind him.

Nolan picked up his glass. "Do you think he suspects?"

"That we used him as bait? Not yet—maybe never, given how close we came to cocking up the whole op."

"What the hell happened out there?"

"Damned if I know—but for some reason, he and Opal stopped in the only blind spot on that side of the mountain."

"Thank God the overwatch team adapted quickly."

Downing nodded. "Your son trained them well."

"And he's been kept in the dark about us tapping his former team for this op?"

"Trevor doesn't know a thing. But how long that will last is hard to say."

Nolan sighed. "I know: SEALS are rough, tough

238

commandos, but they gossip like wrinkled church ladies among themselves. Still, they did a good job."

"No slight intended, but we may owe more to good luck. Things could have worked out very differently. Almost did."

"Well, we still drew the opposition out, forced them to make their move in a time and a place of our choosing, and trumped their hand. And we manufactured the bonding crisis that the psych folks insist will bring Caine and Opal together quickly and surely."

"Yes—but we created more of a crisis than we could handle. I still say it was unreasonably risky, Nolan." Downing would have preferred the word "reckless." "Today's operation came too bloody close to destroying the very asset it was designed to protect."

"Look, Rich, after Alexandria, we have to accept that conventional notions of security are damn near useless. Whoever's after Caine has proven that they can hit a stationary target using methods we don't even understand. So I stand by my decision: drawing them out for a preemptive counterstrike was actually less risky than digging in and hunkering down. And now, Riordan's worries *are* over. Our local security is good, EU forces are pouring into the area in preparation for tomorrow's meeting, and our opponents know they've lost the element of surprise. We're out of the woods."

A nice theory. Downing sipped the Metaxa. *Let's hope it's accurate.* "Even if they were amateurs, it would have been damned helpful to get some identities."

"Yeah, as is anything that might show us who's after Riordan. Speaking of which, any word of the forensics analysis on Alexandria?"

Downing nodded. "The final after-action report

came in this morning's pouch. The analysts are now speculating that Riordan may not have been the only target; they may have been after *all* the coldsleepers."

"What has the analysts thinking that?"

"Well, the power outage killed almost all the sleepers within minutes: with both the main current and the backup generator out, those early cryocells had only five minutes of emergency battery power."

"You said the power outage killed *almost* all the sleepers?"

"Yes: three others were in modern cryopods, so their systems defaulted to long-duration self-power when the generator went offline."

"So they're alive?"

"No, they're dead too."

"How?"

"The intruders shot them."

Nolan's glass froze in the transit from tabletop to mouth. "Say again?"

Downing nodded. "You heard me correctly: the intruders shot them."

Nolan returned the glass to the table. "Not good."

"No, no good at all. That's why the analysts are rethinking why the attackers were there in the first place, and the rationale behind their tactics. Did they cut power to make it easier to infiltrate and secure local tactical control . . . ?"

"Or was it to kill off all the sleepers?" Nolan finished for him. "Christ, Rich, you were dead right when you suggested we replace the original sleepers with death-row inmates. If we hadn't, we'd have another forty or fifty innocent corpses on our hands."

"Sixty-three."

"Okay, you can rub it in: you're entitled." Nolan bolted back most of his Metaxa. "When the intruders killed the other sleepers, did they bother to open the cryocell lids and check for identities?"

"No. So the enemy strikers could not have learned that we switched the occupants. Which brings up yet another related issue: when should we inform the penal authorities?"

"About the untimely demise of sixty-three of its sociopaths and axe murderers? Not until after we know who hit the facility and why. And *how*."

"Yes. About the 'how': the final assessment on the site's power loss indicates there was no sabotage: no sign of explosives, wire cutters, or computer hacking. As a matter of fact, there's no sign of physical intrusion at all."

"What do you mean?"

"There is no sign that the control panel for the building's generator was ever opened. Indeed, they never even entered the generator room."

"Then how the hell—?"

"As best we can tell, the power was cut by an intensive but very narrowly localized EM pulse that shorted out the internal regulators. At least, that's what it looks like."

"How localized an EM pulse are we talking about?"

Downing double-checked his notes. "Essentially pinpoint: half a cubic meter, at most."

"Rich, that's impossible."

"I did not say the report establishes that it *was* an EM pulse—just that it looked like one. But just because we aren't aware of anyone with the ability to create that kind of focused EM pulse—through very thick reinforced concrete, no less—it doesn't necessarily follow that it is impossible. However, our analysts in Newport insist that it would be a large device, and would require a tremendous burst of power—enough to show up on the spectral imaging sensors that are dedicated to orbital overwatch of the DC metro area."

"Which showed nothing."

Downing nodded. "And given the thoroughness of the after-action sweeps, we can rule out a buried device."

"So we've got a locked-room mystery."

"Seems so, Holmes."

"Ha ha, Watson. And still nothing on the intel leak that gave the attackers the location of Riordan, or the sleepers—or whatever the hell they were after?"

Downing shook his head. "No—and we've exhausted our investigatory options."

"So, someone was able to obtain access to our various computer systems without leaving any traces of doing so."

"Precisely. That is why I've suspended all our operations, other than those here in Greece."

"Could that have been part of their plan?"

"To compel the Institute to initiate a precautionary shutdown?" Downing shrugged. "I doubt it. Everything we've seen so far suggests their information on us is far from complete. In fact, it's quite sketchy. Consider: they know that the sleepers are in Alexandria, but they don't know the originals have been moved. They know the one-half cubic meter of space at which to aim a focused EM pulse, but they have to go on a room-to-room search for Riordan. If they really had a solid conduit into our information pipeline, they would have had much better tactical intelligence."

Nolan nodded. "And if I were them, I'd want to achieve my objective *without* leaving any locked-room mysteries."

"Why?"

"Because now we know we're up against something we don't understand. Unfortunately, we can't do anything about that right now—not until Parthenon is over."

"So, how long do we suspend our other operations?"

"Let's decide that after tomorrow morning's preliminary meeting."

"Excuse me: what meeting is that?"

"Just before you returned, the Indonesians called. They are in Athens and they want an early morning confab out here."

"Wonderful way to start the day. One final question: the planning for Riordan's Trojan Horse invasion defense tactic—do we keep working on it?"

Nolan nodded. "We've got to—even if only to continue gathering personnel and prepositioning hidden caches of munitions and other supplies."

"Very well. And what case code do we assign to the operation?"

Nolan stared then smiled. "Case Timber Pony."

"How droll. Goes with the theme, I suppose. Do we need codes for anyone other than Odysseus and Calypso?"

"Yes." He aimed a finger at Downing. "'M' for Mentor."

"'M?' You're giving that label to me, a British overseer of spies? That's either a very bad joke or you have a very poor knowledge of tawdry spy fiction."

"Neither: it's just a code from *The Odyssey*—and it fits."

"Very well. Any others?"

"Yes. Whoever—or whatever—is responsible for our closed-room mysteries will be—"

"'Circe'?"

"See? You're getting the hang of this." Corcoran tossed back the last of his Metaxa. "And now I will walk off my daily indulgence. Could you get a security detail to cover my sunset stroll to the temple with Riordan?"

Downing reached for the handset of the secure land line. "I'll get you two."

CIRCE

He leaned his brow against the binoculars: two dim figures moved slowly up the drive toward the fading silhouette of the Temple of Poseidon. He leaned back, checked his watch, jotted down the time on the notepad.

He turned to face the plate that was perched on the edge of the laundry table. Dominating the center of the unadorned white porcelain dish was a barely diminished cube of feta, surrounded by a litter of olive pits and a dusting of crumbs. He reached over the spoor of his dinner, closed his fingers gently around the orange resting at the center of the table. He lifted it slowly, studying it. He bobbed his hand once, as if feeling the heft of it, then brought it closer, up to his nose. He sniffed, tentatively at first, then sniffed again. He exhaled, then breathed in deeply through his nose: as he did, he smiled. He turned the orange round in his hand, rubbing his finger over its surface, inspecting both its stem and base briefly before cradling it

upright in his left hand. With the precise and focused
intent of a surgeon, using the two-centimeter-long
fingernail of his right middle finger, he made three
quick, successive sweeps around the stem. He studied
the incisions carefully: then, using a neatly trimmed
right index finger, he pried away the top of the orange,
which—already having been mostly sheared from the
rest of the skin—came off easily. He held the fruit to
his nose once more, breathed in deeply, smiled again,
put it down next to his dinner plate.

He turned and leaned toward the binoculars, rotated
them to the right. The two figures were already at the
end of the headland, walking across the ruin's flat central
expanse. One silhouette—lean, long-legged—seemed to
be wandering a bit. The other silhouette—perhaps two
centimeters taller and more thickly built—moved with
unswerving surety to the center of the ocean-facing row
of columns. That silhouette stepped down the stairs leading toward the overlook and came to a halt, staring out
to sea; the other silhouette hopped down to join him.

He smiled, counted the number of pillars to the
right of the two silhouettes, counted the number to
the left, checked his watch, wrote it down on his pad.
He leaned back toward the binoculars while reaching
for the orange. Both silhouettes remained motionless.

Still watching, still smiling, he inserted his right
index finger under the lacerated skin of the orange and
pushed it down toward the base, as far as it would
go. Then he pulled his finger slowly outward, away
from the heart of the fruit.

The skin bulged and ripped and released its life
in a dense, fragrant spray.

Chapter Twenty

ODYSSEUS

Sounion National Park's meeting facility was hardly what Caine pictured as the setting for a rendezvous with global destiny. Collages of photographs sent by appreciative visitors took the place of the somber busts of statesmen. Simple prefab construction did not deliver the sense of dignity that would have been imparted by well-varnished wood paneling and brass fixtures. No, to judge from the surroundings, the fate of the world was going to be determined in a trailer-park meeting hall.

But first, the facility would host a brief session with disgruntled representatives from Indonesia. Nolan, who had told Caine about the meeting the night before, had openly resolved not to let it spoil their walk up to the Temple of Poseidon. He had been successful: as they stood in the twilight calm and watched the stars come out, he had not uttered one word.

The Indonesian delegation had already arrived, dominated by a squat, late-middle-aged man. As they approached the central table, another, ethnically mixed contingent emerged from the alcove that housed the automated coffee dispensers.

"Bloody hell," Downing whispered.

—which was fortuitously—or was that carefully?—drowned out by Nolan's loud and expressive, "Vassily! You're early today—and you brought company."

Vassily Sukhinin—Nolan's Russian equivalent, and old comrade from the Highground War, if Caine remembered his reading—frowned apologetically. "I bring this company like a sheep brings wolves." He jerked his head vaguely to the rear. "I apologize, Nolan, but I did not bring them. I forced *them* to bring *me*."

Nolan turned toward the leader of the new and apparently unexpected group: a spare, immaculately tailored man of youthful middle age, flanked by two nondescript aides. The man wore a tie sporting what looked like a modernized heraldic pattern. Nolan's tone was interrogative: "Mister—?"

"Robin Astor-Smath. It's rather pleasant not being known on sight."

Astor-Smath. *Robin Astor-Smath. CoDevCo. From the news in the car just yesterday.*

Nolan gestured toward a seat at the table. "To what do we owe the honor of this unexpected visit?"

"That is a gracious question—particularly since I must assume you had a hand in ensuring that corporate entities were excluded from the proceedings."

"The proceedings, Mr. Astor-Smath, were initiated on behalf of the citizens of the world's nations. And it is solely on that basis—the lawful and sovereign representation of *citizens*—that the leaders of the five blocs are meeting to discuss matters of state. Mr. Astor-Smath, I believe you represent shareholders, not citizens."

"All of those shareholders are citizens with equal rights."

"True, but not all of the world's citizens are equally privileged shareholders—and that is the crucial difference. You represent the interests of a very privileged few, far less than one-tenth of one percent of the world's population."

"Well, Admiral, we'll see if that distinction holds up after you hear what my friends from Indonesia have to say this morning. I imagine you may have met Indonesia's Minister of Finance, Mr. Ruap."

The squat, late-middle-aged man nodded.

Nolan returned the nod. "I haven't had the honor until now. And while I am unsure how Mr. Sukhinin—Russia's Minister of Foreign Affairs—learned of our unofficial meeting, I am most grateful that he came along. Vassily, where is all your security?"

"If one would move quickly, one must carry few bags."

"Moscow is not going to be happy, my friend."

"*Shto*? I care? There was no time to send a message—and it would have attracted too much attention."

"It's your career, Vassily."

"Yes, and it would be a kindness to be asked to retire."

Nolan smiled—Caine saw a flash of the same gentleness that he had seen yesterday—and then Admiral Corcoran was on stage again: "I'm sorry to rush things along, but we don't have much time. Mr. Ruap, what can I do for you?"

The Indonesian Finance Minister folded his hands. "I am here to serve notice to the five blocs that, if the Parthenon Dialogs are to be truly global in nature, then the blocs need to provide a place for the many nations that are inadequately represented by them. Therefore, on behalf of these nations, Indonesia is demanding that these underrepresented nations be included as the World General Assembly bloc, which wishes to ensure that any global confederation will remain secondary and subordinate to the legal authority and primacy of the United Nations."

Nolan leaned forward. "Mr. Ruap, as the Dialogs' mediator, I am charged with assessing whether your World General Assembly is genuinely a sixth bloc. And here's what I've learned: as of this morning, almost all the nations you claim to represent remain committed to one or another of the five blocs. Similarly, the General Assembly has not charged nor endorsed any sixth bloc to become a watchdog over our proceedings here.

"So I can only think, Mr. Ruap, that you are here on what we Americans call 'a fishing expedition.' You don't have a committed bloc behind you: rather, you're a purchasing agent for a collection of nations that want to do some comparison shopping. You are free to do so—but not here. This is a meeting for duly constituted blocs. You do not have one yet, and therefore, we cannot accommodate you with a seat at the table."

Ruap spread his hands. "It is hard to see how Indonesia can continue to work with its American partners on the Mass Driver Project, then. It is a great shame, given all the joint work and expenses that have been incurred to date. However, our friends in CoDevCo will help us bring the project to swift and successful completion."

Sukhinin's shoulders came forward sharply: "I can no longer sit here and watch this charade. This is not about UN preeminence, or a sixth bloc, or even your mass driver: this is an attempt to scare us into helping you improve Indonesia's standing in the TOCIO bloc."

The rapid change in topic disoriented Caine, but Ruap's reaction told him that the Indonesian Finance Minister certainly felt the relevance of Sukhinin's words. Ruap sat very erect, face impassive: "Mr. Sukhinin, your implications are an insult to my gov—"

Sukhinin waved his hand in the air as if he were brushing away a fly. "*Gospodin* Ruap, it is *your* government which insults *us*—by wasting our time and recruiting this vulture"—he jerked his head at Astor-Smath—"to help you in your petty bid for more power within the Trans-Oceanic Commercial and Industrial Organization. Let us speak plainly: Indonesia was disappointed when Japan acknowledged Brazil and India as its two most important partners in the TOCIO bloc. So here you are today, trying to prove them wrong by showing how much trouble you can make: leading your own bloc, getting access to CoDevCo's big bank account and finishing the mass driver with their money. But tell me, if Tokyo called and said, 'Oh, do not leave us: we were wrong not to recognize you as equal to Brazil and India,' would you still be so eager to argue for a sixth bloc? It is all a farce, and the audience for whom you have staged it isn't even here. They are sipping sake and, I hope, laughing at you. Bah."

Ruap was still: his face had grown very dark. "Mr. Sukhinin, my nation shall remember your nation's slander."

Astor-Smath leaned into the space between them. "Gentlemen, please. These harsh words are unproductive and unbecoming. Let's get back on track. Clearly,

Admiral Corcoran and Mr. Sukhinin are not willing to recognize Indonesia's leadership, or even the existence, of a sixth bloc. However, that doesn't alter the fact that we have agreed to fund the completion of the Equatorial Mass Driver."

Downing shrugged. "Mr. Astor-Smath, you might want to examine the history of the Mass Driver Project before you become overly sanguine about its completion. After talking about it for twenty years, Indonesia finally persuaded China to help with construction and funding. When Beijing withdrew from the project, America got involved. That was fourteen years ago, and it has now cost the Commonwealth's governments and industrial investors about one hundred twelve billion c-dollars. I hope CoDevCo is prepared to take on that kind of job—and debt."

"We are ready to do so—because we believe it is not only a good investment, but is an important step towards global economic and social equity. The mass driver will give Indonesia and its bloc a monopoly on low-cost, high-capacity launches to low Earth orbit."

Caine watched Astor-Smath's chin rise into his topic, recalled the bio: born in Wichita, then enrolled in private schools—from daycare onward—in Madrid, Rio, Hong Kong, Johannesburg. A thoroughly heterogeneous background: Anglo-American, Chinese, Indian, Afrikaans, Polish, Bantu. Astor-Smath was a man for all seasons—and a mercenary for all occasions.

"With the political leverage provided by the mass driver," he was saying, "the Developing World can not only begin to compete in space commerce, but can pressure the Developed Nations to redress the imbalance of wealth throughout the globe."

A different voice jumped into the pause in Astor-Smath's speech: "I'm curious: at what point in the last twenty-four hours did you have a transforming moral epiphany?" Caine was somewhat surprised to find that the voice was his own.

"I beg your pardon?" Astor-Smath was not able to thoroughly mask his surprise. Nor was Nolan, who turned to look at Caine: his left eyebrow was raised, as well as the left corner of his mouth.

"Well, you see, just yesterday, I was listening to your apologetics for CoDevCo's mistreatment of workers from the Developing and Undeveloped Nations. So I can't help but wonder at what point in the last twenty-four hours you decided to become a crusader for those very same downtrodden peoples?"

"That is a separate matter. Those are isolated complaints—"

"Really? That doesn't match up with what I've read recently. Your ghastly working conditions on gray worlds and asteroids are experienced almost solely by laborers from the Undeveloped World, whose contracts resemble letters of indentured servitude. You talk about the wonderful revenues they send back to their families, but thousands of those families have filed class-action suits complaining that the payments are already five years in arrears, and are reduced to pennies on the dollar after you subtract the life-support charges that were in the small—or would that be invisible?—print of the worker's contract. So, since you don't appear to have the money to pay your workers, I'm curious; how do you plan to finance the Mass Driver Project?"

Astor-Smath did not appear to have an answer at the ready. No one spoke: the silence dragged on until it became sharply uncomfortable. Nolan rose. "It appears that we are done. Oh, and Mr. Ruap—"

Ruap, halfway to his feet, paused.

"It's possible that if you pull the plug on the mass driver partnership, Congress and American industry might be tempted to reexamine other deals they have with you." Nolan opened the door to leave, smiled; it could have been a wolf displaying his teeth. "Just a thought."

Caine had planned on remaining quiet until they reached their vehicles, but halfway there, Nolan took his arm. "I thought you already *had* breakfast."

"Huh? I did."

"Then I guess you were still hungry enough to eat Astor-Smath alive."

"Hope I didn't make any trouble."

"I doubt it. He didn't get any policy surprises here—although I suspect you caught him off guard when you put him on the spot personally."

"Which was not wise," added Downing at Caine's other elbow. "Astor-Smath seems unflappable, but he's got an ego—and the memory of an elephant."

"Okay, Rich," Nolan scolded, "stop scaring the new guy."

"I'm scared enough as it is." Caine sighed.

"Why?"

"Because CoDevCo must have foreseen this outcome."

"Naturally," agreed Corcoran.

"Then what was their real purpose in coming here? What are they up to?"

Nolan shook his head. "I haven't a clue. But right now, we don't have any way to find out. So we wait, watch, and—above all—remain completely focused on today's business."

CIRCE

The Sun, almost exactly overhead, duplicated itself in the man's wraparound sunglasses, which were aimed skyward as if he were scrutinizing the details of the stellar disk. He returned his attention to the small earthenware bowl that had three small black olives left in it; a white dish beyond it sprouted a modest heap of well-chewed pits at its approximate center. Their brine still glistened on his index finger; he licked it tentatively. He smiled, stretched, sighed, checked his watch.

"More black olives, sir?"

If the man was startled by the young waiter approaching quickly from behind, he gave no sign of it. He shook his head, pointed to a jar of green olives: each was larger than the top half of his thumb. He paused. "Today, I may also have some wine. Red wine."

The waiter smiled: the man tipped well and was not like most foreigners, who were constantly inquiring about different dishes, Greek food in general, the local sights. This man was quiet and very still, unusually so. And always alone. "I will get your order," the waiter said with a nod, and was gone.

The man kept looking through the space the waiter had just vacated, kept looking up at the end of the Sounion headland.

Chapter Twenty-One

ODYSSEUS

Upon reentering the meeting hall several hours later, Caine expected to find it a hive of activity. What he found, when the security guard on his left opened the door and the one on his right ushered him in with outstretched hand, was an utterly still tableau made up of concentric rings of expectant humanity.

The innermost ring of ten persons was incomplete: seated about a round table, their circle was broken by two empty chairs. The next ring was that of the advisors, aides, assistants, and chroniclers who were seated behind their delegates. The outermost ring—as numerous as the other two put together—were (mostly) men whose eyes could not be seen: square-jawed and sunglassed, the security personnel projected the aura of waiting automatons, creatures who had long ago ceased to move in accordance with their own will. Caine could see the eyes of the other two rings, however—and they were all on him.

Nolan had been waiting beside the door, smiled when Caine noticed him, accompanied him to the two empty chairs at the round table, indicated the one on the right. Nolan stood behind the other, cleared this throat.

"Ladies and gentlemen, you have all heard about Mr. Riordan, and what he found and experienced during his three weeks on Delta Pavonis. Please remember that Mr. Riordan is not here in a political or official capacity. His credentials today are those of a well-regarded researcher and writer who, on the advice of Senator Arvid Tarasenko, was sent to assess conflicting reports regarding advanced life forms and structures found on Delta Pavonis Three. You already have his report—except for one footnote that he will now present to you himself.

"Mr. Riordan, allow me to introduce the bloc representatives gathered here today. Starting on your right: Ms. Hollingsworth of the UK and Mr. MacGregor of Australia; Mr. Sukhinin of Russia and Ms. Durniak of the Ukraine; Mr. Ching of China and Mr. Demirel of Turkey; Mr. Karagawa of Japan, and Mr. Medina of Brazil; and Ms. Visser of Germany and Mr. Gaspard of France."

Caine noted which delegates offered a nod or some other sign of recognition: both of the Commonwealth delegates, Sukhinin of Russia, Visser of Germany, Medina of Brazil. The last he dismissed: at this point, it was impossible to distinguish warm but impersonal Brazilian cordiality from a sign of personal receptivity. He was similarly undecided about Durniak's lack of response: she was somewhat young and very intent, probably too focused to even think of personal interaction, at this point. No surprise in Ching's silence: he was the Great Sphinx of international relations.

China's Foreign Minister for almost eighteen years now, one journalist had quipped that Ching could go days without speaking—even if he was China's sole representative at a two-nation summit. An exaggeration, but not by much: according to Nolan, Ching had not spoken a word during the first day at Parthenon.

All five blocs. Two representatives from each. The US was conspicuously absent, probably because the mediator—Nolan—was a fairly famous American, and also in deference to providing a seat at the table for the Commonwealth's newest (and still probative) member state: the UK. Was this the shape of things to come? The first *de facto* sitting of the Confederation Council, meeting to will itself into existence, to midwife its own birth? *Ex nihilo—a new world order.* For a moment, Caine felt himself as the watcher, not the watched, immersed in the surreal quality of being present for the unfolding of a historical moment, and sharply aware that the neat beginnings and endings of history as reported had nothing to do with history as made.

Nolan's voice was gentle. "Mr. Riordan, whenever you're ready."

"Uh, yes—sorry." *Wonderful beginning. Ass.* He glanced down at his palmtop, at the notes he knew by heart, and calmly decided to ignore them. "Ladies and gentlemen, one hour before departing from Delta Pavonis on July 10, 2118, I returned briefly to the main ruins at Site One—"

—and he was there. His own voice became distant; he fell out of the council chamber and emerged into—

—The glare of Delta Pavonis, low on the horizon, glinted off the semi-rigid body armor of the Marines who, face shields down and weapons in an assault carry, preceded him out of the landing craft. Caine could hear the second fire team milling eagerly behind him, ready to follow him down the ramp. Overhead, a transatmospheric fighter orbited lazily. Caine wasted no time, moving through the swirling dust even as the whine of the landing thrusters was still dying away. Every second counted, now—and would until he got back to Earth. He walked past the right-angled dig pits, clambered over the berm, the first group of Marines hustling to keep in front of him.

He popped over the rise, side-footed down to the base—where the head archeologist was waiting, pudgy hands on pudgy hips, rounder, dustier, more gnomelike than Caine remembered. "I'm here," said the Gnome.

Caine couldn't decide whether he was more struck by the superfluity or petulance of the utterance. "Thanks for coming."

Gnome snorted: Caine's "request" to meet had been, in reality, merely a polite ultimatum. "What do you want?"

Caine debated whether he should try to apologize for the ruse he had used to get information out of the Gnome when they first met, but pushed that aside: there was no time. Gnome was never going to like him, so this had to be all business, pure and simple. So he went straight to the heart of the matter: "I have something you want."

"Oh? Maybe a time machine, so I can undo the past and *not* ruin my career by talking to you?"

"No, better than that."

Gnome's truculence gave way to interest. "How much better? What kind of 'better'?"

"The kind you really want: a ticket out of this place. Here's the offer—and you've got one minute to consider it.

"Someone has to write up a full report on the collective archeological findings from this dig site. That report will be presented at a global summit, sometime next year. That summit will remain a secret until after it has occurred, but I'm offering you the chance to write the report—and be the first to publish on what's been found here, and its archeological implications. That means a free trip back to Earth, and—I should imagine—the endowed chair you've been craving." Actually, it meant a lot more than that, but Caine hardly needed to explicate: Gnome's eyes seemed to grow as large as the round glasses that were in front of them. His lower lip flopped about a little.

"Does that mean you accept?"

Gnome sputtered and nodded. "Yes, yes—what do you want? How can I help?"

"When we met last time, you were about to explain something more about this ruin, about to show me something else, and then you stopped yourself."

A furtive look returned to Gnome's face. "I suppose I did."

"Show me now."

Gnome nodded and beckoned with a crooked finger. He went to the side of the temple, disappearing around the corner from which he had emerged the first time. Caine followed him down into a narrow slit trench that had been dug along the southern, leeward side of the structure, exposing its foundation for at least twenty meters. Five meters in, Gnome stopped, pointed. "Look."

Caine looked, saw a hole, about the size of his thumb, maybe a bit narrower. And then he saw the brown, rusty stain rimming it. He reached out, held his hand back, his breath coming short and fast.

"Go ahead," said Gnome, "all us researchers do. Those of us with any sense of a larger universe, that is. Go ahead. Put your finger in."

Caine did. He felt around. Felt a smooth, cold surface recessed half an inch from the exterior wall, restrained the impulse to either giggle or yell.

"Rebar," supplied Gnome. "Eerie, if you ask me. Chemical composition consistent with mid-grade industrial steel. The stereobate—that's the foundation—is actually risers of dressed stone, alternating with reinforced concrete. Probably the only reason the base held together all this time. The rebar was sunk a meter down, at even intervals all along the side." He paused. "You know what it means, don't you?"

Caine barely heard him, could not remember if he nodded or even waved farewell. He scrabbled up the berm and back toward the Marine lander. He was short of breath when he reached it, but not as a result of the exertion. Rather, he was overcome by a sudden, absolute, even desperate desire to begin his journey: to return home and discharge the burden of this final secret—the one which was the explanatory key to all the others...

Caine once again became aware of the faces ringing the round table. The looks were hard to read for a moment: fragments of many expressions were rippling up through the studied detachment of career diplomats and politicians. He saw shock, doubt, wonder, distrust, maybe even fear: too many threads, too tangled to separate.

They kept looking at him, as if they were waiting for more.

Nolan stood. "I think you see why we saved Mr. Riordan's footnote for last. It is—singularly provocative. I'm sure there are questions. Who'd like to start?"

Visser leaned forward. "You finished by saying that the presence of the rebar explains all the other secrets of what you found. What did you mean by that?"

Where to begin? "I'm going to jump ahead to the most important conclusion that can be deduced from it." Caine took a deep breath. "Taken along with the local's ability to point out the Sun as my place of origin, it means that we have been on Delta Pavonis before."

There were sounds of restlessness among the delegates. "How long before?"

"I can't be sure, but I'd say at least fifteen thousand years. Probably more like twenty thousand."

The first moment of stunned silence spawned its opposite: Gaspard snorted the word "outrageous" through pinched nostrils; Medina laughed; Karagawa smiled; MacGregor raised his eyes toward the ceiling. But Sukhinin, Ching, and Hollingsworth only looked more thoughtful. Durniak's eyes were wide as if she were already seeing how the logical dominoes inexorably fell toward this conclusion.

Nolan had his hand raised for order, but Caine was suddenly weary of having to rely on someone else's authority: "Listen: do you want to hear why this conclusion is inevitable, or not?"

Sudden stillness. Nolan was hiding a pleased grin behind the hand upon which his jaw was resting.

Caine leaned forward. "First, the facts: the local's indication of our star was absolutely unmistakable, once I realized what he was doing and what he was pointing at. And he did so repeatedly. Until I understood. I think it safe to say that there are no grounds for suspecting that I misinterpreted his gestures."

"So once we've established that he does know where I came from, the question becomes: how could he know? There are two reasonable answers, excluding blind luck and divine inspiration. One: he learned this from us, directly or indirectly, since our arrival on Delta Pavonis in 2113—but neither his behavior nor our records show any possibility that this could have occurred. Two: that he and his people knew of us—and our star system of origin—*before* we arrived in 2113."

Durniak was thoughtful. "Could *they* have visited *us*? Were they once a starfaring civilization?"

Caine nodded, impressed by the rapid flexibility of her mind. "That's one possible mechanism to explain their prior knowledge of us. But the data argues against it."

"Why?"

"Lack of gross physical evidence. Let's use ourselves as an example. If Earth reverted to a primeval state, and never rose up from that again, later visitors would still be able to infer some of our contemporary technological capabilities from the alterations we made to the surface of our planet."

"Such as?"

"Such as mountain passes and roadways that have been blasted out of solid granite, the plumb-straight line of canals, perfectly level roadbeds, old quarries, tunnels. The probability that the locals on Dee Pee Three could have reached Earth via supraluminal travel without having first gone through an industrial era is extremely unlikely. On the other hand, there is strong evidence that we were present on their planet. Long ago."

Gaspard scoffed. Sukhinin—eyes narrowed, nodding—asked: "Evidence such as . . . ?"

"Such as the main ruin." Caine picked up his palmtop, switched it over to remote control mode, called up the first image on the room's display screen: a view of the stairs leading up to the humble remains of the micro-Acropolis.

Gaspard sneered. "And how is it that *their* ruin proves *our* presence?"

"Because this is not their ruin. It's ours."

Chapter Twenty-Two

ODYSSEUS

Again, absolute silence. Then Ching leaned forward and spoke: "Please continue, Mr. Riordan."

Caine wasn't sure whether his claim, or Ching's unprecedented decision to participate, made the greater impression on the rest of the delegates. "Thank you, Mr. Ching. Allow me to first suggest something that should be common sense: creatures tend to build what is comfortable and convenient to their own physiognomy. We place our windows at heights convenient to our heads and arms. We shape doorways so that they accommodate our dimensions as we walk.

"So, before we turn to the specifics of the two ruins on Dee Pee Three, let's look at the creatures we think might have built them. Here is a rough anatomical study of the Pavonians." Caine called up another image, superimposed on the mini-Acropolis: a "Da Vinci's man" representation of Mr. Local. "In particular, I want to call your attention to the arrangement of the Pavonian legs and feet. They are, as you can see, splay-footed, and while usually plantigrade, they come up into a digitigrade stance when they run. Their foot also has a long, bifurcated back toe, evidently evolved both for stabilization and as a climbing aid, since they remain very arboreal. So the length of an adult Pavonian's foot, from the tip of their front toes to the end of their rear one, is about forty-five centimeters, or roughly eighteen inches.

"However, at the main ruin, each riser of the stairs averages about thirty-six centimeters in width, or about fourteen inches. That's much less than the length of a Pavonian's foot. So if a Pavonian tried walking up these stairs using his leisurely plantigrade stance, three to four inches of the back of his foot would always be hanging over the edge of each riser, making this design not only stupid, but painful. Each step would be, in human terms, the equivalent of pounding one's sole down on a narrow, hard transverse bar. The only way for Pavonians to avoid this discomfort would be to rise up on the ball of their foot, but without adopting the long, loping stride for which they employ that stance. In short, that would be like trying to tiptoe up a stone staircase in snow shoes.

"So, unless the locals are innately masochistic, the stairs on the main ruin were not made for the Pavonian foot. However, consider *these* stairs." Caine summoned an image of the hidden amphitheater.

"Here, each riser is fifty to fifty-one centimeters wide, but only ten centimeters high. With a width of fifty to fifty-one centimeters, these steps handily accommodate the length of the Pavonian foot. But why only ten centimeters high?"

He had meant it rhetorically, but Durniak, like an

overeager student, supplied the answer: "Because they are reverse-kneed."

"Exactly. Watch a dog going up stairs; the reversed-knee design of its leg is optimized for running and springing, but not for the close up-down movement of climbing stairs. The dog's leg has to bend, pull back a bit, lift up, thrust forward, and then plant on the new surface. The more elevated the new surface is above the prior level, the more awkward this action becomes. It would be even worse for a biped with such legs, lacking the stabilizing contact of the two front limbs—but these problems are all eliminated by the stairs at the amphitheater. They are, in fact, perfect for the Pavonians' leg and foot arrangement."

The next image was of the alcoves and scalloped risers at the back of the arena. "Observe the tendency to avoid straight lines and right angles; everything is rounded, sweeping. Perhaps that motif reflects how a creature whose limbs are flexible, whose digits are prehensile, and who swings through the trees, experiences and sees the world: not as a rigid grid, but as a seamless dance of curves and arcs.

"And lastly, let's consider the nature of the construction: hewn from the rock of the mountain itself. It has no architectural elements that would have necessitated cranes, hoists, pulleys. It is so profoundly *pre*industrial that it is tempting to call it a highly advanced Paleolithic structure.

"Now let's go back to the mini-Acropolis." Caine brought its images to the foreground. "The risers here match the dimensions of those we usually provide for the human foot: fourteen to fifteen inches. A bit wide, but we are not talking about a staircase in your house; these steps lead up to the entry of an imposing, columned structure of some kind. Each rises up about eight inches: again, a comfortable human standard.

"Taken as a whole, this building's design emphasizes lines over curves, and it is a composite structure built from pre-cut pieces that had to be moved to the point of assembly, lifted or rolled into place, and trimmed to fit. Furthermore—and this is an important point—it only *mimics* an ancient construct, since its base is actually reinforced concrete."

"So you conclude that this ruin—the main ruin—was built by humans?" Demirel's voice rose to an almost adolescent pitch.

"Mr. Demirel, we can't know who built it. But it clearly doesn't fit the Pavonian physiology. Conversely, it's clearly a good fit for ours. Now, expand this analysis to include the incident where the Pavonian identified me with our home star. Taken altogether, these facts lead to only one reasonable conclusion: that humans were present on Dee Pee Three long ago. That's why the Pavonians already know about us. That's why the main ruin is not only ancient, but perfectly designed for humans."

Gaspard's fuse had burned down. "Yes, but how could this be? Your deduction follows the rules of logic impeccably—but posits an answer that is preposterous: that humanity somehow developed rebar—and interstellar travel—even as our Neolithic ancestors were hunting the last of the wooly mammoths."

"No, Mr. Gaspard: that is not the only conclusion that is possible."

Gaspard rolled his eyes. "Please, Mr. Riordan: do spare us the idiocies of the Lost Wonders of Atlantis myths, or the equally ludicrous Tenth Planet fabulations."

"You won't hear them from me, Mr. Gaspard"—*you snide bastard*—"because all the evidence is conclusively against such a theory. Where on Earth are the mines, the cities, the terrain modifications that such a culture would have left behind? Where are their artifacts—advanced or rudimentary—and why would they have had contemporaries who were still trying to master the creation of fire and painting homages to elk spirits in caves?"

MacGregor's voice was as dismissive as Gaspard's had been. "Oh, so you're going to give us the old von Daniken bilgewater about humans being descended from ancient astronauts: that we did not evolve on, but came to, Earth—and now Delta Pavonis—by the Chariots of the Gods?"

"No, not at all. The evidence, both in terms of the fossil record and genetic conformity, overwhelmingly indicates that we are not interlopers, but are native to Earth."

Demirel spread his hands. "Then what are you suggesting?"

"I am suggesting that another race—which *had* developed rebar and interstellar travel—transplanted humans from Earth to Delta Pavonis at some point in our prehistory."

MacGregor leaned forward. "That's pretty farfetched."

Gaspard leaned away from the table. "It is absurd."

Caine held his voice steady. "Really? Why? We've relocated species whenever we've settled new lands."

Visser's voice was careful, neutral. "So. When were we transplanted, and by whom, and why?"

Caine turned a smile upon her, received a surprised response-in-kind. "Those are good—and productive—questions, Ms. Visser. And even though we cannot answer them conclusively, simple deduction will help us make a few educated guesses. The main ruin has been authoritatively dated to nineteen thousand years ago, plus or minus three thousand years. This helps us determine when human transplantation occurred.

"Who transplanted these humans? Impossible to say, but probably not the Pavonians or their forebears—unless, of course, the Pavonians are not from Delta Pavonis either. If they were originally travelers from yet another world, that would explain why we do not see evidence of an earlier civilization on Dee Pee Three. But it seems improbable that even a marooned colony would have become—and remained—as primitive as they are now, so I tend to discount that possibility."

Durniak nodded sharply. "So either the Pavonians are a primitive species native to Dee Pee Three, or—"

"Or, similar to our own forebears, they were imported there."

Gaspard's hands seemed to flutter upward toward the ceiling. "What are you proposing: that Delta Pavonis was a game park where the zookeepers were little green men?"

"No, but we must explore all possible answers to Ms. Visser's question of *who* brought humans to Dee Pee Three. Because *that* is the truly crucial issue of these Dialogs—not the discovery of the Pavonians."

"Why?"

"Because, Ms. Visser, it means that there is not just one, but multiple exosapient species, and that at least one of them already had interstellar capability twenty thousand years ago. From a strategic standpoint, that's rather daunting information."

A dour silence: the practical ramifications were starting to hit home. Visser tapped her finger in cadence with her words. "So, now: *why*? Why move primitive species from one star to another?"

"Well, we can observe ourselves for some possible clues."

"What do you mean, 'observe ourselves'?"

"Ms. Visser, sometimes we extract animals from their native habitats simply to ensure their long-term survival."

"Like the Bengal tiger and the panda bear."

"Yes, and the same may have been done with us—or other species—that seemed interesting to an advanced exosapient race. But usually, we relocate species for more practical reasons."

"I'm not sure I understand what you mean."

Nodding, Durniak provided the answer: "He means like horses in the American West."

"What?"

Durniak's nod seemed to be contagious: Sukhinin's head now bobbed in sync with hers. "*Da*: the cowboy on his mustang is a symbol of the United States—but just six hundred years ago, there was not one horse in America."

Hollingsworth's voice was only a murmur, as if she was remembering something from a history lesson thirty years ago. "Of course; they were brought by the Spanish."

Visser was still staring at Caine. "So you are suggesting that almost twenty millennia ago, Neolithic humans were taken from Earth. But being so primitive, of what use would they have been to an interstellar culture?"

"Their primitiveness may have been exactly what made them useful: they couldn't really resist, had no greater sense of the cosmos, had only rudimentary social structures. So what if an advanced race takes a few hundred Cro-Magnon and gives them three generations to safely reproduce—naturally or otherwise—while being taught to function in a post-industrial society? Only the original generation would experience any regret or disorientation. By the third generation, their offspring would be fully domesticated."

Hollingsworth stared at Caine with raised eyebrows. "So you are saying that we were bred to be oxen—or lab rats?"

"Perhaps, but our lab rats and oxen don't get special attention—or special buildings. However, other species have long been recipients of our extra care and consideration, species that lived closely with us, that were domesticated to assist us with important, even life-and-death tasks. Case in point: humans started by domesticating wolves: why?"

Sukhinin nodded again. "To hunt down the wild wolves."

"Exactly. Our forebears fought fire with fire. They found creatures that could help with—or could wholly take over—tasks that were both important and dangerous.

"Now, let's apply the same logic to the relocation of humans. There's certainly no reason to use us for dragging around heavy objects: hell, we're not particularly good at that. But to serve as overseers, builders, administrators, even soldiers for a race which does not want to be bothered with the dirty business of managing its own empire? History illustrates how very effective we might be in such a role—because we have done just that with other humans for millennia. Mr. Medina, you might tell us about the special class of mixed-race overseers that were once common on Brazil's plantations. I could outline the role played by house slaves in the management of the field slaves in the antebellum American South. Ms. Hollingsworth might recount three hundred years of imperial management of the Raj, where the queen's small British cadres directed an immense native infrastructure of bureaucrats, soldiers, even doctors and engineers, who served efficiently and loyally in the perpetuation of their own subjugation. What happened on Dee Pee Three may not have been very different."

"And then what? These human servitors were simply abandoned? Were allowed to die out?"

"Mr. MacGregor, why should we be surprised by an aftermath of neglect? Did the Spaniards remain as game wardens for the horses they left behind? No: empires rise and empires fall, and in their wake they leave fragments of their long-forgotten actions and ambitions. The main ruin on Dee Pee Three may be just such a fragment."

"And so what about our old masters? Are they all dead and gone—or tarrying around some distant star, ready to re-adopt us if we find our way back home to them?"

"Possibly. Or possibly, they'd just see us as a species gone feral. And of course you all know what we do to feral dogs."

"Oh," said MacGregor. Who fell as deathly quiet as the rest of the room.

Chapter Twenty-Three

ODYSSEUS

Gaspard was the first to break the long silence. "Mr. Riordan, I wish to return to the less esoteric matter of your experiences on Delta Pavonis Three. It is said that you are the first person to encounter an exosapient—but in fact, you are not: correct?"

"Technically, correct. However, as far as I know, I am the first human to *communicate* with an exosapient—unless you consider Mr. Bendixen's shotgun a communication device. In which case, it surely does bear out the axiom that the medium is the message."

"Er...yes." Gaspard cleared his throat. "I wonder if you could tell us what happened after your encounter with the Pavonian."

"Certainly. I decided that I couldn't risk normal communication channels anymore. So I activated the orbital beacon/transceiver that Lieutenant Brill had given me and called in a Commonwealth military assault boat, which extracted me within the hour. I was flown directly back to Downport, where I spent the next three days preparing for my journey back home."

"'Preparing'?"

"Yes, Mr. Gaspard: I suspected that the threat to me would not end when I departed Shangri-La. After my last chat with the head archaeologist, I surmised that well-groomed versions of Mr. Bendixen would be following me all the way back to Earth."

"Hmm...I recall reading that there was also a final exchange between you and Mr. Helger, just before you spoke to the archaeologist."

"Yes, that is correct."

"In which you threatened a great deal more than simple interdiction of traffic and messages."

"That is true."

"On what grounds?"

"On the grounds that I had to force him to end his campaign of xenocide, sir."

Gaspard moved back an inch: Caine couldn't tell if it was from his words or his tone. "Xenocide? I'm afraid I don't understand why you—"

"Then I will explain it—sir. Admiral Silverstein gathered detailed orbital images of Site One immediately after I was extracted. Thermal lookdown showed a number of humans, all in pairs, pushing well north of the main site, and in the direction of my encounters with the locals."

"Prospectors?"

"I doubt it."

"What then?"

"Hunters. CoDevCo was trying to finish the program that Mr. Bendixen had started."

"What program do you mean, Mr. Riordan? I do not follow you."

Caine was sure Gaspard did, but he wanted it on

the record. "They were trying to exterminate the Pavonians, Mr. Gaspard. Before I arrived, it was clear that they had already hunted them like animals and killed them by the dozens. If CoDevCo was going to have a free hand developing Shangri-La, it had to eliminate all evidence that they existed. And once they began that campaign, it became more urgent that they complete the job."

"Why?"

"Because there was overwhelming evidence that the Pavonians were not merely an interesting species: they were intelligent. Which meant that, in any practical sense of the word, CoDevCo's crime was not environmental abuse: it was premeditated mass murder. And the only way CoDevCo could cover it up was to get rid of all the evidence and all the witnesses. That meant every single Pavonian—and me. So in my last conversation with Mr. Helger, I mentioned that he might want to consider voluntary cessation of those activities, lest he be brought before the Hague for the equivalent of crimes against—well, not humanity, but intelligent beings."

"And this worked?"

"The hunter teams returned to Site One. The Pavonians were not molested after that."

"And so it has been concluded that it was CoDevCo that tried to kill you aboard the *Tyne*?"

Nolan interrupted. "Mr. Gaspard, that investigation is ongoing and the confidentiality essential to that process precludes discussing it in this forum." He stood up. "Ladies and gentlemen, our time together has just about come to an end."

CIRCE

Seated at the same table, in the same sidewalk café, the tall man looked up as the same young waiter rushed past. "I will have a few last olives."

The waiter stopped as if one of his feet had suddenly been nailed to the floor. "Last? You are leaving us?"

"After I finish my work today."

"Well, I hope you will return."

The man smiled. "We will see. My olives. Please."

The young waiter hurried away, scattering two flies off the tabletop with a quick swish of the towel he usually kept draped over his forearm.

The tall man checked his watch, looked up.

Toward the tip of the Sounion headland.

ODYSSEUS

Nolan stuck his hands in his pockets. "I'd like to close these proceedings with a few strictly personal thoughts." He began a slow-paced orbit around the table. Heads turned with him. "Yesterday's creation of a true world congress is a laudable achievement—but it was brought about by fear. Fear of war, fear of change, fear of the different and the new. Fear of a universe where we are no longer alone, no longer certain of our future, and not even entirely sure about our past. Sadly, then, it is due to fear that one of the oldest hopes of humanity—world government—has begun to move from being a dream to being a reality."

"Family disputes are frequently put aside when the neighbors become a threat." Gaspard smoothed his tie.

"Yes, so they are, Mr. Gaspard. But the wise family

learns an important lesson from the experience: that it has the ability to lay aside old squabbles and to forget past hurts and insults."

Medina of Brazil smiled and brushed his pepper-and-salt moustache. "An apt metaphor, but the purpose?"

"The purpose is to take this as an opportunity for action, Eduardo, not re-action. All our talk has been framed in the anticipation of dire necessities. Defense against extraplanetary exploitation, invasion, even extermination. But what if, when you all meet again, you were to use this unity as the foundation for taking proactive steps for the betterment of our species, our world? Why allow history to characterize Parthenon as a gathering of cunning old wolves? Why not give posterity a legacy of something better: something that will prompt the teachers of our descendants to say; 'And on that day, they strove to actualize their ideals, even as they prepared for unknown threats.'"

Gaspard released a slow, exasperated sigh. "Impressive propaganda."

Ching's response was quiet but swift. "I do not think so, Mr. Gaspard. It is true that we started this meeting with fear in our minds, but who is to say that we may not have something different—nobler—in our hearts as we leave? It is propaganda only if we ourselves are too cynical to believe it."

CIRCE

He heard the noise of the waiter approaching, did not open his eyes, but let the sun continue to shine full upon his face. He heard the expected plate of olives touch the tabletop. Then he heard a heavier thud. He opened his eyes, looked down.

A ceramic jug. Just below the rim of its wide mouth, red wine oscillated from side to side.

He looked up. The waiter's hand—lowering a glass to the table—stopped. So did his smile.

"Just olives. I gave no final order for wine."

The waiter opened his mouth—but then closed it, picked up the jug, half-bowed himself away from the table in haste.

When he was gone, the tall man smiled and picked up an olive. He rubbed it against his teeth, feeling it slide smoothly back and forth. He pressed harder: the slick skin of the olive began to squeak, like a trapped animal being tormented by a capricious predator. He smiled more widely and opened his mouth...

ODYSSEUS

Nolan walked to his chair before he spoke again. "One of our American presidents stated that a house divided against itself cannot stand. What he knew is that unity is not a tangible object or commodity, not something that can be made or unmade by convening councils and signing accords. It is an idea, and you either subscribe to it in your innermost heart, or you don't. The trade agreements and military cooperation pacts that you've made here will all fall into obscurity and be forgotten. What shall endure is the influence of the belief you take back home with you: that we can collectively protect *and* better our species—or that we cannot. That belief—and your commitment to it—is what will last, and will determine all our fates."

Nolan sat, the creak of his chair echoing in the high corners of the meeting hall.

Ching lowered his head slightly, as if staring at the table in front of him. After five silent seconds, he began to speak, without raising his head. "Mr. Corcoran speaks a great truth when he points out that we stand at a crossroads in the history not just of our nations, but of our entire species." He turned his gaze slowly about the table. "Two days of meetings have not changed the world, or us, for the better. But there is nothing to prevent us from deciding that today is the day on which those changes should begin. The wisdom I would offer has been made trite by inclusion in fortune cookies throughout the West, but it is no less true for all of that: a journey of a thousand miles *does* begin with a single step. Is this the time to commence such a journey? I answer with a Western axiom: if not now, when? And if not us, who?"

Caine was surprised—and misled—by the unprecedented Sino-American solidarity for only a moment before he realized what it really signified: *Ching is going to be the first Proconsul. He and Nolan worked it out ahead of time: a public burying of hatchets, and a mutual testimony of faith from the two most culturally disparate of the blocs. And if the Commonwealth and the Developing World Coalition can swear their separate oaths to the same ideal, which of the other three blocs would—could—decline to join?*

And Caine could tell, by looking around the table, that the tactic had worked. Scattered nods, thoughtful stares at the tabletop, a few smiles. Even Gaspard, his eyebrows a pair of matched, surprised arches, tilted his head slowly from side to side, as if weighing the merits of a mostly attractive investment.

Nolan stood. "Honored delegates, these proceedings are concluded."

CIRCE

Using thumb and forefinger, he extracted the fourteenth and final pit from between clenched teeth. He let it fall to the center of the plate: the impact upon the china made a dull musical sound.

The waiter looked up, wary.

"I am finished," the tall man said. He rose, reached into his pocket, scattered the fistful of remaining euros across the pit-littered plate.

He turned, spied the second story of his duplex above the other buildings, walked in that direction.

Chapter Twenty-Four

ODYSSEUS

Nolan, Caine, and Downing emerged into a stiff breeze. Nolan squinted up the slope, leaned into the ascent. "You have a knack for this, you know."

Caine looked at him. "I beg your pardon?"

"You asked me not to be coy, yesterday. Now I'll ask the same of you. You're good at this, and people saw it. You're going to be on a lot of watch lists."

Downing smiled ruefully from Caine's other side. "You're caught well and good, and only yourself to blame."

"Thanks."

A light tread behind them: Downing turned, veered away from Caine. Ching nodded his appreciation as he stepped into the vacated space. They walked on. And on. Then:

"Mr. Riordan, I hope when you are speaking to the media that you will not include any political speculations."

"Why? Are you afraid I will reveal what was said here?"

"No: I fear that you will reveal what was *not* said here." Caine turned toward Ching—who looked him full in the face. And smiled: it was possibly an invitation to further acquaintance; it was definitely a sign of respect. "Mr. Riordan, you have much skill at a diplomatic table for one so young and so unaccustomed to it. But I saw your eyes when I offered my closing comments. You understood. You know."

Nolan's voice came from the other side: the tone was casual, pitched so as not to attract notice as Demirel passed them. "Nothing to worry about; Caine knows how to keep a secret."

Walking between these two men, calmly discussing undisclosed manipulations of the global power structure, left Caine with a feeling of greater otherworldliness than anything he had experienced on Dee Pee Three. "So I'm right: the Commonwealth has assured the Developing World Coalition that it—in the shape of you, Mr. Ching—is going to be source of the first Proconsul."

The silence indicated assent.

Caine uttered the insight as it arose. "And since the DWC was given the first slot, that implies that there had to be some kind of arrangement regarding the subsequent slots." He paused, checked the almost identical smiles flanking him, one on Nolan's face, one on Ching's.

"Let me guess: since China is first, Russia insisted upon the second slot. That provides Moscow the opportunity to immediately correct any 'imbalanced' decisions arising from Beijing. And, since Beijing anticipates this, it will wish to preemptively cultivate a reputation for evenhandedness, and so will pursue a more temperate course, anyway. Which will in turn encourage the Russians to be more temperate when their turn comes."

Ching's smile was broader. "He has promise."

Nolan shrugged. "He learns quickly, I have to admit."

Undaunted by their needling, Caine unfolded the rest. "Next will be TOCIO. Japan needs the political clout that will come from an early Proconsul slot in order to stabilize their bloc and fend off CoDevCo's attempts to poach from their membership."

"And then? The order of the last two?" Nolan's tone was amused, as if he were testing a pupil who had no chance of failing the exam.

"Europe, then the Commonwealth."

"Why?"

"Because Europe is the best bloc for stabilizing the Confederation. After the other blocs have each had their two years in the big seat, the Europeans will be the ones most able to come in and build a durable equilibrium."

"And the Commonwealth is forced to wait until last."

Caine looked at Nolan, then at Ching, whose eyes were still friendly, but also incisive, almost challenging. Caine looked back at Nolan, unsure whether he should—

"Go ahead; say it. Mr. Ching knows."

Caine shrugged. "No: the Commonwealth *wants* to be last. Needs to be. It has the most advanced space program, the best position in terms of interstellar expansion, military capability. If it took an early leadership position, the other nations would balk, might feel that they had become satrapies of the Commonwealth. And—"

"It's okay; don't stop."

"And it makes it possible for the Commonwealth—and particularly the US—to let the other nations and blocs take the heat for any mistakes or inequities that persist through the early years. America has been resented for its inordinate wealth and power for so long that, if it started in a leadership position, there would be a reflex to blame any problems in the Confederation upon the US."

Nolan looked over at Ching, eyebrows raised—but both were surprised when Caine pressed on.

"But there's another advantage."

The gait of the two older men slowed. *They thought the list was done. Maybe they haven't seen it, since they are so focused on the political maneuvering.*

"Which is?" Ching sounded mystified, enthralled.

"Optimal timing for logistical benefit."

Silence. Gravel ground and snapped under their shoes. It was Nolan who took the bait. "What?"

Caine smiled at the two of them. "The US is still the leader in defense and aerospace technology. In some ways, it has too great a lead. Unless the US wants to bear the brunt of a potential interstellar war all by itself, it needs a greater diffusion of higher technological capabilities throughout the globe. Right now, there's a good amount of that from the Federation and the Union, but—with all due respect, Mr. Ching—"

"No, you are quite right. Continue."

"The largest populations, and therefore production potentials, are in the TOCIO and DWC blocs. If their general technological level can be upgraded in the first eight years, they can become integral participants in a truly global effort to establish an interstellar buffer zone. And, after eight years, those nations might be ready to follow the Commonwealth's leadership in the energetic business of rapid expansion—which is, let's be honest, a particularly strong trait among the nations of our bloc."

Nolan's smile was surprised, a little baffled. *Did I just give away some of his deeper game? Well, if I did, he should have stopped me...*

Ching was staring at Caine as though he was a rare antiquity that had turned up in his soup bowl. "Fascinating. And astute." He smiled at the sun, now accelerating in its plunge toward the horizon. "This is a day of much change." They had arrived at the buffet tables—olives, wine, a few white-coated attendants—and he turned to Caine. "Perhaps you will advise me on the wines, Mr. Riordan? I seldom partake."

Caine shrugged, stole a fast sideways look at Nolan, who did not return his glance, but was smiling into the sun himself. Eyes back upon Ching's, Caine gestured to the tables. "I'll try, but I'm not sure I'm any more of a connoisseur than you are, Mr. Ching."

He reached down, picked up a bottle, tilted it toward a glass—

CIRCE

He reached down, picked up the binoculars, tilted them to snap into the short tripod. He swung them around to aim up at the end of the Sounion headland, leaned over to check the view: the columns of the Temple of Poseidon were slightly off center to the left. He tapped the front right lens rim slightly, looked in: centered.

He looked to his right: the false olive container was open, most of the sharp, acidic fumes carried away from him by the prevailing winds running in from the Aegean.

MENTOR

The breeze from the Aegean tore the cocktail napkin out of Downing's hand. "High winds," he commented, then looked back at the milling delegates. "And we'll soon be heading into others, I wager."

Nolan kept looking out to sea. "It can't be 'we' any more, Rich: you'll have to steer the ship on your own from here on. We've got to make IRIS your organization now."

"Rubbish. Nolan, you are not so old that—"

"Richard."

Downing stopped: Nolan had used his proper name.

"Richard," Nolan repeated, "it's not just a matter of age. It's a matter of policy. Caine isn't the only one who's going to be watched, now. For the last twenty years, I've operated under the media radar, but here at Parthenon I was running a public show, approved by the leadership of all five blocs. How do you rate my public profile now?"

Downing looked out to sea, felt a sad, cold knot coalesce in his stomach. "You're through. You're a newsmaker, so they're going to watch you." It was going to be lonely without Nolan...but then there was a deeper reflex: *You don't want to be in charge. You are a good XO—but not a CO. Good God, how will I do this?* He took a long drink of his wine to drown the anxiety. "So what now?"

Nolan smiled. "Now, I eat an olive."

"Hilarious. And then?"

"Then I eat another olive. And I take a vacation: a long one."

"With Pat?"

"Yeah, and the kids too. Particularly Trev."

Downing felt Nolan's pause, looked over, saw a pair of blue eyes that were suddenly old, tired, and very serious. "Richard, there's something I need to tell you, something I—"

"Admiral Corcoran—"

Ching. *Bloody hell.*

"Mr. Riordan seems to have good instincts for wine, as well."

Nolan looked at the returned pair. "I'm not surprised."

"And, Mr. Downing: which wine did you select?"

Downing turned toward Ching, smiled as a prelude to his response, peripherally saw Nolan take Caine's upper arm and steer him gently for a walk down toward the oceanside peristyle.

Damn it, Nolan, what were you going to tell me? You've got to—

But Ching was waiting and watching. Downing widened his smile and prepared to feign interest in their impending conversation.

CIRCE

He put his hand in his pocket, pulled out a small, featureless black cube, six centimeters per side. He rested the box on the weather wall to the left of the binoculars and stared at it for a moment. Then he brushed his finger over the side that was facing him.

The side of the cube shivered slightly and fell open, as if hinged at the bottom. The man's nose pinched as a carrion-scented musk diffused into the air around him. Then slowly, deliberately, he inserted his left index and middle fingers into the box.

A moment later he grimaced. Then he breathed out slowly, as if following a yogic discipline, and lowered his eyes back to the lenses. With the temple now centered in his field of vision, he started counting across the columns...

Chapter Twenty-Five

ODYSSEUS

Caine and Nolan exited the ruins of the Temple of Poseidon just to the right of the central column and looked out at the sea. "Ching likes you, you know."

"Seems to."

"He does. It's not an act. When you pointed out the logistical advantages of having the Commonwealth take the last place in Proconsular rotation, you showed him something he hadn't seen yet. That doesn't happen to him very often. And you're an articulate Westerner who is not a loudmouth, and who understands the value of listening instead of talking. You're a rarity, for him—and he knows that you have a future."

"I'm glad *he* knows that."

"He can smell it. He's been in this game a long time, and he is its consummate professional."

"Do I need to watch out for him? Be cautious?"

Nolan chewed down an olive. "For now, you need to be prudent. As time goes on—well, I think you'll have a friend in him. That's only a hunch—but sometimes, that's all you've got to go on."

"Which seems insane."

"How do you mean?"

"Well, maybe you've forgotten how the world of global statecraft looks to all us little people who never become a part of it. We presume it's all a well-orchestrated dance, but in actuality..."

"In actuality," Nolan finished for him, "it's just as haphazard an enterprise as any other. But the chaos can be managed if you understand one basic rule."

"Which is?"

"There are only three variables governing the outcome of any given situation. Power—political, economic, military, whatever. Intelligence—the information you have and how cleverly you use it. And chance."

"And that's it?"

"That's it. Leaders get themselves too tangled up when they fail to break a situation—any situation—back down to those basics. Or when they forget the fundamental differences between the three variables."

"Huh. Any more sage advice?"

Nolan smiled without looking over at Caine. "I hope that I can give you reason to move past the resentment fueling those little digs, Caine. Although it's true enough that we—IRIS—have had to play pretty rough, sometimes."

"Like with the megacorporations?"

"And with the desperate groups and states that they use as proxies, yes. One of the harshest lessons of intelligence work is that, to borrow your phrase, sometimes you have to fight fire with fire. It's an unpleasant but inescapable fact—which, as you also remarked, was appreciated even by our primeval forebears when they bred domesticated wolves to hunt the wild ones. Sometimes adopting the methods of your adversaries is the only effective strategy—and I suspect you're going to come face to face with just how true that is in the coming years."

"You mean that we have to keep fighting the mega-corporations by using their own tactics against them?"

Nolan stared off into the blue. "I mean that you're going to have to think about how even the best-intentioned states and leaders occasionally have no choice but to fight fire with fire. I've lived that truth. Yet, having lived it, I just don't know that our ends, no matter how worthy they are, can ever justify the means—the 'fire'—we've used."

"Seems to me you had little enough choice, most of the time."

"Maybe, but we—Rich and I—could have chosen not to get involved."

"And then who would have achieved all this?"

"Caine, there's always someone else. No one is that indispensable."

"No? That's what I used to tell myself—before the *Tyne*. Sometimes, we get to choose if we're willing to be a link in the chain of history—but sometimes, history chooses us. Puts us in a position where we have no choice but to act."

Nolan looked over at Caine abruptly, as though his companion had, without warning, jabbed a needle into him. Caine looked closely at the seamed face and he suddenly realized how all Nolan's secrets had started. "Because that's what happened to you, isn't it? You found yourself in a position where you had no choice but to act, because you knew—*knew*—that there *are* exosapients. You've known from the very start."

Nolan did not look at Caine, but turned his eyes back toward the blue-on-blue horizon where the Mediterranean met the cloudless sky.

"When did you learn about them—and how?"

A number of others—Ching and Downing among them—were approaching. Caine guessed he had about twenty seconds before they were in earshot. He put a hand on Nolan's still-considerable shoulder, felt no startled flexure in the smooth expanse of trapezius. "*When* did you learn? And *how?*"

Nolan turned, then smiled. The gentle curve of his lips and relaxed creases in his forehead and around his eyes suggested that he was not merely about to share a secret, but jettison it, cut it loose as he would a millstone. He opened his mouth—

CIRCE

He finished counting across the columns and found the silhouette he was looking for. His face relaxed, his shoulders almost slumped, as if he had lost awareness of himself. However, almost visible through his shirt, his heart began to quake, to race, gaining speed, like an engine building up to overload—

ODYSSEUS

Nolan's lips and eyelids flicked open a little wider. His head went back slightly, as though someone had surprised him by poking a finger into his back. The olives went tumbling out of his hand.

Caine grabbed toward him, but Nolan's body was

already in motion, falling backward, slamming down against the foot ramp and rolling off to one side.

Caine was around the ramp and kneeling beside him while everyone else on the promontory stood immobile for a moment that seemed to stretch on and on and on—

Caine roared: "Call a doctor! Now!"

As if released from a trance, the gathering crowd burst into a criss-crossing rush of chattering and yelling activity. Caine propped Nolan up, felt and saw his chest spasming irregularly, the shocks centered on the sternum. *Oh, Christ*—

Nolan, eyes wide, was trying to gasp out words.

Downing half stumbled over the ramp, almost pushing Caine out of the way, desperate to ask a question: "What were you trying to tell me, Nolan? What? *What?*"

For a split second, Caine could not make any sense of the question, then he shoved Downing back in disgust. *Always business with you, isn't it, asshole?* Caine looked down. "We're getting help. We're—"

Nolan swallowed, closed his eyes as his chest continued to buck irregularly. When he opened his eyes again, he was able to gasp words between the spasms. "Sorry, Trevor...Elena..." His eyes—uncertain—sought Caine. "You. Too. Sorry."

"It's okay, Nolan. They've got doctors on the way. They—"

Nolan interrupted with a smile that seemed more rictus. He lifted his hand toward Caine—who had the fleeting impression that the redoubtable warrior and canny statesman was attempting to touch his face. But no: his eyes were losing focus. He couldn't see. *He's alone with the pain, with the approach of death.*

Caine reached up with his right hand, intercepted and held Nolan's faltering one in a firm, and he hoped soothing, grip. "We—I'm here," he said.

Nolan's eyes roved, then closed. He smiled faintly, nodded, tried to breathe, seemed unable to do more than gasp in a shallow breath. With which he said, "Trev."

The hand Caine was holding went limp. Nolan's body was still; there was no sign of respiration. The surrounding din of frenetic activity either stopped or Caine became deaf to it.

Caine choked back nausea, surprised by the rush of emotion that went through him: *Why Nolan? Why now? Why not Downing, that bastard? Nolan—liked me. In a world where no one knows me anymore, he liked me.*

The circle around Caine and Nolan had grown still. Somewhere, beyond the ring of witnesses who would soon be mourners, clipped, urgent orders were being given by the security entourage in the ongoing attempt to save a life that was now beyond saving.

Caine looked at the surrounding faces without seeing them. "He's gone."

He laid Nolan's hand down, and withdrew his own.

CIRCE

He withdrew his two fingers from the box, closed it, caught it up and dropped it in the open container of acid. A gout of steamy, acrid vapor shot straight up, accompanied by an agitated hissing and a short, rising squeal that clipped off abruptly—not unlike a small animal being killed sharply, painfully.

Using the two fingers that had been in the box—which were now mottled red, as if they had been scalded—he produced a final olive from his shirt pocket and popped it in his mouth.

His other hand had already uncoupled the binoculars from the tripod. Carefully, leaning away from the container, he dumped these two components—one after the other—into the jar. A slower, roiling bubbling and guttering brewed up out of the container. He waited for it to subside, making sure that there was not much more gas being produced by the reaction, and then recapped the jar. He looked out over the blue Aegean and, smiling broadly, spat out the olive pit in the direction of the Temple of Poseidon.

He turned and headed for the stairway that led down and out of the duplex.

MENTOR

The rough stairs that led down and away from the Temple of Poseidon were a writhing Brueghel tapestry of chaos, panic, and counterproductive activity. Emergency workers rushed up, rushed down again to get additional gear from their ambulances. Security types spiraled out, produced guns, stood uncertainly, called for further instructions, reholstered their weapons, cycled back inward. Several of the delegates were trying to get away quickly; several realized that help was no longer possible and were trying to stay out of the way; others who had held back from the first saw that the crisis had resolved and were now putting on the face-saving skit of attempting to offer assistance.

Downing looked at Nolan and couldn't move, could

only think: *How could this happen, here, now? Nolan, this was your triumph. This was what you had lived for and had put aside your loves in order to accomplish. And now this? This is the reward for good and true service, for the countless missed dinners, Christmas pageants, baseball games? For the smiles you were not there to receive, the hugs you were not there to elicit, the "I love you's" that were not said because you were not there to hear them?*

"Downing."

Richard looked up, hearing hostility in the tone. Caine was facing him across Nolan's body. But Riordan must have seen something in Richard's face, because his own became less rigid, his eyes less accusing. "Richard," he revised, more neutral.

"Yes?"

"This may not be a simple heart attack. But either way—orders?"

At first, Downing didn't understand. Then he realized that Riordan was already thinking again: Nolan's death needed investigating—and quickly. And then the real blow hit him: he was in charge of IRIS, now.

Whether he liked it or not.

Chapter Twenty-Six

MENTOR

The tilt-rotor banked steeply as it angled toward the city center vertipad. Downing turned his head, caught a glimpse of the Reflecting Pool as it swept behind them. The sun winked briefly off the dark bar of water; almost noon. Not enough time for the government car to get him to the Capitol Building on time. But Tarasenko would be running late, too—and after all, it was Downing who was in charge now, who was the unofficial heir-apparent to IRIS.

But like a monarch dying intestate, Nolan had left behind no definitive instructions as to how, and by whom, succession was to be effected. It was possible, even likely, that Tarasenko had the complete blueprint for how to proceed—but if so, that put him in position to take control of IRIS himself, to falsify or withhold postmortem directives—

Downing started: he wasn't sure whether it was at the slightly off-center landing of the tilt-rotor, or at his own cynicism. *Good grief, man, you've worked with Arvid Tarasenko for over twenty years: he's a good man.* But losing Nolan so suddenly had Downing running from pillar to post, trying to pick up the pieces, even wondering who could be trusted and who couldn't. *So I wind up suspecting everybody.*

And having Caine go missing a day ago had not helped matters. No word from Opal either. *Some covert bodyguard she's turned out to be.*

But that was unfair and he knew it: there had never been enough time to do more than assign her and clean up after the ambush in Greece. And less than twenty-four hours later, Nolan was dead and Downing was scrambling to fill his shoes and figure out what to do next. Not easy, particularly since the outcome of the Dialogs was to have determined their future operational agenda.

Downing grimaced as he unfolded from the narrow seat of the cramped commuter craft. As it turned out, advance planning would have been a waste of time, because none of the scenarios would have begun with the operational presumption that Nolan was dead. There had been plans for how best to handle his death *before* Parthenon. But this—losing your leading man not at the close or rise of a curtain, but between the acts—this was *terra incognita.*

Downing exited the aircraft into the bright sun and cool air of DC in April and experienced a surge of anxiety that he imagined was indeed akin to those felt by ancient mariners whose journeys had carried them past the edges of their maps, compelled them to sail into deep, unknown waters.

As I do now, Richard thought, glancing at the Capitol dome as he walked to the black sedan waiting discreetly beyond the edge of the tarmac.

❖   ❖   ❖

The traffic was moderate but progress was fitful, sudden rushes of speed alternating with a bumper-to-bumper crawl. Unpredictable and unsettling—just like the immediate future. *If Arvid can help me forge, or better yet, inherit, the same political and industry links and relationships that Nolan enjoyed, then IRIS should be able to continue along on much the same footing. But if not...*

Downing willed that thought to die, but another—just as troubling—rose to take its place: Trevor, arriving at Dulles, would be joining him at Tarasenko's office within the hour. There, Nolan's son would stolidly endure condolences, stolidly sit through lunch with Uncle Richard, and then stolidly shake hands, depart, and carry on a fighting withdrawal from his own feelings until he reached the safe refuge of his one-bedroom townhouse in Georgetown. By that time, Downing would be on his way out to visit newly widowed Patrice in Silver Spring, who would smile gratefully through bright, wet eyes that would not brim over until the intrusion of consolers had ended.

But the eldest child, Elena, was the wild card. Her father's daughter in almost every way, Downing was certain of only one thing: she would be devastated, no matter what she showed the world, or Miles, her teenage son. On the other hand, although being a single mother had been hard on her, maybe it would be a strange blessing now: from his own experience, Richard knew that parents could often be strong for their children even when they felt themselves too weary and weak to carry on.

"Mr. Downing, we're here."

Downing sighed, looked up at the Capitol Building. An hour from now, he'd know the fate in store for IRIS—and himself. A part of him wanted to stay in the car, and just keep driving.

Right: none of that, now. Downing forced himself to exit the vehicle briskly, waved the driver on, went up the steps two risers at a time. He kept up that pace as a matter of principle, stopping only where the security checks—the chemical sniffers, metal detectors, Geiger counters, badge and retina checkers—slowed him down. Tarasenko's assistant looked up as he swept around the door jamb. "Mr. Downing, Senator Tarasenko is expecting you."

"Has he been waiting long?"

"Not quite a minute."

"Thank you, Daniel."

"My pleasure. Go right in."

Downing did, willing himself through the doorway that would put him on his future path as well as bring him face to face with Arvid Tarasenko—

—who was staring at him as he entered. The senator was sporting a small smile, half-reclined behind his desk, hands folded over a midriff that had, in the last two years, started to expand. "Richard: join us."

"Thank you, I—" *Wait: 'us'?* Richard looked, saw that the chair in the room's right-hand corner was occupied.

Caine. Smiling. Or, more accurately, with teeth bared. "Hello, Richard," he said.

"Hello, and—and I'm damned glad to see you. But why didn't you tell me where you were going? I had no idea—"

"I think that *was* the idea, Richard." Tarasenko smiled, a bit ruefully: "Unless I'm quite wrong, you were not supposed to have any idea where Mr. Riordan was or where he was heading."

"What do you mean?"

Caine's voice was flat. "I'm out, Richard. No more IRIS."

Downing was too surprised to feel surprise, but clearly, Caine had come to the wrong place to make such a pronouncement: Tarasenko would never let it stand. "Come now, Caine, there's simply no reason—"

Tarasenko did something he rarely did: he interrupted: "He's right, Richard."

Downing felt his palms grow suddenly cold. "Right about what?"

Caine smiled. "I'm busted."

Tarasenko nodded. "He's contaminated goods."

It was moving too fast. "He's—?"

"Compromised by having direct contact with me, particularly so soon after Nolan's death. To any half-witted newsperson, his coming here will look like he was running back to the home office. Leaves folks wondering if he came here on his own—or if someone sent him. Someone like you, Richard, since I'd lay odds that he made sure the press saw him leaving the villa he shared with you and Nolan. And I'm guessing, in the past two days' chaos, you haven't had the time—and he never gave you the reason—to think to have him watched, or have his mobility restricted." He turned to Riordan. "Damned shrewd. You'd have been pretty good at this line of work, Caine."

"Thanks—but no thanks."

Downing discovered he had wandered over to the chair next to Caine's. He sat heavily. "I don't understand."

"You don't understand what? Why I'd leave? Or how I got in here without an appointment?"

Downing looked at Arvid. "How *did* he get in to see you without an appointment?"

"Same way he's probably going to get in just about any place he wants to for the next two or three years—twenty, if he stays in the spotlight: he just gave his name."

"And you let him in?"

"*Jesu Kristos*, Richard, why the hell wouldn't I? He shows up, unannounced, no appointment, Nolan's recently dead, IRIS is mute: what am I supposed to think? He could be a courier with something you can't trust to any of your remaining commlinks; he could be coming to tell me that now *you* had been eliminated, too, and he was the only survivor. He's not just anyone, Richard—and these days aren't just any days. He knew that, and therefore knew I'd open my door because I had to presume that his appearance here was necessitated by some kind of emergency. He played us both like a pair of violins, Richard."

"And now—"

Caine shrugged. "And now, because I've been observed to have immediate, on-demand access to Senator Tarasenko, the press will assume that I report to him. And that connects back to you, again, since you're also known to have a long association with the senator—and collectively, that all points to IRIS."

"Which means that it still points to nothing: IRIS is still thoroughly secret despite its data leaks."

"Listen, Richard, my running straight home to Senator Tarasenko like his pet dog will start at least a few of the smarter investigative reporters down the same path I followed in my own researches. They're going to start unearthing the same 'coincidental associations' that I found, start making some of the same conjectures, and then start asking some of the same questions—but in public.

"However, I've only come here *once*. So if I drop off the radar—and you leave me alone—then the news media just might overlook this, or deem the evidence too thin to warrant a follow-up."

"How kind—and condescending—of you to walk me through all the implications, Caine, but I quite understand what you've done. I just wonder if *you* understand—really understand—the consequences of your actions."

"What do you mean?"

"I mean that Nolan and IRIS have been a force for good. Roll your eyes if you like, but you've said it yourself on occasion: if there are exosapients, then IRIS was a necessity. You don't like our methods? Fine: neither do I. You don't like what I do for a living? Fair enough: most days, I don't like it much either. But does that mean it shouldn't be done? Can we afford to hope things will just turn out all right? You're the military analyst, writer, historian: you, above all people, should know that those who decline to take a hand in controlling events surrender the ability to influence them. And now you may have broken our one useful control mechanism."

"Firstly, it's not broken—not yet. And it won't be, unless you force me back into it," Caine countered. "But more importantly, if you had only had the common courtesy of *asking* me to join you—directly, without half-truths and coercion—then I would probably have volunteered to help. But you can't *force* someone to become a willing volunteer for a cause. That's not how loyalty works—and you and Nolan should have realized that."

"Caine, Nolan and I tried to *protect* you—"

"Oh, you mean like at Sounion, at the overlook?"

"Nolan admitted that was a mistake and that he and I—"

"Are liars. The ambush at Sounion was not a mistake. That was a sting operation—*your* sting operation—to snare enemy agents, with me and Opal staked out as a pair of Judas goats."

Downing felt his face grow very hot very quickly. *Bloody hell: Caine caught us—well and good.*

And he did not appear to be in a forgiving mood.

Chapter Twenty-Seven

MENTOR

Downing opened his mouth, hoping that a glib, convincing lie would cooperatively spring forth from it—but he remained mute. Tarasenko stared politely out his window toward the throngs of sightseers headed toward the National Mall.

Downing let his lips close, looked down at his folded hands. *Bugger all: nothing left but the truth, I suppose.* "So you figured that out. About the overlook."

"Oh yes, I figured it out." Caine's voice was as hard and level as a steel ruler. "Too much coincidence. And too happy an outcome. You sent us out there as bait—because the best way to draw the opposition into the open was to give them a target they couldn't resist."

"And that's how you figured it out? Because you retroactively conjectured how their attack might have been to *our* advantage?"

"No, what tipped me off was what happened to that thug you shot—or rather, the thug you *didn't* shoot." Caine shook his head. "So much went on that day, and then the next, that I didn't realize it at first: when you

305

saved me by shooting that assassin who had come around the front of the car, there was no sound of a gunshot. And when I thought back, I distinctly remembered seeing your pistol: no silencer. So who shot him?"

Downing tried to swallow, found his mouth too dry.

Caine's smile was cold. "I guess I'm just about the luckiest man alive, considering that there was a sniper—my own personal guardian angel—someplace higher up the mountain, waiting to put a hole the size of a tailpipe though that assassin's head. I should have realized it sooner: the angle of the impact and the way his head went over so sharply couldn't have resulted from any shot that would have come from your handgun. It had to be a bigger, high-velocity weapon."

Tarasenko glanced back at Downing once, then out the window again.

"And once I realized that, then everything else started falling into place. It wasn't my landslide of PVC pipes which sent that second car over the embankment; it was another well-placed shot from another guardian angel. And why did that vehicle burn so handily? Because while Opal and I were fighting for our lives, the sniper put an incendiary round into the engine and transmission—or maybe a few, at least until the oil in both systems caught fire.

"I think what really kept me from suspecting a setup right away was that clever lie you told—so quickly, too—about the road worker at the detour being part of the assassins' team. But no, she was *your* agent, because it was her directions which sent us to that deserted overlook, where your snipers were already in overwatch positions. Pity it got a little messy, but you still got what you wanted."

Tarasenko's head turned back from his sustained gaze out the window. "Which was?"

"Mr. Tarasenko, you're no stranger to special operations, so that question is pure theater. Richard needed to get the opposite side to risk their assets so that he could pull their fangs in one fell swoop. Because after assassinating their assassins, IRIS was in control again.

"From the moment you took out their operatives, the opposition was running out of time and options. They wait to hear from their assassins, don't, try to contact them, can't. So it takes them hours to learn that their assassination attempt has failed, takes even more time to learn how their first crew of thugs was liquidated, and still more to start moving new forces into the area. By then, it was the next day and I had sung my song at Sounion—and was no longer a crucial target."

Richard leaned back in his chair. "So, if you understand all that, how can you fail to see that we did it for your own good?"

"Why was anyone looking to kill me in the first place? Who was responsible for putting me on a hit list to begin with—*Richard?*"

Downing tried to look Caine square in the eyes. "That ambush was the only option we had to secure your safety. Once you stepped off the VTOL in Greece, we knew the clock was ticking and that if we waited for the opposition's inevitable attack, we couldn't be sure of the outcome. For all we knew, they might have had the time and resources to conduct multiple attacks: first on the villa, then, the next day, a bomb at the Dialogs. And what would have been left when the dust cleared? International discord, finger pointing, mutual suspicion—"

"Well, congratulations. And feel free to risk my life again—and Opal's—whenever it's convenient for you."

Downing kept his voice calm. "Like it or not, we were right. There were counter-operatives at Sounion, we did eliminate them, and Parthenon did come to a successful conclusion."

"Sure, you were right, but that just reinforces your assumptions that you can always outthink everyone else—which you can't—and that your ends justify your means. But your means—your *lies*—are always part of your ends, too. *How* you achieve something always leaves its imprint upon *what* you achieve."

Tarasenko looked out the window of his office and scratched his ear. "Mr. Riordan, you speak as eloquently as anyone I've ever heard. But I wonder: do you really—*really*—believe that our preferred method of operation is misdirection and deception?"

Caine snorted a laugh. "How could I *not* suspect that? You covered up my disappearance on Luna. The Pavirus was clearly your hoax. You staked me out as a Judas goat at Sounion. One hundred hours of my most important memories have been erased. Every time I'm told I'm free, I get pulled back into cloak-and-dagger land again. So you tell me: where does the duplicity end?"

Tarasenko continued to smile; they waited.

After five seconds, Downing noticed that Tarasenko hadn't looked away from the point in space at which he had been staring. Nor had he blinked. As Caine rose from his chair, Downing's breath caught and jammed in his throat: "Arvid?"

The next thirty seconds were utter, hushed chaos. Once they had Tarasenko on the floor, CPR produced no results, and Downing noted the encroachment of the same rapid pallor that had swept so quickly up and over Nolan's face two days earlier at Sounion.

After thirty seconds, Caine jumped up, abandoning the chest compressions, grabbed for the phone.

"No," said Downing.

Receiver in his hand, Caine froze. "What do you mean, 'no?' He needs—"

"No," repeated Downing, leaning back from Tarasenko's body. "We need to control this."

"Control this? How?"

"We have to think how this will look, how the media will begin to probe us if we call this in right now, without any prior—"

But Caine had dropped the phone just a sharply as the stunned expression had dropped off his face: he was moving toward the door.

"Where are you going?"

"To tell Tarasenko's assistant that his boss needs medical help—now."

"Caine, I can't let you do that. Don't make me order you—"

"Richard, now it's *your* memory that's faulty: I've stopped taking your orders. Remember?" He opened the door.

Downing was surprised by a sudden, dizzying panic so intense that his vision blurred. "But you can't leave—"

"Oh no? Why?"

Downing reached for an answer, had none. "I'm in this alone, now."

"Richard, you always have been. Nolan, Tarasenko, you—each trapped in your own private bubble of secrets and uncertainties. Maybe that's the nature of organizations—and relationships—built on lies." And he was out the door before Downing could find a suitable reply—because, Richard realized, there was no such reply to be found.

CIRCE

The tall man leaned away from the binoculars and breathed again. Robin Astor-Smath wondered what would happen next.

The man removed his two fingers from the small black cube, used his other hand to replace his sunglasses.

"Well?" Robin said in a higher pitch than he had intended.

"Well what?"

"What happens now? When do you—?"

"It is over; it is done."

Astor-Smath blinked. "Over? How?"

"That does not concern you." The man backed away from the window, which was half-filled with the bright white façade of the northern side of the Capitol Building. Behind him, the dome rose up over his short-cropped hair like the top half of a guillotined egg.

Astor-Smath looked at the box: what was it? A communication device? A remote control for some weapon planted in the Capitol Building? If so, its appearance was quite odd: no external marks of any kind. Not even any seams suggesting manufacture—but now, an odd smell was emanating from it, a troubling smell that was akin to a shudder-inducing mix of musk, carrion, and patchouli—and something else that he could not place.

The man shook the two fingers that he had placed in the box—much as if he had scalded them—and closed the container, none too gently.

"Naturally, we take your word for the successful completion of—"

"You will have independent verification soon enough." The man picked up the box and put it in his pocket. "I believe I hear sirens."

If he did, then either his ears were extraordinary, or Astor-Smath's were in need of retesting. "Excellent, most excellent. However, this is hardly what I—we—expected. Your methods—"

"Are my concern alone. You requested an accommodation; it has been provided."

Astor-Smath cleared his throat—and heard, faintly, a single approaching siren. "Well, regardless of your methods, you have done us a great service today." The tall man moved away from the window: if he was listening, he seemed unaffected by Astor-Smath's words. Robin tried a little harder. "This marks a major step forward in our cooperative agreement, and you have also struck a significant blow against the agents of national sovereignty, who stand in the way of—"

"How gratifying. I would welcome another dish of olives."

Then the tall man sat down in the shadowed corner. He did not speak again.

Chapter Twenty-Eight

CALYPSO

Opal saw Caine emerge from the Capitol's West Face at a brisk walk that carried him straight to the descending flight of stairs at the southern end of the portico. At the same moment, a small horde of medtechs started charging up the staircase on the northern side. The EMTs were accompanied by a smattering of suit-and-sunglass security types who were about as unobtrusive as a flock of condors in a day-care center.

Caine fast-foot-shuffled down the second, lower flight of stairs, headed straight toward Opal but didn't show any sign of stopping near her. She took her cue, fell in beside him. "What's the excitement?"

He smiled—too brightly and cinematically for comfort—and said nothing, only looked past her at the taxis on First Street, scanning from one to the next.

What the hell is he looking for? His favorite brand? "Caine—"

He peered down to where First Street emerged from the Maryland Avenue traffic circle. He snapped straighter, flung up a hand: "Taxi!"

A cab—one of the few driven by a human—swerved to the curb. Caine scanned its interior—and driver—quickly: *What the hell is he looking for?* It seemed an odd choice: a dilapidated gypsy cab, and a primitive one at that, without any comm or call number stenciled on the side, just the rather battered legend, "Sim's Taxi Service."

The window edged down unevenly. Caine's question sounded strange, even to her: "Who are you?"

The driver started. Too surprised to come up with a retort, or a lie, his response was gruff: "I'm Sim. Who wants to know?"

"A high-tipping fare."

Sim's eyebrows went up. "Glad to hear it." He reached over the back seat toward the rear door.

"Not so fast. You own and operate this cab yourself?"

"Do you think I'd be out here if I had anyone to do it for me?"

"Are you subscribed to a dispatching service, or a fare-share cooperative?"

"What, and go bankrupt between the fees and the percentages I have to share out? Listen, buddy, I just barely get by as it is."

"Then you're taking us to Reagan International."

"Suborbital or orbital terminal?"

"Orbital. And if you get us there in thirty-five minutes, there's a fifty dollar tip in it."

"Luggage?"

"No luggage."

"Then hop in."

Caine pulled open the door. Opal stepped forward, paused, started to look back up the stairs of the Capitol Building—

Caine put a hand on her arm: it was not gentle. "Don't look back. Get in."

She waited until they had crossed the Potomac and then toggled the privacy screen. After it was done grinding and groaning closed, she turned to Caine. "Mind telling me what's going on?"

Caine was removing his collarcom. "I'm taking a trip."

The first person singular pronoun left a burning feeling along Opal's brow. *Okay: keep it relaxed: don't give yourself away.* She looked around the soiled interior of the cab. "Well, you've certainly picked some first-class transportation for this leg of your journey."

He did not smile: at first, she wasn't even sure he had heard. However, as he began fishing around in his pants pocket, he finally replied, as if in afterthought: "Actually, this cab is exactly what I need. It's not automated, so there's no commlink. It's self-owned, so no central dispatcher. And he's not connected to any of the gypsy cooperative services. So the only way Downing—or anyone else—can find me is to trace the signal of my phone." Which he had now extracted from his pocket.

She decided to ignore the first-person-singular pronouns with which Caine continued to frame his responses. "So it's the same plan as yesterday: we travel incognito as much as possible?"

He checked that the privacy panel was still up, scanned the corners of the rear compartment quickly— *looking for fiber-optic snoopers? Here?*—and then jammed his hand down into the gap where the rear cushion abutted with the seat cushion. He pulled the seat away from the backrest: a lint-and-litter crevasse yawned at them. He pushed the phone and collarcom down into it as far as they would go.

She chose to arch her left eyebrow. "I understand ditching the phone, and letting them chase it around D.C., but the collarcom?"

He dusted off his hands. "I got the collarcom from Downing. Which means I got it from IRIS. For all I know, they have a transponder chip in it."

She nodded. *Act cheery, but not overly interested or concerned.* "So, where are we going?"

"I'm going to Mars."

Mars? "What? Why?"

He looked out the window at a spaceplane lumbering aloft. He watched it disappear into the low-hanging haze before he answered: "Tarasenko is dead."

"Dead? While you were in there?"

"Yeah."

"How?"

"Good question. An apparent heart attack."

"'Apparent'?"

He looked sideways at her. "Doesn't it make you a little bit suspicious, Tarasenko dying of a heart attack—just two days after Nolan?"

"Well, both of them were getting on in years—"

"Yeah, but both of them received superior medical care, got a reasonable amount of exercise, were not engaged in any strenuous activity at the time of their death—and were the two key power brokers for IRIS."

"But how could an assassin—?"

"I don't know how, but I've learned that just because I don't know *how* something might be done, doesn't mean it *can't* be done."

"So why Mars?"

"Because that's the best way to put some distance between myself and IRIS. Tarasenko's death is going to send Downing—and IRIS—into a twenty-four-hour tailspin, at least. By then, I want to be well beyond easy reach. That's why I'm climbing straight onto the first spaceplane I can catch, and then taking the LEO shuttle out to Highport."

"And just how are you going to pay for that?"

"My book royalties have been accumulating for almost fourteen years. And while we were over the Atlantic, my agency was holding a fast, invite-only auction for publishers who wanted the right of first refusal on my Dee Pee Three diaries."

Huh. Caine sure works fast. And so quietly that I never suspected it. "So: onward to Mars. And once you get there—what?"

Opal had the distinct impression that this was the first time she had ever heard Caine utter ideas as they came to him, without prior assessment and editing. "I'm not sure. I'll just be happy if I can keep away from anyone associated with IRIS."

Then get the hell away from me, you poor guy. Aloud: "Sounds prudent, but you could probably get lost in the sauce more easily by staying Earthside. More room to run, more places to hide."

"Maybe, but Mars is a much longer reach for Downing. And right now, he's short of trustworthy manpower, so he's not going to want to strand an operative out there."

"Caine, before you go running off to another planet, I've gotta ask: why are you so sure that Richard will still want to keep tabs on you? Maybe he'll just let you go. Maybe you don't have to run so far. Maybe you don't have to run at all."

"Maybe—but it sure didn't sound that way back in Tarasenko's office. I think Downing wants to pull me deeper into IRIS."

"But that just doesn't make any sense. Downing knows that you don't want to be an agent, and now you've made yourself too high-profile for him to use, anyway. So why would he try to keep you as a resource?" *Yeah,* thought Opal, with a sense of ominous realization, *why does Richard want to keep Caine in the game so badly? Why does Caine still need to be watched?*

Riordan had obviously been thinking similar thoughts. "You're right, of course: Downing shouldn't have any further use for me—not after today." His tone became jocular. "Unless, that is, he expects to find some more exosapients that need to be 'contacted.'" But Caine's initially sardonic tone faded over the course of his quip: indeed, he looked very thoughtful as he finished.

"That's a pretty unlikely scenario, Caine—keeping you around as an escort for the little green men who might land and say, 'Take me to your leader.'"

Caine smiled, but was still thinking—hard. At last he looked up. "I don't like running away from my home—it's wrong and it pisses me off. But damn it, on Earth, or one light-second away on the Moon, Downing's got all the advantages. So right now, I need distance."

"That's not exactly a sophisticated plan, Caine."

"No, it's not. But that's what happens when the other guy holds almost all the cards: things get really simple, because you've got so few options. In this case, it's just like Sun Tzu says: a weak force must go where its adversaries have the least power. And for me, that means Mars."

Okay, so there's no stopping him. Let's see if I can hitch a ride, instead. "So: Mars. Quite the hotspot, I hear."

Caine's smile was more relaxed, now. "Yeah, it's not exactly a Mecca for fun-seekers, but I just want a place where I can gather more information on those one hundred lost hours, and keep my head down while I do it."

"Why keep your head down?"

"Downing may not be the only person monitoring web traffic for inquiries into the background of one Caine Riordan. The opposition may be looking for that, too."

"'Opposition'? Wasn't the working assumption that, with Parthenon behind us, you're safe?"

"I can't afford to subscribe to that assumption— because if I do, and I'm wrong, then I'm dead."

Opal had to admit that Caine's conclusion was unassailably commonsensical. "Sounds like a pretty lonely life you're making for yourself."

Caine nodded, looked at her slowly, almost cautiously. "I wouldn't wish it on anyone else, that's for sure."

Careful now, Opal: don't scare him off. "Oh, I don't know: it doesn't sound all that bad. Sometimes a bit of enforced peace and quiet is just what a person needs. Hell, since Downing gave me my honorable discharge, all I can think about is diving under a rock somewhere and trying to figure out this new world at my own pace. Maybe planet Earth has always been a madhouse, but it seems more so now."

Caine nodded, looked forward again. After a long pause, he said: "Mars is a lot less chaotic than Earth or Luna. Not too big, not too busy."

"See? So how bad does Mars sound when you describe it that way?"

He looked at her. "Come with me?"

She wanted to smile but stomped down on that reflex. *Careful: if you say "yes" too quickly, he might become suspicious, might start wondering if this isn't happening just a bit too easily.* "Well, no offense, but I'm not in the habit of being anyone's traveling companion."

"Okay—then how about being my bodyguard?"

Oh, Christ: he's offering me the job I'm already doing. "Do you really think you need a bodyguard?"

"Maybe; I don't know. And that's the whole problem: I don't know much of anything just yet. I don't even know who I can trust." He turned to her, and after a moment, he smiled. "Except you. I trust you."

Damn it, this just isn't right: "Are you sure you want me tagging along?" *Say "no"—for your own good.*

"If you want to come, that would be, well— wonderful." Then his eyebrows raised a little, and the corners of his eyes crinkled, the way they did when he became jocular. The cab swerved across two lanes of traffic and up onto the exit ramp for the spaceport, just as he leaned towards her. Almost nose to nose at that moment, there was mock conspiracy in his hushed voice as he asked: "Because I *can* trust you—can't I?"

She looked him in the eye—and realized that, asked so directly, she could not lie to him. She also realized that, alone in the world as she was, and as he was, she could not leave him, either. And if, one day, being loyal to him meant disobeying Downing's orders? That was merely illegal—but it sure as hell didn't feel wrong. On the contrary: it felt—

"Right," she breathed out through her own sudden, surprised smile, "you can trust me." And, still smiling, leaning back to see his whole face more clearly, she realized:

You can *trust me. More than you know.*

BOOK TWO

CONVOCATION

PART FOUR

Mars and Deep Space

September, 2119

Chapter Twenty-Nine

MENTOR

Richard Downing waited patiently while the lieutenant—big, wide-eyed, and increasingly florid—shouted at him.

"No, sir, I don't have to recognize your authority. And to hell with your cosmic clearance level. We've been on patrol in the Belt for six months now, bypassed twice for rotation off this god-forsaken boat. I've got a wife and kids back in Syrtis City, a mother dying on Earth—"

Downing closed his eyes. "Lieutenant Weuve—"

"—and now you just want me and my whole crew to obligingly pop ourselves into the emergency cryo-cells with no explanation why, and no guarantee of when—or if—we'll wake up in this century? Not on your life—sir."

"Lieutenant, I'm sorry—but this is a matter of national security. Actually, it's a matter of global security: I'm here at the express orders of the World Confederation."

"I don't care if you're here to announce the Second Coming, Downing. Neither I, nor my men, are hopping into the meatlockers on your say-so. I want more verification."

"I'm sorry, but I can't accommodate that request. This must remain an entirely compartmentalized operation. No external communications, not even by encrypted lascom."

"Then you're out of luck, Mr. Downing."

"Then I am afraid I must relieve you of your command, Lieutenant."

Weuve's shock became a smile, then a smirk. "Oh, really? Didn't see you bring a Marine detachment on board with you from the other ship."

"That's because they are also, along with the rest of that crew, in cold sleep now. Besides, I don't need any Marines."

"No? Why's that?"

"I think I can handle this myself."

Weuve's eyes went wide again, then narrowed. "Mr. Downing, I think you've seriously overestimated your authority and your combat power on this hull. Mister Rulaine,"—the lieutenant hooked a finger in the direction of his security chief—"please take Mr. Downing into custody and place him in the brig."

Rulaine—tall, spare, silent—produced his NeoCoBro liquid-propellant sidearm. "Are you sure you want to do this, Lieutenant?"

Weuve turned to stare at the query. "You may be new here, Chief, but on this hull, you don't question your orders: you obey them."

Rulaine shrugged. "Yes, sir." He quickly raised the gun—but aimed it at Weuve's cheek.

Who took a drift-step back in the microgravity. "Hey—"

The NeoCoBro uttered a weak cough—consistent with the low propellant setting used for nonlethal rounds—which sent a gel-capsule splatting against the side of Weuve's face.

Who was shouting: "McDevitt, Gross, get—" Weuve's orders to his first pilot/XO and second engineer slurred into a groan and then a rough sigh; his feet drifted up off the deck and he floated slowly toward the bulkhead, already senseless.

Downing breathed again. "Those new tranq rounds work rather quickly."

Rulaine nodded as he steadied his own recoil-induced drift with one hand, trained the gun on the other two bridge crewmen. He nodded at them. "Are we going to have any trouble with you two?"

McDevitt swallowed and shook his head. Gross was actually smiling. "Hell, no: I'd have been happy to pop the CO myself."

"That's insubordination, mister: your CO was out of line, but he's still your CO. Be glad I don't put it in your record. Now, take the lieutenant, and get the others ready for cold sleep."

"Yessir." The two of them skim-trotted off the bridge, towing Weuve. As the bulkhead door started sealing, Richard heard McDevitt ordering the ship's complement to gather in the galley.

Downing put away the Executive Orders that Weuve had—erroneously—dismissed as forgeries. "Very well done, Captain Rulaine. Obviously, you roused no suspicions when you replaced their 'ailing' security chief a week ago."

"Guess not, sir. But I have to say this is the strangest assignment I've ever been given; what's it all about?"

"I can tell you what some parts are about, Captain. But I can't tell you what it's *all* about—as I suppose you have already surmised."

"I suppose I have, sir."

Glancing at the green beret's patient hazel eyes, Downing wondered what unusually gifted recruiting sergeant had seen beyond the insubordination of Rulaine's undergraduate years, and had instead discerned a spirit that would not only accept the practical dicta of a military life, but would thrive under them. As an OCS candidate, Bannor Rulaine had not been the average shave-tail—and afterward, he had not been given average assignments. To date, his battlefield choices had been frequently unorthodox and overwhelmingly successful. More importantly, his discretion was legendary, having brought him to the attention of intelligence chiefs, and hence, to Downing.

Downing shrugged. "What I can tell you about your part of this mission is that we will be consigning this hull and its complement to the care of another ship once we reach Mars orbit. From there, we will make planetfall at Syrtis City, where you will be responsible for overseeing the protection of ten extremely important persons. It is not merely their lives that you must protect, but the information that they will soon have: they must not be buttonholed, seduced, drugged, kidnapped, or otherwise made susceptible to any kind of debriefing or interrogation. Any questions?"

"Just ones you can't answer, sir."

Downing wondered how much Bannor's unconventional brain had already answered on its own. Certainly, he had inferred the extreme sensitivity of the mission from the outré secrecy precautions he was witnessing.

Downing had arrived via a special military clipper, its crew put into cold sleep before docking with Weuve's patrol boat. A third craft—a navy transport—would soon make rendezvous and, after depositing Downing and Rulaine on Mars, would then tow the other two ships to an outbound shift carrier. Which, upon arriving at Alpha Centauri, would inter their crews in a secure facility for a long, secrecy-assuring sleep. Hardly standard operating procedure.

Rulaine glanced at the internal monitors, frowned when he saw some of the crew becoming restive in the galley, turned up the sound: surprised complaints, but nothing mutinous. Yet. He turned back to Downing. "Not to rush you along, sir, but—orders?"

Downing nodded. "Seal the bridge. Route all controls directly through here. Engage the antitamper failsafes, if they are not already active."

Rulaine double-checked the control panels. "Already active, sir. Switching all control to bridge; auxiliary is now deactivated."

"Very good. And be sure to keep one eye on the crew."

"I'll keep both eyes on them, sir." Rulaine drifted closer to the monitor. Without looking back toward Downing, he asked, "Sir, am I allowed to know the identity of the ten persons I'll be babysitting?"

"Eventually. But right now, we need to focus on the one who's likely to attract—and possibly cause—more trouble than the other nine combined."

"A rabble-rouser, sir?"

"Nothing of the sort. But he does resent me—and for good reason."

ODYSSEUS

Caine pried open the malfunctioning door sensor he had removed: hair-thin fiber-optic connectors coiled around chips that should have been called "specks."

The doorbell's secure tone announced a recognized "friend" rather than an "intruder." Opal breezed into the suite, then his room—and stopped, surprised. "Is that sensor busted again?"

"Yep, which is damned odd, considering it was just repaired. This time, I'm running the diagnostics myself."

Opal frowned at his tone. "Do you think that someone has been tampering with it?"

Caine smiled. "No, probably not. As Napoleon said, never ascribe to malice what which can be adequately explained by incompetence. But either way, the only way to be sure the sensor works is to fix it myself."

"Can I help?" she asked brightly, sitting down very close to him.

He looked at her. "You're very cheery. Too cheery. So I'm guessing today's news is bad."

Opal's smiled faded. "Well—yeah. Just as we expected; the Scarecrow will be here soon. Sorry."

Caine went back to examining the sensor. "It was only a matter of time before Downing came sniffing around. And with Nolan's memorial being held on Mars, he has the perfect excuse."

Opal responded in the flat, utterly reasonable tone that signified she was digging her heels in. "Well, just because Scarecrow is almost here doesn't mean we have to waste the afternoon. I was thinking that, before he takes our lives away from us again, perhaps we could—"

"Yes?" Caine looked up, trying not to look hopeful or lecherous or shallow.

"I was thinking that we could get in one last visit to the dojo."

"Oh." Caine tried to sound enthusiastic. "Sure. Great." *Not the direction I hoped our activities would take during our last day of privacy.*

But that hope was, Caine admitted, pure fancy. After months of uncertainty regarding where his relationship with Opal was headed (if anywhere), it beggared belief that she'd initiate a change now, in a few final hours.

When they'd left Earth, Caine had hoped their traveling together would segue into their *being* together. But the frenzied rush of their departure hardly set the tone for budding romance. Getting off Earth had meant getting through security before Downing—or anyone else—thought to red-flag their IDs. Fortuitously, the back-to-back deaths of Nolan and Tarasenko had generated enough chaos to prevent that.

Or so Caine had thought. But he began to question that hypothesis when they made the journey to Mars without interference or even a message from Earthside. It wasn't as if they had vanished without a trace: they'd had to use their own IDs to get to orbit, and then to book passage to Mars. So maybe Downing had left them alone because he couldn't risk sending orders through his leak-prone intelligence net. If so, that might explain why he was now coming himself.

But for what purpose? To coerce them back into the cloak-and-dagger webs that he habitually spun? *No way.* IRIS was a magnet for death: Nolan's demise, Tarasenko's, and three attempts—at least—on his own life were all the proof Caine needed. And if his efforts at filling in the one hundred hours missing from his past were proceeding slowly, at least no one had tried to kill him, either.

He mustered a smile for Opal. "So, when should I meet you at the dojo?"

"Sixteen hundred hours sidereal. We'll work on releases, maybe a few throws, then *kumite*."

"Ugh." He smiled more broadly. "Sparring."

"You don't like getting a workout?"

"Oh, I like the workout. But getting my ass kicked every time does deflate my ego."

Opal's own smile faltered a bit and she turned quickly—even awkwardly—and strode into her room, apparently suppressing a wistful sigh as she did.

MENTOR

Downing checked his watch. "Mr. Rulaine, we need to establish contact with two of the other people on your security list. Nolan Corcoran's children—Trevor and Elena—are on Mars presently, for their father's memorial ceremony."

Rulaine raised an eyebrow. "Admiral Corcoran's memorial is being held on Mars? That's a little—remote—for a person of his stature, isn't it, sir?"

"That's partly why it was chosen. His children are expecting me, but I'm a bit ahead of schedule, so we'll need to call ahead. Please contact Comm Ops at Syrtis Major Naval Base and have them locate and collect the Corcorans."

Only a few moments passed before Rulaine responded. "Syrtis Major confirms that the contact orders for Corcoran's children are received and being acted upon, sir." Pushing back from the commo panel, Rulaine slowly and carefully unfolded himself into a standing position: only three weeks in zero-gee, and he already moved like a seasoned professional.

"Very good, Captain. It also seems like the disturbance in the galley has died down."

Without looking sideways at the relevant monitor, which showed the crew going through preparations for cold sleep, Rulaine nodded. "Seems so, sir." Rulaine evidently had impressive peripheral vision, as well.

"Then let's start reviewing—"

"Sir, before we get to that, I have one more question about Riordan."

Downing nodded.

"Beyond his resentment of you, is Riordan going to present me with any—problems—that I have to take into consideration?"

"What do you mean?"

"Well, sir, there's a rumor in the news—and elsewhere—that Mr. Riordan was not exactly a 'fellow traveler' when given his mission to Dee Pee Three."

Downing kept from working his jaw. "He was not a completely willing recruit, no."

"Then, sir, do I expect that he'll cooperate, or be—problematic?"

Downing considered avoiding the question, redirecting it, even lying outright, but instead he turned to look at Bannor Rulaine and said, "I wish I could tell you, Captain, but I don't know the answer myself. You see, when we activated him—"

"Mr. Downing, I'm sorry to interrupt, but I've got a response from Syrtis Base regarding the Corcorans."

"And?"

"There's a problem, sir."

"You mean the Shore Liaison Office doesn't have them in hand, yet?"

"No sir; I mean that, according to the SLO, they're not in Syrtis City—or anywhere else on Mars." Rulaine looked straight into his eyes. "They're missing, sir."

Chapter Thirty

The face that looked out the airlock window at him was ill-shaven, eyes indistinct behind a lank forelock of dirty-blond hair. *Thank God,* he thought. *If they're terrorists, then they're sloppy ones. Most are highly disciplined, attentive to personal grooming not only by inclination, but by training. Conversely, personal sloppiness usually means operational sloppiness.*

As the face backed away from the airlock door, he felt the wind push fitfully against the heavy life support unit on his back. He turned: a rusty-brown expanse of stone and sand was surrendering occasional sheets of dust up to the growing wind. Not good and not expected. The Navy meteorologist had agreed with the civilian service for once: from Syrtis Major to Isidus Planitia, twenty-kph winds, steady from the west, a relatively constant –12 degrees Celsius. By Martian standards, a calm and balmy day. But that's not how it was shaping up for Trevor Corcoran, and the disguised SEAL officer was not pleased with the discrepancy.

335

He heard the airlock door squeak and sigh and he turned—to find himself looking down the barrel of a ten-millimeter Sig Sauer caseless handgun. *Okay, their equipment isn't top-shelf, but it's not all antiques, either.*

He raised his hands. The figure—wearing a generic spacesuit that was the same model as his own—gestured him to approach. Trevor did, keeping his hands high. The figure stepped to the left, motioned him past—and slammed him forward against the inner airlock door, the pistol pressed into the side of his helmet. The figure's free hand roved and snatched at his spacesuit, tugged open the thigh pockets, then pulled him about-face by the shoulder. With the gun now snugged up against Trevor's neck, his chest pockets and utility pouches were subjected to the same hasty inspection. Then the spacesuited figure stepped back and, gun steady, reached back with his free hand to pull the outer airlock door closed. A moment later, the hatch autodogged and a rising hiss indicated that atmosphere was being pumped in.

So far, so good. There had always been a chance that they would shoot him down the moment they saw him. But that was one of the many operational hazards that there had been no way to avoid.

The inner airlock door swung open—and Trevor found himself staring into yet another muzzle. This one *was* an antique: a nine-millimeter parabellum MP-5 machine pistol. Almost a century out of date. *Okay, they're definitely not the A-team.*

Pushed roughly from behind, he staggered forward and—knowing that they'd have his helmet off in seconds—reasoned that this was the last moment he could conduct a visual assessment without looking like he was doing just that.

And Trevor liked what he saw. The three in the main room were ethnically diverse. None over twenty-seven. All male. All had tattoos, piercings, long—and in one case, grotesquely unwashed—hair. Complete heterogeneity of weapons. The central table was an overcrowded parking lot for used coffee mugs and pots. Several dozen ration-pack wrappers had been discarded on the floor, as well as other trash and—was that a pair of dirty socks under a chair? One of them—the big, sleepy-looking guy with the greasy hair—clearly had track marks on his left forearm. T-shirts, several sporting the logos of Slaverock bands. In short, nothing to imply or even hint at the kind of discipline imparted by any formal training in operations. *Terrorists?* He smiled. *Or gang-bangers?*

The "terrorist" behind him grabbed his helmet, popped the side clamp and ripped it off.

The smell of unwashed bodies and stale air almost made Trevor gag.

"You've got five seconds to tell me who you are and why you're here. You give me an answer I don't like, and you're meat."

"My name is—hell, it isn't important. Call me Trev. I'm just a guy hired by the girl's family. And I've brought money to pay for her release."

"What the—what the hell are you talking about?"

"Look: I know you've got the girl. And all these guns prove it."

"Yeah—and you'd better prove you've come alone or this conversation is going to end. Real soon."

"You can send a man out to see. You'll find a

pressurized buggy three hundred meters due east. There's no one in it. But before you send someone to check it, you might want to pick up the aluminum attaché case just outside the door."

"Why?"

"Because the payment is inside."

The kidnapper with the machine pistol turned to give an order to the man in the spacesuit. "Scan him." He turned back. "Now, how do I know you're not just the inside man for an assault team?"

"Because when you send your man out, you're going to find that there's no one in sight—which means by the time anyone could join me here, I'd be dead. Right?"

The one with the machine pistol spent a moment thinking, then his eyes flicked over toward his man with the RF scanner.

Who shrugged. "He's clean; no signals coming off him."

"And none will. Take his helmet off. Check for a backup radio. Take his gloves off, too."

"Yeah, yeah."

Trevor looked around while they spoke. The interior was exactly what he'd expected from the schematic: large primary dome, centered on the "storm room"—a shielded core that provided refuge during solar flares and other radiological anomalies. There was one opening off to the right that led to the installation's single reinforced corridor, which was the spine to which all the other, smaller expansion domes were attached. No change from the original layout—and no sign of the meteorological and geological monitoring teams that were supposedly stationed here. The last was not a good sign—but, sadly, not a surprise, either.

The one in the spacesuit was finished, handed Trevor's gloves back to him. "He's clean."

"Fine. Tape him up."

Trevor's hands were pulled out in front of him and wound with four wraps of three-inch reflective duct tape. Standard, even amongst amateurs.

The terrorist with the machine pistol waved him over to one of the three chairs at the room's only table, then waved one of his flunkies toward the storm room.

Who asked: "Whaddya want me to do?"

"Just—check her. See if she's—I dunno: expecting something, or someone. Christ, do I have to think of everything?"

Back to Trevor: "So you're here to give me money. That's very nice of you—and I'll check into that right away,"—he waved the spacesuited one back outside— "but there's just one thing that still puzzles me."

"What's that?"

"I didn't ask for any money. As a matter of fact, no one should even know I'm here. So you'd better start shedding some light on your arrival, or I'll be looking at daylight through the holes I put in you."

Lines straight from the late-late show. You're too into the role to remember that you're just doing a job, huh? Bad for you; good for me.

Trevor made sure to never maintain eye contact very long, to appear moderately nervous. "I figured you were here—"

"*You* figured?"

"Yes—because when the family called me and reported her missing, I started looking for anything strange outside of Syrtis City."

"Oh? Why outside?"

"For the reason I'm guessing you left. Pressurized cities—they're too tight: behind every wall, there's another room, a corridor, a ventilation shaft. There's no safe ground. And there's too much surveillance: the cameras you can see, the fiber-optic peekers that you can't. You could think you're safe and sound and well-hidden—and the next thing you know, a SWAT team is blowing a hole in the wall right behind you."

"Smart boy. Go on."

"So I figured you'd be heading out—getting distance. You'd want something small, easy to grab, easy to control. Something without a lot of traffic. So I started checking the science outposts—and sure enough, this one was overdue for its commo check. But, since no one else knows the girl is missing, no one knew to think that might mean something more than a malfunction or a downed antenna."

"But you knew. Because the family called about their pretty, pretty—but not too young—baby."

"Uh—yeah."

"And who are you?"

"I do—jobs—for people."

"Oh?" The gun came up. "What kind of jobs?"

"Please, don't—no, not *those* kinds of jobs. Not with guns. But rich families get in trouble sometimes—more than most people realize. And I—I take care of those problems for them."

The gun went down. "They must be paying you a lot to come out here on your own, not knowing if we were gonna let you in or let you have it."

"Well—" *Careful now: just the way you rehearsed it. Use as much truth as possible: that's how you'll get away with the lies.*

"Yeah?"

"I know this family. I've worked for them before." *True.* "And now the father's dead and the mother's back on Earth and they didn't have anyone else to turn to." *Also true. And now the lie.* "And yeah, the money's good."

"Good enough to risk your life?"

"Good enough that I'll never have to risk it again."

The kidnapper with the machine pistol became thoughtful, only looking up when his partner returned from outside, carrying an aluminum briefcase. "How's it look?"

The other put the briefcase down, popped his helmet. "As advertised. All clear, as far as I can tell."

"What the hell does that mean, 'as far as I can tell'?"

"Look, man, you wanted me back quick, right? Well, that means I can't go wandering around behind every hill and big rock within five klicks. But the buggy's where he said it is, and empty."

The one with the machine pistol was about to open the case, halted, thought a moment, reached out and put it on Trevor's lap. Then he walked behind Trevor, his arms coming around from behind to prepare to undo the clasps.

"You mind being a human shield?"

Trevor shrugged. "Fine by me."

The clasps snapped, and the briefcase opened without incident. "Good: we're off to a promising start. No tricks."

Trevor nodded, thought: *No tricks that you can see. But the concentrated CO_2 canister in the false bottom has started dumping its contents—which will trigger the atmosphere alarms soon enough.*

The kidnapper had pawed through the bills in the attaché case. "One hundred K?"

Trevor nodded.

"Light, man; way too light."

"Don't worry: there's plenty more where that came from. This is just a taste."

"Just a taste, huh? Well, I'm ready for the full meal. But how do I get it? You don't get to leave until she does—and I'm not going to let in any more visitors."

He had taken the bait—which all but proved that they weren't from a group of religious or political fanatics. *And they're not seasoned professionals or they'd have already debriefed—and then greased—me. That's the problem when you don't use professional operatives; always the greed factor.*

"Getting the rest of your money is easy. It's on my bomb-rigged buggy."

"Bomb-rigged? How did you get explosives? Even the black market is tighter than nun-pussy on those."

Tighter than nun-pussy? If you took a course on how to talk like a tough guy, you should get a refund. Out loud: "The family has some clout. But you know that already."

"Yeah,"—he was a bad actor—"I guess I do."

No, you really don't. Someone sketched out the basics, but didn't fill you in on the reasons for taking the hostage. You're just hired muscle, following orders. Good for me now; bad for the follow-up investigation. Because when the authorities start checking into these guys, it'll be a dead end. They're on the outside of the operation. Way outside.

"So, now you give us the information on how to disarm the bomb."

"No, because the second I do that, you put a bullet in my head."

The wiseguy considered for a moment, then waved listlessly with the machine pistol. "Ah—you're right. So how do we do this dance?"

"You get a spacesuit for the girl, we all walk—"

"Nope. Not happening, hero. She stays here."

"Until?"

The wiseguy frowned, got agitated. "Until I say so, asshole. Listen, I call the shots here."

No, you don't. You were told to sit on her and await further orders. Kill her if someone tries a rescue op. And you're starting to realize that that may have been your employer's plan all along: they want her dead, and you dead, and a lot of chaos and worry in the bargain. It's only a matter of time until someone comes looking, you start shooting, and it all goes to hell.

"The way I see it, you might need the buggy as much as the money. More."

"Yeah? And why the hell do you think that, asshole?"

"Because whoever hired you to do this hasn't told you how the whole show ends, has he? And the radio he gave you is quiet—and he didn't tell you how to signal him, did he? 'Don't call me; I'll call you'?"

The wiry man's face became very red and he stuck the gun straight out, quivering, the muzzle half a foot from Trevor's forehead. "Listen, asshole—"

Trevor waited. The gun trembled, wavered, was yanked away.

"Shit! Shit, shit!" The wiseguy put his other hand to his own forehead, as if trying to still it.

The big sleepy-eyed one crooned, "Hey, Mingo, man—we just need to wait. We just need—"

"Shut up—just shut up! And don't use my name—not even my street name."

"Okay—but listen, man. He's just messin' wif you. We got a deal we can trust, a deal—"

"Yeah? We do? Why? 'Cause they said they want to keep her anyway? That's bullshit, man—and we were bullshit to believe it. We were doing too much ice, man: they messed us up, messed up our heads so we wouldn't think it all the way through. Shit, man—" And then he spun back toward Trevor, gun up and steady. "You. Hero. Why are you here? You lie, you die."

As if you'd know whether I was lying. "I'm here to get the girl. The family was smart enough to know that if they went to the cops, they were as good as killing their daughter themselves. By the time a rescue team got to her, you'd have killed her."

"Damn skippy on that, hero. Okay, so you've got a buggy, and we've got the girl. How do we do this?"

"We all go to the buggy together."

"How big is it?"

There's an open door for me to gather some tactical intel. "How big does it need to be?"

"I got eight—and her."

"And me."

"You can ride on the outside, hero."

"Okay. And you'll need to put one other out there. I've got six seats, room for two more as cargo."

"Fine. So we're at the buggy. Then what?"

"We drive to another outpost—I know you won't accept going back to Syrtis City."

"No shit, genius. So we're at another outpost."

"She walks away. You have the money and the buggy. And me."

"And then?"

"When she's safe, then I disarm the bomb. And you drive away."

He brought up the gun quickly; Trevor let himself flinch a little.

The wiseguy smiled. "Not so brave after all, huh, Mr. Hero? So tell me, how do you know I won't grease you as soon as you've pulled the plug on the bomb? And how do I know you haven't bugged the vehicle—a hidden radio, a transponder?"

"You'll know the vehicle isn't wired the same way you knew I wasn't—your friend's RF signal detector. And as for shooting me—you might, but right now, she's just an unreported missing person. And she can stay that way. And you don't have to be accused as kidnappers. But you shoot me, and now there's a crime that can't be ignored or unreported: the law gets involved. And you don't want any news getting out on how you got away, do you? Because if your employer finds you, that will be worse than the police. Right?"

Chapter Thirty-One

TELEMACHUS

Wiseguy's eyes widened: he hadn't thought of what his employers might do if they found out he skipped on the job. If they had meant him to be killed by the cops, they'd need to finish the job themselves if something went awry with that plan. He swallowed. "Okay, okay—but we do it my way. We go to the outpost I choose. And you're blindfolded until we get there." He forgot Trevor, started giving orders. "Peak, you get the others; tell 'em we're moving. Now. Just suits and guns. Mel, you—"

A klaxon started shrilling. Wiseguy whirled, aimed the gun at Trevor, saw it couldn't be his doing, started a spastic circle dance in search of the cause. "What the fuck, what the—?"

"That's an enviro sensor, man: we got a leak, or somethin'."

"Great. Fucking great. Probably broke a seal when you capped that guy in the back. I told you—"

The boss—Mingo—stalked past Trevor, intent on berating his flunky and checking the atmosphere gauges

346

that were next to the inner hatch. Peak was halfway out the door that led further into the compound; Mel was standing flat-footed, following Mingo with slow, heavy-lidded eyes. *No one watching and no one close.*

Trevor kicked himself over backward in the chair, touching his heels together as he pushed. The contacts in each heel closed, and he felt the base of his life-support unit blast outward, the bottom panel cutting through his suit leg as it went spiraling into the room like a runaway circular saw. White hexachlorathene smoke vomited out of the bottom of the backpack unit in a wide, gushing plume.

As Trevor bounced to a stop on the floor, he joined his hands into a composite fist and hit the sternum-centered strap release: the life-support unit came loose, and he rolled toward the densest accumulation of smoke. Coming out of the snap-roll into a sitting position, he brought his left foot up between his arms, pulling his hands as far apart as he could. He angled his foot sideways, so that the black-painted razorblade taped to the sole of that boot was pressed against the duct tape. He sawed his foot up and down twice, felt the fibers of the tape give—just as gunfire erupted, spanging off the bedrock floor near his chair.

"Mingo, man—don't shoot! There's too much smoke: you could hit me—"

"Shoot, asshole—get him! Don't wait—shoot, shoot!"

By the time they had worked out their sophisticated tactical response, Trevor had pulled apart the remains of the duct-tape cuffs and grabbed down under the collar ring of his spacesuit to pull up the slimline thermal imaging goggles taped there. He tugged hard, felt a moment's resistance, then heard a plastic pop

348 *Charles E. Gannon*

and a metallic crunch. Shit: busted an eyepiece. He got it out and around his head in a quick motion and snap-rolled again, coming up into another crouch.

The unit—already on—only worked in the right eyepiece now. But with that one eye, he could see the kidnappers' white silhouettes plainly as they moved around the smoke-filled room, following around the walls, guns out in front, firing occasionally. Mingo was particularly trigger-happy: he'd be dry in another moment. *And in the land of the blind, the one-eyed man is king—*

Trevor grabbed one of the mugs off the table, threw it away from himself, against the wall that was directly opposite Mingo.

Who, along with his crew, promptly blasted away at the sound. Mingo's response was short-lived, however: "Shit! I'm out." His silhouette jabbed a finger frantically at his gun's magazine release. Trevor moved toward him, pressed against the same wall, keeping his weight on the sides of his feet.

Mingo had a new magazine out, snapped it up into his weapon—

As he did, Trevor shoved his body against Mingo's flank, rotating him slightly out from the wall as the thug finished reloading. In the same instant, Trevor reached over the kidnapper's left shoulder with his left hand and grasped the right side of his jaw, just as Trevor's right hand locked in a secure grip on the left rear side of the thug's neck. Trevor uncrossed his arms in a sharp X motion: his left hand yanked Mingo's head swiftly to the left; the right kept the neck from rotating with that sudden turn. There was a sharp snap, like a piece of well-dried kindling broken over a knee, and Mingo went limp, a shout dying out of him as a breathy gasp.

Trevor snagged the MP-5 in mid-fall as he dropped to one knee, made sure the slide was back, and snapped the selector switch to semiautomatic.

"Mingo—Mingo, man—"

Trevor aimed for the center of Peak's mass and squeezed twice in rapid succession. Peak screamed, went backward, firing wildly, still screaming without words. Mel froze in place—*thank you, stupid*—and, taking about half a second to aim, Trevor centered two rounds into him, as well. Staying low, Trevor crossed the room, knowing what he would have to do when he got there.

Peak was still screaming, heard someone approaching. "Help me, man—oh, oh, shit—fuck, help—"

Trevor crouched so he was very close and fired a single round into the center of Peak's bucking forehead. He snatched up the thug's pistol—another ten-millimeter Sig Sauer caseless—and headed back to the airlock's inner door, which he opened wide before returning to the center of the room. He snatched up his life-support unit, reached in through the jagged hole where its base plate used to be, and burned his hands as he yanked out the empty smoke canister that had been installed in place of the second air tank. He reached in again, pulled out a black disk the size of a hockey puck, flipped back a cover, pressed the single concealed button, and placed it in the center of the floor, looking away as he did. There was a flash that he could see quite clearly in his peripheral pickups: the thermite filament fuse had lit—and would burn for about three minutes. He pulled a small packet out of the ruined base of the LSU before strapping the unit back on.

Then over to the table as he pocketed the small packet, found his helmet, latched it on and toggled the communicator as he started moving in the direction of the storm room. "Crossbow, this is Quarrel. Crossbow, this is Quarrel."

"Quarrel, this is Crossbow. Go."

"I am in. Beacon is set. Have you acquired lock?"

"Negative, Quarrel. I'll have to come closer to see the heat from the fuse. Not getting the UV phased-spectrum signal from your beacon at all."

"Roger. Any sign of laser targeting beams?"

"Negative. Looks clear. No sign of fixed defenses or heavy weapons."

"Take no chances. Use the antilaser aerosols as you approach."

"Pretty marginal effect, Quarrel. Wind is over forty klicks, here. And rising."

Trevor had spun open the storm-room hatch. "Use the aerosols anyway. Out."

"Out."

He swung the hatch inward—and found the hostage, taped to a chair in the center of the room. The duct tape was so thick on her that she seemed half-mummified.

He slung the machine pistol, stuck the barrel of Peak's weapon through a utility ring on his belt, grabbed her chair by the backrest, dragged it out of the door's sightline, speaking as he went: "We're getting out. No time to talk. Answer my questions—and only that." She nodded as he pulled the razor off the sole of his boot, and started sawing at the tape binding her legs.

"Nod for yes. There were eight of them, all told?"

Nod. He moved on to her arms and hands.

"See anything bigger than a machine gun?"

She shook her head.

"You know how to use a rescue ball, right?"

A pause. Then a tentative nod.

Great. That pause meant she didn't really know. He began to slice at the wraps that bound her midriff to the chair. There were a lot of those. And there was some distant, tentative shouting: the rest of the rogues' gallery was on the way, no doubt.

He pulled the pack off of his belt, dropped it on the floor in front of her. "Rescue ball. Listen carefully. When you pull the tab, the ball will balloon out at you, so stand back. It's in two halves, joined by a hinge at the bottom. Sit in the middle. There'll be a zipper at your feet: pull it up over your head; the ball will expand more as you do. When the zipper can't go any further, you'll feel a click. That means you're sealed in. You'll find a mask to your right, on the floor. Put it on right away; that's your O_2 with chemical rebreather. Gives you about forty-five minutes of air. The hissing you'll hear around you is okay; that's inert gas, creating point five atmospheres of pressure in the ball. Wait here."

Trevor slipped away from the chair, listened beyond the door. The smoke was not quite as thick, but, having filled a single room with only two narrow exits, its dissipation was slower than usual. He knelt, ducked his head around the corner.

One bright white silhouette was just entering the main room, the suggestion of another one, maybe two, hanging back in the corridor's entryway.

Trevor pulled Peak's pistol out, sighted carefully, high in the first silhouette's chest, and fired twice.

The silhouette went down, and after a quick, blind fusillade, the other two ducked back.

So did Trevor—only to discover the hostage trying to pull the tape off her mouth. For one incongruously mischievous moment, he was tempted to make her leave it there—but toggled his radio, instead: "Crossbow, I have the package."

"Copy that, Quarrel. I see the fuse now, and have locked on. Ordnance is hot and ready to fly. Waiting your mark."

"Roger, Crossbow. Out." Turning: "Into the ball. Right now. No talking. We've got to go."

To her credit, she was already pulling the activation tab. The ball's two halves burgeoned outwards; she sat between them. Trevor nodded approvingly, sidestepped back to the doorway; a thermal glimmer suggested the kidnappers had returned to their earlier covering position at the doorway into the corridor.

This was the tricky part—how to get the loaded rescue ball from the storm room to the exfiltration point he'd chosen. He hoped the last four of the bastards hadn't had the time to fully suit up; if they had, his plan might not work. But their lack of both time and discipline was on his side. Of course, there was also the backup plan—to call in the heavy artillery—but even in the storm room, there was no guarantee that he and the hostage wouldn't wind up as corpses themselves. Rockets tend not to be discriminating about who they kill, and the walls of the storm room were designed to keep out brief bursts of solar radiation—not hypersonic projectiles.

Trevor turned back, found himself face to face with a Day-Glo orange and reflective-white bubble, topped by a set of heavy handles and a winch loop. He grabbed a handle, moved the ball to one side of the pressure door, then set the MP-5 to full automatic. Twenty-five rounds left: not enough to win a gun battle, but that wasn't his plan anyway. He just had to make sure that they kept their heads down for a few seconds.

Releasing the MP-5 to hang on its sling, and taking Peak's Sig Sauer in a steady, two-handed grip, he swung to the opposite side of the pressure door and leaned out a bit. From that angle, he could just see the small window in the outer airlock door: a plate-sized thermal anomaly. Taking careful aim, he started to fire. On the third shot, he hit it—

The klaxon started to shriek yet again—now in the triple-time yowling that meant a critical pressure breach. The smoke gusted out in that direction, along with a slow cyclone of papers, napkins, and other rubbish. Trevor stowed the pistol, grabbed the MP-5—just as one of the kidnappers poked his head around the corner. Trevor sent a snap-burst—three, maybe four rounds—in that general direction. The figure ducked back—hit or not, Trevor couldn't tell.

And didn't have the time to ascertain: grabbing the top of the rescue ball, he lifted its sixty-three kilos as though it were twenty-five—thankful for the 0.37 Mars gravity that made such a feat possible. He sprinted out the door—the ball and occupant bouncing sharply off the jamb as he went—and then through the already-diminishing maelstrom of escaping air. Halfway across the room, he spun, fired a quick burst at the corridor entry without stopping to check if there were any targets. Trevor just wanted to keep their heads down long enough to get out, because once the kidnappers had all clambered into their spacesuits, there would be plenty of real targets—too many.

As Trevor reached the far wall, he pulled out the ten-millimeter pistol and emptied the remainder of its magazine in two vertical lines, about four feet apart. The rounds did not penetrate, but the metal prefab sheeting was bent, and, at the impact apexes, ruptured. He snapped down his helmet, produced and opened the last small packet he had removed from his LSU: a 1.5-meter cord of C-8 plastic explosive with a pinch-contact igniter—all together, about the size of a shot glass. He stuck one end of the plastique on the wall above the left set of bullet holes, unspooled the rest in a chest-high arc to end at the top of the other vertical line of scars, yanked the four-meter microwire igniter leads out straight—and turned on his heel to fire another burst back at the passageway behind him.

Just in time: an emerging figure ducked back, firing two wild rounds.

Wild rounds, yes—but they weren't blind, this time: they could see him just as well as he could see them, now that the smoke had been sucked out. Time to go.

Dragging the rescue ball so that it was behind his body, Trevor let the MP-5 fall loose on its lanyard and pulled the safety sleeve off the pinch contacts. He pressed them together.

The blast was not loud in the thin Martian atmosphere, but it tumbled him off the side of the rescue ball. Catching up the MP-5 in his right hand, and the ball in his left, he toggled his helmet's commo bar with his jaw. "Crossbow, I am removing the package."

"Quarrel, I see your new doorway. We are locked and off-safety."

At the jagged hole that he had blasted in the side of the dome, Trevor had to pause to maneuver the rescue ball through without slicing it open on the torn edges of the prefab, all the time keeping his body angled so he could keep an eye on the passageway. Good thing: two spacesuited figures came around that corner, one high, one low—the high one firing with his own MP-5.

Trevor crouched, aimed, dumped the entire magazine: the standing shooter went down, the other one put a crease in the left arm of Trevor's suit before ducking back behind the doorjamb.

Trevor rolled the rescue ball through the gap— feeling the contents thump awkwardly around as he did so—and popped out into the tan-pink dust swirls of a fifty-kph Martian breeze. "I am out—and it is a hot exfil, Crossbow. Repeat, hot exfil."

"You call it, Quarrel. I have you only five meters from the target zone, and I see thermal blooms in the building behind you."

"Do you have smoke?"

"Negative: live warheads only."

"Give me my range."

"You are at twelve meters from target. Do you see the gully—at your two o'clock?"

"Roger. Good eyes."

"You are still danger-close."

"Just fire on my mark."

Trevor swerved in the direction of the gully, felt something clip him in the rear of his right thigh as he pushed the rescue ball over its edge. As he dove into the natural trench himself, he yelled, "Mark!"

There was a half second of silence, and then, even through the thin Martian atmosphere, there was a momentary, soaring roar—like an up-dopplering freight train driven by jets—which passed almost directly overhead. It was cut short by a tremendous blast behind him, which sent fragments of stone and metal spattering into and over the trench, and which painted the surrounding rocks with a flickering glaze of orange and red light. Then the light was gone, and, a moment later, the concluding rumble of the detonation had faded as well.

Trevor stood up as the last pieces of debris came down. The entire northeast corner of the dome was gone, some of the edges pounded inward, others torn outwards. Thermal imaging showed the heat of some quickly smothering fires—and one or two prone, rapidly cooling biomasses. Any others were either cowering further inside—or had been reduced to protoplasm.

"Quarrel, we show all clear. Confirm."

"Crossbow, the LZ is clear."

"We'll be there in fifteen seconds. Quarrel, your biomonitors are showing us three suit breaches, two wounds. One of those breaches hasn't been fully autosealed. Recommend you use suit patches all speed."

"Already on it, Crossbow."

Ten seconds later, the transatmospheric assault VTOL—a cubist wasp with ordnance bristling under its wings and belly—swerved into sight, sucking up coils and curlicues of the tan-pink dust as it banked, straightened, and hovered, just a foot off the ground. Trevor picked up the rescue ball, discovered that his left leg was wobbly, got a hand from a tan-and-gray spacesuited figure who hopped down from the payload bay. Together, they hoisted the ball inside the VTOL with one heave.

"Thanks, Carlos."

"N'sweat, sir. Up you go."

Leg shaking, Trevor rolled into the VTOL, heard the warning klaxon and saw the orange lights: imminent high-speed closure of the bay's pressure door. Which it did with a bump and a metallic slap. Trevor lay still for a second, feeling the noradrenal rush begin to fade, prepared to suppress the post-op shakes his body—and mind—always wanted to have, but which he never permitted. Then he propped himself up on his elbows—

And saw a woman emerge from the rescue ball like Venus on the half-shell, her figure still discernible through the heavy clothes and tattered duct-tape remains. She must have seen him looking at her: raven-black hair fanned out as she quickly turned her head toward him. Her startling green eyes smiled when they met his—and tears started to run down her cheeks.

Trev smiled back. "Hi, sis. It's good to see you, too."

Chapter Thirty-Two

Commodore James Beall leaned back and glared at Trevor Corcoran. "So let's add up the list of violations to which you have already admitted. Exercising multiple command prerogatives in a unit to which you are not assigned, including illegal access to communication logs, orbital imagery, meteorological projections, and counterintelligence databases. Conceiving, planning, and executing an operation with the assets of said unit, without consulting or even informing its actual command staff. Requisitioning combat equipment—including a fully loaded attack sled—and authorizing the application of lethal force. Suborning three persons of this command, and inciting them to desertion—"

"Hold on. I gave them orders—and they didn't know I didn't have the authority to do so."

"Nice try. They already told us they were operating as volunteers."

"Bullshit. They're lying. They're just trying to keep me out of the brig."

"Commander Corcoran, you're the one dishing out

358

the bullshit. You have personal connections to all three, and they all know damn well that you're not a part of this command. Hell, just three years ago, you were their CO. You'd be a shitty SEAL officer if your men *weren't* ready to volunteer to get your ass out of a sling."

The door opened. "Not *his* ass, Commodore: his sister's." Downing walked in, Elena behind him.

The commodore stood, stiffly, but also cautious. "Sir, I'm not sure what you think you're do—"

Richard already had his credentials out; he handed them to Commodore Beall as he walked past, moving to Trevor's side.

Beall looked at the credentials, eyebrows rising slightly. Then he put them on the table, slid them down toward Richard.

"Very well, sir. You certainly have the authority to be here and to watch these proceedings, but—"

"Commodore, I also have the authority to end these proceedings and dismiss whatever charges you have recorded against Lieutenant Commander Corcoran."

"Mr. Downing, with all due respect—"

"Commodore, Commander Corcoran was operating on my orders."

Trevor managed not to start in surprise—or smile.

Beall frowned. "Sir, you'll forgive me if I find that extremely improbable. You've been Marside less than three hours."

"I wasn't aware you were monitoring my travel itinerary."

"You'd be surprised what we monitor here, Mr. Downing—or actually, you shouldn't be surprised, of all people."

"Regardless, rescuing his sister was an urgent and immediate priority, and had to be done without taking any chance of alerting her captors to the operation."

"Well then, Mr. Downing, I would appreciate you telling me why it was necessary to leave me out of the loop—and, sir, if I don't like the answer, I will have no choice but to lodge a protest."

"Feel free to do so, Commodore Beall—and I recommend that you skip all the intermediate steps and send it to your very highest superior."

"Admiral Tanaka?"

"No, President Liu. Or didn't you note the clearance and rank-equivalent on my ID?"

"I did sir, but—"

Downing just kept staring at Beall.

Who ultimately shrugged and looked away. "Sir, why did it have to be this way—or are you just retroactively covering Trevor's ass?"

Trevor wondered if Downing would be able to avoid smiling at Beall's insightful question. Elena—still standing at the other end of the room—continued to look tense. She'd never seen high-stakes interagency poker, in which each party plays its authority cards until someone blinks and the game is over. And Beall had blinked.

Richard's voice was level, nonconfrontational. "Commodore Beall, I am unable to answer your question due to matters of national security."

"Oh, fer Chrissakes—look: I'd have been happy to help. And I can keep a lid on things. We could have worked together—under the radar, out of sight of the higher brass."

"I know, and I appreciate your willingness to help.

But, Commodore, do you realize that that same kind of willingness has now landed Lieutenant Winfield, Chief Petty Officer Witkowski, and Petty Officer Cruz in your brig?"

"Okay, I'll let 'em off—as Trev always knew I would."

Downing shook his head. "Commodore, I wasn't trying to get them released, nor call attention to the rather striking inconsistency in your own insistence upon proper chain of command procedure—"

Beall flushed. "Now, listen—"

"What I was trying to indicate is that we had to keep Ms. Corcoran's name completely out of all reports, and out of all media. As far as anyone knows, she was never abducted. And that means you do not have to lie about having mounted a rescue operation—because you didn't. Nor did your superiors." Downing paused. "Do you understand?"

Beall turned round to look at Elena, looked back at Richard. "Yes, I do. Sir."

"Very well. I have one last directive for you to expedite."

"Very well."

"I would like the three SEALs you have in the brig released and issued immediate medical furloughs, with transport passes for Earth."

"What? Why? My men—"

"Commodore. Those men are no longer 'your' men. We can't have them talking to their teams."

"And I can't spare them, Mr. Downing. I'm pretty shorthanded up here; I've only got two teams in the shack and these three are my most experienced—"

"Commodore, I'm sorry, but this cannot be a matter of debate. And I would also appreciate your writing them sterling letters of recommendation should it become necessary to discharge them from service."

Beall went back in his seat as if he had been hit in the chest. "Discharge them from—? Downing, this can't be necessary. These are good men—the best. They can keep a secret—Christ, they're already sitting on a few. You don't need to—"

"Commodore. Your appreciation of them is duly noted. And I assure you, this will not in any way damage their careers. Now, if you would kindly begin the necessary paperwork..."

Beall frowned. "Not as though I have much choice, anyway."

"I'm sorry, but no, you don't."

Beall looked over at Trevor and jerked his head toward the door. "We're through. And Trev—"

Trevor heard the shift in tone, stopped.

"Sorry about your father. You too, Ms. Corcoran."

"Thank you, Uncle Richard," Trevor said. "Those were some inspired lies."

Downing shrugged, smiled as they entered the transit car.

"But how did you find out that Beall had detained me? Hell, I didn't even know you were on-planet yet—"

The car's doors closed with a rough sigh. "No, but evidently Elena did."

Trevor slid into the seat next to his sister, smiled at her. "Nice work, sis." The car started its pneumatic journey down into the residential levels of Syrtis City.

"One good rescue deserves another, I always say."

Richard leaned back as he looked at her. "You do seem remarkably well-collected after your ordeal."

"Which only goes to prove that you were right about my having missed a career in the theater," she said. "I'm just looking forward to getting into a hot bath. And then shaking. A lot."

Trevor resisted the impulse to nod in empathy. "I'm sorry, El, but I've got to ask: have you remembered anything else about the bastards?"

"No, just what I told you in the VTOL. They were careful not to talk around me and wouldn't answer questions. But they seemed impatient—as though they were waiting for orders and didn't know what to do next."

Richard nodded. "Cat's-paws. Pawns in someone else's game."

"Whose?"

"Don't know. Maybe the megacorporations—but kidnapping the daughter of a recently deceased hero is daft. Frankly, I can't see how it would benefit any of the players we know about. And I've got another mystery I'd like solved." He turned to Elena. "How in blazes *did* you know I was here already?"

"Because you've been fussing about Dad's memorial for two months, making sure we'd all be here on time, were not traveling together—and making sure it was timed so that Mom's schedule didn't allow her to come out. Don't give me the big-eyed innocent look: it might not be obvious to her, but it was to me. If the main purpose for this memorial was to honor Dad's memory, you'd have made sure that Mom was here."

Trevor was suddenly aware that his mouth was open: *What was* this *all about?*

Richard's response only made his confusion worse. "No fooling you, eh, El?"

Trevor felt the car buck sideways and then drop: they were in a descent tube, now. "If it's not too much trouble, would one of you please tell me what the hell you're talking about?"

Elena nodded toward Downing. "Dad's memorial is a cover for something else. Richard and Dad used to do this sort of thing all the time. They created social events which were an excuse for them to be in the same place at the same time—so they could get their work done. And that's what this memorial is: a cover."

Richard shook his head. "That's not entirely accurate either, Elena. Your father's become quite a provocative figure in the last three months, particularly in certain nations of the Undeveloped World. From both the standpoint of his memory, and security for his family, an immediate post-mortem ceremony on Earth would not have been prudent."

Trevor frowned. "But you didn't deny that his memorial is, at least in part, a cover for something else."

In the uncomfortable two seconds of silence that followed, Trevor felt as though the Uncle Richard he had always known was undergoing some swift and horrible transmogrification into an unknown entity, a creature which, if stuck with a pin, would bleed shadows and mist. "Why didn't you tell us?"

Downing looked at his hands. "I couldn't. Things have been changing dramatically since Parthenon. And they're about to change even more dramatically."

Elena's eyes had never left Richard's face. "You're bringing us inside, aren't you?"

Inside: the word that Trevor and Elena had adopted as the shorthand label for whatever it was that Dad and Uncle Richard did together—and could never talk about. *Inside* was the forbidden place—so forbidden that they intrinsically knew to keep Dad from learning that they even had a special word for it.

Richard had been nodding. "Yes, you're being brought inside. At the request of others."

"Others? What others?"

"That's part of what we'll be talking about after the memorial."

Elena looked up as the car began slowing. "This is where I get off."

"Not anymore." Downing's tone was sad, not imperious.

Elena stopped, half-risen, to look at him. "What do you mean?"

Trevor nodded, understanding. "He means you can't stay on your own. You were kidnapped, and we can't even be sure of the reasons yet. Right now, we've got to arrange security for you, keep you close."

"For how long?"

The car had started again; Downing looked out the narrow slit window into the rushing darkness. "I wish I could say."

ODYSSEUS

The attacks seemed to come from every direction. First a low kick, which Caine reflexively downblocked, but before he could launch into a counterpunch, he was battered back by a flurry of strikes: a downblow (fended off with a rising block), then a front snap kick that he narrowly backstepped and a quick right-left sequence of punches (inside block, outside block) followed by a roundhouse kick—

—which did not come. But having anticipated it, Caine had started to turn inside the expected arc of the kick, intending to interrupt the attack before it could come around.

But suddenly, there was no attacker there—not standing, anyway. Caine felt the sole of a small, hard foot slam into the back of his knee. He had just enough time to realize—*she dropped low and then kicked straight*—before he went down.

He broke his fall—and was then knocked flat as she landed on his back. The air went out of him with a sound that was part groan and part hoot—a noise so comical that instead of feeling disappointment at being dropped again, he started laughing into the floor mat. A moment later, he heard—and felt in her body—that she had joined in.

He rolled over—and found Opal's face very close—unnecessarily close—to his. He smiled. "You win."

"I ought to. But you're getting better. Pretty good, actually."

"Well, I have a great teacher." He decided not to move.

She apparently made a similar decision to continue their conversation nose-to-nose. "And I'll keep teaching you—as long as you keep it our secret."

"That's a deal. Time for another fall?"

"Yeah, I guess I've got enough time to kick your butt again." Her eyes widened. "Shit! The time! I'm late!" Her weight was suddenly off of him, departing with a farewell waft of her shampoo.

"Late? Late for what?"

"For a meeting with our favorite spy guy, Downing.

He paged me just before we started. Shall I send him your regards?"

Caine just looked at her. "Have a nice time."

"Yeah. Sure. It'll be a party. I'll be dancing on his desk."

"That I would like to see. But maybe you'll consent to tell me about all the fun later. Over dinner?"

He held his breath a little: *It's a small step, but all our prior meals together have been happenstance or convenience. This time, there's no real reason for us to eat together—which means it can almost be interpreted as a "first date."*

His anxiety over her response was short-lived: her smile was quick and very wide. "Great! That's—great! I'll call you as soon as Scarecrow lets me loose."

"Deal."

Chapter Thirty-Three

MENTOR

For the first time since making planetfall, Downing entered the suite's living room and relaxed. Reclining in the one of the adjustable console chairs, he glanced at his secure palmtop: the "message waiting" light was flashing. *Oh, bloody hell.*

He listened carefully to the other sounds in the suite. Further down the hall, Trevor was audibly unpacking; further still, he could hear Elena filling the tub in the master bath. So he had a few moments of privacy, at least. He opened the communication.

It was not voice, but coded text. The encryption program worked briefly and then revealed the message.

It was Opal's response to his pre-landing page. It began without preamble.

> Downing, you have one hell of a nerve arriving on Mars and immediately repeating your instructions that I must make my relationship with Caine "more intimate."

Right now, everything I have done with Caine is a lie—and will continue to be a lie, until I can tell him that I'm your hired eyes, ears, and guard dog.

When I can tell Caine the truth, I will—very gladly—take the next step in my relationship with him. Until then, I won't. If that makes me a failure, then fire me.

Downing sighed, wrote back:

And what if *he* initiates intimacy with *you*?

Downing considered expanding upon that response, realized Opal was never going to answer such a poignant challenge anyway, and so simply sent that one line, which—he was fairly sure—would help erode her resolve when and if Caine pushed past his gentlemanly reserve.

Disgusted at himself, Downing tossed the palmtop down on the table. He had thought, twenty-two years ago, that the worst part of this job would be setting aside one's own scruples. While that had been miserable enough, the worst part of it was actually coercing and compelling people who still had scruples to set theirs aside, also.

"Wow," said Trevor, entering the room with an appraising glance at the walls. "Got enough space here, Uncle Richard?"

Downing schooled his expression into one of casual congeniality. "I hope so—because this is going to be home for all of us, now."

"And who is 'all of us'?"

"You, me, Elena, two security I brought from Earth, your three friends from the SEAL detachment—"

"What?"

"They've just become our—or more properly, your—assets. We need the very best security, and more of it."

"Why?"

"Well, I would think that after your sister was kidnapped, you'd hardly need to ask. But there is another reason: Caine Riordan."

Trevor nodded. "The guy we were babysitting on the sub—and who was with Dad, when—" His voice lowered, became unsteady. He looked away.

Downing watched Trevor's jaw steady into a rigid line: *Poor Trev.* He had loved his father—maybe too much—but they had never worked out a medium through which to exchange and share their emotions. Perhaps that was because Trevor had been the son that IRIS had orphaned. He had only been six months old when Nolan's life became hostage to the tasks which ultimately consumed all his time and energy. The more school plays and baseball games that Nolan missed, the harder Trevor tried—as if his father's absence signified indifference to his achievements. *Would Trevor have gone to the Academy, and then into the Teams, if it had been otherwise?* Downing paused: *How would it be if I reached out—right now? This very second?*

But the moment had passed: Trevor had turned back to face him, eyes so grave and controlled that they looked more like rectangles than ovals. "Okay, so I'm in: what's my job?"

Downing adopted a similarly businesslike tone. "You will coordinate special security, for now. Later on, you might oversee strike operations."

"Okay, but you still haven't told me who, or what, I'm working for."

"It's called IRIS: the Institute for Reconnaissance, Intelligence, and Security."

"Wait, I know that name. That's your little think tank in Newport."

"It's a lot more than a think tank. And it's not so little."

"So it's a US intel agency? What umbrella is it under? Navy?"

"Well—no. It's not under any umbrella."

Trevor's eyes widened a bit. "It reports directly to the Executive Branch?"

"For the most part."

Eyes wider, his eyebrows moved upward. "What the hell does that mean?"

"Trev, I can't give you a detailed explanation right now. But I can reassure you that joining it is not a contravention of your Constitutional loyalty oath."

Trevor's eyes—and eyebrows—returned to a more quiescent state. "Okay, we'll sweat the details later. What needs doing right now?"

Pure Trevor: always ready to act. "First, we ensure the safety of our group."

ODYSSEUS

Halfway through Caine's post-sparring shower, his apartment's fire alarm started shrilling.

He stumbled on the wet tiles as he tried to make it out the bathroom door in a single long stride. He caught himself on the countertop, the fingers of one hand hooking down securely into the basin. But for some reason, he wasn't steadying as quickly as he expected; staring into the sink, the drain swam lazily at the approximate center of his blurring vision. *What the—*

O_2 leak? CO_2 concentration too high? But no—there was also a new smell, slightly medicinal. Like—gas! Christ—assassins. Again.

Grabbing a towel and sticking it under the shower's spray, he dropped to the floor . . .

MENTOR

Downing handed the rest of the group's dossiers to Trevor. He glanced at them, then asked, "So, am I Riordan's only security?"

"No. Primary overwatch is assigned to another former sleeper—Opal Patrone. Captain, US Army."

"What's her story?"

"On the surface, she's simply a security asset that we can be sure is *not* a double agent."

"And beneath the surface?"

"She's close security for Riordan. He doesn't know. And neither do you."

"Understood." Trevor looked sideways at Downing. "'Close security,' huh? Just how *close* is she?"

"Yes, you have the idea. But there's no intimacy— yet."

Trevor shifted in his seat. "Christ, Uncle Richard, what do you use to check up on them? Hidden cameras?"

"No, her reports. Yes, I know: it's a beastly thing to monitor, but it's imperative, in this case. If she doesn't become intimate with Riordan, then she has no plausibly deniable reason to remain with him almost constantly. Which is the kind of overwatch that we need to maintain on him."

"Why?"

"Because, before Parthenon, there were at least three attempts on his life." Trevor sat up straighter. "That's why your father had you babysit him a mile under the Atlantic."

"Christ, Dad never told me that. Neither did Riordan—although we had orders not to talk to him, anyway. Something about minimizing potential intel leaks?"

"Yes—which reminds me: we have to give you a code name. Homeric. Your father's idea, I'm afraid."

"Okay."

"Your code name is 'Telemachus.'"

"Okay, so I'm Telemachus. What's Riordan's code name?"

"Odysseus."

"Wait: if I remember my *Odyssey*, that makes me his son."

"What is it with you Corcorans and these code names? They're just labels. Telemachus was a loyal and helpful family member: good enough?"

"Sure. I guess. So, what's the larger mission?"

Downing feigned puzzlement. "What do you mean?"

"Uncle Richard, please. Elena's right: the memorial is a cover, and bringing all these people out to Mars means you're assembling a team of some sort. And a team means a mission."

Downing relented. "We'll talk about that tomorrow. With everyone present. Be advised, though, that once we depart from Mars, your security personnel will return Earthside, where they will await further instructions."

The door chimes—a muted three-tone hum—sounded the same moment that Richard's collarcom beeped. He tapped it, listened to his earbud. "Yes? Very well; send her straight back."

"We have a visitor?"

Richard replaced the handset. "Yes." He rose. "She's expected. Actually, she's late."

ODYSSEUS

The door leading from the foyer into the living room was already opening, and whoever it was, they moved pretty quickly. From his prone position, half in the hallway closet—wet towel over his nose and mouth—Caine could see that the intruder was in a light-duty hard suit, the helmet's black visor sweeping from side to side.

But where's the gun? Caine disciplined his curiosity: *you don't have time to look, and there's at least one more moving in behind him.* He tightened his grip on the plastic comb he had snagged while crawling out of the bathroom and pushed.

The comb shoved the hastily grabbed butcher's knife into the access panel he had just pried open at the bottom of the closet wall. Caine turned his face away as the steel blade made contact with both of the two splicing screws that connected the apartment's wiring to the community power mains.

There was an angry squeal, a sharp blue-white flash—and then all the lights went out. From the entryway, a sputter of curses rose in response.

Before the first monosyllabic profanity was complete, Caine had the knife in hand and was taking long leaping strides to close the distance.

Before the emergency lights snapped on, he saw the first intruder's bioreadout panel glowing. On a hardsuit, that marked the location of the left clavicle. *But my target is fifteen centimeters lower.*

Caine leaped, knife point first.

The emergency lights flickered as the knife point hit, and bucked against, the body armor. But, glancing downward, it found and slid through the articulation point that separated the breast plates from the belly panels. The intruder—visor now up, and struggling with a pair of night-vision goggles—grunted and went down backward.

Caine, landing on top of him and already trying to locate the other assassin, realized that his knife hand was now coated in hot, rushing wetness. He pulled himself up, hoping he could get to the other attacker before—

But he never made it to his feet. The world—sounds and images both—seemed to be rushing away from him, pulled further and further down a darkening tunnel. *The gas. I've got to...*

He was sucked into the tunnel, felt it close around and behind him.

TELEMACHUS

Trevor noticed that the small hand shaking his was both very shapely and very strong. Uncle Richard was talking—as usual—but the words were a lot less interesting than the eyes staring up into his. Richard was saying something that sounded like: "Opal Patrone, I'd like you to meet Trevor Corcoran."

"Pleased," she said. "Wait—Corcoran? I'm sorry; are you the admiral's son? I mean, the late—" She blushed: it looked good on her, he thought. "I'm sorry. I didn't mean—I didn't know—"

"No, that's fine," he reassured her. "That's okay."

"Well, I just—I just want to say that I'm very sorry about your father. I only met him once, right before—" Her blush intensified.

Trevor sent some reassuring pressure through their handshake. "I appreciate your sympathy. Really."

She smiled, nodded gratefully, glanced over at Downing—and when she did so, her expression became a whole lot less friendly. "Sorry I didn't get here on time. I got busy. With work."

"I see." Downing stared at her gi. "Well, I won't keep you long. I just wanted to get our security precautions put right, which means that you two had to meet. Opal is the only security asset who is not in your table of organization, Trevor."

"Since you bring it up, Uncle Richard, who else *is* in my tee-oh-oh?"

"Just your three friends from the Teams and the two associates of mine that I mentioned earlier."

"Yeah, 'mentioned.' Details, please?"

"One is on detached duty from the Special Forces. He's an expert at working with indigenous groups. He had five combat commands leading two-stick A-teams on extended insurgency ops."

"The other?"

"Secret Service. On leave. President Liu will express

official regret over his resignation a month from now. Of course, she's already approved it."

"I see. IRIS seems poised to become the beneficiary of several 'fortuitous retirements.'"

"So it would seem. Get them working together ASAP, Trevor: they're all going to be needed at tomorrow's memorial service—particularly given the incident with your sister."

One of Opal's eyebrows rose slightly. "And what incident is that?" she asked.

"Ms. Corcoran was—abducted—late last night."

"And?"

Downing's eyes flicked over at Trevor momentarily. "Commander Corcoran recovered her. Unharmed."

Both of Opal's eyebrows were now raised as she looked over at Trevor. She looked both impressed and mischievous as she asked, "Tough day at the office, Commander?"

Trevor smiled. "I command a desk, now. And I'm only a *lieutenant* commander."

"No, you're not." Downing pushed a small black box across the table. Trevor frowned as he opened the box, glanced down—and kept staring.

Richard's smile was somewhat pinched. "A field promotion, lad. You've earned it, and you might have to re-earn it many times over in the coming months."

"But I wasn't up for—"

Richard waved his hand in a circle to indicate the suite. "It may not look like it, Trevor, but this is the field. And this promotion is necessary."

"Necessary?"

"The more direct authority *you* have, the more direct authority *we* have."

Trevor nodded. "Got it."

Opal put out her hand. "Let me be the first to offer you my congratulations, *Commander*."

"Not so fast." Downing jumped in before Trevor could respond. "You're in line for your own congratulations—Major."

"Me? Major?" Her voice was high and girlish with surprise: Opal salvaged the moment by getting tough. "Okay, Downing; what gives?"

"I beg your pardon?"

"What's with the promotions?"

"I think I just explained that. The more rank you have—"

"That's not what I mean. There are two times you get promotions in the field; right after the shit has hit the fan and empty saddles need to be refilled, or right *before* you expect the nastiness to hit the spinning blades. And since we don't seem to be in foxholes already—"

Downing nodded slowly. "I see your point. And yes, I suspect things are going to go pear-shaped sooner rather than later. But not in the way you mean, Major. I only know this: the more rank you have, the more orders you can give, and the easier it is to requisition, commandeer, or just plain nick what you need. And that could become very important in the coming months."

Opal shrugged. "So—I'm a major. New pay grade." She laughed. "My salary has just jumped from nothing to next-to-nothing. What *will* I spend it all on?"

"I'm sure you'll think of something. Here."

Downing pushed another black box toward her, along with a rather well-stuffed envelope. "The contents of the box, you know. The envelope is current—plus back—pay."

Opal opened the envelope, removed its contents:

various bills of various colors. "What the hell is this? Monopoly money?"

"Universal Economic Credits. Thirty-two thousand, one hundred ten of them, to be exact."

"Great. What the hell *are* they?"

Trevor leaned towards her, still grinning. "Don't worry: they're for real."

"Okay, so I've got a fistful of somethings. Now, why don't you tell an old-timer like me what I really want to know: what's it worth in *dollars*, please?"

"The credit's value—which is, very roughly, an average of the c-dollar and the euro—is about one-point-one c-dollars. So you have about thirty-five thousand, three hundred dollars."

Opal looked down. "Well, this funny-money looks a lot more serious now." She thumbed through it, looked at Downing. "Damn. Is this back pay for the whole fifty years I spent as a popsicle?"

"No."

"So this is just for the time since you thawed me out?"

"Correct."

Opal seemed to run the numbers mentally. "Okay, not that I'm eager to be poor again, but that jump in pay grade makes me at least a full bird colonel."

Downing looked her directly in the eye. "As I've already said, you are on special duty. This is special pay."

Downing frowned when the commmplex's handset started chirping: an external call. He picked it up: his frown transmogrified into an expressionless mask that brought Trevor to his feet. "Yes," Richard said. "I see. Do it quietly. Yes, I want the whole squad. I will be on site in"—he checked his watch—"six minutes. Update me as you learn more."

Downing was up beside Trevor in a single motion. "There's been another—incident. Major, you come with me. Trevor, you are acting site CO."

"What's happening?"

"Not sure. There was a fire alarm—and some irregularities—in the suite that the Major shares with Mr. Riordan."

Opal's voice was so tightly controlled that it conveyed more panic than a scream. "Where's Caine?"

"No word on that yet. He's probably fine."

Opal did not blink. "Or he could be dead."

Downing moved toward the door. "We should hurry."

Chapter Thirty-Four

TELEMACHUS

Trevor watched the small gathering in the ecumenical chapel rise and approach the side room in which he was waiting. *For them, it's all about what Nolan Corcoran had said, or what he did, or what he stood for. All that is fine. And all that will be forgotten. But this endures: he was my Dad, and I loved him, and I didn't say it enough. And now I never can.*

Except Trevor couldn't afford to feel that, not now. Officially, he was here as one of the major mourners: the grieving son. In actuality, he was working: coordinating the activities of his meager security staff while keeping an eye out for the incipient signs of yet another incident. He angled toward Elena, who had emerged from the chapel and quickly became the focus for a spontaneous receiving line. He slipped in behind her, nodded for Rulaine—Downing's green beanie—to rotate into a position that could cover the area he'd vacated.

Trevor leaned toward Elena's ear. "How are you holding up?"

Elena was looking intently at the chapel doorway,

where Caine was emerging—walking with a limp and his left arm in a softcast and sling. "I'm fine, Trev. I've done my own mourning for Dad."

He followed her eyes; she was looking at Caine, all right. She wasn't blinking. "You know his story?"

"I'm sorry: who are you talking about?"

"Him. The guy you're looking at. Riordan."

"The one who was attacked last night?"

"Yup, that's him. He was with Dad—at the end— you know."

"I thought I heard that."

Trevor leaned back to look at his sister. "El, you must know who he is. He's the guy from the Parthenon Dialogs. You know—exosapients on Delta Pavonis? That's *him.*"

"Yeah—I guess I just wasn't thinking about that." She looked away—as if it were a considerable effort— and smiled at her brother.

"Oh? And what were you thinking about, Sis?"

"How people connected to Dad seem to be targeted. Maybe Dad was himself."

"We'll find out at the meeting with Richard, right after we wrap up here. Seems they've got the final coroner's report."

Trevor saw Opal edge into the reception hall behind Caine. *I wonder if she'll see me looking at her—*

Elena turned back to him during a short lull in the commiserating handshakes. "You're staring, Trev."

"Uh...oh. Yeah."

"Who is she?"

"Her? Oh, she's his—" And the words staggered to a stop in his head and his mouth: *I haven't lied to my sister since I was a bratty younger brother.* But

Richard had been very clear regarding the confidentiality of Opal's real job.

"His what?" Elena's head was tilted to one side, the way it did when she was on the scent of a secret—or knew that she was being snowed.

"She's his friend. And she works for Richard. Security. Seems she and Riordan have a lot in common, though."

"How so?" Elena's voice sounded strangely flat.

"They're both reanimated sleepers. He was down for fourteen years, all told."

Now her voice sounded careful, as if she were weighing every word. "That must have been very hard on him—losing so much time that way."

"More than you know. He hardly remembers a thing from the last few days of his old life. Shame. Seems like a nice enough guy."

"You *know* him?" She had turned to face him.

"Well, yeah—sort of. I babysat him on a sub for a couple of weeks." He looked at her. "Didn't I tell you?"

She was already looking back at Riordan. "No. You didn't. And what about the girl—I mean, the woman?"

"She was in cold storage for fifty years. What she remembers no longer exists. She's entirely alone in the world."

Elena turned back towards him. "Uh-oh."

"What do you mean, 'Uh-oh'?"

Elena smiled. "I mean, I know that tone of voice. Trevor, look at her. She and Riordan are—well, it looks like they're more than friends." She put a hand on his arm. "I'm sorry—I just don't want to see you get hurt."

"Yeah. Me neither." He checked his watch; 1258 hours, local. Which meant that, any minute now—

A medium-sized, nondescript man in black fatigues

slipped into the room sideways. He scanned faces, stopped when he saw Trevor, nodded once. Trevor leaned toward Elena's ear. "I'll be back in a few."

"Trevor, the guests—"

"Are all trying to talk to you because you're the pretty one—and none of them knew Dad personally, so I'd be happy to stop playing charades. Besides, I've got to get back to work."

She nodded, scanned down the dwindling line. Caine was toward the end.

Trevor walked back to the position he had originally occupied. Rulaine saw him approach, moved toward the other side of the hall.

The nondescript man met Trevor at the exact point Rulaine had vacated. "How's it going, boss?"

"All quiet. What's the word, Stosh?"

"Lot of shack chat. By the way, is it true?"

"About what?"

"That I've got to stand a little straighter when I salute you?"

"Like you ever salute me."

"Hey—I salute you. Sometimes. Sir."

"Yeah—but I mean without that big shit-eating grin."

"Well, it's just hard not to remember you blowing chow during the last run of hell week."

"Oh, you just loved that."

"Made you the grunt you are today, Commander."

"You're a sadist, Chief."

"Masochist, too—since I asked to serve under you. Figured you'd want to return the favor to your old instructor."

"Right now, I just want my old instructor to clue me in on the shack chat."

"Aye aye, sir. Hardly know where to start."

"The most unusual stuff first."

"That's just it, sir: it's all unusual."

Trevor looked over at the man who had nearly busted him out of his SEAL training: Chief Petty Officer Stanislaus Witkowski was nearly fifty, unflappable, and renowned for his extraordinary capacity for understatement. "It's *all* unusual?"

"Seems so to me." He nodded in the direction of the receiving line. "For instance, take what happened to that guy last night."

"Riordan?"

"Yep. Something funky about that whole deal."

"Well, sure: someone tried to off him in his room. And then tried to make it look like arson."

Stosh shook his head. "Not what I mean, boss. First off, do you know that Riordan apparently tagged one of the bad guys with a knife?"

"What?"

"Yeah. Turns out the blood the cops found on the floor wasn't Riordan's."

"How do you know that?"

Stosh grabbed a canapé off a passing tray. "From a friend in base security. We've bent our elbows on the same bar a few times. He's Force Recon, so I have to keep telling him how he's really supposed to do his job."

"Okay, so how does your leatherneck beer-buddy know anything about the blood on the floor of Riordan's apartment? How does he even know that anything happened to Riordan?"

"Well, that's where the serious weirdness kicks in. Seems that when the bad guys broke into Riordan's apartment, the alert didn't go to the police first. It went straight to the duty officer in the State Department's Marine contingent."

"What? How?"

"My jarhead pal didn't know. But out he goes on the call. They get to the suite and there's already one guy he knows—a 'translator'—on site, checking Riordan's vitals."

"Some translator."

"Yeah, I'd say his spook-cover is pretty much blown. Anyway, they're mopping the blood up off the floor and the translator grabs a Marine to evac Riordan to the base hospital. But so far as my pal can see, Riordan's not wounded."

"They sent him to the *base* hospital?"

"Yeah. Now, as he's being ferried off, the police arrive and start arguing procedure and maintaining a pristine forensic site and etcetera etcetera etcetera. Result: jurisdictional tug of war. The locals are grabbing what they can, just as the station chief shows up from the State Department, claiming precedence due to matters of national security. That three-way clusterfuck goes on until your pal Downing shows up. A few words with each of the contenders and all is calm."

"So the blood—?"

"So some of the blood has already been taken off site by the locals. They type it: A negative. But when I spoke to the orderly who was present when they admitted Riordan to the base hospital, he was O positive."

"Wait: I don't get it. If the hospital blood-typed Riordan, he *had* to be wounded, right?"

"Nope: no sign of a wound. But they *already* knew Riordan's blood type at the hospital. Before he ever arrived."

Trevor frowned. "Is he in an armed-service database?"

"Nope. I told you it was weird. Seems our non-bleeding Mr. Riordan was nonetheless rushed into surgery a few minutes after he arrived. And that's where my buddy's story loses sight of Riordan."

"But that's not the end of it?"

"Nope. I've got another pal in the Russian Ministry of Foreign Affairs. We argue the merits of bourbon and vodka occasionally."

"And he figures into this—how?"

"Well, late last night, my pal Sasha comes hang-dogging into the Red Planet Lounge, looking like he'd lost his best buddy."

"What had happened?"

"Well—he'd lost his best buddy. Turns out his good friend was reportedly knifed near the dives around the passport and quarantine control zones. Or at least, that's what the bigwigs in the Russian Embassy told Sasha."

"What do you mean?"

"I mean that Sasha's deceased buddy was reportedly alone when he was attacked, so there were no witnesses. And when Sasha tried to track down more information about it, he ran into a wall: his pal's murder had been called in by 'an anonymous local tip.' So Sasha got really curious, and tried to get a look at the forensics report of the crime site: nada. No cooperation: just a lot of locked jaws and unfriendly eyes, both from the intel guys in the Foreign Ministry and the watch sergeant in the local precinct. But because Sasha is the senior NCO in the Ministry's security contingent, he has access to all the medical records of his team."

"And?"

"And his pal, the one supposedly knifed in an alley, had a very interesting blood-type."

"Let me guess: A negative."

"Bingo: same type as on the floor in Riordan's suite. Doesn't prove anything, but—"

"Yeah: 'but.'" *What the hell was going on? Why would the Russians have sent someone after Caine?* That made less than no sense—unless these Russians were moonlighting, were being paid to do it by someone other than their superiors.

"Commander, even if the Russians were involved somehow, there's something I can't figure."

"What's that, Stosh?"

"Well—the outcome. They bust in on Riordan and through some miracle, he takes one out. But that means there must have been at least two intruders. Otherwise, who removed the body of the first guy that Riordan tagged? But if there were two attackers, the second guy should have been able to grease Riordan and *then* remove his buddy's body. But our guys find Riordan still alive, just unconscious. It doesn't add up."

. "No, it doesn't, Chief. You've got more?"

"Yeah—but not on this."

"What on?"

Witkowski looked down, moved one foot slowly toward the other and away again. "Boss, some of this—well, some of this is about your dad. Sort of."

Trevor frowned. "Go ahead, Chief."

"Yes, sir. Well, one of the ratings who was on liberty last night was new to the team—just got in

a few days ago. In fact, he arrived on the ship that
your pal Downing came in on."

"So he's just in from Earth."

"No, sir, that's the weird part. He was stationed
out in the asteroids at a secure site. And although
Downing came in from Earth, he changed ships along
the way. And conducted a little business beforehand."

"Such as?"

"Well, it gets pretty thirdhand, here. But here's
how it seemed to go down.

"Our newbie from the asteroids pulled special duty
as security on board a Navy transport. It was carrying a replacement crew for a patrol boat that was
approaching Mars with a government clipper in tow.
A day before the rendezvous, our newbie is standing
a comm watch when the transport makes contact with
the patrol boat. It turns out the guy minding the
secure lasercom on the patrol boat is his buddy from
Basic. Said buddy shares some interesting scuttlebutt
about the clipper's departure from low Earth orbit.
Turns out that rather than heading straight for Mars,
the clipper went way up out of the ecliptic and picked
up a small package—less than a cubic meter. Downing was the only one who knew the coordinates, and
later, he cryoed the whole crew just before docking
with the patrol boat."

"Ooooo. Cloak and dagger. Frozen men tell no tales."

"It gets better. Before our newbie from the asteroids
signs off, his buddy proposes they share a meal during
the crew swap. So the next day, the Navy transport
makes rendezvous with the patrol boat. But before the
crew swap, the transport sends its medical officer and
the XO aboard the patrol boat. About an hour goes

by. Then comes the green light for the crew swap. Our newbie on the transport expects to find his friend waiting for him. What he finds is Downing, the XO, and the medical officer."

"Just them?"

"They were the only ones he saw—awake, that is. Seems that the crew of the patrol boat—including our newbie's pal—were all put into cryogenic suspension by the CMO and XO before the swap. Just like the clipper's crew. Meaning that Downing built a one-hundred-percent info firewall around his activities from the time he left Earth.

"Then all the cryocells—from both the clipper and the patrol boat—were transferred to the Navy transport. Which was also given new orders."

"Not back to the asteroid belt?"

"Nope: a deep-space rendezvous with the next outbound shift carrier. And if I was a betting man—and I have been known to indulge in that vice—I'd take decent odds that both cryoed crews are already outsystem, the whole bunch of them in some popsicle holding yard at Alpha Centauri. Or beyond."

Jesus H. Christ: what the hell was Uncle Richard up to? "You mentioned something about my father?"

"Yeah. When they were moving the cryocells, they moved some cargo, too. One item was a coffin for space burial. Our new guy—given his EVA rating—was sent to check out its seal integrity. He recognized the occupant: it was your father. In full dress whites."

Trevor's first reflex was one of the most useful he had acquired during more than a decade of active service: to put on a poker face when his mind became a roiling chaos of conflicting ideas and emotions. What the hell was going on? His father had wanted to be buried around another star, if possible, but his own instructions had precluded that: after Parthenon, the outbound cargo priorities became absolutely rigid. But Dad's body was now outward bound for Alpha Centauri—and without consulting his family? What the hell was Richard playing at?

And in the very moment that he decided to confront Richard about it, Trevor realized he couldn't afford to. *If I catch him on this, he'll know I'm aware that he's not coming clean with me. So he'll 'fess up to this—but then play any subsequent cards closer to his chest. If I'm to have any chance of learning the other things he might be trying to pull, then I've got to play dumb. But—I've got to watch* Richard? *Him? Of all people?*

"Commander?"

"Hmmm?"

"Orders?"

"None right now, Stosh."

"Yes, sir. And, sir?"

"Yes?"

"Condolences. Your father was an outstanding man. We were on liberty when we heard. We raised our glasses and hoo-yahed him. Three times."

Trevor kept a lump from rising into his throat. "I'm sure he heard it—and smiled."

"Yes, sir. I'm off."

Witkowski sidestepped away, finger-signed to Rulaine that he was ready to swap places. Trevor started back toward Elena, saw that the line had almost exhausted itself: Caine and Opal were next.

But then, four men entered, all wearing ties, two

with bold corporate logos. Their leader—a balding, late-middle-aged man whose generous girth was a sad compensation for his meager height, came in with his head forward, scanning aggressively. When he saw Caine, he headed straight for him—the other three in tow.

Trevor looked at Stosh—who, of course, had seen it too—and shook his head slightly. The megacorps wouldn't try anything here.

Or would they?

Chapter Thirty-Five

ODYSSEUS

Caine felt his palms grow moist as the elderly couple directly in front of him moved forward, hands extended toward the woman that was, he hypothesized, Corcoran's rather stunning daughter: straight nose, high cheekbones, large eyes, and a strong jawline blended together in a concordance of sure, graceful arcs.

"Admiring the view?"

Caine started at Opal's voice, heard the playfulness in it—but something else, as well. A hint of worry? Maybe—jealousy? He turned to confer a reassuring smile upon her—and instead found himself face to face with a tall, expressionless man. He was dimly aware that there were three other men, but could not bring himself to look away from the first one, whose features were as strangely nondescript as they were alarmingly symmetrical.

The shortest of the three men looked up. "You're Riordan, right?"

Still looking at the unblinking eyes of the smooth-faced, almost featureless, security guard, Caine nodded.

"That's me. And I'm guessing that you're from the megacorporations."

"Yeah, but let's be real clear—I'm not from CoDevCo or any of its subsidiaries." He fixed his eyes upon Caine's. "I've got a few things best said in private."

"Okay." Caine took two steps away from Opal, reached the wall: he stopped and looked at the shorter man.

Who shrugged and joined him. "Look, before we start—try not to stare at the guy, will you?"

"Stare? At which guy?"

"Our—security operative. His situation is—well, awkward. For everyone."

"What awkward situation are you talking about?"

The short man's eyes opened a little wider. "You don't know? Really?" He saw the answer in Caine's face. "He's a Tube."

"A what?"

"A Tube." Seeing that Caine still didn't understand, he emphasized. "A *test* Tube. He came to term in vitro."

Caine felt his mouth drop open. "He's a clone?"

"Shh. Not so loud. Christ, you want him to hear?"

"But I thought that cloning—"

"Look. You need to get out of your ivory tower a little more often. Yes, ex-vivo cloning of humans is against international accords. But not all places on Earth—or beyond—are under routine governmental supervision. Some aren't even under national jurisdiction anymore."

"Which is where you come in?"

"No. That has nothing to do with why I'm here."

"Then why *are* you here?"

"I'm here to tell you—first of all—that not all corporations are the same. The admiral—" he nodded at the memorial flame with a deferential lowering of his voice "—he knew that well enough. But after yesterday's events—well, some us started to worry that maybe you new guys might forget the distinctions."

You new guys. That was a mix of good and bad. Good in that it suggested that some of Nolan's old acquaintances were ready to recognize a transfer of power and authority to Downing and—God forbid—himself. Bad in that this emissary had elected to contact Caine, which suggested that his connection with Nolan's old activities was already presumed.

"Look: that last comment makes me think you're talking to the wrong person."

"Oh? Why's that?"

"Because I'm not sure what or who you mean when you're referring to 'the new guys.'"

The shorter man looked up out of narrowed eyes, then nodded once. "Maybe not. But still, I was sent to talk to you. Even if you're not one of the 'new guys.'"

"But why talk to me? I'm nobody."

"Sure. You're nobody. You're the 'nobody' who closed down CoDevCo's site manager on Dee Pee Three and then pinned back the ears of their fancy-boy, Astor-Smath, at Parthenon."

Caine managed not to wince at the slur. "You don't sound sorry that I did."

"I'm not. A lot of us aren't."

"Who's 'a lot of us'?"

"I work for an aerospace firm. And like a lot of the other industrial megacorps—well, we *like* working with government. We've got a good relationship. And I'm guessing you know that our boardrooms look like reunions for the various service academies, right?"

Caine nodded. "I've been to a few."

"So the mood upstairs in my firm—and a lot of others—is that companies must remain secondary to, and ultimately serve the interests of, nations. Period."

"I'm glad to hear it."

"Yeah—but then there are the other companies. The ex-oil companies, the consumer service industries, the 'resource extraction' firms, and big investment and credit conglomerates. They think that the rule of nations is old-fashioned, inefficient."

Caine looked down at the necktie and its almost heraldic design.

The shorter man looked down also, then rolled his eyes. "Yeah—it's getting a little crazy with the tie thing. Even with us Industrials."

"So maybe you're not so different from the other megacorps, after all."

"Look: this is just a stupid tie. Bottom line: there are certain things we Industrials will *not* do."

"Such as?"

The shorter guy took a step closer. "Look: we—I mean the Industrials—had nothing, and I mean *nothing*, to do with the abduction of Corcoran's daughter. And word on the street is that not even CoDevCo had a hand in what happened to *you* last night."

"Did CoDevCo send you to tell me that?"

"I'll tell you one more time: I'm not a messenger for those ass-lickers. But that doesn't mean that there aren't back-channel communications between my company and theirs. And I was given to understand that they had nothing to do with your—personal mishap."

"What about Ms. Corcoran?"

He looked away. "Can't say."

"Can't or won't?"

"Can't. They contacted us about you. They didn't say anything one way or the other about abducting Corcoran's daughter, and we didn't ask."

"But you're guessing that they did."

"Hey." He turned back. "I don't guess. Guessing about things like that—then talking about them—could be very unhealthy for someone in my position. So I don't do it."

"So you think it was random terrorists."

"Nah."

"Or third-world fanatics who hated Nolan."

"Christ, no. I hear this bunch were gang bangers."

"So it was one of the other blocs."

"You kidding? Among the leaders of the big powers, Corcoran is turning into some kind of folk hero. Dying at just the right moment can do that, you know."

Caine looked at the man and smiled. "So you're telling me that you're pretty sure that *no one* was behind the abduction of Corcoran's daughter."

The man smiled slowly. "Yeah, I guess—by process of elimination—that's who must be behind it. No one at all."

"Except you really don't know about CoDevCo."

"Right."

"And saying *that* doesn't get you in trouble, does it?"

His smiled broadened. "Nope. Not a bit." He straightened up, stuck out his hand. "I'm glad I was able to come and give you the inside scoop on—absolutely nothing. And on the people who have absolutely nothing to do with it."

Caine smiled. "Your failure to impart any information has been very illuminating."

He shook Caine's hand a moment longer, looked at him as if he'd first seen him that very second, and then left with a chuckle and a wave.

Caine smiled. So. CoDevCo was responsible for the move against Elena Corcoran, but not the move against him. Interesting. Probably useful. He suppressed a shudder as the short man's bland-faced security operative exited behind his employer—and then started as a hand grasped his left bicep.

"A little jumpy, are we?" Opal's frown matched her concerned tone. "What was that all about?"

"Lots. Not much. I'm not sure." He smiled down at her. "I'll figure it out later. Might concern you too, since I think it's going to concern Downing. And while we're on that topic, how's it feel taking a soldier's coin working for the Prince of Lies again?"

"Ugh. Don't remind me. But I couldn't just keep freeloading off you." Opal preempted Caine's attempt to object. "Besides, duty calls: Scarecrow's getting kind of antsy over in the corner. I think we'd better pay our respects so they can wrap things up here."

Caine nodded, turned, found Corcoran's daughter right there, staring straight at him with glass-green eyes. He extended his hand into hers, but before he could say anything, Trevor—who had apparently been at her shoulder the whole time—nodded after the corporate emissaries. "Friends of yours?"

He can't be serious— And then Caine saw Trevor's rueful grin. Caine returned it. "Yeah. Bosom buddies. Good to see you again, by the way. I wish the circumstances were different."

"Yeah, me too. I don't think you've met my sister, Elena. Elena, this is—"

Her voice was a smooth mezzo. "Trevor: I do watch the news occasionally. Mr. Riordan, a pleasure."

He looked at her directly, a little anxiously, since he

had been intermittently staring at her since entering the room.

Trevor's voice was part intrusion, but also part hint. "And *this* is Captain—excuse me, Major—Opal Patrone."

Caine became aware that he was still holding Elena's hand, pulled his back a little too quickly, smiled to cover the awkwardness, decided that he was quite an ass and should not be allowed in public. He was vaguely aware of Opal shaking Elena's hand and that she had just finished saying something in a sympathetic tone. *Good grief, I forgot to—*

"Ms. Corcoran—excuse me: I—"

"Please: call me Elena."

"Elena, I'm so sorry. About your father. I hardly know what to say. I didn't know him very long, but—"

She was not smiling, only nodding: was she angry? No; just very serious. "I know. Richard—Mr. Downing—has told me a little. I can tell that my father must have liked you. And trusted you."

And voluble Caine felt his brain lock up: what response could he make that was both reasonable and truthful? Could he really claim that he had reciprocated the trust of a man who had permitted (maybe ordered?) his fourteen-year internment in a meat locker, and who then thawed him out only to perform a politically expedient task? Could Caine claim that he had liked this august figure who also covertly manipulated people and nations and facts and events? "I only knew him a day—but I will miss him. A lot. I would like to have gotten to know him better. I think he was—a good man."

Elena had stopped nodding. Her eyes had become very grave—but he didn't feel any disapproval in them. Then she faced Trevor. "We should go. Richard's meeting is in five minutes." As she turned to leave, she looked back over her shoulder. "Thank you for coming. Please excuse us."

Trevor, with a quizzical look after his sister, shrugged an awkward farewell, and followed Elena's abrupt exit. Opal stood looking after them.

"*Soooooo*—" Opal let the vowel sound drag out— "you never met her before?"

"Uh—no. Why?"

Opal smiled sideways at him. "I guess it just looked like you wished you *had* met her before. It also looks like you're recovering from your injuries pretty fast. But I guess we'd still better keep your karate lessons on hold for now."

"Yes, but you can still critique my form over dinner."

"Oh—you mean you're hoping I'll give you a raincheck for the dinner you *didn't* bother to buy me last night?"

"Yeah." He hefted the softcast meditatively. "Sorry. I was . . . uh, detained."

"Well, I guess I'll give you another chance—but no more lame excuses about homicidal intruders and emergency surgery, okay?"

Caine nodded, saw they were among the last people in the room. "Well, I suppose we ought to head to Downing's briefing."

"I suppose." Opal looked back at the memorial flame as they walked toward the exit. "So strange."

"What is?"

"Having met the admiral only once," Opal paused as they entered the corridor and made for a nearby conference room. "He seemed like such a nice man—a fun man—"

A canny man . . . thought Caine.

"—and he seemed in good shape for his age. Amazing shape, given what I am—no, *was*—used to seeing when I met people who were in their mid-eighties. Did he have heart disease for a long time?"

"Well, he had cardiac problems for thirty-five years—but it wasn't disease: it was damage."

"Damage? How?"

"In 2083, Admiral Corcoran was the commander of the mission that went to intercept what has come to be called the 'Doomsday Rock.' You've heard of it by now, right?"

"Just that it was heading straight for us. And after that, there was a much higher commitment to space development."

"Yeah. It gave us a good scare. The rock came straight in from the far reaches of the Kuiper belt. Normally, we would have expected a culprit from that area to be a comet. Because it wasn't, we didn't see it until very late."

"Why?"

"Because comets leave visible tails of vapor and debris; asteroids do not. And it was approaching on a retrograde trajectory. Meaning less time to intercept."

"Okay, but how did Nolan get injured? EVA accident? A crash?"

Caine shook his head. "Nothing that dramatic. Just too much acceleration. For too long."

"So that's what killed him, cardiac failure?"

Downing came up behind them in the hall. "No, not cardiac failure—although it looked that way at first."

Caine glanced sharply at Downing as they entered the conference room, acoustic-damping panels lining the wall like immense gray waffles. "What do you mean? What else have you found?"

Chapter Thirty-Six

MENTOR

"We found this in Nolan." Downing moved to the head of the conference table, dimmed the lights and snapped on the display screen. The diagram of a torso—the heart outlined in muddy maroon—faded in. A moment later—in Day-Glo green—a sinuous collection of filaments sprung into existence on the heart itself, first winding along the external walls of its chambers and then sending strands into the spine and upward from there. There was a second of silence.

"What the hell is that?" Trevor's outburst was raw, emotional.

Downing shrugged. "We don't know, despite a painstaking post-mortem analysis that took Bethesda the better part of two months. Even so, they almost missed it."

Trevor gaped at the intricate windings. "They almost missed *that*?"

"Yes. Because, by the time they were conducting the post-mortem, there was almost nothing left of it. This is only an approximate reconstruction of what was in Nolan when he died. By the time they were examining his body in detail, these filaments had almost totally denatured. They deliquesced even as the specialists were trying to run tests. All that was left were traces: simple proteins, amino acids, nothing definitive."

"So, was this some kind of infection?" Elena sounded lost.

It was Opal who spoke, and with singular decisiveness. "That's no infection. Not in the regular sense of the word. Look at how it went straight from the heart toward the spine, and braided itself up toward the skull. Excuse me, Elena, Trevor, but there's no delicate way to ask these questions—"

Elena nodded. "Certainly; we understand."

"—but what was found upon examination of the cerebral cortex?"

"Nothing definitive. If there was something there, it decayed before the rest of—whatever this is."

Opal stared. "It's a parasite," she announced.

"Or—" The voice was Caine's. Downing saw him staring at the screen over steepled fingers.

"Or?" prompted Opal.

"Or it's a symbiote."

She looked surprised and turned back to the screen. Then she nodded. "He's right. There's no way—looking at this—to tell how the organism functioned in relation to its host. But if it was Nolan's cause of death—"

Caine smiled and looked at Downing. "But it wasn't, was it?"

Downing felt the small hairs on his neck rise up: *how did he know?* "No, it wasn't. At least, we have no conclusive evidence that it was."

Everyone was staring at Caine, except Elena, whose eyes were aimed off into the darkness.

Trevor sounded truculent. "Okay, I've had just about enough of this episode of Mystery Theater. This is my father we're talking about, and I'd be a lot happier if people start talking plainly."

Caine held up one hand. "Hey, look: I'm no expert. I'm just guessing."

"Yeah—but you're guessing pretty well."

Caine shrugged. "Look, Opal—Major Patrone—is the one with the zoology degree, so I'm sure she's already way ahead of me on this, but look at the lay-out of that 'organism.' And then add that to the fact that it spontaneously denatured upon the death of its host, leaving no signs of toxins or virus, or bacteria, or foreign DNA. This thing—whatever it is—broke down into the same goo that you'd get if our own biochemistries were broken down. And I'll bet the remains are a close or exact chemical match for a particular part of our bodies: our nervous system."

Downing nodded. "Caine is correct."

"So then what was it?" Trevor sounded a little more patient again.

"Best guess?" Caine shrugged. "An independent nervous system of some kind."

"Which could have turned off my father's heart."

"Maybe, Trevor, but let's look at some of the other facts." Caine's voice was calm. "First, it's a pretty extensive organism if that's its only purpose. And I do mean purpose, because I'm guessing this thing can't be natural—not in the evolutionary sense of the word."

Opal nodded. "I'm about a half-century out of date in terms of designer organisms, but this doesn't look natural at all. Particularly its speedy decomposition into materials that mimic the body's own byproducts."

"So you're saying that thing was designed to disappear as soon as it killed Dad."

"If it *did* kill him," Caine persisted. "And we're still waiting for Mr. Downing to tell us what the coroners found in that regard."

Now all the eyes came back to rest on Downing.

"They found very little—except that when they polled the chip in Nolan's coronary controller, they found that it failed to operate at the moment he went into arrest."

"Preposterous." Elena's voice was sharp, declarative. "Dad always had the best controller available, and Mom's colleagues at Johns Hopkins always reviewed his test results."

Riordan's eyes hadn't left Richard's face. "But Mr. Downing didn't say the coronary controller broke; he said that it 'failed to operate.' I'm betting that it's not a typical malfunction either, is it, Richard? Any more than the security system and power failures at Alexandria were typical malfunctions."

Trevor looked from Caine to Downing. "What are you talking about?"

Downing shrugged. "During Caine's sequestration at a safe facility in Alexandria, the internal power and security systems were mysteriously 'turned off' right before he—and Opal—were attacked there."

"You mean someone broke in and cut the systems?"

"No. That has been ruled out. It looks like they were shorted by a focused EM pulse."

"That's damn near impossible."

"Perhaps. But that is the closest the scientists can

come to an explanation of what happened—in *both* cases."

"So you're saying that this...thing"—Trevor waved at the screen—"*didn't* cause my father's death? That it was an EMP burst?"

Downing shrugged. "It's possible that this organism could have been capable of the electric discharge itself, like an eel. In that event..."

Opal frowned. "In that event, Richard, wouldn't there be other gross anatomical signs of such a trauma? And wouldn't the chemical residues be different and the controller burnt out?"

Downing sighed. "It's true that there are weakness with that explanation—but the alternative is the ranged EM pulse theory, which, as Trevor rightly points out, seems impossible."

"No, Richard, we don't know it's impossible." Caine leaned forward. "We only know that it is beyond our present capability. But so is generating, and sending, enough of an electrical spike from this filmy organism. And to have it send that discharge straight into Nolan's cardiac controller? That's a feat of bioengineering that's at least as 'impossible' as a focused EM pulse. More so, I should think."

It was Elena who engaged the conundrum head-on. "So what is your point, Mr. Riordan?"

"I'm saying that there may be a connection between the controller malfunction and this organism, but it may not be the simple connection we're postulating. Even if this organism was the means whereby Nolan was killed, that only gives us more questions to ask: how was it implanted, and when, and by whom?"

Elena nodded. "Perhaps by whoever put in the

coronary controller. Probably the last time it was replaced."

"Right. But that's how many years ago? And how did they—whoever 'they' are—manage to get the organism to respond, to cause his cardiac failure, so soon after Parthenon?"

Elena was staring at the strange tendrilled mass on the screen. "It would mean that someone had to be able to send commands to this 'thing.'"

Opal shrugged. "Which makes it an even more amazing piece of bioengineering. And that still doesn't explain how none of Nolan's interior tissue shows any of the signs of thermic trauma that would be consistent with electric discharge."

Trevor had nodded at each separate point. "Okay—so let's assume this 'organism' didn't kill my father. Which means it was put in for a different reason."

Caine pulled closer to the table. "And, therefore, maybe by entirely different persons with entirely different motives."

"Okay." Trevor kept nodding. "But either—or both—of those persons would have to know about his cardiac weakness. And both can use his treatment visits as either a way to insert a foreign body—the organism—or to fiddle with his coronary controller."

Opal leaned forward. "Well, at least you can find out who performed the last surgery for his controller upgrade. Someplace in that file, there is the name of a person we can interrogate: if not the surgeon, then a nurse or technician or somebody who—"

Downing shook his head. "No."

Opal and Trevor looked at Downing in surprise. Elena just looked. Caine didn't bother: he was the one who answered: "Because an investigation would reveal to them that we're aware of their actions. And that we know what to look for from this point forward. And that will render this knowledge useless: they'll change their game. Besides, we don't know that this organism was malign. For all we know it was benign—or even beneficial. Maybe Nolan's cardiac weakness would have been more profound without it. Maybe the organism was turned off along with the controller—"

Downing blinked: *Crikey, he has a point—*

"—But even if the organism was beneficial, it's pretty clear that whoever put it there wanted to remain anonymous. And something else is pretty clear: whoever did either or both of these things has access to some technology that defies the boundaries of what we generally consider possible. That's got to be factored into all future operations."

Elena had half risen. "I don't mean to be rude, but this seems a likely point for me to excuse myself. From the sound of it, you are about to begin secret discussions with persons who are evidently going to be the new 'insiders,' Uncle Richard." She looked around the table meaningfully.

Downing waved her back down. "That is true. And you need to be a part of those discussions."

"Uncle Richard, I haven't the qualifications or the desire—"

"Actually, for what I'm announcing today, you have urgently needed qualifications. And as for what you desire—I'm afraid that doesn't really factor into our decisions."

"So now you're telling me what to do, Richard? On what authority?"

She's got her father's anger, too. "Let's not call it authority; let's call it an invitation—which you must accept because of your obligations."

That stopped her. "My obligations? To whom, or what?"

"To your father: his life, his work, his legacy."

"Richard, you'll have to come up with a more compelling recruiting pitch than some vague—"

"Elena, this isn't my idea, and this isn't my pitch."

"Oh? Then whose is it?"

Richard allowed himself to smile. "The request was made by a group calling themselves the Dornaani."

Silence. *God, how I do love shutting them all up. And those priceless, confused expressions. Except Caine, damn him. Those suddenly wider eyes: he's already half-guessed what I'm leading up to. Nolan was right about him.*

Opal was the first to speak. "Who or what are the Door-Nonny? Secret society? Rock band?"

"No, Major. The Dornaani are exosapients."

Chapter Thirty-Seven

ODYSSEUS

Exosapients. Of course. "That's why you had this meeting scheduled right behind Nolan's memorial service. And that's why you had it on Mars. It's all cover for this briefing, and puts us in a spot where there's far less press and far fewer possibilities for intelligence leaks."

Downing nodded. "I'm afraid so."

Judging from Trevor's face, Nolan's son still wasn't sure that he had heard what he had just heard about exosapients. Opal was that much further behind the leading edge of the culture-shock wave. "What do you mean, 'exosapients'? You mean, the critters—er, folks—that Caine met on Delta Pavonis?"

Caine shook his head, kept his eyes on Richard. "No. These are different. Not from Dee Pee Three. They're what you and I grew up calling 'aliens.'"

Opal gaped, then grinned—still not believing, he guessed: "Oh, you mean little green men. 'Take me to your leader' and all the rest?"

Downing shook his head. "They're rather more a gray

410

olive-drab, according to the single image they relayed. And they do not wish to be taken to our leaders. Nor do they expect our senior leaders to be taken to them. They are calling for a delegation to attend a meeting that is part induction ceremony and part summit."

Opal's grin became open-mouthed disbelief. "You're serious."

"I'm afraid so, yes."

Caine noted that Elena was the first to recover, pick up the earlier threads. "And these—Dornaani—asked for *me* to attend this . . . meeting?"

Downing shrugged. "Not by name; they simply asked for an adult child of Nolan Corcoran."

Now it was Elena's turn to be flustered. She looked around the table, as if their eyes were accusing her of something. "Well—send Trevor. He's part of your organization now, anyway. And he's military, so he'll be of interest to them—and of use to you. Good grief, I'm just a semiotic anthropologist—"

Downing smiled. "I seem to recall that your appointment to the State Department is as one of the section heads of the xenoculture analysis task force."

Trevor leaned back. "So, I'm off the hook?"

"No. We can't know which of you they will consider Nolan's best representative, so I need both of you. And, Trevor, you will also be the delegation's unofficial expert in military technology. And we will definitely need a pair of eyes and ears that are dedicated to immediate security. So that's your other job. And since we need at least two people watching our backs, we'll be taking Major Patrone, as well."

"Whoa, wait a minute. You're taking me to meet ET? I don't think so."

"Major, I think so, and I say so."

"And what is my essential expertise for this mission?"

"That you can help keep us out of trouble and can follow orders." Downing's head was suddenly very stiff and erect upon his neck. "You all seem to think that this assignment is voluntary. With the exception of Caine and Elena, you are active duty members of the United States Armed Forces and these are your new orders. End of discussion." Caine could tell from the pause that Downing had saved him for last. No reason to wait for it.

"So let me guess; I'm coming along, too."

"Of course."

"What happened to my new life of freedom, Richard?"

"I'm afraid you'll have to take that up with the President, Caine."

Oh, shit. "What do you mean?"

"I mean that President Liu is formally asking you to serve your country, the Commonwealth, and your planet by accepting the position of Senior Negotiator of the Deputation."

Caine sighed, then nodded. "Okay. But—fair warning—I'm no politician."

"And no one is asking you to be one. You will not make policy; that is for other members of the delegation. Your role is as liaison; you are the conduit for contact and exchange."

"So I get to make the introductions at the cocktail parties?"

"No: you get to decide how and when to communicate with the other species at the meeting."

"Other species? As in, *many* species?"

"There are five, counting the Dornaani."

Caine felt the urge to throw up. "Richard, I don't have the training for this sort of thing."

"Neither does anyone else. And you are the only human who has ever handled a first-contact situation. And successfully, I might add. There are no other meaningful credentials for such a role—an assertion which was made by the Confederation task force that determined the complement of the delegation three weeks ago. Indeed, you were the only nominee for Senior Negotiator."

Great. "Lucky me."

"Actually, I think you'd be rather honored, given some of the people who nominated you."

Caine wanted not to ask, but he couldn't resist. "Who?"

"Ching. Sukhinin. Visser. MacGregor. And even Gaspard."

"What? Did they reconvene Parthenon just to decide how to staff the delegation?"

"More or less. The delegation had to have representation from each bloc, and staffed by people who had sufficiently high clearance. And two had to be senior enough politicos to make diplomatic decisions, on the spot, if need be."

"And who are those two?"

"Visser accepted the first chair on the delegation. Durniak is joining us as her advisor and second chair.

"The rest of the team are all leaders in their respective fields. Bernard Hwang was tapped to be our expert in life sciences. Lemuel Wasserman—yes, the nephew of the inventor of the Wasserman drive—will be our engineering and physics analyst. And Sanjay Thandla is going to be our expert in IT, data management, and robotics."

"What?" Opal sounded distressed. "No assistants? Who'll go get our coffee?"

"We will. No assistants. That was the decision made by the commission, since the Dornaani restricted us to a ten-person delegation." Downing leaned back. "Questions?"

I've got to ask. "Richard, why did the Dornaani contact us now?"

"They didn't say. But I have a hypothesis: convenience. The Dornaani indicated that we will not be the only first-time participants at this convocation." He frowned. "What troubles me is that the Dornaani also indicated that they make first contact soon after a species has achieved interstellar travel capabilities. I think it odd that they have two new races standing for membership during a single gathering."

Caine nodded. "I agree. Very odd."

Opal was looking back and forth between them. "Okay, I give up; what's odd about having one meeting instead of two separate ones?"

"If Caine and I are thinking similarly, that is not what we find suspicious, Major. Rather, it's the fact that two separate species would be attaining interstellar capability at almost exactly the same time."

"Okay, I see your point: the odds are really against that kind of timing. But then how do the ruins on Dee Pee Three make any sense? If that civilization fell twenty thousand years ago, it doesn't seem plausible that four or five brand-new interstellar species could have risen up since then."

Caine shrugged. "Maybe they didn't."

"What?"

"Maybe the first bunch of exosapients didn't all die out—in which case today's exosapients would have some overlap with the ones who were running things about twenty thousand years ago."

Downing nodded sharply. "Caine is absolutely right. Indeed, without such an exosapient collective constraining the colonizing activities of its members since then, new species would have no chance to develop independently, either on their homeworld or beyond."

Trevor snapped his fingers. "Sure. Otherwise, all the green worlds we've colonized in the last eight years would have already been filled with the other exosapients. Unless we are way the hell out in some interstellar backwater, why would they have left all that nice green real estate alone, unless it had been set aside for us?"

Opal nodded. "Like property held in trust for when we 'come of age.'"

Caine shrugged. "That's the theory. And that's all it is: a *theory*. But it does account for what we know of this area's past, and what we see in its present." *And it could be that our rapid push outward also triggered this invitation: maybe we're about to cross over some neighbor's property line. Maybe we already have . . .*

"We may be walking into a very complicated situation," Elena said quietly.

Downing sighed. "Exactly. But as long as different powers exist, so too will rival interests, and therefore, many of the basic rules of foreign relations and *realpolitik* should continue to apply."

"And when do we get to learn if that hypothesis is accurate, Uncle Richard?"

"We are due to arrive at preset coordinates—ten AU above the ecliptic out near Saturn's orbit—in sixteen days. That means we need to depart tomorrow."

MENTOR

Opal was the first to break the stunned silence. "So we've got only two weeks to prepare?"

"The convocation will be very simple, and very brief. We have not even been given any advance guidelines."

"I'm not talking about guidelines. I'm talking about being ready for—" Opal stopped, at a loss for words.

"For facing the unknown, the outré?" supplied Downing.

"Yeah. Something like that."

Downing shrugged. "The Dornaani indicated that we don't need to actually meet—or even see—any of the exosapients except them. Also, the other races are sending cross-species liaisons who have become experts in several of our languages and cultures in anticipation of this event." Downing looked around the table. "Besides, all of you, and the other members of the delegation, tested low—very low—on the xenophobia index."

Apparently in response to the puzzled expressions, Elena expanded upon the topic. "The xenophobia index was originally a test for anthropological field workers—usually buried inside another test—to measure how aversive they'd find unfamiliar conditions. Some people are so xenophobic that they freeze up just going to an authentic foreign restaurant; others thrive best when plopped down in a wholly different culture."

"Well, I never took any test like that," grumbled Opal.

Downing smiled faintly. "Major, when you were recuperating from your liver surgery, do you remember that vocational survey you filled out?"

"Yeah. Wait. Are you telling me...?"

"That test told us a great deal more about you than your long-term work preferences. A great deal more."

Opal looked up from under sullen brows. "Still. Only two weeks to prepare?"

Trevor raised a finger. "Actually, Uncle Richard, I've got my own problem with that two-week time frame. If my math is right, two weeks is not enough time to make a stationary rendezvous. We won't be able to get there and also counterboost enough to come to a full stop. However we slice it, we're either going to be late, or we'll be hitting the target point at a pretty decent velocity."

Downing nodded. "The Dornaani simply requested that when we reached these coordinates, we were not traveling any faster than zero-point-two C."

Trevor's eyebrows rose. "Wow. Sounds like we've got a lot of questions to ask the Dornaani."

Downing's lips quirked. "And we have only a few days to choose and prioritize them, Trevor. For now, let's just get a good night's kip." He started moving his many papers back into folders.

The others exited, Opal lagging, waiting for Caine, who smiled and held up a pausing finger. He turned toward Downing when they were alone. "You knew this day was coming, didn't you?"

Downing looked up from his papers. "No. Not me."

Caine remembered Sounion, remembered the last look on Nolan Corcoran's face. "So—Nolan knew."

Downing looked away. "I'm not sure...but I think

418 *Charles E. Gannon*

he suspected we might find ourselves in this situation. And that we'd need you. Again."

"So you guys never planned to cut me loose at all, or help me piece together my lost hundred hours. You just wanted to keep me dangling, forcing me to choose between living out on Mars, where I've got almost no access to information, or down on Earth, in easy reach of IRIS."

Downing closed his eyes momentarily. "Caine, I'm sorry. Yes, we hoped you would continue to work for us. As to having access to the right information—well, you chose to come up here; you weren't exiled."

"So you're telling me you *do* have information on the one hundred hours now? That you can help me?"

"Caine, it's not that simple. It was Nolan who kept all the relevant files, who knew where they were and how to access them. But when he died, well—"

"Oh, I see. You can't help me because Nolan's gone. Blame it on the dead guy. Very original."

"Damn it, Caine, it's the truth!"

"The truth? Since when has anyone connected with IRIS ever cared about the truth?"

"Caine," Downing pleaded. "This is not how it was supposed to be. But I can't undo the past, and I can't get information from dead men. All I can tell you is that we need you. Again."

"Well," said Caine, turning to leave with Opal, "thanks to the President, you and IRIS have me. Again."

Chapter Thirty-Eight

ODYSSEUS

As soon as Caine got the news, he bolted out of his stateroom, across the corridor, and into Opal's berth. She looked up with a big smile. "And to what do I owe—?"

"The Dornaani are here—and we've got pictures." He put his hand on her firm upper arm, drawing it gently towards him: a dancer's cue to "follow."

They left the delegation's hab mod at a trot, dodging around the stacked cargo bins and duffle-bagged supplies that were still being loaded into it. As they cleared the end of the luggage-slalom, Caine saw Lemuel Wasserman crossing the T-intersection ahead of them. Caine grabbed Opal's hand, pulled her in the direction Wasserman had gone.

She almost stumbled, looked at Caine: "What? Where are we going?"

"Wherever Wasserman goes."

She looked ahead as Lemuel disappeared around a corner. "Follow him? Why?"

"Because he'll have the inside track on where to see the first sensor results."

"But that will be the bridge—"

"Don't bet on it. This corvette is rigged for spec ops. There's a section amidships which has a couple of unlabeled rooms. And I bet he's heading toward them."

"You're thinking a passive sensor suite?"

"I'm thinking the works: passive, active, every spectrum you can think of and more. The intel folks knew they were going to get a look at a Dornaani ship, so I'm betting they loaded this hull with every sensor known to man—and probably a few that are still in the experimental stage."

"And how would Lemuel have located it?"

"I figure he shadowed folks in the mess, listened to their chatter, figured out which ones had the advanced science backgrounds."

They rounded a corner—and saw, in addition to a single unmarked door at the end of the passageway, Lemuel Wasserman reasoning with two Marines. The look on the smaller—and senior—leatherneck's face was not promising. "C'mon," whispered Caine as he tugged Opal forward.

They arrived just in time to hear Lemuel's voice rise a decibel and a whole octave: "—and who do you think needs to see those results the most? I'll tell you who: they picked *me* to go on this mission to do exactly what you are now *preventing* me from—"

Caine stepped alongside Lemuel and brought out the biggest and best smile he could muster. *Damn: I must look like Nolan, right about now. A large, congenial grin to put all the restless natives at ease.* "Hello, gentlemen. Can I help?"

Lemuel looked sideways at Caine and grunted.

The shorter Marine, a gunnery sergeant, looked him straight in the eyes. "I doubt it, sir. I was just explaining to Mr. Wasserman that our orders are very clear regarding security and clearance in this section. If he can't show me the correct ID, then I can't let him pass. Or you either."

Caine's smiled broadened. *Good preemptive move, Gunny. But I'm heading toward higher ground.* "I'm sure this is all just an oversight. I wonder if you—or your team member—could call in to Mr. Downing and have him wave us in?"

The sergeant's face did not move, but his eyes wavered.

Gotcha. "Mr. Downing got the jump on us—got here first—and probably overlooked the special clearance protocols. He expects the entire delegation to join him, I believe."

"He didn't say anything."

Thanks for confirming that Downing went through already. "Probably too excited himself; pretty historical stuff happening in that room down the hall."

"Essential stuff," piped Wasserman from over Caine's shoulder.

Caine turned, shone his smile at Lemuel, used his eyes to say "shut up," turned back to the gunny. "I guess we're all a little worked up. So if you'd be kind enough to give Mr. Downing a call, that should set everything straight."

The sergeant nodded at the larger leatherneck, who did a crisp one-eighty and tapped his collarcom, walking away as he started to speak in quiet tones.

"Thanks for your help, Gunny."

"Don't thank me for anything yet."

But the bigger, younger Marine had already returned and nodded once at the gunnery sergeant.

Who seemed a bit surprised, then shrugged and stood aside. "Sorry for the mix-up, sirs, ma'am."

Lemuel leaned forward to respond: Caine put a hand on his shoulder. Surprised, Lemuel stopped with his mouth open, looking at Caine. Who jumped into the silence, determined to save Wasserman from himself: "No problem, Gunny; you're just doing your job the way it's supposed to be done. Thanks for your help."

The corners of the sergeant's mouth crinkled: probably his equivalent of a smile. Caine nodded, towed Lemuel past the checkpoint, noting Opal's suppressed grin.

Lemuel shrugged off Caine's hand. "Thanks—but I had every right to tell that guy—"

"Lemuel. That guy—that *Marine*—was doing his job. And if there was a crisis on this ship, accidental or otherwise, he'd be one of the people most likely to save your life. You might want to consider that."

Lemuel looked away as they reached the unmarked door. His retort was a grumble. "Okay, so I need to play nice to stay on Jarhead's good side."

Opal drew abreast of them and pinned Lemuel in place with unblinking eyes. "'Jarhead' would give his life trying to save yours, whether or not he liked your sorry ass. Being nice—hell, just being *polite*—to him is the least you can offer in return." She opened the door, turned her back on Wasserman, and went straight in.

Lemuel stepped after her, head thrust forward, cheeks reddening. "Hey—"

Caine took Lemuel's arm again. "No. Don't start it.

I won't allow you to give Major Patrone any trouble. Besides, there's one more thing you might want to consider."

"Like what?"

"That she's right."

Lemuel looked up at Caine, then away. "Yeah. Maybe. Okay. Let's go."

They entered a room filled with screens and a few small holotanks. Three sensor operators were adjusting controls, studying results. Standing at the center of their triad, Richard turned, nodded, went back to watching the screens. In the most distant corner, wedged between two consoles, shoulders hunched together, Visser acknowledged them with a tight, perfunctory smile. Had she been wearing a sweatshirt emblazoned with the legend "I am a technophobe," her discomfort could not have been clearer.

Evincing a diametrically opposed set of affinities, Lemuel pushed hurriedly into the suite, shouldered past Downing and almost dropped into the lap of one of the Navy ratings in his single-minded attempt to get at the machines. Opal sidestepped over toward Caine's side; he felt her shoulder brush into contact with his upper arm and stay there. "Jesus, I see why they call Wasserman 'Le Mule' instead of Lemuel. What gives with him? Does he take jerk pills?"

Caine shrugged. "From what I hear, he's usually less prickly than this. But either way, he's the real deal when it comes to high-energy physics."

"But I thought you and Richard had your doubts about his being assigned to the delegation."

"Yeah, we did. We were worried that he might be an overpraised heir-apparent to the family's reputation for genius. He's got a lot to prove if he's going to be someone other than the nephew of *the* Wasserman who invented—as much as any one person did—the shift drive."

"But he's got the goods?"

"And then some. Mark my words: he's going to outdo his uncle. He's rough around the edges, but in all our meetings, it's been obvious he really knows his stuff. He can almost see the next generation drive."

"So in the Wasserman family, the lightning of genius struck twice."

"Looks like it." Half of the screens starting scrolling off reams of data. Caine stepped forward. "What've we got?"

Downing gestured. "Come take a look: first visuals of the Dornaani's arrival."

In the largest screen, there was a sudden flash and then a blurred shape arrowed out of view to the left.

Lemuel—by dint of expertise—had effectively taken control of the suite. "Get me the first frame image of that ship, and zoom in on it. Ladar 3-D interpolation and densitometer sweeps?"

"Working through them now."

Caine leaned forward to study the still image that popped up. "Lemuel, did that ship put out any thrust—did it accelerate—as it arrived?"

"Nope."

"So it came in moving at that speed?"

Lemuel turned around, a smile on his face and one eyebrow raised. "Yeah—so you understand."

Caine nodded, staring at the screen again. Opal cleared her throat. "Why is it important that their ship came in moving?"

"Because ours can't do that. In order to achieve the power levels necessary to effect a shift, our shift carriers have to both accelerate to near-relativistic velocities and *then* use the energy output of an antimatter reactor. The shift drive uses up every bit of that energy, so when our ships come back into space normal, they're at full stop."

"So that means—?"

Lemuel's tone was almost congenial. "So that means that the Dornaani either don't need as much energy, or are much better at generating it, because they just came out of shift moving at one hell of a clip. The mere fact that they have any exit velocity means they can generate excess energy—kinetic energy, in this case—before shifting. That means that they might not even need the weeks of near-relativistic preacceleration that our ships require. And here's another indicator of just how far ahead of us they are: take a close look at the hull design."

Caine did: it wasn't at all akin to the long modular frames of Earth's gargantuan shift carriers. Shaped like a blunted arrowhead with down-angled edges, the Dornaani vessel was essentially a delta-shaped design. As Caine studied the finer details, he noticed what seemed to be vents or intakes on the underside of the ship's drooping "wings." "Are those—?"

"Fuel scoops, yeah."

"And the significance of that is what?" Elena's question announced her arrival: Caine turned, saw Durniak, Trevor, and Hwang file in behind her.

Wasserman leaned far back in his chair. "Well, if the Dornaani can use any gas giant—and maybe any water world—as a gas station where they can tank up on hydrogen, then their experience with interstellar travel is going to be entirely different than ours. In every one of our systems, we have to maintain a multi-billion dollar infrastructure to provide fueling and cargo handling for our shift-carriers. But with a ship like theirs, you could conceivably go anywhere that there's a gas giant insystem. Interstellar travel made fast, cheap, and easy."

Trevor squinted at the arrowhead image of the Dornaani ship. "No sign of fuel booms or receptacles for tanker interface?"

"Maybe theirs don't look like ours, or are hidden, but I'm guessing they work with internal fuel only. The architecture is all wrong for drop tanks."

Caine turned to look at the ship again. "So that tiny hull also holds all the fuel they need."

"Looks like it."

"So how in the hell...?" Caine let his astonishment swallow the many different technological puzzles posed by the ship they were staring at.

"How the hell, indeed." Lemuel shook his head, kept scanning the data.

Downing frowned. "It's disconcerting that they can put that kind of performance in this little box."

"And it's a damned mystery box," interrupted Lemuel. "We're hitting it with ladar scans, but I'm getting garbage back."

"Garbage?"

"Yeah. Beam reflection is shot to hell. I'm just getting a froth of photons pushed back at me. And I've got no return at all on the radar—no, wait: radar is registering their hull, now."

Caine studied the screens; he couldn't make much

sense of the reams of data. But he had a guess. He leaned toward the lieutenant who was the suite's ranking officer. "Tell me: as you got radar contact just now, did it look like anything you've seen before?"

She thought for a moment. "No—wait, yes: like when you're trying to get through electronic counter-measures and then the target's ECM goes offline. The garbage straightens out and you've suddenly got clean data. Except here there wasn't any signal at all—and then, all of a sudden, there was."

Lemuel turned around. "What are you thinking?"

"That they decided to give us a better look by turning off their electronic stealth measures."

"But active stealth measures would put out an energy signature—and we're not getting any electromagnetic emissions *at all* from their ship."

"That's because they must have the system built right into their hull material: probably some kind of electrobonded matrix—"

Lemuel's down-curving eyebrows reversed upward into an arch of surprise. "Sure, some kind of radar absorbing and reflecting material that only works when they're pushing current through it. Like stealth materials, only you've got an off-switch, since the antiradar molecular structures—or whatever—only have that property when they're getting juiced." Lemuel smiled at Caine. "And now, I'm thinking the same thing regarding the problems with our ladar. Probably some kind of hull coating that works like a scattering prism: breaks up coherent light. Might be a good defense against lasers, too."

"Could be—but let's not get ahead of ourselves."

"Hey—it's like you said about the Marine sergeant: I'm just doing my job."

Caine smiled back. *Good: Wasserman may occasionally be a jackass, but he doesn't hold a grudge. And he may be right in another way about the parallel between him and the Marine sergeant: for all we know, the information he's gathering in this dull little room may ultimately save us all.*

The external commo screen was suddenly bright with data. Caine moved toward it, announced, "We've got activity on tight-beam commo," and thought: *Here I go, Speaker to Aliens.*

Chapter Thirty-Nine

MENTOR

Downing turned toward Caine. "What is it?"

"Don't know yet. If I'm reading this screen correctly, the signal we're receiving is high-speed, high-compression encrypted."

Downing turned to the suite's operator. "Is it the same data protocol as their first communiqué, four months ago?"

"Looks like it, sir. Decompressing and decoding now."

"Excellent," affirmed Visser with a decisive nod. "Mr. Wasserman, you will please continue to share your findings with us so we can collectively assess their strategic significance."

Downing suppressed a smile. Visser was trying to sound like she had a firm grasp of the military implications of scientific data. However, the past week of joint preparations had proven that she did not. On the plus side, she took counsel well and not only listened to all the facts, but all the conjectures and hypotheses. And that was more important in a leader than a mastery of the theoretical sciences—or of any other esoteric discipline, for that matter.

However, Wasserman turned to look at Visser with an expression that was more sneer than smile: "Which findings are you most interested in, Ms. Visser? Spectrographic analysis of their hull materials and thrust exhaust? Gravimetric anomalies? Or maybe their bizarre shift signature? Or maybe you're interested in something that I've overlooked?" When the ambassador did not rise to the bait, Wasserman's sneer became more pronounced. "I'm ready to follow your scientific lead, Ms. Visser." Visser tried to glare at him, but looked more like a deer caught in the headlights of advanced physics.

Downing bit his lip, wished Lemuel would let Visser off the hook. *Hopeless git; a genius in his own right but soured by living in the eclipsing shadow of a celebrity uncle.*

Visser converted her failed glare into a severe look. "Tell us about the shift signature."

"What—exactly—do you want to know about it?"

Visser sounded as though she had swallowed lye. "Start by telling us what a 'shift signature' is."

Wasserman's smile dimmed into a smug curve. "A shift signature is a collection of anomalous physical sequelae that result when extremely high energy-density levels induce space-time disruption of real-space interstellar superstring traces—"

Visser held up her hand. "Mr. Wasserman, please—you are the expert. Not us. In terms we understand, please."

Wasserman leaned back, smiling, taking his time, letting Visser squirm. "So where would you like me to start, Ms. Visser? With high-school physics?"

Visser became very pale, then very red. She was slowly raising her finger. *Crikey; here it comes.*

Caine stepped into the space between them. "Actually, Lemuel did a fine job of familiarizing me with the basics the other day. Major Patrone and I were, uh...napping when the shift drive was introduced, so we needed a review of its oddities. Maybe you could repeat that explanation here, Lemuel?"

Lemuel's sneer faltered into a frown.

Downing almost nodded at Wasserman. *Take his lead, man: Caine's trying to help you save yourself, even though you* are *a right bastard.*

Wasserman's frown faded away. The rest of the delegation relaxed—gratefully, it seemed, since every prior word and second had been taking them toward an in-group conflagration.

As Wasserman started to speak—cocky, assertive—Downing noted that Visser's gaze occasionally migrated over to Caine's face. In another scenario—had the ages been closer, and Visser not already been furnished with a same-sex spouse—Downing might have suspected that she was discreetly fueling a romantic infatuation. But her expression was attentive rather than adoring: specifically, as Wasserman spoke, Visser was monitoring Caine's reactions. *She trusts his judgment. She's listening to Riordan very carefully, and with a strong positive predisposition. That's good—and useful—to know.*

Wasserman had already warmed to his subject. "To understand what a shift signature is, you have to understand how a shift drive operates. First, get it out of your head that the ship travels faster than the speed of light. It doesn't."

Durniak nodded. "It is impossible to exceed or even achieve the velocity of light. Relativity."

Wasserman seemed about to disagree, then shrugged. "More or less. The Wasserman drive works by creating a field effect that ruptures weak spots in normal space-time. Although we accelerate for weeks to make the shift possible, speed really has nothing to do with it: the velocity is just a way of storing energy.

"What?"

"Trevor, think of the mass of the entire shift carrier as a battery. At zero velocity, it has only its rest mass energy—not useful for our purposes. However, as we accelerate it, every atom in that mass is also being moved to a higher energy state. In essence, the ship itself becomes a kind of energy capacitor—which is the only way we can store the energy levels required to effect shift."

"Then why do we need the antimatter reactors?"

"To push us over the hump. As you begin to achieve significant sub-relativistic velocities, it takes increasingly more energy to add more speed. So, the efficiency of using the ship's mass as a capacitor begins to drop sharply. That's where the antimatter reactor comes in."

"It provides a final burst of speed?"

"No, Trevor. I *told* you: it's not about velocity. The antimatter reactor powers the Wasserman Drive, which works by compressing a seed of superdense material into a borderline implosion. That creates what laymen call a 'pseudosingularity.'"

"And which you call—?"

"An 'incipient event horizon,' Ms. Visser. It's way too small to become a full-fledged black hole. However, it does create a strong, albeit brief, time-space distortion—which, if it's generated right on top of an interstellar superstring, is what triggers the shift."

Visser frowned. "Go back, please: an 'interstellar super-what'?"

"A superstring. It's nothing you can find in space-normal. It's—well, how do I explain this? It's a vestigial subquantal umbilicus that connects nearby stars. Kind of an echo of their dispersal from the same pool of matter, even though they are now *almost* completely discrete stellar objects."

"Sounds a little like an interstellar version of quantum entanglement," mused Thandla.

"Yeah. Some theorists even claim the two phenomena are related. Kind of."

Downing looked quickly around the room: Thandla, Riordan, and Hwang were still following Wasserman. Durniak and Elena were struggling to keep up. The rest were attentively and hopelessly lost.

Wasserman continued without missing a beat. "So, when you activate the Wasserman Drive atop the space-normal 'ghost' of the weakest part of the superstring between two stars, you create a field effect that journalists have mislabeled a 'transient wormhole.' Once that hole is open, the ship goes through."

"And pulls the hole shut after itself," supplied Elena.

"Not exactly. Actually, not at all. When I say that the pseudo-wormhole is transient, I mean it is *extremely* transient. Its expression is measured in microseconds. But because the ship is traveling so quickly, it's through the rupture before space-normal can reassert."

"So it's more like pulling open a trapdoor and dropping through the hole before it falls shut on you."

Lemuel nodded and almost smiled at Elena. "Yeah, more like that."

"So now the craft is traveling in shift-space."

"Well—no. Shift-space is just a made-up word that the press likes to use. There really isn't any shift-space that we can tangibly experience or measure. We can only represent it as mathematical formulae and relationships. Which I'll spare you."

Visser muttered, *"Gott sei Dank."*

"You see, a ship doesn't really 'enter' a superstring: it 'interfaces' with it. It's not moving, not in the material sense of the word. What it does is more akin to electron tunneling."

Elena's eyebrows rose slightly. "'Electron tunneling'?"

"Yes. To put this really simply, atoms on either side of a barrier can, under the right conditions, swap electrons. But not because the electrons physically push through the barrier: they don't. Instead, when an electron winks out of existence on one side of the barrier, another electron blinks in to replace it on the other side. That's called 'tunneling.' How it happens—well, that's a longer topic. Suffice it to say that the cosmos is keeping score, and when it tears a particle down in one place, it has to reconstruct it in another place."

"And that's how the shift drive works?"

"Well, it's the same principle. Stars are, in some ways, like these atoms. They can, under the right conditions, exchange particles—or, more accurately, they can 'communicate changes' along the superstrings that link them. Like a tunneling electron, a shifted ship is not being physically propelled to another place: instead, the superstring transmits its 'potentiality' from one place to another."

"So, in the same instant that the Wasserman Drive makes the ship wink out in one place, the same ship has to be re-expressed further along the superstring."

"Now you get it. And what you'd call the 'wormhole' is more like an entry ramp onto the superstring free-way that connects the two stars. When the wormhole's distortion of normal space-time grazes the underlying space-time irregularities that exist at the weak spot of a superstring—boom! You get a shift. And the precise conditions of how that happens is what determines—finally—a ship's shift signature."

"Which is—what?"

"A bloom of high-energy particles, rays, photons, and heat."

"What creates it?"

"Well, the Wasserman Drive's incipient event horizon grabs everything nearby—and I mean *everything*: solar particles, photons, cosmic rays. All the background noise and garbage of space-normal comes along for the ride during a shift. So when all that gets re-expressed, one of two things happen. If the object was at a high-energy state when it shifted—gamma rays, cosmic rays, the ship itself—it comes out just the way it went in. But that means you get a brief Cerenkov flash and a spike in the background radiation signature, because you just imported high-energy crap into a system which is already awash in high-energy crap of its own."

"And what about the less energetic objects that get shifted—like dust or gas molecules?"

It was Durniak who hypothesized the answer to Visser's question. "Logically, because they are not moving fast enough, they would be torn apart before

crossing the threshold. So they would come out as—
what?—heat, energy, subparticles?"

"All of the above. But their annihilation is too
brief and diffuse to present either a radiological or
thermal hazard. However, against the background of
space-normal—which is comparatively cold, empty,
inactive—this burst shows up like a signal flare in
night-vision goggles."

Visser visibly drew in a large, relieved breath. "Very
well. So, now: the Dornaani shift signature."

"Well, like I said, I'm not sure it *is* a shift signature."

"Why? Did they not shift in?"

"I think they did—but it's not like any shift I've
ever seen, or ever heard theorized."

"Why?"

"First, they came in at speed. What that implies about
their power generation and/or storage capabilities—"

"You have already made very clear. For which we
thank you. Next?"

"Well, there was no initial shower of particles. However, a microsecond or two *after* the Dornaani ship
shifted in, *then* we got the signature. And it's like no
signature we've seen before. Far fewer photons, cosmic
rays, radiation. Instead, we detected a stern-wave of
mesons decaying back into normal space-time—"

The senior duty officer leaned forward. "Makes me
want to reopen the book on the concept of tachyons."

Wasserman shrugged. "I'm not so ready to go down
that path—but it sure did look like we were watching
ultra high-energy particles crossing back down through
the lightspeed threshold, undergoing a rapid—uh,
'decay'—into normative particles."

Visser nodded. "I will not pretend to intuit the

significance of all these facts, nor do we need them explicated here. Our module is scheduled for transfer to the Dornaani vessel in"—she checked her watch—"less than an hour. So tell us this: what do these facts suggest in terms of the Dornaani drive technology? Or other practical accomplishments?"

Wasserman rotated his hands into a palms-up gesture of uncertainty. "I can only tell you this much: the Dornaani approach to supraluminal travel is way different from—and way beyond—ours. But I don't know when I'll be able to tell you anything specific about it. If ever."

"Why?"

"Because this is like being a paleontologist who's shown a single fossilized footprint and is then asked to produce a sketch of the dinosaur that made it. I mean, there are certain features you can *eliminate*, but just how reliable and accurate an image are you going to generate from a single footprint? And right now, that's all I've got to work with."

Visser's pout was one of grudging acceptance. "Very well. Mr. Riordan, can you tell us any more about the communication we received from the Dornaani?"

"Yes. The Dornaani relayed the accords of the interstellar organization they told us about."

Durniak's smile was genuine, yet rueful. "I am guessing this means many days of reading, no?"

"Erm—no."

Downing heard the pause and looked at Caine. "How long is it, Caine?"

Caine took the hard copy from the printout tray, checked front and back. "Not quite two pages."

"How many accords are there?"

He scanned the sheet. "Twenty-one."

"Only twenty-one?" It was the first time Downing had ever heard Visser sound surprised.

"Only twenty-one. Here you go." Caine started the thin stack of sheets around the room.

Trevor, the first to finish reading it, turned the document over, as if searching for fine print. "And that's it?"

Caine nodded at him. "That's it."

"Makes me think we're looking at a very hands-off kind of organization."

Visser answered with a sharp shake of her head. "This is not an organization. It is a league of non-aligned states that have committed to a universal nonaggression treaty."

"And who've made rules for how to act toward each other when they meet on the playground." Opal's comment earned a smile from Caine, a broad grin from Trevor.

Visser folded the sheet and slipped it into a pants pocket. "So. Much to discuss in the days to come. But, if we are done here, let us call—"

"Already here." The drawl from the doorway seemed to carry in a long, spare man in the blue unipiece fatigues of the USSF. Captain Dale "Tex" Flannery (who was, Downing had learned, from Nevada) waved the suite personnel back into their seats. "Folks, my CPO is about to have kittens, we're cutting it so close. According to the instructions, we are not going to make a hard dock with the exosapients. So that means we have to cut your module and its intership coupler loose in about thirty minutes. They will then maneuver to pick you up. We will observe from a range of thirty kilometers."

"That's pretty far off if something goes wrong," muttered Hwang.

"Doctor, if something goes wrong, there is probably squat-all we can do about it, anyway. I'm sure you folks have been chatting about the ship that just came in so you're probably guessing the same thing I am: that if these Dornaani wanted to put their foot up our ass and wriggle their toes out our nostrils, I doubt there's a thing in creation we could do about it. On the other hand, if they mean to harm us, they're going about it in an awful neighborly way. If I was you, I wouldn't worry about any problems during the transfer—or after."

Flannery edged back toward the door. "Now, I've got a ship to run and a transfer to effect, so I must politely insist that you get your asses into your module, button up, and batten down. You've got twenty minutes." He paused, then saluted. "Do Earth proud, folks." One long, lanky step had him out the door and gone.

ODYSSEUS

Caine checked his watch—just about fifty minutes since Flannery's brusque farewell—and then felt a reasonable amount of gravity pushing him down into the acceleration couch once again. Trevor's voice came out of the ceiling speakers a moment later. "Okay, folks. That bump you felt a few minutes ago was indeed the Dornaani connecting to us via our intership coupling node. Instruments now indicate a spin-generated equivalent of 0.97 gees. Be careful if you get up—we don't know our rotations per minute yet, so we can't be sure how bad the inner ear or Coriolis effects are going to be."

Visser's voice followed Trevor's: "Might the gravity be natural? Could we have already shifted, and come out near a planet?"

Caine felt a sudden flush of embarrassment for Visser, was glad that Le Mule did not jump down her throat. It was fairly common knowledge—even for someone who had been asleep for fourteen years—that you couldn't come out of shift near a planet. The proximity to a gravity well would deform the ship's re-expression pattern and—*pfffffftttt*: you came out as a whole lot of nothing. And as for the possibility that they might have felt a shift...

Caine toggled his own comm link. "I doubt we've experienced shift yet, Ms. Visser. You feel a little jolt when you shift. Not painful, just a start—like when you wake up from a falling dream."

Movement at the entrance to his stateroom caught the corner of his eye: Opal, in a low-cut T-shirt and shorts. Which looked very fine on her. Caine tapped the commlink which was dragging awkwardly at the neckline of his own tee, rose, smiling—but then saw that her face was as rigid as a mask. He moved past her, closed the door, and steered her toward the acceleration couch on which he had been sitting. She didn't resist or speak.

He sat down next to her, put a hand on top of hers. She clutched his fingers so quickly and so tightly that he almost cursed. "Opal, what's wrong?"

Without looking at him, she spat words. "You heard that braying jackass, Le Mule. Shifting is just a nice way of saying that we're going to be torn into trillions of tiny, subatomic particles."

"It is a pretty strange concept," Caine started agreeably.

Opal shut her eyes. "It is suicide."

He studied her face, started at what he saw there. "Why are you crying?"

She blinked, looked even more surprised than he was, and yelped out a short laugh. "What? I'm what? Crying?"

Caine only nodded: clearly, this was more than just fear.

Opal waved an airy hand. "Oh, that's nothing. I was just—"

Caine reached out and drew her close slowly, gently. She exhaled and put her arms around him. She was in that position, unmoving, for so long that he wondered if she might have gone to sleep. "Opal, are you—?"

She let out a long sigh. "I'm sorry. I'm—God, I'm such a coward."

"You?" He held her back to look at her. "*You?* This is a joke, right?"

"It's this whole shift business."

He doubted that, but asked, "What about it?"

"Well, the mere thought of being shredded into subatomic particles—didn't it scare you, the first time?"

Caine shrugged. "It couldn't: I was in cold sleep. And by the time they woke me up, I had already been through three shifts. I guess some part of me accepted that if shifting was going to kill me, it would have already done so. But instead, here I am." He smiled.

And then, she was grabbing his head in both hands and was kissing him. He also felt her shaking, as if she had started crying again, but a moment after he began to respond—eagerly—she stopped trembling. And by that time, he had stopped thinking.

Several seconds—or minutes—later (he could not tell), the compartment intercom toned twice: a priority message. "Folks"—it was Trevor—"if you're still in your acceleration couches, you might want to stay there. We just received a communiqué from our hosts. Seems they're ready to initiate shift. For those of you who've never experienced one, you might feel a little vertigo, so just make sure you're seated or lying down. Fifteen minutes, they tell us. See you on the other side. Out."

That reminder—about her impending discorporation—made Opal start away from Caine, who put his arms back around her. He tilted his head down until she could not fail to look him in the eyes: "Look: think of it this way. Your body is pushing around—sometimes destroying and rebuilding—electrons all the time."

Opal shuddered. "Sorry, but logic doesn't help. I've faced death a few times, you know. Getting too close to it on one occasion is what got me banished to the future. But here's the funny thing: I always knew I wasn't going to be killed. I have known—all my life—that I wasn't going to die young, that I was going to outlive all my siblings and live on into advanced, and probably testy, hag-dom. But this—it makes me feel like I'm about to dissolve into nothing."

"Well," Caine said and his arms tightened a little more, "you certainly feel real enough to me."

He did not expect what happened next: she pushed herself into him with a sinuous motion; her reluctant vulnerability sudden transformed into forceful wantonness. "You'd be surprised how real I can feel," she said in a tone that sounded like fierce annoyance.

As Opal pulled herself against him, Caine imagined he felt various needs tightening her fingers—needs for love, for safety, for escape, for him, for release. But now, those separate needs were losing their distinctions, were fusing together into one impulse—

And Caine, as distracted as he was by her profoundly suggestive words and motions, finally understood where her tears had come from: she had wanted this to happen for a long time. And now, made desperate by a fear of imminent annihilation, that unfulfilled want had cracked the emotional container in which she kept herself, had started leaking out...

Caine stood away and extended a hand. "Come with me."

She had risen and put her hand in his even before she said, "Where are we going?"

"To a therapeutic environment."

She blinked. "And where on this tin-can would that be?"

He smiled, checked up and down the corridor, and led her aft. And as they approached the last door on the module's central corridor, she understood: "The buoyancy tank? Now?"

"When better? You like baths; think of this as the ultimate bath." He opened the door; a muted glimmer of moving water moiréd against the walls.

She seemed slightly more collected as she wondered: "Damn, is this even allowed?"

"Hey—I thought you were the bad-ass, maverick major."

"Bad ass, yes: exhibitionist, no. How do we know that no one will—?"

"We just passed all their doors. Closed tight. Waiting for the shift. Lot of first timers like yourself. All probably a little anxious, and eager to hide it from everyone else." Caine pulled off his T-shirt. "So this may be the one time we can indulge in a little—" he slipped into the water "—hydrotherapy."

"Okay. Give me a sec." She moved towards the changing booth.

"What for?"

"My grand entrance." She slipped inside, but he still could see her: she didn't bother to close the door. In a moment, she had shed her outer clothes. She primped for all of one second in the mirror, making sure her bra and briefs were trim and taut, showing off everything to its best advantage.

When she left the booth, she did not meet Caine's eyes, but stepped daintily into the water on the other side of the tank and then waded across to join him. She leaned back against the rim of the tank, her body only a foot away from his. The water raised her breasts slightly. His arms—spread out to either side—suddenly felt very heavy. He felt the water lap against his side, shifted his body slightly, wondered if—*oh Christ, stop thinking!*

Smiling at his own awkwardness and tendency to overexamine everything—even this—he turned toward Opal.

She was not smiling.

And then, thinking became extraneous.

PART FIVE

EV Lacertae and Barnard's Star

October, 2119

Chapter Forty

TELEMACHUS

Downing was tapping his lower lip meditatively with a compupad stylus. "So Mr. Thandla, you have confirmed our final position?"

The Indian nodded. "Starfield configuration and parallax measurement both put us in the EV Lacertae system."

"That's some rather fast travel, I must say. And no communiqués except this morning's?"

"Correct."

Downing turned toward Riordan. "I'm assuming that they sent us a list of the systems included in Earth's 'allowed region of development'?"

Caine nodded, and activated the holotank. A two-column list of star names glimmered into existence. "Excluding our home system, there are fifty-eight systems that have been reserved for us. I've highlighted the ones where we've already pitched our tents."

Trevor read the glowing words. Other than the highlighted names, they didn't mean much to him. A few systems—such as Luyten 726-8—he had only seen on military navigational charts and tables. They had been visited once, maybe twice, to serve as routing alternatives in the event that main-line systems were interdicted or had to be avoided. But other than that, he didn't know much about the other systems, except they were all relatively close.

Elena asked the first question. "Those star names—did you have to do some kind of translation, or—?"

Caine's smile was sly. "Nope. That came from them."

"So they already knew what we called all these stars. Interesting."

"Yes. I'd say with each passing hour, we're finding more and more evidence that we've been pretty thoroughly monitored prior to contact."

Downing poked at his palmtop: the list shrank down and zoomed backwards, displaced by a slow swirl of bright particles at the center of the 'tank. Another jab and they stopped rotating.

Durniak came to stand by Downing. "So that is a map of the systems we are permitted?" He nodded.

Visser stared at the star map then looked over at him. "Is this bad?" she asked.

"Most of it is just disappointing. We ignored the systems that are not highlighted for a very good reason."

"Which is?"

"They are mostly M-class stars or white sub-dwarfs."

Durniak nodded her understanding. "Fewer planets, and almost no chance of finding any with biospheres. Gray worlds only."

"Exactly. But there is one serious problem: a very significant omission from the list of allowed stars."

Visser nodded. "70 Ophiuchi."

Trevor looked at the list again. *Good God, they're right.*

Opal cocked her head. "And why is it so important that 70 Ophiuchi is not on our 'Mother-may-I' list?"

Downing shrugged. "Because we have a colony in that system."

Opal nodded. "So we went off the reservation there."

"Yes."

"So what are we going to do?"

Visser smiled. "You ask direct questions and are not afraid of direct answers: you are good to have with us, Major. Come, we will think on it together before I go to meet the Dornaani."

Opal smiled and set off with Visser. As she passed behind Caine, she gave the back of his left bicep a quick squeeze. Trevor looked away, wished he had done so a moment earlier. But, of course, he was going to see everything she did.

Because he was always watching her.

ODYSSEUS

The door into the Dornaani ship—an iris valve—dilated. A smooth corridor—the walls curved up gently from the floor and arched subtly overhead into a ceiling—yawned before them. Caine waited: they hadn't worked out an entry order. Caine had presumed that Visser, as ambassador, would take the lead. But she seemed very still—almost rigid. Another second went by: *Oh, what the hell—*

Caine stepped through the round portal, did a quick sweep with the atmosphere analyzer. The green light never wavered. "The air is okay; actually, less CO_2 and marginally fewer contaminants." As if the Dornaani had brought them all this way to either murder them with toxins or asphyxiate them through incompetence. *But protocols are protocols...*

Visser stepped over the low lip of the valve, eyes slightly lowered. As she drew abreast of Caine, she glanced up with a quick, faint smile. Caine understood the look as *thanks*, responded with a smile of his own. Visser's broadened in response before she moved further into the Dornaani ship with her usual assertive stride.

Downing came next, followed by Elena. Behind them, still in the airlock, Opal stared at Caine without blinking. "You four be careful," she whispered, still looking at him.

Caine raised his hand in farewell, just before the panels of the iris valve contracted with a swift, breathy hiss. He turned; found the others waiting for him. The milky walls stretched away into a dim haze. *Uncharted territory: "Here be dragons"—or what might be stranger and more dangerous still.*

Elena studied the walls as they moved forward. "Any idea where we're going?"

"Nope. The Dornaani simply asked us to—"

"Please," interrupted a new voice, apparently speaking from the ceiling, "continue forward for twenty meters. You will find another portal. Place your hand on the round panel beside it."

Visser cocked her head to one side. "What accent is that? And what gender?"

Downing smiled faintly. "I can't make out the gender. And I would say there is no accent at all. Does sound a little nasal though, so I'm guessing that he—or she—was taught by a Yank." Downing shot an amused glance at Caine.

Who wasn't really in the mood to smile at any of Downing's jokes. "There's the portal."

This iris valve was somewhat smaller in diameter—just sufficient for average human height, so Caine stooped a bit as he grazed his fingers across the saucer-sized pad. The panels scalloped away from the center point, retracting back into the walls, floor, ceiling. Visser glanced at Caine, crinkled her eyes slightly, then stood slightly straighter and briskly stepped over the threshold. Caine followed, resolved to be ready for anything.

Chapter Forty-One

ODYSSEUS

The one thing Caine hadn't been prepared for was the anticlimax of the moment. The room was a plain white ovoid, all the fixtures of which reprised a curvilinear motif—except for one gray rectangular table furnished with four black chairs. Across from it was a crescent-moon table. Standing squarely between the two tables was, evidently, a Dornaani.

Caine, having girded his loins for a profoundly alien being, had not been prepared for yet another conventionally arranged biped. The Dornaani—not quite one and a half meters tall, raised long arms and long fingers into the air slowly. "Please feel free to look at my form: be certain you are comfortable before you come closer."

"Should we? Come closer?" Caine had spoken before he realized he should measure his words carefully now: he wasn't flying by the seat of his pants in the jungles of Dee Pee Three anymore: he was an official negotiator. Whatever that meant.

The being's fingers widened further. "You may approach if you wish. Indeed, with the exception

452

of this meeting, you may elect not to see, or even directly hear, any exosapients at all. It is our intent to minimize any shock that might arise from your first encounters with alien species."

Caine inclined his head slightly. "We thank you for that accommodation. However, our delegation was selected, in part, for our receptivity to unfamiliar situations. Accordingly, we look forward to having as much direct contact with other species as is possible." *And gather more intel in the process.*

The Dornaani inclined its own head in response. "We welcome this. It is not our custom to shake hands, but we know that it is yours. If it will make you feel more comfortable to do so, I am happy to comply."

Caine was surprised by the next voice: Elena's. "What is *your* customary greeting?"

The Dornaani's upper arms drew in somewhat, the forearms went out at right angles from the body: the fingers—three very long tapers directly opposed by a rather stubby digit—splayed wide, like rays emanating from the ends of the sinewy arms. "'Enlightenment unto you.' It is an auspicious beginning, that you ask of our ways. However, we shall use your ways and language, for now: whereas we are accustomed to sentient species other than our own, you are not."

Elena seemed ready to add something—*possibly what she read about my experiences with Mr. Local on Dee Pee Three*—but Downing put a hand on her arm and responded. "That is very considerate."

"It is simply prudent. You may call me Alnduul, you may gender me as male, and you are free to ask any questions. You may also approach and inspect my form in greater detail, if you wish."

Caine approached, reflecting that, after the Pavonians, the Dornaani hardly seemed alien. The two large, slightly protuberant eyes appeared pupilless at first—until Caine realized that a nictating inner eyelid was currently in place. The diminutive mouth seemed set in a permanent moue—until Alnduul lifted a widemouthed bottle of water to it. The mouth everted into an unsightly sucking protrusion, seeking the neck of the bottle much the way a tapir's short trunk would snuffle after fodder. Caine repressed a shudder as small cutting ridges reminiscent of a lamprey's clicked lightly against the container. Alnduul's nose was almost nonexistent; a single nostril perched over the bony promontory that housed the mouth.

At the base of the almost pelicanate mouthflap and jaw arrangement, about where a human's Adam's apple would be, there was a set of slits or gills, above which there was a triangular flap: probably a foldable ear. The cranium itself—for there most definitely was one—was very rounded and smooth, and seemed to have a rearward extending shelf, so that if seen from above, the outline of the head would present as a teardrop.

Caine felt that mental image of a drop suddenly superimpose itself over everything on the Dornaani physiognomy, and even the motif of the room and the ship, and so he understood: "Excuse me, Alnduul. Are the Dornaani native to water?"

The nictating lids fluttered. "We are. We prefer to rest in water, but as we have evolved, more of our waking activity takes place in air-space. And thus I am reminded: if you agree, I would like to change the room's environment slightly."

Visser nodded. "Of course. What changes do you wish to make?"

"We prefer higher humidity and slightly higher temperature. However, while wearing this suit, I will be comfortable with approximately eighty-five percent humidity at thirty degrees centigrade."

One of Downing's eyebrows raised slightly; he tugged open his collar. "By all means." Caine imagined him in a pith helmet and found the image an apt—and deserved—parody.

As Alnduul manipulated controls embedded in the table, Caine noted the profoundly sloped shoulders: evidently streamlined for arms-tucked swimming, but reaching overhead had to be awkward, at best. The short, high chest was perched upon an abbreviated abdomen that tapered quickly into what, in a human, would have been an absurdly waspish waist. Short and powerfully muscled "thighs" winnowed down into long, thin lower legs, which ultimately flared out into wide, spatulate duck-feet. In silhouette, Alnduul presented a broad parody of the female hourglass figure—but with fingertips that came down well beneath the knees, immense feet, and a total absence of hair. Even so, it was a more humanoid shape than any envisioned by the most optimistic predictions of xenophysiologists.

The room was already becoming warmer; Caine felt the first bead of sweat form at his hairline. He tugged open his collar, watched as Visser and then Downing went forward to shake Alnduul's hand. They smiled, introduced themselves, muttered something low and congenial, were the very pictures of human decorum. *And that's the problem.*

Caine stepped forward, tucked his elbows in against his floating ribs, rotated his arms out like stunted wings, spread wide his fingers. Alnduul seemed to stare for a moment, then his gills audibly popped open and he returned the gesture. Caine bobbed his head slightly. "Is it proper for me to wish you enlightenment?"

Alnduul's nictating lids cycled slowly and his speech was measured, deliberate: "It is always appropriate for one sentient to wish another enlightenment. You do us honor. What is your name?"

"I am Caine Riordan."

"Ah." It was a confirmatory sound, as if Alnduul had just received the expected answer to his question. "And you are here in what capacity, Caine Riordan?"

Well, this was as good a time as any for introductions. "I am here as this delegation's negotiator and—er, spokesperson."

"So you are the leader of the delegation?"

"No, that would be Ms. Visser, our ambassador."

"So your job is to communicate, not to deliberate?"

Caine was trying to figure how best to answer the question when Visser stepped in: "Mr. Riordan is our primary communicator, but he is also one of our most important advisors and plays a crucial role in our deliberative process."

Caine turned to look at Visser, who once again crinkled her eyes at him. *Good Christ, have I just been promoted? And is that a good thing or not?*

Then she continued: "And this is Ms. Elena Corcoran, who is our specialist in xenocultural signification and semiotics."

Elena stepped forward—Caine tried not to notice her dramatically long legs—and made the splay-fingered gesture. She carried it off with a sweeping grace that made it seem balletic.

"Enlightenment unto you, Alnduul."

"And you, daughter of Nolan Corcoran. We are pleased you have come and that you sit at this table. Your father was much—appreciated—by us." From the way the statement had begun, Caine had expected the concluding qualifier to be that Nolan was someone the Dornaani "admired," rather than "appreciated."

If Elena noted the same peculiarity, she did not reveal it: "I am happy to learn this. My brother—who is also here—and I both wondered at your request for our presence. How did you know our father?"

"How could we not? He was a famous human—and I foresee that his fame will grow, not diminish."

"So you knew of him through monitoring our broadcasts?"

The nictating lids closed slowly, did not open immediately. "Let us speak of this later. I would invite you all to be seated, if you feel comfortable doing so." Alnduul made a gesture with his fingers that looked like streamers waving in the wind. "Where is the rest of your delegation?"

Caine looked at Visser, who nodded. "After some discussion, it was felt that it would be difficult to keep our conversation focused if we had ten persons here. So the other six members of our delegation will be listening, and sharing their input, by radio, assuming we can make a connection through your hull."

"Your radio will be allowed to operate. We are observing a similar protocol. Many are listening, but I shall be the only one speaking. Indeed, my role here is akin to yours, Caine Riordan."

Caine smiled. "Perhaps. But I do not have your authority."

"I have less authority than you might suspect. I am not at all among the first voices of the Dornaani."

"Then why were you chosen to speak for your people?"

"Why were you made negotiator?"

"Because I am—supposedly—the member of my species most familiar with contacting exosapients."

"My situation is analogous."

"You specialize in first contracts?"

"Not exactly: I specialize in humans."

"As a scholar?"

"That too. But mostly as an—an administrator."

"I beg your pardon?"

"We—the Dornaani—are the Custodians of the Accord. Among us, I am one of those responsible for overseeing the Custodial policies and activities that involve your species."

Caine sensed Visser's posture become more erect. He did not need her prompting: "Does this mean that you are also the one who will determine whether or not we may become a part of the Accord?"

"Proffering membership in the Accord is determined by vote of all the Accord member states. Matters which involve interactions between the Custodians and your species are reviewed by the Custodial group of which I am a member."

Caine felt a vast, significant silence at the end of Alnduul's explanation. "And may we reasonably hypothesize that you are the primary advisor and senior expert in that group?"

Alnduul's lids nictated several times, ultimately

remained open: "This would be an extremely reasonable hypothesis."

Well, I guess we'd better not piss you off.

Alnduul had positioned himself at the convex center of the crescent table. "Let us start with any questions about our contact with you to date, or the accords. We shall conclude with an overview of the protocols and itinerary of the upcoming Convocation of the Accord. Please begin."

Caine checked the list on his palmtop. "Our delegation's first item is more an observation than a question. We found it...curious...that we did not receive copies of the accords until an hour before we shifted to this system."

Alnduul half-lifted one long hand. "We believe that first contact should emphasize unconstrained experience, not detailed analysis. Consequently, we encourage you to use your first Convocation to explore the Accord not as abstract dicta on a piece of paper, but as a living entity. You are here to witness the Accord in action: how else could you reasonably decide whether or not you wanted to be a part of it?"

Visser shook her head. "But—with respect, Alnduul— had we been given a few months of lead time, had you relayed the accords along with your invitation, we could have examined them—and any relevant precedents and interpretations—more closely."

"And had we sent you the accords ahead of time, it would only have served to give your many leaders enough time to make something very complex out of something that is very simple. They would have succumbed to endless abstractions and hypothesizing and would have paralyzed themselves—would they not?"

Visser was smiling now. "Unquestionably."

"It is the nature of organizations: the larger they grow, the more ponderous they become. I imply no criticism: to use a saying from one of the nations of your planet, one should not expect an elephant to scamper like a mouse. An organization large enough to govern a planet cannot also be flexible enough to react easily to new ideas or situations."

Visser nodded. "Thus the size constraint you placed upon the delegation."

"Yes. And also the short notice and lack of advance documents. For, given the opportunity to inspect the accords, your government would have encumbered you with all manner of constraints and objectives and questions and conditions. Indeed, they would not have sent *your* group at all."

"I do not understand."

Downing leaned forward. "If I may: I believe Alnduul is suggesting that, because the blocs did not have the opportunity to create a policy in advance, they had to choose a delegation that would be flexible, versatile, and unperturbed when dealing with unknown situations and species."

Alnduul's eyelids nictated slowly. "Precisely."

Caine checked his palmtop, moved on: "Our next question concerns the Twelfth Accord. Specifically, why is radio and high-power microwave broadcasting prohibited?"

"Primarily, to ensure the normative maturation of young cultures."

"You mean, you are trying to protect them?"

It was Elena, not Alnduul, who answered: "It's simply an extension of their rules regarding first contact. They are attempting to ensure that any young culture—including ours—has the chance to develop without advance knowledge of exosapients. To learn too early that one is not alone in the universe would almost certainly have a profound sociocultural effect."

Alnduul's nictating lids closed, then opened slowly. "Just so."

"But what of new races who are using radio before they are contacted for membership? Such as ourselves?"

Alnduul's fingers spread wide: "Most species sharply limit their use of high-power broadcasts long before they venture out into space. Indeed, only one other member state has failed to do so."

"Which one?"

"I may not say. It is unlawful for any member state of the Accord to provide information regarding any other member state."

Caine leaned forward. "I'm curious: why do most races terminate radio transmissions before they achieve spaceflight?"

"There is no single answer to such a question. But suffice it to say that not all species await first contact before they begin to speculate upon the possibly dire consequences of sending signals—intentional or inadvertent—out into space."

Caine shook his head. "So we spent almost two centuries showing everyone else how stupid we were."

"Let us say that you revealed yourselves to be ingenuously optimistic."

Caine allowed himself a small, ironic smile. "You are quite the diplomat, Alnduul."

Again, the slow close of the eyes, but this time,

a ripple distressed the small, perpetual moue of a mouth. "I thank you."

Caine smelt sandalwood coming closer, just before Elena whispered, "I think that was amusement."

"Looked like it." Caine considered his list of questions—and decided to ignore it for a moment. "Alnduul, our next question concerns one of the extraordinary conditions mentioned in the Twenty-first Accord." Downing looked up suddenly. Caine pressed on. "It indicates that the Custodians will intervene in the event of an 'impending and probable destruction of a biosphere.' I take it you are not referring to supplanting indigenous life, but wiping it out summarily. As occurs with weapons of mass destruction."

"Yes: this is the intent of that clause."

"Earth must have come awfully close on that one about one-hundred-fifty years ago."

"We were poised to intervene on several occasions during that period. And it occurred at a difficult moment for us: our monitoring resources were over-taxed at that time. Indeed, this was what compelled us to revise the Eighteenth Accord to allow a sharing of monitoring duties."

"So we were monitored by another race, also?"

"Rarely, but yes."

"So, back then in the middle of the twentieth century, were there any unplanned or planned contacts made with humans?"

Alnduul's lids nictated closed, then opened just a sliver. "That is a topic for another time."

Uh-huh; I'll bet it is. But now it was time to return to the list—and arguably its trickiest question: "Alnduul, we noticed that the accords seem to be written with the presumption that all who apply for membership will receive it. But what would happen if we were not offered membership? Or if we declined it?"

Alnduul's gill flaps shut with a soft slap. Caine didn't need Elena's input—"A negative reaction, possibly a rejection or deep concern"—to interpret the Dornaani's reflex.

"The Accord would decide upon a policy for dealing with you as a non-Accord state."

"But what if one of our interstellar neighbors decided to seize our systems, wasn't interested in waiting for an Accord policy? The accords are silent on independent actions taken by a member state against a nonmember state."

Alnduul's gills pinched even tighter against his neck. "There is no precedent, so I cannot speculate. It would be a very undesirable turn of events, and we would mitigate strongly against it. However, the accords do not abridge the political autonomy of the member states, nor constrain their freedom of action, except with regard to each other."

Now it was Downing who jumped in with a topic of his own spontaneous creation. "I understand that you cannot reveal information pertaining to other member states, but since you are permitted to disclose information regarding your own, I wonder if I might ask for the location of the Dornaani sphere of influence?"

Alnduul's gills rippled faintly, once. "I must refuse your request. Even though I am personally inclined to answer."

"I am perplexed: why withhold this information?"

"All information is intelligence. Once you are a member state, you are entitled to certain limited information on all states: for instance, you must know the location of each member state's homeworld."

"Why?"

"Because attacking a member state's homeworld will trigger a sharp Custodial intervention, as outlined in the Twenty-first Accord. So, if you are to observe such constraints, you must know the worlds to which they apply."

"So how does our knowing the Dornaani homeworld put anyone else's at risk?"

"A member state could legitimately—if speciously—contend that by prematurely revealing our astrographic siting to you, we have contributed to your ability to deduce theirs. By process of elimination."

Downing smiled sardonically. "So by knowing where you are, we know where they are *not*."

"Yes."

Caine felt the break in the pace of Downing's line of questioning, took back the initiative. "While we are on the topic of astrographic locations, we have a question about the allowed pathways of expansion outlined in the accords. Specifically, do all species receive fifty-eight systems, with the same general mixture of stellar classes and planets?"

"Unfortunately, there is no simple answer to your query. However, I will attempt to furnish you with a crude overview." The center fingers on each of Alnduul's hands rose slightly. "We attempt to balance the number of stars available to each race, maintaining proportionality of type and sequence. We make every effort to ensure that there is no astrographic overlap between the current member states and the developmental pathways that are held in trust for possible future member species. This was the case with your developmental pathway; it remained off-limits to other races so that you might have the sole use of it."

Caine nodded, looked down the list of worlds, then the list of further questions—and then his eyes returned to the list of worlds. They settled on 70 Ophiuchi. He was supposed to ask about that next. But his attention was instinctively drawn to a different planetary name, a name that was dragging him away from the line of safe inquiry toward one that was potentially quite perilous. In the next moment, Caine realized that his instincts were actually pulling in the same direction as his conscience. Alnduul might be conducting a subtle test here, to see if they'd have the nerve—and integrity—to ask about this other system. Caine realized he'd have to take a chance in order to find out, which meant asking—

"What criteria do you use to determine if a primitive protected race needs to have a pathway—or world—set aside for it?"

Caine felt Downing's fast, reflexive lean toward him: *he'd probably have tackled me bodily if this wasn't first contact.* Visser looked up quickly; her mouth had sagged open. *Took you a second longer, Fraulein, but you see where I'm going.* She winced and put her hand over her ear: even so, Caine could hear Wasserman's tiny, muted voice shouting: "Oh, Jesus Christ. Riordan—!"

But Alnduul did not seem to intuit or heed the potential discomfiture in the human delegation. "For a species to be given 'protected race' status—and therefore, have worlds reserved for its use—it must demonstrate sapience, or the imminence thereof."

"What would happen if the Custodians—uh—missed detecting a race requiring such protection? What if it was first discovered by another starfaring species, which had already colonized the world in question?" Caine heard chairs squeaking, fingers drumming, and more Lilliputian outcries from Visser's earpiece: they all knew where he was heading now. *But this is the right—and the smart—thing to do—*

"It is hard to imagine how such an oversight would occur," Alnduul answered. "Sapience leaves clear marks of its presence."

"But if it *did* occur?"

"We must end this line of inquiry, unless it has immediate pertinence. Tasking the accords to respond to every hypothetical situation can only—"

"I beg your pardon, but my question is not hypothetical."

Alnduul paused. "Indeed?"

Visser tugged sharply at Caine's elbow and hissed in his ear: "Don't you dare tell them about—"

Caine didn't stop: "I feel it is our responsibility to bring such a possible oversight to your attention."

Alnduul stared. And repeated: "Indeed?"

"Yes. After we had established several colonies on the third planet in the Delta Pavonis system, we discovered various artifacts indicating prior, and possibly persistent, sapient habitation. We eventually confirmed a relatively small group of this race is still extant."

Alnduul was silent for a long time. Then his gills flared and rippled. "This is known to us, Mr. Riordan."

The nervous chair squeakings to either side of him stopped. *Hah: thought so.* "Then why was this world on our pathway of allowed expansion? I would have expected it to be excluded—along with others held in trust for those sapients."

"A reasonable deduction. And a most reassuring display of self-declaration and good faith not specifically mandated or required by the accords. However, the situation on Delta Pavonis Three is a special case: there has been no oversight."

"But how—"

"Mr. Riordan, I cannot share the specifics of the case with you until Earth receives and accepts Accord membership. To do otherwise would be to violate the Accord's confidentiality protocols."

Violate the protocols? That would logically mean— "So some other member race is somehow connected to the sapients on Dee Pee Three? And therefore, you can't discuss the situation without violating your Custodial restraints upon sharing information that pertains to other member races?"

Alnduul's gills flared outwards with a pop: a signal of surprise? "A most stimulating conjecture, Mr. Riordan. But I cannot respond to it, either."

"Of course he can't," whispered Downing. "Not without revealing it to be the very reason he *can't* respond—thereby confirming what you asked in the first place. Well played, Caine: very well played indeed."

Caine smiled tightly, but thought: *This is no game, you ass. They may be allowing us to ask the questions, but we're under a microscope, being watched and judged.* "Alnduul, I must finish by pointing out another problematic situation pertaining to the fifty-eight worlds we have been allotted."

Alnduul's lids nictated slowly. "Yes. 70 Ophiuchi. This is a difficulty."

"Had we known—"

"You are blameless in this. The fault lies within the Accord."

Caine waited for him to expand upon his comments; he did not do so. "And, once again, that is all you can say."

"Just so. Naturally, you must anticipate that the topic of 70 Ophiuchi will be raised. However, the member states know that you cannot be pressed to decide your species' policy on this matter. At most, you can be charged to bear the Accord's—and the individual states'—perspectives on the matter back to Earth."

Caine looked at Visser and Downing: they exchanged satisfied pouts and nodded at him. "Very well, Alnduul. We thank you for your answers and your candor. That is, I believe, all the questions we have at this time."

"Very well. Allow me to acquaint you with the itinerary and protocols of tomorrow's Convocation . . ."

Chapter Forty-Two

ODYSSEUS

Caine looked over at Visser. "Ready?"

She didn't look back. *Nerves again*, he thought. Then she nodded tightly. "*Ja.*" She clutched her palmtop and papers unnaturally close to her chest.

From just behind Caine, Thandla sounded as anxious as Visser looked. "Mr. Riordan, if you could clarify once again—"

Thandla's question was drowned out by Le Mule Wasserman's favorite, brayed interjection from the rear rank of the delegation: "Jesus Christ. Thandla, what's with you? He handed out the procedural guidelines last night."

Thandla turned toward Lemuel slowly. "I have been memorizing the communication and data protocols that the Dornaani insist we use. Some of the data handshakes are quite complex. Regrettably, this left me little time for memorizing the agenda itself. I hope you do not find that excessively distressing."

Downing interceded before Wasserman could make whatever riposte he was readying. "Mr. Thandla, after introductions, the current members have an opportunity to question our bona fides as the legal representatives of our species. Then they are allowed to interrogate our government's dossier, including the legitimacy of its claim to being the definitive source of power and decision-making for our species."

"I thought the Custodians had already submitted a report on us to the rest of the Accord."

"Yes, but the Custodians' report is general, and other than what the other member states have learned from our own broadcast signals, that's pretty much all they know about us. Protected species like us are entitled to the same informational privacy the members have, except in regard to Custodians."

Caine heard a faint hiss emanating from the large iris valve before them. "I think we're on," he muttered into his collarcom to Opal.

"Okay," she answered from the security monitoring console back in the module. "The Dornaani just sent a message informing me that we can't send signals into or out of the Convocatorium. So good luck. I'll be waiting by the phone when you come out."

The iris valve opened—and Caine felt someone's toe bump against his heel. He looked back. Elena, sheepish, green eyes looking up from under a front-fallen raven wing of hair: "Sorry. A little too eager to get in there, I guess. Or nervous. God, can't they open the door any faster?"

Trevor, head visible despite being at the rear of the group, smiled. "Our grand entrance, El. Savor the moment."

"You savor it. I just want to get it over with."

You and me both, Elena. Out loud, Caine prompted Visser, "Ms. Ambassador, after you?"

Head and eyes fixed forward, Visser nodded and led them over the low lip of the valve as the plates scalloped away.

They entered a large, hexagonal amphitheater. Instead of rows of seats, six raked expanses descended gently to meet in a hexagonal central plane. Centered on that flat hub was the Dornaani delegation, seated in a transparent hemispherical dome. Caine looked overhead at the canopy bounding their own chamber, then to those on either side: they were made of the same nearly-invisible substance. However, unlike the central dome, their own chamber and those of the member states were all in the shape of a teardrop or flower petal, tapered tail pointing back in toward the hub occupied by the Dornaani. One such petal was set into each of the other five slopes of the amphitheater.

Trevor stared around. "So this is where we make it or break it today."

Downing ran an RF sensor around their gallery. "Technically, the membership decision is made on the second day. But, as you say, success tomorrow depends upon making a good impression today."

"Yeah, well, let's not be so eager to make nice that we give away the farm for free." Wasserman sounded truculent.

Visser, who was running her fingers against the almost frictionless canopy, countered without bothering to turn toward him. "Mr. Wasserman, we are not here to drive a hard bargain. Indeed, I suspect we have little, if anything, to bargain with." She walked to the narrow, down-sloping point of their flower petal and nodded toward the central dome. Looking up at her, Alnduul splayed his fingers in response.

Durniak pointed across the chamber at the gallery directly opposite their own. It was currently transparent and the shapes within it—akin to water heaters on wheels—were moving slowly from console to console.

"*Bozhemoi.*" Durniak usually spoke her mother's language—Ukrainian—but she slipped into Russian when distracted. "What are they?"

"I guess we'll find out soon enough." Caine offered.

Hwang looked over the top of his reading glasses. "Whatever they are, I suspect they are the most physiologically alien exosapients we have encountered thus far. It's possible they're not even carbon-based."

Elena turned toward Hwang. "Why do you say that?"

"Those massive cylinders. I'm guessing their atmosphere is either too corrosive or laced with lots of hydrogen, making regular seals and pressure-suit materials useless."

"What if they're just—well, like fish or water-snakes? They might like a big tank." Trevor was adjusting his commo-set; apparently, he had not yet established connection with Opal.

Downing nodded. "Perhaps. Or perhaps there are limits to just how extreme an environment these galleries can support."

"Well, we won't find out by looking at the member races to our right." Elena pointed her sharp chin in the direction of the two galleries that were located counter-clockwise from their position: both were opalescent, glowing from within—but opaque.

"The same with the member race just to our left," Thandla observed, pointing.

Caine shook his head. "That chamber belongs to the other new candidates, Sanjay. Alnduul explained that while a candidate race is being questioned, the Custodians keep the canopy opaque: being watched might distract a newcomer, cause them to act or speak hastily when—"

"Welcome." Alnduul's voice seemed to emanate from all around them. Caine looked down: Alnduul had come to stand at that part of the central dome closest to their own gallery. "We are completing our inquiry of the other candidate race now. Are you prepared?"

Visser nodded at Caine—but her lips were a tight, sealed line. *She can't even say "yeah, hi, thanks for inviting us"?* Aloud, Caine responded: "Yes, we are ready, Alnduul."

"Very well. We shall soon interdict the transparency of your gallery. However, introductions first: directly across the Convocatorium is the Ktor delegation."

"The water heaters," grumbled Wasserman.

"Moving clockwise from them toward your gallery is the Slaasriithi delegation and then the Arat Kur delegation. To your immediate left are the Hkh'Rkh, who were heard first today."

"Why?" Eight pairs of eyes turned to glare at Lemuel. Who stared back. "Hey; it's a fair question."

Alnduul's answer disrupted the silent, growing consensus that Le Mule Wasserman was about thirty-three years overdue for a truly life-altering spanking. "Unfortunately, I cannot answer that question without disclosing data regarding the Hkh'Rkh. However, the clockwise order of the galleries reflects the order in which the member states have joined the Accord." He paused. "You will note that your gallery precedes the Hkh'Rkh's in the sequence."

"But we are not yet a member state. Nor are they."

"This is true, Ambassador. However, should you both become member states, the gallery order you see now is the order that will be retained. I will signal you again shortly."

Trevor was the first to speak. "So we have seniority."

Elena's hair hung down, concealed her face from Caine. "But we don't know why."

"And we don't know if that is good or bad." Durniak rubbed her elfin chin.

The world around them faded to cream; the canopy was no longer transparent. A light flashed on the console in front of Thandla; he opened the link at a nod from Caine.

Near the gallery's narrowest point—the tip of its teardrop-tail—a very convincing hologram of Alnduul appeared. Thandla leaned forward to study it; Wasserman leaned back, squinting at the image and glancing quickly at the walls.

"We will begin," said the Alnduul hologram. "When Dr. Thandla opens a channel, you may see one of us from each gallery, and we may see and hear those of you who stand within the sending circle." A faintly glowing ring—maybe big enough for two—appeared in the floor. "If you wish privacy, simply close the channel and reopen it when you are ready. To do so abruptly or unannounced will not be taken as rudeness. We understand that the need for confidential discussion will arise throughout this meeting. If you are ready, I will introduce the spokespersons of the other delegations."

Caine realized that if he swallowed now, he would make a loud gulping sound. "We are ready."

"May I present he whose name translates as Wise-Speech-of-Pseudopodia of the Ktor." Another hologram—this of one of the water-heaters they had seen on the opposite side of the amphitheater—snapped on. The voice was clearly a machine simulacrum: "The Ktor are honored to encounter the human species."

"And we are honored to meet the Ktor."

Alnduul resumed. "May I present Vishnaaswii'ah of the Slaasriithi."

There was a pause and then a blinking green quatrefoil pulsed into existence to the right of Wise-Speech. Caine waited: no further image appeared. After several very long seconds, he started: "Alnduul—"

"My apologies, Caine Riordan. It seems that the Slaasriithi delegation has elected not to share their likeness with your species at this time."

"It is their right," added Wise-Speech mildly.

Caine heard various rustlings in the gallery behind him; people were standing, sitting up straighter, taking notes. "Is this expected, Alnduul?"

"It is not."

"Are they receiving our signal?"

Another simulacrum voice answered, this one from the green quatrefoil: "We mean no slight by withholding our image. We would understand if you wish to do the same."

"A little late for that now, isn't it?" snapped Wasserman, quite loudly. Caine saw Downing turn to glare at him, but not quite so harshly as before: after all, "Le Mule" did, once again, have a point.

Vishnaaswii'ah's voice was puzzled. "I did not hear your last utterance clearly, the Riordan-who-is-Caine."

"One of my colleagues was commenting on the awkwardness of this situation. However, we will continue to make our image available to you."

"This is a kindness—made greater, since we are currently unable to reciprocate. We shall not forget."

Hmmm: an unpromising start to that introduction, but a rather reassuring finish.

Alnduul's voice sounded very flat now. "And finally, may I present Darzhee Kut of the Arat Kur."

Another pause; another quatrefoil—this one yellow—flicked on and pulsed next to the green one. More rustling from behind; Visser looked at Thandla, made a slicing motion with her hand. The connection broke. She turned to Caine. "A *second* race chooses not to share its image? What does this mean?"

He shrugged, looked over at Elena, who shrugged back. "Let's find out." He nodded to Thandla: the water heater, the quatrefoils and Alnduul reappeared. "Our apologies. We are somewhat surprised at our inability to view so many of the species we came to meet." No response. "Darzhee Kut, can you hear me?" Still nothing. Then a third artificial voice whispered out of the yellow diamond: "I am Zirsoo Kh'n. Speaker-to-Nestless Kut is indisposed. We, too, decline to share our image."

Caine felt Visser look at him, then back at Downing: there was no mistaking the tone. Curt, clipped, no-nonsense: not exactly hostile, but certainly not friendly. "We are pleased to make your acquaintance, Zirsoo Kh'n."

"We are gratified to participate in this process."

But nothing nice to say about us, *huh?* Caine looked over at Elena, whose eyebrows were lowered into a shallow vee: she shook her head slowly. *Nothing to add yet, evidently.* "Alnduul, we are ready to begin."

Alnduul's fingers flared momentarily like pinwheels. "Very well. The member states have received the personal bona fides of your delegation. They are now permitted to inquire into them."

Silence. At least ten seconds of it. Caine was surprised at just how long ten seconds can be.

Alnduul prodded the other members again: "I remind the delegations that if they ask no questions, and make no challenges, the governing construance is that silence grants consent. Once accepted, the personal credentials of the human delegation is immune to subsequent interrogation or challenge."

Five more seconds—even longer ones—went by.

"So noted. The human delegation's personal bona fides are accepted without reservation or question. We may now proceed with the legitimation of the government they represent, which has been outlined in the dossiers you received yesterday. If there are questions—"

"Yes." The voice came from the yellow quatrefoil. The Arat Kur. Of course. "We do not understand some of the claims of the human government, which is referred to as the Earth Confederation. Specifically, it claims to be the collective medium whereby the will of humankind is solicited, represented, and made manifest. Do you dispute this?"

"Not at all," answered Caine. "If I remember correctly, you are quoting our own statement."

"I am. However, we find this claim suspect, since it seems that some nations were pressured into joining this Confederation."

"There were some fierce debates, yes. However, any exertions of political pressure were strictly in keeping with the normal principles of democratic process."

"Nonetheless, in the end, the greater nations imposed their will upon a number of weaker—albeit quite populous—states."

"Speaker Zirsoo, I would express that differently. No nation was compelled to join the Confederation. However, the great majority of nations—and through them, a majority of Earth's population—did agree upon a set of requirements that had to be observed by any country that desired membership in one of the Confederation's five blocs." Caine paused. "Just as the Accord imposes requisites for membership upon its member states."

"Touché." Caine could hear the smile that accompanied Lemuel's interjection. He also saw Alnduul's holographic mouth half-twist about its axis.

"He's trying not to laugh," supplied Elena.

But the Arat Kur were not finished. "We have another question. You categorize the Confederation's governmental structure as 'modified bicameral.' Please explain."

"Well, bicameral means—"

"Two houses of representation, now common among many of your nations. This we understand. We are interested in how this has been 'modified.'"

Caine looked at Visser—who was clearly nervous. *Yeah, I think this is where they try to put us in the bag.* "The first house of representation—called the

'Forum'—is the one in which all nations have equal representation: it is a 'one state, one vote' system.

"The second house—called the 'Assembly'—is the one in which national representation is proportional to a metric which balances population against productivity."

"This is what we noted with interest. As we understand it, nations with lower per capita productivity suffer a reduction in their total votes."

"That is correct."

"In other words, their populations are deemed less worthy of equal representation. Which, as a simple matter of mathematics, means that their citizens have a proportionally smaller number of votes representing their interests. This makes them, in your language, 'second class' citizens."

"I would not agree with that categorization."

"Perhaps not. But the fact remains that their representation in the Confederation's Assembly is not proportionate to their numbers."

Visser was shaking her head. Caine raised a— hopefully—stilling palm. "That is true."

"So the structure of the Confederation actually contradicts its claims to legitimacy: it does not provide equal and full representation."

"With respect, Speaker-to-Nestless, that is not what the Confederation claims. You cited the key passage yourself just minutes ago: the Confederation is—" he checked the paper that Visser had pushed into his hand—"the means whereby the 'will of humankind is solicited, represented, and made manifest.' There is no promise made regarding precisely equal representation."

"Your terms are misleading."

"Our terms are precise in what they claim and in

what they do not." Visser made a motion to stand alongside Caine: he nodded.

She leaned inward. "Honored delegates, pardon my intrusion. I am Ambassador Visser. As one of those who helped craft our Confederation, allow me to assure you that the language was not intended to be misleading. We could not claim equal representation at the global level because we cannot ensure it at the national level. Many nations have different limitations upon voting: age, sex, cognitive competency, group affiliation. If the political voice of each state is therefore created by excluding and including different segments of their society, how could we claim that the Confederation offered uniformly equal representation? Our objective was to produce the *most* representative, and yet workable, government that we could, with minimal intrusions upon each nation's sovereignty. I thank you."

Alnduul cycled his lids once, slowly. "Thank you, Ambassador Visser." They waited for a similarly polite response from the Arat Kur. After a second, Elena—eyes no longer rounded but oddly angular—shook her head: "Don't wait; they're not going to acknowledge her."

When the Arat Kur resumed, the simulated voice was slower, more cautious. "We are curious: was there a world organization before your current Confederation?"

"Yes."

"And what became of it?"

Caine looked around the gallery; there were frowns on the faces of Visser, Downing, Durniak, and Elena. *They see where this could go.* Visser shook a hand at Thandla: she waited until he had cut the connection. "I think we must decline to answer."

Elena spoke before Caine could open his mouth.

"Madame Ambassador, I do not think that is wise. They are clearly seeking to indict our credibility and integrity."

"So we must not allow them to by discussing this matter any further. We must convince them that we are worthy of their vote."

"With respect, Ms. Visser, their vote no longer matters."

"What?"

Caine nodded. "The Arat Kur have already decided against us. So our strategy must focus on how our actions make us look to the other member states."

Visser narrowed her eyes, nodded, gestured toward Thandla.

Caine resumed. "Our apologies for the brief silence. The organization which preceded the World Confederation was called the United Nations. We are currently in the process of shifting most of its responsibilities and activities to the Confederation."

"So the United Nations elected to willingly transfer its authority to the World Confederation?"

Damn. The Arat Kur had smelled the blood of human political discord and were on the scent— but how? Their questions were not just precise and penetrating—they were *too* precise, *too* penetrating, almost as if—

Visser had once again instructed Thandla to cut the connection. "This is over. We should never have agreed to respond to this line of questioning."

Caine looked at where the Arat Kur's blinking yellow quatrefoil had been. "No—we're fine."

"How can you say that? If we continue to answer their questions, they will soon be claiming that the

United Nations was illegally sidestepped. They will thus decide that the World Confederation is illegitimate, and that Earth is too politically factious to be a member state."

Caine shook his head. "No: the Arat Kur are already well past that point."

"What do you mean?"

"I mean that we've been wrong about the Arat Kur. Their questions aren't an attempt to acquire knowledge about us, or even to discover flaws or contradictions in our dossier."

"Then why are they asking these questions?"

"Because they already know the answers and hope that when pressed, we'll lie. Somehow, the Arat Kur already know about the uproar over how the Confederation usurped the power and prerogatives of the UN."

"How could they know?"

Downing had moved toward the center of the gallery. "It's impossible to know *how* they got the information. But we do know that it's illegal for them to have it. And that's a weapon we can use against them. We can expose them in front of the whole—"

"No." Visser's voice was unusually calm. Arms folded tightly, she was completely still, eyes closed.

"With all due respect, Ambassador, you said it yourself: we have to stop this line of questioning. I put it to you that this is the only way to really put an end to it. If we—"

"No. I am no longer concerned with ending this line of questioning." She opened her eyes. "The Arat Kur have laid a deeper trap."

Chapter Forty-Three

ODYSSEUS

Downing blinked. "A deeper trap?"

Visser nodded. "They know we will realize that their questions arise from illegally acquired knowledge."

"And that is precisely why we must expose them."

"Mr. Downing, they *want* us to expose them."

Durniak forgot her composure and her English in the same instant: "*Shto?*"

Visser shrugged. "It is the only reasonable conclusion. They knew we would figure this out. And they must logically presume that we will then expose their violations. But if they foresee this course of events, then it follows that they must welcome it."

"But why? What could they achieve?"

Elena's response to Durniak was slow but certain. "Discord."

Visser was nodding again. "*Ja.* Discord. This Accord is not so stable, I think."

Caine found himself nodding, too. "During our first contact, Alnduul mentioned the possibility of 'specious' actions by other member states. And then there was his reaction to our question about what would happen if we were declined membership: his gills snapped shut with a sound like a popgun going off."

Downing chimed in. "And then there's the anxiety over us blundering into someone else's 'pathway of expansion.' That should merely be awkward, not a crisis."

Visser furnished the deductive capstone. "If the Accord was politically coherent, then this entire candidacy process would simply have been a pro forma exercise. No: the Arat Kur's line of questioning is an attempt to use us to widen the rifts already present in the organization."

"And to put our candidacy in the trashcan." Elena was looking directly at Caine as she said it.

Caine forced himself not to be distracted by her eyes and pressed on. "What we really need are answers about *why* the Arat Kur are trying to spoil the party."

Lemuel rolled his eyes. "Yeah, sure—but what the hell do we *do* about the Arat Kur? If we let them keep asking questions, they uncover Earth's dirty laundry for everyone else to see. And if we tell them we're on to them, they call us liars and everyone goes home angry. Or, we can simply lie about the UN. Then they'll expose our lies, we'll expose theirs—and we all go to hell together, anyway. So with choices like those—hey, Riordan; what're you doing?"

Caine had moved to the very end of the gallery, the tip of the teardrop's sharp tail. He touched the canopy. "Dr. Thandla, the Dornaani gave us the opacity for privacy. Do we have an override?"

"Er . . . yes, we do."

"Please restore the transparency."

"Wha—?" Visser gasped. Wasserman brayed a counterorder, but it was too late: the opalescent curve above them faded away.

Caine looked down at the Dornaani delegation. They were all—*all*—facing toward the human gallery. Eyes unblinking. Caine nodded at Alnduul, who made no movement in return.

Visser cleared her throat behind him. "Mr. Riordan—Caine—"

Caine felt all the Dornaani eyes looking directly at him, kept looking back at them as he spoke: "Here's what we do: we tell the Arat Kur—and the Accord—the truth. Everything. We deny them nothing. Give them every sordid detail they want to pursue."

"And when it becomes obvious that the Arat Kur have illegal advance knowledge?"

"We let someone else point it out. But I don't think that's going to happen."

"Why?"

"Because the Dornaani already know what's going on."

"What? How—?"

"They monitor us—legally. So they know about recent events on Earth, too: how else did they know about Nolan? So they *already* know that the Arat Kur have illegal access to information. But the Dornaani aren't pointing fingers, so I'm thinking that they'd like this to play out nice and calm. Which means that right now—oddly enough—the fate of the Accord and their Custodianship could be in our hands. Whether we publicly prove the Arat Kur, or ourselves, to be liars, is equally harmful to the Dornaani: both outcomes indicate that they have failed as Custodians, and it weakens the Accord."

Trevor was nodding. "Yup. That's how it would play out, for them. So they'd be happiest if we play dumb and go along with the charade."

"And thereby keep the peace."

Downing shifted his weight from one foot to the other. "Risky business, giving the Arat Kur any info they want."

Caine shrugged. "Except, if we're right, the Arat Kur came here expecting to cause an incident, not actually gather intel. So if they try to interrogate us without a prior investigatory game plan, we're likely to learn more from them than they will from us."

Downing's eyebrows went up. "Yes, that's probably true."

Visser was looking back and forth between them. "I do not understand."

"Caine is quite right, Ambassador. If we do not tip our hand—if we 'play dumb'—then the Arat Kur will want to keep asking more questions. But each one of their questions tells us a great deal about what they already know about us—and what they don't. With some careful analysis, we might even be able to reconstruct what sources of information on Earth they had access to—or at least those they didn't. The more questions they improvise today, the more we learn about them and their intelligence operations."

Caine nodded. "And it puts the ball back in the Arat Kur court: they'll damn themselves with their *own* actions."

Durniak nodded. "*Da.* And if the Arat Kur act like brutes, the undecided powers should be more likely to side with the Dornaani. But I wonder: are the Arat Kur alone in this?"

Caine rubbed his chin. "Maybe, but it's also possible that they're the patsies of one of the other two powers."

Trevor looked up. "What about the Slaasriithi? I find it pretty suspicious that they refuse to show themselves."

"Yeah, but so far, they've been affable, even if they're shy and cautious. It could all be an act, I suppose, but they seem pretty temperate: not as likely to be the movers and shakers in this club."

"And the Ktor? What about them?"

Caine looked across the amphitheater at the wheeled water tanks. "What about them, indeed. The wild cards."

"And what about *them*?"

"Who?"

Hwang pointed to the left. "The other new kids on the block." Caine turned, looked into the now-transparent gallery that had been assigned to the other candidate-race.

Rough brown-gray fur covered most of their pebbly hides. They were upright but digitigrade, standing at least two meters tall even without raising up on their long rear legs. A thick, round, pointed tail sent a faint line of lighter fur up the spine. It thickened into a crest where it divided the blocky haunches, mounted the barrel-shaped back between arrestingly large shoulders, and then ran along the ventral ridge of a neck that was the shape and thickness of a small pony's. As Caine's inspection reached the head, he heard Durniak gasp and Trevor mutter, "Christ."

The head was hardly a separate object; it was a seamless, curved continuation of the neck, which ended in three pronounced nostrils arrayed as the vertices of an equilateral triangle. On either side of that nose, two glinting obsidian eyes were mounted under bony ridges that flared out from whatever skull might be extant beneath the sheath of flesh and muscle that blended back into the neck. The rounded "head" was long, rather like a cross between that of a sloth and an anteater, but the underslung jaw was vaguely reminiscent of a sperm whale's. The spinal fur was heavier and thicker on the head, rising into a high, tufted crest. Caine's eyes met those of the—creature? It was hard to think of it as a person, just yet.

"Do you think they're part of the Arat Kur plot?" pressed Hwang.

Trevor exhaled emphatically. "Good God, I hope not," he said, staring at the short, wide swords that swung from each one's back-slung baldric.

Caine stayed silent, surveyed the group's reactions: Durniak seemed to be having the most profoundly xenophobic reaction—odd since her xenophobia index had been one of the lowest. But tests and reality are two very different things. Hwang and Thandla evinced almost spiritual detachment, whereas Wasserman seemed too contentious and self-involved to be affected. Elena looked captivated, not terrified. Visser seemed rigid, but was still coping. And Trevor's outburst struck Caine more like a means of purging anxiety rather than a declaration of it. All in all, the delegation was doing pretty well handling the sight of such profoundly different—and potentially ominous—exosapients.

The one who was looking at Caine raised a four-fingered hand—a thumb on either side of the palm—in what seemed a gesture of greeting, or maybe threat, or even warding. Caine raised his hand in response—

—just as the privacy screen reasserted. Caine turned; Visser had given the signal to Thandla. "We must resume our conversation with the Arat Kur; they are waiting."

Caine nodded to Thandla, then cleared his throat. "My apologies, Zirsoo. There was some debate as to how much detail we should use when responding to your question regarding the relationship between the World Confederation and the United Nations."

"You have finished your deliberations?"

"Yes. Please feel free to ask any question you wish."

And so began the dull recitation of the sad facts—which, in retrospect, read like the decline and fall—of the United Nations: its lack of efficacy; the interminable deadlocks in the Security Council; the self-interested posturing and dickering in the General Assembly; its successes in the areas of social welfare and education; and its dismal failures at ensuring, or even increasing, peace, security, and economic parity. As the questions became more specific, Visser and Durniak had to intervene more frequently to provide precise data. After receiving Durniak's long—and to Caine, baffling—answer regarding the accounting procedures used in the calculation of each nation's per capita productivity, the questions stopped. Everyone waited.

The yellow quatrefoil pulsed steadily, but no further queries came forth.

"Are there further queries regarding the legitimacy or authority of the government represented by the human delegation?" Alnduul folded his hands, waited. "Very well. If any delegation wishes to formally contest the legitimacy of the World Confederation of Earth, they must do so at this time."

A brief pause, then Zirsoo's simulated voice: "The

Arat Kur delegation must contest the human government's legitimacy. The covering dossier claims that it enjoys the approval of seventy-eight percent of the human population and that its leading nations control ninety-two percent of all global productivity. However, the approval percentages were not generated by universal one-person/one-vote polling, but by extremely disparate national surveys and referendums. Furthermore, we are concerned that the human delegation has not shared all the relevant facts regarding the legal creation of the World Confederation."

Alnduul's voice sounded exceedingly composed. "The Arat Kur delegation clearly must be dismissing the Custodians' observations, and preliminary report, that the World Confederation's practices—and origins— conform to their stated policies."

Sitting, Caine leaned his chin into his palm: *I wonder who else might have gotten their hands/paws/ pseudopods on that report before today?*

Zirsoo elected not to comment on the Custodial report. "We contend that our arguments warrant the deferral of this Convocation's consideration of human membership status until such time as a special investigation can resolve the discrepancies we have cited. Furthermore, we point to the illegal means used by the World Confederation to replace the United Nations. Even if the Confederation enjoys the majority support it claims, it is the fruit of a poisoned root: its illegitimate origins compel us to disallow it as a legitimate government."

Alnduul's mouth seemed to stretch into a line. "Very well. Are there any other challenges to the legitimacy or authority of the human government?"

Silence.

Alnduul parted his arms. "The objections of the Arat Kur have been noted. However, the Custodians find them to lack sufficient substance to warrant special investigation into the representativeness of the human World Confederation."

Smiles were springing up around the gallery, but Caine leaned forward: *If the Arat Kur were front men for someone else's agenda, the real heavies would have to step in right about now—*

Wise-Speech-of-Pseudopodia's voice was mild. "Would it not be appropriate to poll the member states to determine if an investigation is warranted?"

Alnduul's hands stopped in mid-gesture. "It would hardly seem necessary. The Arat Kur did not contest, but simply ignored the detailed—and contrary—findings of the Custodial observation group."

"Even so, is not a call for investigation at least a matter upon which we should all vote?"

"No other member state challenged the legitimacy of the Earth government. And it is within the Custodians' purview—indeed, it is among their express responsibilities—to chair all Accord proceedings to ensure not only fairness but to prevent obstructionism."

Wise-Speech's response was slow and careful. "So you are accusing the Arat Kur of raising their issues simply to obstruct this process?"

Alnduul's mouth stretched into a thin, flat line. "I am suggesting that, since the Arat Kur present no evidence that challenges the findings of the Custodial observations, there are insufficient grounds to convene an investigation. I am surprised that the Arat Kur did not perceive that from the outset."

"And we are surprised at the Custodians' autocratic handling of this matter. Perhaps issues of unfair and unequal political practices are not restricted to the governments of Earth."

Caine heard breath sucked in hard and sharp between clenched teeth: Trevor. Downing and Visser seemed to be engaged in a frowning contest. Wasserman sprawled back, stuck his tongue so far into his cheek that it looked like he had dislocated his jaw: "Well, *that* wasn't very friendly."

But Alnduul proceeded without responding to Wise-Speech's sharp—if oblique—rebuke: "The legitimacy of the World Confederation of Earth is recognized. Member states may now submit general inquiries to the human delegation."

A long pause. The voice of the Slaasriithi, Vishnaaswii'ah, emanated from the blinking green quatrefoil: "Has the human delegation prepared an encyclopedic self-reference for distribution to interested species?"

Caine nodded. "We have. We had thought the appropriate time to offer it was in today's final step—that reserved for unofficial inquiries."

"Your conception of protocol is correct. If you feel it is a fair and thorough almanac of your species, then we feel no need to ask any specific questions at this time. Rather, we shall compile a list of queries occasioned by our perusal of your self-reference."

"That seems quite prudent."

Wise-Speech's simulated voice followed quickly: "The Ktor elect to follow the same procedure, in the interest of shortening the official portion of these proceedings."

Hwang wiped his glasses. "Sounds like he's had enough for one day."

Alnduul gestured up at Caine and Visser. "The Convocation now invites questions from the human delegation. In the interest of brevity, please do not ask more than twenty questions of any given member state."

Caine, standing outside the sending circle, smiled ruefully. "Never thought I'd be playing twenty questions again."

"Yeah, well, this time, you're playing for keeps." Lemuel was not smiling.

"True enough." Caine moved forward into the communication node again. "Alnduul, honored delegates, we have prepared our questions beforehand, and elect to submit the same twenty questions to each member state. Transmitting our questions now." Caine nodded to Thandla, who pressed a virtual button on the touch-sensitive control screen, and leaned back.

Downing broke the silence. "Bombs away."

Trevor looked over at him. "Which set of bombs are we dropping, anyway?"

"Given the arm's-length attitudes we've encountered today, we decided on sticking with the basics: where they're from, what they're made of, how long they've been puttering about the stars, when they joined the Accord, which stars are on their allowed pathway of expansion. And of course, a few key questions on the state of their technology. We'll use it all to construct a timeline, an astrographic map, project their capabilities."

Elena cocked her head. "And culture and language—?"

"We will get to that in the unofficial information requests, Ms. Corcoran." Visser had started to pace from one side of the gallery to the other. "Such sociological data are crucial. But with only twenty questions, we must secure key strategic data first."

Wasserman looked up. "Speaking of strategic data, if the Arat Kur—and the other member states—were playing by the rules, they shouldn't be able to do any more than listen from the edge of our space. And that means that all their information about Earth should be at least nine or ten years old, since that's the number of light-years between the outer edges of the zone they've reserved for us, and the nearest other stars. So if the leak isn't from that Dornaani report—"

Downing nodded. "Then someone has been eavesdropping from just outside our home system. Or even inside of it."

"And to get to Earth, they would have to violate a lot of our other systems first—and be able to do it on the sly."

Visser looked from Wasserman to Downing to Caine. "You are all assuming that the exosapients, like us, have to start their shift from a solar system. If they don't, or if they have shift ranges of fifteen or twenty light-years—"

Wasserman jumped in. "If the Arat Kur can pull off stunts like that, then we're so screwed it hardly matters."

"Why?"

"Because that would mean that their technology is so far beyond ours, that we're just a bunch of grunting Neanderthals compared to them."

"Which is possible."

"Possible," commented Elena, "but I think not."

"Why?" Visser asked.

"Because the Arat Kur seem worried about us. Genuinely worried. Don't misunderstand me; I, too, suspect that they might be cat's-paws for another member state. But I also believe that their objections to our candidacy reflect their own fears."

Downing nodded encouragement. "Go on."

"Uncle Richard, they are being rude to us. Pointedly and unnecessarily rude. And that behavior has clearly surprised the Dornaani, which suggests that it is not typical for the Arat Kur."

Visser was staring at her. "So what is the significance of this?"

Elena folded her hands. "It may be an unwarranted—a humanocentric—generalization, but when one group perceives itself to be in conflict with another group, the members of the first group tend to dehumanize the members of the second group."

Durniak nodded. "War propaganda. Racism."

"Exactly. But that is the extreme case. The far more common variety of this is a daily dynamic in every culture: being snubbed. That's what the Arat Kur have been doing to us."

"And why is that important?"

Elena turned to Visser. "If they were so much more powerful than us, then they would not bother to snub us. Think back on all those British novels that were obsessed with class tensions: a nobleman could freely chat with a tradesman. Why? Because his position was so much greater that his status was unthreatened by associating with the lesser being. But—"

Caine smiled. "But the middle classes would stick up their noses and snub the tradesman. Because they were still close enough to his level that any suggestion of intimacy with him threatened to lower their status by dint of association."

"Exactly."

Visser was frowning, but not at Elena. "So you are saying—"

"I know it seems circuitous, but I believe that the Arat Kur's rudeness, even hostility, suggests that they see us as possible rivals. And that suggests that they can't have the immense technological edge that would allow them to shift about the cosmos without having to obey the same laws of physics that we do. If they did, the worst we would experience from them is benign indifference."

Downing sat, hands on knees. "It's only a hypothesis, but a bloody good one. However, we're going to need more information in order to push this deductive process further along."

Visser nodded. "Very well. So how do we go about doing that?"

Caine coughed politely and looked around the room: all eyes were trained on him. He shrugged: "Well, here's what I was thinking—"

Chapter Forty-Four

ODYSSEUS

Alnduul's image stood with hands folded as Caine stepped closer. "Alnduul, just a moment ago, we detected a crucial oversight on our part: we neglected to send questions to one other important group."

"If you refer to the other candidates, the Hkh'Rkh, they are not yet a member state, and so your inquiries may only be made informally, at the end of today's official proceedings."

"Alnduul, the Hkh'Rkh are not the group to which we wish to address our questions."

Alnduul's inner eyelids slowly closed. "I am perplexed. There is no other group."

"With respect, there is: the Custodians."

Alnduul's mouth seemed to squirm. "I remain perplexed: you are obviously aware that the Dornaani are the Custodians. Answers to your questions on the Dornaani sphere are currently being crafted by Third Arbiter Glayaazh."

"Alnduul, the questions we would ask the Custodians are different than those we would ask the Dornaani."

"How so?"

"We have asked the Dornaani questions pertaining to their history. But if we were to wish information on the history of the Accord itself, it seems only right to ask the Custodians. And I must believe—since Custodianship is not a permanent position—that the Dornaani and the Custodians are separate political entities. Or is the voice and will of the Dornaani the same thing as the voice and will of the Custodians?"

Alnduul's lids slowly cleared his eyes: the pupils were fixed upon Caine. "None before have made such a distinction when submitting their questions."

Caine felt several retorts and appeals rush up like an incipient, reflexive shout. Trusting instinct, he pushed them back down—and waited.

Alnduul's eyes did not waver. "However, it is an apt distinction. And perhaps more necessary now than in the past."

Behind him, Lemuel's "We're in!" drowned out a chorus of relieved sighs, all from outside the sending circle.

Alnduul gestured to himself. "I shall be the one to answer your questions. You may proceed."

"Before beginning, we wish to clarify: the Custodians may not withhold information pertaining to their own activities, is this correct?"

"Fundamentally, but there are two key exceptions."

"Which are?"

"Until you are conferred membership, we will not indicate the existence of, nor discuss any of our activities involving, any protected species."

"Understood. And?"

"And, if in answering your questions regarding our activities as Custodians, we would be forced to disclose information on other member states, we must decline to answer."

"We assumed so. However, did you not, during our first contact, indicate that another race had been recruited to augment the Custodians in a variety of routine functions?"

"This is so."

"So we may also ask questions regarding the performance of those functions as well, correct?"

A pause. *Gotcha. But maybe you're glad we've found this loophole—*

"You may."

"By extension, then, we may ask the identity of these auxiliary Custodians?"

A longer pause. "We have never considered this particular line of inquiry. However, revealing any of the activities of a member race would violate the race-privacy protocols of the accords."

"Allow me to verify that I am accurate in my understanding: is it true that this other race has served as Custodians?"

A long, long pause. Then: "Yes, they work as Custodians."

"Then I do not understand how questions pertaining to them, or their identity, are protected under the accords. The Custodians themselves have no such protections."

"No, but the racial identity of our assistant Custodians is irrelevant. Their species of origin does not alter their responsibilities or their performance of them."

Caine had foreseen that rebuff: "Alnduul, do you believe that the nature of an observer influences what they observe, and thus, what they report?"

"Yes: we hold this to be a fundamental tenet of the limits of empirical method."

"So do we. So I must insist that the speciate identity of a given Custodial team will ultimately shape the work they do. By inescapable deduction, then, their identity is pertinent to any detailed inquiry into the overall history and performance of the Custodial function within the Accord."

"Please excuse me for a moment."

No one in the gallery spoke. Alnduul's "moment" was seven minutes in length. Then: "Thank you for your patience. Although we have no extant policy on this matter, your reasoning is without flaw. In the absence of explicit rulings to the contrary, we hold that you may inquire as to the identity of those who have been solicited to assist us in routine Custodial tasks."

"Good job, Riordan." Lemuel's mutter was triumphant. Visser was smiling fiercely; Downing only nodded and mused. Elena seemed to be carefully staring somewhere else.

And now, the 64,000-credit question... "Which member state has been assisting you in Custodial matters?"

Alnduul's pause was peculiar in that Caine could not see any reason for it. "The Ktor."

Eyes closed, Downing nodded vigorously to himself.

"May we ask how the Ktor were chosen, and why?"

Again a long, strange pause. Alnduul's thumbs seemed to flex downward slightly—

—and Elena was on her feet. "He's embarrassed—or apologetic—or annoyed."

"Annoyed at us?"

"No. At himself."

Alnduul stood straighter. "I cannot reveal all the circumstances surrounding that choice, for to do so would violate the privacy of several member states. However, I may tell you that the Ktor volunteered to serve in this role. Furthermore, the requirements of Custodianship make it most prudent to solicit help from other member states in descending order of their technical competencies."

Downing and Visser exchanged confirmatory nods.

"Logical," Durniak whispered. "As the most senior member state after the Dornaani, the Ktor are probably their closest technological rivals."

And therefore, Caine thought, *even more likely to be the ones behind the Arat Kur obstreperousness. But why? Well, we'll circle back toward that later—* "When was the Accord established?"

"Approximately seven thousand years ago."

The quiet in the gallery was absolute. Caine couldn't be sure, but it seemed as though some were holding their breath.

"Are the Dornaani the architects of the Accord?"

"For the most part, yes."

Huh? "There were other architects?"

"Not at the time of the Accord's formal institution seven thousand years ago. But the spirit and structure of the accords was borrowed from the founders of an earlier, analogous organization."

Just how far back are we talking about? But first things first: "Have there been other members of the Accord?"

"No."

"How long have the Dornaani served as the Custodians?"

"Approximately seven thousand years."

Whoa. "So you have always been the Custodians?"

"Yes."

Hmmmm... "Have other member states expressed interest in becoming the Custodians?"

"I am not allowed to say: it would imply the official actions or attitudes of other member states, not the Custodians. However, I may say this: the Dornaani are interested in identifying another species that would be willing to serve as Custodians."

I could interpret that about twenty different ways—and I don't have the time now to even ask about one. "Have the Custodians ever had to intervene in wars waged between species of the Accord?"

"No—not since the accords were established."

Well, that was either a big slip—or a big hint. "So, the Dornaani *were*—at some time over seven thousand years ago—involved in a war against one of the species that is now a member state of the Accord?"

"We may not answer; your question concerns events that predate the Accord. Consequently, you are inquiring into the history of different species, not the Custodians."

"My apologies for overstepping. It was unintentional."

"Your apology is noted and appreciated, but unnecessary. It was plain that the question arose from eagerness, not guile." A pause, a slight rotation of Alnduul's mouth. "My entire delegation notes your deductive—inventiveness—with interest, Caine Riordan."

Thanks for the pat on the head; next you'll be giving me a cookie—"Have Dornaani Custodians ever landed on any of our planets?"

"Yes."

Now, let's find out who else has been poking around our backyard. "Have Ktoran Custodians ever landed on any of our planets?"

The pause was marked. "They have received no such orders or authorization, and we have received no such reports."

Hmm—not a "yes," but not a "no," either. "Has a species ever been considered for membership which ultimately did not become a member?"

"No."

"So the Custodians know of no races other than the ones that are presently in the Accord?"

Alnduul's fingers fluttered. "There is historical record of other races. However, there has been no official contact with them—if they still exist—since the institution of the Accord. Therefore, knowledge pertaining to these races is the province of those species which have retained records of their contacts with these other species."

Tell your non-Custodian Dornaani pals to expect a tidal wave of questions on that *topic. And now, the key question*—"Other than the Custodial report to the Accord, is there any condition under which it would have been legal for the Custodians to share information about Earth with any member state?"

"Absolutely not." *Ah hah.* "Even the Dornaani Collective is not allowed such information, despite the fact that it is the member state charged with Custodianship." Alnduul's lids half-closed. "We trust that this answer provides additional context to several of the inquiries that were addressed to your delegation earlier today."

Visser smiled. "*Ja*, he has confirmed that the Arat Kur have obtained information illegally."

Wasserman snorted. "He all but winked."

Caine wondered how much time they had left before the other member states relayed their responses to the twenty questions. No time to waste. "Why was Earth not contacted prior to, or shortly after, our entry into the 70 Ophiuchi system?"

Alnduul's thumbs opened downward, longer fingers waving listlessly, fitfully. "The Custodians' Human Oversight Group received conflicting field reports regarding your interstellar expansion. This resulted in a very late first report to the Accord, which then debated—for two years—over delaying your hearing in order to combine it with that of the Hkh'Rkh. By that time, your race had not only visited but commenced the settling of 70 Ophiuchi. I cannot say more without revealing—" Alnduul held up his hand in what seemed to be a universal "stop" gesture. "The member states have all submitted their responses to your questions. We must consider your inquiry of the Custodians to be ended. I have also been asked to inform you that the Dornaani member state has been pleased to answer all your questions in detail."

—*Well, no surprises there*—

"Now please open your channels to the other member states."

Caine nodded at Thandla. Wise-Speech and the green and yellow quatrefoils returned.

Alnduul spread his arms. "The delegates of the member states will now respond to the inquiries of the delegation from Earth."

Wise-Speech managed to produce a tone at once apologetic and sympathetic. "The Ktor delegation welcomes the keen human interest in our species. Indeed, their questions are so far-ranging and pregnant with greater implications, that we cannot answer them in the sterile format necessitated by these proceedings."

Damn: strike one—

"We would welcome an opportunity for more expansive, less rigidly structured discussions."

"'Let's talk over drinks.'" Wasserman's paraphrase even got a smile out of Visser.

Vishnaaswii'ah began a moment later. "The Slaasriithi also feel that, given the diverse questions posed by the human delegation, we would prefer not to proceed until their species has a more complete concept of us."

God damn; strike two—

"Accordingly, we shall send our response in the form of a primer, used to associate our very young with our history, our language, our planet, our polity."

Wasserman rolled his eyes: "See Dick run. Run, Dick, run."

"This primer," continued Vishnaaswii'ah, "and the supplemental materials, are an excellent foundation from which to develop further lines of inquiry. We hope you are not offended that we offer this in place of direct answers to your inquiries."

Caine raised his voice over Wasserman's sardonic guffaw. "We will look forward to receiving your primer, Vishnaaswii'ah. And we take no offense: we are thankful that you took it upon yourself to furnish us with what you feel is the best and most helpful first exposure to your race."

"And our thanks for your patience and gracious response. I think, upon close consideration, you will find the text and the supplementary materials quite— illuminating."

Caine looked around the gallery; Elena was the

only other one who had apparently noted the faintly stilted diction of the last comment. She looked at him, eyebrow raised: "Why mention the supplementary materials twice? Why mention them at all?"

He nodded. "And why emphasize that they would be 'quite illuminating' upon 'close consideration'? That sounded like a surreptitious prompt, to me."

Downing nodded. "Yes, but right now, let's hear what the Arat Kur have to say."

Caine felt the delegation's eyes turn, along with his, to the blinking yellow quatrefoil. Ten seconds later, they were still waiting.

"Speaker-to-Nestless Zirsoo, there may be a problem with the communications equipment; we are not receiving your responses."

"The communication equipment is operating properly. We decline to respond to your questions."

Strike three—a blind miss—and out. Not a single question answered.

Alnduul folded his hands. "The human delegation has received all formal responses."

Caine stepped closer to the image of the Dornaani. "Alnduul, we would like to ask a question."

"Yes?"

"Have member states elected not to answer the formal questions of candidate races before this?"

"Yes."

"How many questions have been declined—in toto—over the course of all the prior candidacy hearings?"

Alnduul folded his hands more tightly. "Two."

Caine turned to face the others. "Yep. We're in deep shit."

❖   ❖   ❖

After the long silence that followed, Visser's voice sounded very tired. "So, any ideas what we should do now?"

Elena looked over at Caine—inquisitively, tentatively—before suggesting, "We could have a party."

The room was more silent than before. At the words "have a party," Hwang commenced looking sidelong at Elena, as if assessing her for signs of impending mental collapse. Wasserman's reaction was even worse: he smiled, kindly and a bit crestfallen, as if he'd just learned that a favorite sibling had been diagnosed with dementia.

But Elena kept looking at Caine—and then he understood. "Yes—of course."

Durniak's head snapped back. "We should have a party? Now?"

Elena's hands were suddenly as lively as Alnduul's. "No, no—not a party for us. For them. A diplomatic reception."

"So that's our show of strength and resolve? They insult us, and in return, we feed them?"

Caine turned toward Wasserman. "No—she's absolutely right. And not just on the level of communications, but tactically."

"Pardon?" Downing's eyebrows were raised.

"Sun Tzu; always do what your adversary won't anticipate. Always find fields of engagement that minimize your weaknesses, maximize your strengths. Always strike them where they are most vulnerable. And Elena's suggestion accomplishes all those things."

Visser nodded. "Yes, of course. Today, almost all the member states either dismissed us or attacked our credentials: the last thing they will expect is a social invitation."

Downing smiled. "And, being the diplomatic victors of the hour, the Arat Kur can hardly reject an invitation without also making themselves look like utter cads. They've got to be gracious in victory—or they come away looking petty and ungenerous."

Durniak was frowning. "What if the other member states do not care how they look? So we give a party. Some do not show. Others say *ne kulturny*, shrug, and turn their backs. How does this help us?"

Elena nodded. "It might not. But I think it will, at least with the Dornaani. And perhaps more importantly, I think it could be very important in our future relationships with the Slaasriithi—and the Hkh'Rkh."

Visser squinted at Elena: "Important in what way?"

Elena leaned back, collected herself—and Caine had the impression of an organist surveying all the keys, pumps, stays, and pushes before starting a complex concerto. "Firstly, I suspect that those two member states are the ones most likely to be undecided about us. The Slaasriithi, in particular, seem not to be a part of the Arat Kur's ploys—"

"Even though they also refused to be seen, and refused to answer our questions."

"True, Dr. Thandla, but they were always very polite and suggested that more complete communication would be forthcoming. The Hkh'Rkh are new, like ourselves, and could hardly have come with any preconceived notions—"

"Unless the Arat Kur got to them first."

She looked at her brother. "And if that's the case, Trev, then the Accord is more sham than substance. Fully half the current or prospective members would be actively involved in subverting its basic principles. How long do you think it will last, if that's the case?"

Trevor met her gaze. "I didn't say I think it *will* last. In fact, if you were taking bets—"

Downing stood. "Agreed—things are looking shaky all around. But I think Elena's making some excellent points. The greatest remaining strategic prize is the good opinion of those races which may be undecided about humanity, particularly since the decision upon our membership is to be made tomorrow. So, if the Arat Kur accept our invitation, we have an opportunity to learn about them; if they do not, they have shown themselves to be aggressive and unfriendly in formal council, and rude and inconsiderate in informal interaction. And in contrast, we will come across as patient, congenial, forgiving—"

"And weak." Wasserman leaned forward. "No member state is going to ally with us against another because someone turned up their nose at our appetizers. Christ, it's just a party."

Caine tried to keep his smile from becoming ironic. "*Just* a party? Lemuel, where do you think most politicking is done, where most deals are made? At meetings? No: on the side. Meetings are for show; the real action is taking place over drinks. Wars are won, land ceded, truces made in the time between the crudités and the canapés. Besides, Elena's plan has another upside."

"What's that?"

"The Ktor. Remember what they said?"

Wasserman smiled. "Yeah, that they would welcome 'an opportunity for longer, less rigidly structured discussions.'"

"Precisely. They asked for an invite, so we're sending them one. And I think they're the ones we really need to talk to."

Visser frowned. "Why?"

Downing jumped in. "Because they've got their fingers—maybe tendrils—in almost all of the issues that involve us. They're the surrogate Custodians who may or may not have visited our systems. They want to talk with us, but not briefly or in public. They don't challenge our legitimacy but they make trouble when the Dornaani try to put aside the Arat Kur objections to it. And their seniority and technology is second only to the Dornaani." Downing shook his head. "We have to talk to them before tomorrow's decision. They know it. They made sure of it."

"You're saying—?"

"That they orchestrated many of today's events? I'd lay odds on it."

Visser raised an eyebrow. "So you think they'll come?"

Caine stepped toward the communication node: "There's only one way to find out—"

Chapter Forty-Five

ODYSSEUS

"You're sure you're okay?" Opal was on the way out of the reception hall.

Caine looked up. "Why?"

"Because you look like shit, darling."

"Tough day at the office."

"Sounded like it, from where I was sitting. And I'll be happy to be back at my boring post for most of this evening." She looked around at the platters that had already emerged from the serving alcove: buffalo carpaccio and kibbe nayyeh *sans* bulgur—Elena's best guess at what the Hkh'Rkh would consider delicacies. Opal wrinkled her nose at the raw meats.

"Finger food," Caine explained.

"Road kill," she countered. "Look, take it easy: you've been working too hard, running on fumes."

"I'm fine—fine." No one was looking; he ran his palm into and around the taut arch that was the small of her back.

Her eyes sprang wide, as if he had pinched her. "Caine—not here!" she remonstrated. But her smile—and her quick half-step closer to him—said otherwise.

"You're such an old-fashioned girl."

Her smile faded, replaced by a look that was more intent. "Yeah, sure. Demure. Passive—" her next half step brought the tip of her right breast into faint, split-second contact with his left upper arm "—Uninventive."

He smiled and looked away. "We'll see about that— later. Now, get out of here."

"I hear and obey, mighty one—at least until you try to last a minute with me on the mats."

What came to mind was not karate. "Or on some other flat surface."

Her smile returned. "Flat surface? No imagination." She headed for the exit, turned, flashed a grin that was also a leer and a promise, and then went around the corner.

Visser, Thandla, and Downing entered from the same spot, escorting close to a dozen Dornaani, several of whom were carrying what looked like immense wooden bowls. The Dornaani immediately dispersed into the room: the humans headed straight for Caine.

"What's with the bowls?"

"Think of them as fruit baskets, sent with the regrets of the Slaasriithi." Downing surveyed the selection of highly spiced fish dishes that the Dornaani had requested.

"So you heard from them?"

Thandla nodded. "They would not explicate why they declined to attend. But they were very polite, very profuse regrets. Very like my great-aunts."

"And what's in the bowls?"

Downing stood aside as Hwang—chief chef along with Elena—swept past with four new trays of food. "I was serious, Caine: the bowls *are* filled with fruit. From their homeworld."

"And have we—?"

Thandla nodded. "One sample of each removed. Scanned for soil residues, but it looks like they've been sanitized."

"Better than nothing," agreed Downing.

"And then there's what our guests unintentionally leave behind—hair, dried skin, saliva, wastes." Caine shrugged. "I don't see how they can object to us collecting it for analysis. But I think our real priority has to be learning more about the intentions of these races—and we may not have a lot of time left in which to do that."

"I think this is twice I hear you suggest that there may be little time to ask questions." Durniak had approached from the other direction, rubbing at a stain on her blouse. "Why do you say this?"

"Because I think this meeting could come apart. Which means we could have a fuse burning in terms of how much time we have to get information. Which reminds me: any word from the Arat Kur?"

Downing shook his head. "Not a whisper. But look who's coming to dinner."

Several of the Ktor suspension tanks were rolling ponderously through the entryway. Visser unfolded her arms. "Mr. Downing, Mr. Riordan, let's welcome our guests."

Caine stared at the tanks. "I promised I'd help arrange the trays as Hwang and Elena bring them out. I'm sure the Ktor won't miss me."

Visser's head leaned sideways. "Or is it you who will not miss them?"

Caine shrugged. "We'll see."

Visser nodded, headed toward the doorway with Downing. Caine straightened out the trays; Durniak trailed behind: her duty—drinks—had been swiftly concluded. Beyond water, there wasn't much that any of the species had cleared for consumption. "How much of our food can they eat?"

"The Ktor passed on everything: not surprising, given they're in a fully sealed environment. The Dornaani seemed interested in lightly cooked and highly spicy seafood—particularly chowders or pastes, but they didn't seem to have any concern about digestibility. The Hkh'Rkh were pretty easy to plan for: Elena consulted the encyclopedic self-reference they exchanged for ours—she's now our resident expert on them—and confirmed that they process complex proteins almost exactly the same way we do."

"Meaning—?"

"Meaning that we're serving them a buffet of buffalo steaks—very rare—raw meats, sashimi, asiago cheese, goat's milk, chocolate truffles, chateauneuf-du-pape, stout."

Durniak stared. "We brought goat's milk?"

Caine smiled. "Yeah. Go figure."

"They seem to like strong tastes."

"Yes, Elena and Ben were warned to avoid serving anything that's bland."

"It seems like they've succeeded." Durniak said with a departing smile.

Seems so. Now where the hell is the Hkh'Rkh delegation and the—

"Here. Hold this." The command came from behind.

Caine turned—and found himself staring into glass-green eyes. He almost dropped the plate that Elena thrust into his hands. He looked down to see what was on it—and looked back up quickly. She had changed into evening wear: a sleek black dress with a plunging and—due to her figure—dramatic neckline. *I'm looking down again—and I'm staring.* He looked up again quickly.

Where he encountered her small smile. "Could you please hold them—both of them?"

Caine tried hard not to blink, but he did. "Could I—?" *I can't have heard that correctly. She wouldn't—*

"Please: hold both of them. Now."

He opened his mouth to speak, realized he had nothing to say, tried very hard not to look down again—but did. And saw that she was holding out a second plate for him to hold. *Oh, Jesus H. Christ.* He couldn't restrain a quick hiccough of laughter as he took the second plate, then looked up at Elena.

Whose long sweeps of black hair shone. Whose swimmer's shoulders sent long graceful lines down into a body that blended them into a composite of curves and arcs. Who was now staring at him—because, he realized, he was staring at her. Again.

Caine felt his face grow hot: *Great; I'm blushing, too.* "I'm—I'm sorry."

She considered him severely for two seconds, then a third, and then—her notably straight eyebrows set in a severe line—she said, "I'll let it go—this time."

And then she smiled. Bright, straight teeth, brighter eyes. The smile became a soundless laugh as she lifted her chin a little—and in that moment, Caine saw that she was indeed her father's daughter, down to the smile and the strange mixture of mischief and personal gravity. And she was, he had to admit, frankly beautiful.

But not in the way he'd already known, had seen (and looked away from) on numerous occasions now. At this moment, with her odd, intermittent evasiveness either forgotten or forsaken, she was intelligence and shrewdness and playfulness all mixed together.

By the time he became aware of his surroundings again, her eyes had changed. They were concerned, then almost panicked: her smile disappeared, she looked away, moved back toward the central alcove. Halfway there, she turned—was no longer radiating herself out toward him, but had drawn back into a weighty composure: "I'll be back with a platter." She turned sharply, moved away at a controlled pace.

He realized, some moments later, that he had not moved his body or his eyes. *I cannot—can* not—*let myself start gawking at her again. But I do wish I knew why she changes mood so quickly when—*

"Caine—they're here; the Hkh'Rkh." Visser was pulling at his elbow.

He turned to look at her, noticed that she seemed anxious. Or annoyed. Or maybe angry. "Where's Downing?"

"Back at the door, meeting them." She looked down, then directly up at him. "You have to go now. Have to go in my place."

"Why?"

"Because the Hkh'Rkh won't speak to me."

"What? Have they hopped on the Arat Kur bandwagon or—?"

"No: it is nothing like that." She seemed about to grit her teeth. "It is because I am a woman—no, a 'female.'"

Caine smacked his palm against his forehead. "Shit. I read that their society is absolutely patriarchal, but I completely overlooked how they might extend that paradigm to another species—"

She laid a hand on his arm. "*Gott in Himmel*, stop. This is not your fault; it is clear in retrospect only. Go; help Richard." She half rolled her eyes. "He needs it." Caine put down the plates he was still holding and made his way to the door.

Richard—who was 6'2"—was still half a head shorter than the smallest of the six Hkh'Rkh who had all but surrounded him. They leaned forward into his words, their immense bodies dwarfing the spare human torso. Caine side-shouldered into the ring of sword-toting monsters and smiled at Richard.

Whose aplomb was still considerable—but Caine could see that he was working hard at it. "Caine, may I present our honored guests, including He Who Is First Voice of the First Family." Downing's eyes indicated the second largest of the Hkh'Rkh, whose spine-tufts were slightly blackened and thinner, even wispy, at the tips. He also had more irregularly pebbled—or was that wart-covered?—skin seamed by cicatrices so venerable that they had begun to determine how the faintly sagging flesh fell in flaps: old, but still tough. "First Voice of the First Family, my apologies that I do not know how to greet you in your own language, or with your own gestures, but we—"

First Voice made a sound that resembled someone clearing their nose into a pipe. "Your ignorance is best: unhonored, your attempt at a formal greeting would be an insult to any who possess honor. The more honor they possess, the greater the insult." His tongue—a long, thin, black whip—sawed out of his nose and roiled about like a garter snake having a seizure. "And it is rumored that I possess some small measure of honor." Four of the other Hkh'Rkh also let their tongues writhe about in response: was this laughter?

The last one—the smallest of the group—stepped in Caine's direction; his tongue had darted out briefly and then away. *What was that? A polite chuckle at the joke of a boor born of the blood royale?*

"I am Yaargraukh, Advocate of the Unhonored," he said. "We appreciate that you accepted our tradition of always bearing our family blades. We may not venture beyond our chambers without them."

"We understand the tradition; there have been similar customs among our peoples. However, I do not understand your title; for whom are you an Advocate?"

Yaargraukh made a faint huffing noise. "I am the advocate of all the Unhonored. This is our term for what you would call 'exosapients.'"

"But you represent—are the spokesperson for—the Hkh'Rkh, are you not?"

"This is how it would seem to you, for I am the one who speaks with you to express the will of the First Voice of the First Family."

"So you are his advocate."

"The First Voice of the First Family needs no advocate; he speaks for himself, and, as First Voice, all Hkh'Rkh."

Ah. "I think I see; you are actually *our* Advocate—since exosapients are unhonored and therefore may not be heard by him."

Yaargraukh's nod—although it recalled a horse pitching its neck—was a surprisingly human gesture.

"Now you perceive. I carry your words to his ears—and add my own to them."

"So you are also a counselor to him?"

"No: I represent your interests, insofar as honor is concerned. The First Voice of the First Family needs no counsel. Allow me to finish the introductions—"

As Yaargraukh went round the rest of the small circle, Caine noted the honorifics: all war-boasts, reminiscent of Nordic deed-names such as *Skull-splitter* or *Gut-render. Okay, it's pretty clear they're not pacifists. And judging from their haughty demeanor, not particularly tolerant, either.* When introduced, they looked over Caine's head. Well, that was simply consistent: since he had no honor, he was—quite literally—beneath notice. Yaargraukh was finishing the introductions.

"—and this is Graagkhruud Great-claws of the Family Hnenkh'hien, First Arm of the First Voice of the First Family and what you would call General-over-all-Generals."

Graagkhruud did not even look toward Caine and Richard; he stared into the room as he was introduced. *For him, we're not just beneath notice—we're nonentities.* "And what is your honorific, Yaargraukh? I apologize if I missed your speaking of it."

"You missed nothing. When working as Advocate, I am not allowed honorifics."

"Why is this?"

Again, the huffing sound. "I would stain a title if I claimed it while representing the Unhonored."

Downing's tone suggested that he had had enough of the indirect denigrations, had forgotten that here, he was a diplomat. "I see. It would be like bringing the title into contact with something unclean?"

Yaargraukh was evidently not the only one who heard the combative tone. First Voice leaned forward again. "This bothers you? Why? Have you acquired honor?" Snakes writhed out of each Hkh'Rkh's larger, central nostril—except for Yaargraukh and Graagkhruud, who probably understood enough of the nuances to foresee that this joke could become deadly serious.

Downing leaned forward—*gotta give him points for guts*—toward the immense creature, his mouth open, no words coming out: self-respect and intelligence were at war, had stalemated his tongue into temporary stillness. But only temporary—

Caine stepped into the space between Richard and First Voice. "We cannot answer the question of First Voice of the First Family—not until we know how the Hkh'Rkh define the acquisition of honor."

The Hkh'Rkh's lidless black eyes became more protuberant, and they leaned back—surprised. All except Yaargraukh, who came closer: his eyes seemed to momentarily retract into the bony ridge that housed them before reappearing. *Hah, made you blink.*

"Spokesmale Caine of the Family Riordan, this is a serious question."

"With respect, Advocate, so was the one asked by the First Voice of the First Family—whom I assume I should not address directly until I have acquired honor."

Yaargraukh and the First Voice exchanged a long look before First Voice spoke to—and looked at—Caine. "You have said two true things, Spokesmale Caine of the Family Riordan. The question is serious, and, yes, by our custom, it is an affront for you to presume to address me directly. You learn quickly. And he—"

motioning toward Downing "—speaks boldly. But you have no way to acquire honor, for being Unhonored, you may not be challenged by, nor offer challenge to, the Honored. This respects the Honored; this protects the Unhonored."

Catch-22: you have to have an initial entitlement to honor to be able to attain it; a closed society. "I see. So we are like—females? Or young?"

First Voice now leaned in also. "So you have read the—" he struggled for the word in English "—the encyclopedia we relayed to you earlier?"

"I regret that First Voice of the First Family must be told that I have not had the opportunity to do so." *Too busy skimming the Dornaani self-reference for anything that might provide hints on their relations with the Ktor.*

First Voice leaned back again with a horselike nod. "So you discerned it yourself, just now. Spokesmale Caine's intelligence makes him an ornament to the reputation of the Family Riordan. A pity you may not acquire honor."

Hmmmm . . . "Advocate, is all honor acquired by challenge?"

Yaargraukh's head bobbed. "In one form or another, yes."

"So females may not challenge, and may not fight— even each other."

"This is so; this is necessary."

"Then what does it mean when a human has challenged a human, is even an accomplished warrior among us?"

Except Yaargraukh, all the Hkh'Rkh blinked. *Ha— gotcha with that one.* Eventually First Voice looked over at Yaargraukh, who turned to Caine: as he did, his neck oscillated in a faint circle around the center of its resting axis—a "shrug?" "We have no answer for this. We have never had an answer for this."

"Never?"

"Never." Yaargraukh studied Caine closely. *Is he trying to read my expression?* Evidently the Advocate succeeded: "You forget that your broadcasts have been reaching us for many, many years. Did you not think it odd that I speak so much of this human language?"

Jesus, am I a dope. "Allow me to compliment you, and the First Voice of the First Family, upon your command of English."

"The First Voice of the First Family chose to learn it for this occasion; I have had the advantage of long training. To return to your question: we have long been undecided how to address one of your warriors. It seemed an unnecessary question to answer—until now."

"Well, Advocate, the quandary you left unanswered now stands before you in the flesh." Caine indicated Richard, who stared at him.

"This male, Richard of the Family Downing, until injured in one leg, was an elite warrior in his youth— and a commander of as many as fifty such elite warriors who were of lesser rank."

Yaargraukh swung far back—surprise? First Voice seemed to rear up higher: he looked down—but directly into Richard's eyes. "You are a warrior? In answering, you may address me directly."

Richard shrugged. "Yes, I was—a long time ago."

"This answer is no answer: one never stops being a warrior. One is, or one dies."

Yaargraukh intervened. "With respect, First Voice of

the First Family, consider your own cousin, Uungsk'srel Swift-Eye: although he lost both legs in the Eighth Zh't'zhree Dispute, he has yet to lose a challenge."

First Voice reflected for a moment. "This is true. And he speaks more war-wisdom with each passing year."

Downing, emboldened, leaned closer to Yaargraukh, mimicking their body language. "Pardon me, but how can a legless Hkh'Rkh prevail in combat?"

"Not all challenge is combat, Richard of the Family Downing. The one who is challenged chooses the means of its resolution. Uungsk'srel Swift-eye, having lost his ability to fight, now always chooses contests of the mind; he is largely held to be invincible, and is now but rarely challenged."

Richard turned halfway toward Caine: "Like the old code duello; the man challenged chooses the weapons."

Yaargraukh had stepped a little closer. "So you remain a warrior?"

"I remain unafraid of challenges."

"This is well-answered—but we cannot yet know what it means in terms of honor."

First Voice waggled his neck. "Some questions are answered simply by living with them. So you may guide us to your food, Richard of the Family Downing— and if you are careful in your tone, so that there is no hint of challenge, you may speak to me directly."

Richard had regained his composure—and his diplomatic acumen. "I am honored, First Voice of the First Family. And I would first take you to meet a human I suspect you shall find even more perplexing in the matter of human honor than I am."

"How so?"

"He is a great warrior and war-captain—and recently

rescued his sister from abductors, slaying half a dozen single-handedly to do so. He is also the son of a great warrior and a great general. His name is Trevor Corcoran; would it please you to meet him?"

First Voice's spine fur had spiked straight up and was quivering. "Show me this human." They went into the room together.

Yaargraukh lingered behind a moment. "It has been gratifying to meet you, Caine of the Family Riordan. I noticed your name in the human self-reference; I would speak with you again."

I'm in the self-reference? What the hell for? Aloud: "I would welcome that, Yaargraukh. If you have heard many of our broadcasts, then you will know humans often agree to such invitations merely to be polite, but I mean it when I say that I look forward to our next meeting. Very much."

Yaargraukh leaned closer; at this range, the odor of his breath was discernible: it was a cross between musk and fresh-mown clover. "We shall speak again before this evening ends." He placed one of his massive hands at the base of the immense, smooth slope of his ribcage. "My honor." He pony-nodded and followed First Voice's entourage.

Chapter Forty-Six

ODYSSEUS

Caine watched as Yaargraukh's hulking back disappeared among those of his fellow Hkh'Rkh. *If most of the Hkh'Rkh are like him, we're in good shape, but if they're mostly like Graagkhruud*—Caine elected not to proceed down that speculative path. He returned to the buffet tables, where a cluster of Dornaani had surrounded Visser, possibly because she was standing in front of—and preventing access to—the seafood dishes.

Caine announced his approach with the Dornaani greeting: "Enlightenment unto you."

Alnduul turned halfway, so that his back faced neither Caine nor Visser; a very wrinkled Dornaani joined him in his change of facing. "Enlightenment unto you, Caine Riordan. I wish to introduce Third Arbiter Glayaazh."

Recent reading triggered a connection: the Third Arbiter was the number three spot in the Dornaani Collective. *So that's who was representing their race down in the dome today.* Caine made the splay-fingered gesture; the raisinlike Glayaazh responded in kind, lids half closed.

Caine spoke as he moved over to Visser's side. "It is a great honor to meet you, Third Arbiter." He took Visser's elbow gently, towed her closer to Alnduul—and away from the food. The other Dornaani moved into the vacated space and began daintily yet greedily emptying the trays. Visser remained oblivious to anything but Glayaazh.

Who spoke softly. "As I was remarking to your ambassador, your patience was exemplary this day. But more important, so was your decision not to reciprocate the inconsideration of others. This is the sign of a mature race; we are honored to have you here."

"I wish others felt the same way."

"Surely, some do. However, I do not believe that any of today's difficulties reflects an attitude toward your species. Rather, these behaviors were intended to exacerbate disputes already extant in the Accord."

"Then it would seem to me, sir, that—"

Glayaazh's mouth made a quick quarter-rotation. "You may wish to know that, according to your conventions of address, it would be more accurate to title me 'madame.'"

Caine felt his face grow warm briefly. "Glayaazh—ma'am—my sincere apologies."

"They are unneeded, but it if puts you at ease, I accept them. Now, you were preparing to offer an observation?"

"I was simply going to remark that if this is the usual degree of discord and tension, then the 'Accord' is a rather oxymoronic title for this organization."

A tiny ripple distressed Alnduul's perpetual pout. "Well said. And, sadly, true. Particularly since any failure to resolve these frictions is indicative of our failure as Custodians."

"That seems an overly harsh self-assessment, Alnduul. But, on a practical level, since we do not know what the Accord's current tensions pertain to, it is difficult for us to know how best to proceed."

"We are aware of, and regret, this." Glayaazh considered the small bowl which, minutes before, had held a thorough sampling of the sashimi: the fish was gone, the rice remained. "I must also remark that despite your artfully oblique inquiry, I cannot tell you more about these disagreements." A pause. "Not at this time."

Caine remained calm, even as he grasped after the thin strand of hope that Glayaazh had just proffered. "Can you tell us more about these disagreements before we return to Earth?"

"I would like to do so."

Visser folded her hands. "May I speak frankly?"

"Of course."

"It is of great importance to us to better understand the frictions to which you allude. So when deciding whether you will share this information with us, what will determine your course of action?"

"Why, *your* course of action." Glayaazh placed her bowl delicately on the nearest buffet table. "You must excuse me: I tire easily. The ceviche was particularly delectable. I thank you." She splayed her fingers— "Enlightenment unto you"—and started toward the exit.

Caine moved his arms to return her gesture—and barely stifled a gasp of pain: there was a sudden uncomfortable spasm in the arm which had been wounded during the assassination attempt on Mars. *Damn.* He rubbed the small scar: the spasm—not really a pain—had been a surprise, since the injury hadn't bothered him for at least two weeks. He looked up: Visser had left along with Alnduul, attending Glayaazh and her retinue to the exit.

Caine considered selecting a quick snack—and heard a desperate gagging sound. He looked up, scanning, and saw both Downing and First Voice trying to choke down some delicacy that obviously failed to appeal to either of them.

"Old Families, old ways, old tastes."

Caine turned. Yaargraukh stood just behind him: his black tongue swished about like the tail of an intrigued cat, but was hidden behind a massive "hand." Caine smiled. "It seems that the Hkh'Rkh do not enjoy the *ikura*."

"Not all of us. Not all humans either, it seems." Downing was trying to wash down the last of the salmon roe with gulps of cold water.

"And you—do you enjoy the *ikura*?"

"The eggs of sea-creatures?" Yaargraukh's neck oscillated. "It is not a taste I am accustomed to, but it is not unpleasant. But then again, I haven't the luxury of only indulging the tastes of my ancestors: I am not of an Old Family."

"I do not understand: what do you mean, Old Family?"

"My regrets: I forget you have not read our self-reference. The Old Families trace their lineage back through dozens, even hundreds, of generations. They are what you would call our aristocracy." Caine was not yet fully accustomed to the inflections and intonations of English as spoken by the Hkh'Rkh, but Yaargraukh did not sound enthused.

"They are a minority of the Hkh'Rkh?"

"No, they are the majority—although that is changing. New Families—like mine—will soon be the most populous. If not in my lifetime, then during the lives of those I sire."

So Earth wasn't the only planet in the throes of dramatic social change. "How does a 'New' Family come into existence?"

"Many ways, but usually it is built from the remains of an earlier Family that was destroyed in war, or which was disbanded into Hearthless individuals. Sometimes, groups of the Hearthless can cohere long enough to establish a New Family, but that is rare."

What a peaceful sounding bunch. "It sounds as though the Hkh'Rkh are constantly involved in— settling challenges."

Yaargraukh looked at Caine directly. "What you wish to say is that we are always at war. You may speak your mind with me, Spokesmale Caine of the Family Riordan. I am your Advocate, and what is more, we have already shared truths that did not have to be uttered. We are on the path to more shared truths. Let us face them frankly."

"Agreed, Yaargraukh. And you may simply call me Caine."

Yaargraukh paused. "Among us, it is a blow to honor not to speak one's Family and title. Or it is a sign of great familiarity, as among members of the same Family. I would not diminish what honor you might one day prove to have, Spokesmale Caine of the Family Riordan."

"Among humans, to address each other by first names alone is to share the hope that one will share more and more truths."

Yaargraukh considered. "When we are in private, or among humans, so shall we speak to each other. But among the Hkh'Rkh—particularly those of the Old Families—we must follow my ways: they will not understand your custom. And they would not approve of it if they did."

"Very well. The Old Families seem less flexible than the New Families."

"Like all generalities, that is an over-speaking, but yes: the Old Families feel that their ways are the only true ways. And that their bloodlines are the most worthy."

"But if a New Family is often built from the survivors of an Old Family—"

"That matters not. An Old Family that falls is deemed to have grown weak: that it could be overthrown proves that its members no longer deserved to be an Old Family. And Old Families no longer fall very often; that is mostly a fate of New Families."

"Are your Families always at war?"

"Understand, Caine. What we mean by 'war' is not what you mean. Only warriors are to fight in wars—and only warriors are to be killed in wars. Our planets—our homeworld included—are not blessed with the riches of yours. So our wars were not like yours. It was a breach of the honor-code—and madness, besides—to destroy cities and farmlands and great masses of the Unhonored." He paused. "At least, it was thus for millennia. But now—" He looked up, but not at Caine: Yaargraukh was staring at his own delegation. Whether he was focused on First Voice or Graagkhruud, Caine could not tell.

Caine proposed the conclusion to his unfinished musing: "Now, things have changed."

A single, slow pony-nod. "Things have changed—since we have factories. Since we have ground vehicles and air vehicles that range far and wide and swift. The honor-code is no longer law, but a tradition, a folkway: obeyed if convenient, ignored if it becomes too great an obstruction. And it is apparently becoming a greater obstruction with each passing year."

"Given what you have said, I do not understand why the Old Families tolerate the growth of New Families, why they do not band together to eliminate them."

Yaargraukh made a sound like a nickering snort. "You sound like an Old Family patriarch, Caine, though you do not mean to. The truth is that we are their pawns; the Old Families hold all power, almost all property, all authority. So the New Families do all of what you call the 'dirty work.' It is we who work mines, build structures under the seas, are granted leases and sometimes fiefdoms in deserts or polar wastes or on the marginal worlds we have found. And since I am your advocate, I may tell you—for you should know this—the Hkh'Rkh have only found marginal worlds."

Caine blinked. "Yaargraukh, if you tell me such secrets, won't you be—?"

"First, these are not secrets. We make the truth of us known at all times; you will see this in the self-reference, when you read it. Secondly, you must understand that I am indeed *your* advocate; it is part of my responsibility to ensure that you understand us so that your interactions with us are not marred by ignorance. And I say again: we have only found poor worlds. Even the best have only sparse vegetation and creatures that are so simple that one hesitates to call them animals at all. Most of the planets are too cold or too hot or too dry, and the New Families struggle to make them of value, so that we may survive—and so that the Old Families may prosper by our labor."

Caine looked up at Yaargraukh. "I can't believe they"—he looked at the other Hkh'Rkh—"would want you to be telling me *that*."

The Advocate's tongue extended, did a quick side-to-side wag, disappeared again: "No. Probably not. But you must know that our hopes—to find green worlds such as yours—have been unrewarded thus far."

"Yaargraukh, I appreciate your candor, but why do you feel that *these particular* truths are so important for me to know?"

The lidless, pupilless black eyes looked at him. "Because, Caine, the Hkh'Rkh are restless. The Old Families had thought the stars would bring them new worlds upon which they would plant new seeds of their power. The New Families longed for worlds where they could claim good, rich land for their own posterity. The worlds we have found have not merely disappointed these dreams; they have made mockeries of them."

"So why not press on further? You're bound to find—"

"We cannot do so. We do not have the shift range. It may be many years before we achieve it."

"But one of the member states might provide you with the technical information you need in order to—"

"Caine, you do not yet understand the pride of my people, particularly of the Old Families. Their assertion of superiority does not allow them to admit the need for assistance. Besides, they see this as fate calling them to a great adventure."

"What great adventure is that?"

Yaargraukh looked at Caine for a long time. "Conquest."

"Conquest? Of us?"

"I cannot say. I do not think First Voice or his counselors have made any choices, but they believe they have exhausted all options for exploration."

"Is our space near yours?"

"Somewhat, but it is not easily reached. We are closest to the Arat Kur—but I cannot say more than that."

Closest to the Arat Kur? But then why aren't the Arat Kur objecting to the Hkh'Rkh candidacy instead of humanity's? What the hell is—?

"Advocate Yaargraukh: there you are." They turned. Elena was holding a plate of various meats in one hand, a glass of foaming stout in the other. "I thought you might enjoy these foods—the ones in which you expressed the greatest interest."

Yaargraukh hesitated, then looked her in the eye. "I thank you, female."

Caine smiled, hoped his correction would not insult the Hkh'Rkh: "In my culture, Advocate, when one addresses women, it is proper to—"

But Elena was moving. Stepping between Caine and Yaargraukh, she snatched up a length of carpaccio on a fork and proffered it handle first—eyes downcast—to Yaargraukh. "We shall make our guests welcome by observing their ways."

Yaargraukh was utterly still. Then he raised a hand and delicately, carefully, removed the fork from Elena's fingers. "I am shown much honor. In truth, it is frustrating that your ideas of honor and ours are not more similar; it is this which most keeps us from understanding humans."

"In truth, there are those among us here tonight who possess great honor." Her semantic emphasis matched Yaargraukh's; *Christ, she's a quick study.*

"I presume you refer to your brother? He is indeed—"

"No, esteemed Advocate: I refer to your present companion, Spokesperson Caine of the Family Riordan."

Yaargraukh and Caine both looked at her as though a second head had suddenly sprouted from her shoulders.

"Indeed?" said Yaargraukh.

"What?" said Caine.

"I speak truth, Advocate. Since he does not have the label of warrior among our people, you might presume that Spokesperson Caine of the Family Riordan has not challenged or met challenge. But this would be incorrect. I list his deeds for you to judge: on Delta Pavonis Three, he defeated a great consortium of criminals with his cunning, and killed a pavonosaur—a swift predator with ten times your mass. Shortly thereafter, he defeated two different groups of assassins. In the past three months alone, he has learned a special warrior art called karate, which teaches him how to defeat armed opponents with his bare hands, and equipped only with that knowledge, a knife, and his wits, he killed another elite assassin who sought to ambush him in his own home." Elena turned and answered Caine's speechless stare with a dazzling smile.

Yaargraukh's held breath now came out as a long, almost inaudible hoot. "So you *are* a warrior. I apologize for not having asked—or intuited—this, Caine."

Elena's eyes opened wide when Yaargraukh called Caine by his first name, but she said nothing.

Caine waved a dismissive hand. "I have had to fight, but I am not a soldier."

"This is a terminological distinction that we find difficult to understand. How is a fighter not a warrior, and a warrior not a soldier?"

Elena leaned in. "On Earth, a soldier is summoned to fight, but does not live for the challenge. He serves his nation's honor, not his own."

"Must he not be honorable in the fighting of the war? Is not his honor one and the same with the nation's?"

"In principle, it might be; in practice, it is not strictly enforced. The war's challenge is not his—nor is the honor that is won or lost. His personal honor lies in performing his duty, not the conflict it entails. This is a soldier."

"Very well."

"Whereas, to human perception, the Hkh'Rkh are warriors, first and foremost. Your wars are but greatly amplified versions of your personal challenges: the same forms of declaration and resolution exist. Is this not so?"

Yaargraukh's facial contortions were identifiable as grimaces. "Up to three hundred of your years ago, this was true. Now, our wars are quickly becoming more akin to yours." He paused. "Holding such opinions makes my current position with the scions of Old Families—unusually challenging."

"How so?"

"They wanted only Old Family scions on this delegation, but none were willing to work as your Advocate."

Elena's smile was slow. "Why? Because when a Hkh'Rkh represents the Unhonored, he begins to be associated with them? Our status as lesser beings rubs off on you?"

Yaargraukh nodded. "It is as you say."

"That is also how a human woman feels when she

is treated as though she does not exist—as simply being a 'female.'"

Caine held his breath. Yaargraukh looked at Elena, who kept smiling at him without the slightest hint of impatience or displeasure. She had managed to offer a correction without also making it a remonstration. "That is exactly how it feels for us," she emphasized.

"Yet—you served me."

"Among you, to be served has a particular meaning, and I was happy to make you comfortable. Among humans—" and she turned toward Caine, with a forkful of carpaccio heading quickly towards his mouth—"it means something else." Caine had just enough time to get his lips and teeth out of the way. But the fork didn't jab in; the wafer-thin shaving of raw meat seemed to land on his tongue like a butterfly. He opened his eyes, found hers less than a foot away. The fork left his mouth slowly; her eyes stayed on his.

"So what does it mean among you, for one to serve another?" Yaargraukh sounded puzzled. "I do not understand; how is that not serving him? He who has met challenges and acquired honor?"

Caine knew, looking at Elena's earnest face, and Yaargraukh's stance—of patient futility?—that a careful delineation of nuances was not going to make the point. He reached over, took the plate gently but firmly out of Elena's hand. Caine made a quick pass with the fork, and then he was tapping her upper lip with a sliver of proffered asiago. Eyes surprised, she opened her lips: as had she, he inserted the utensil carefully, let the slight friction against her tongue drag the cheese off the tines.

Yaargraukh reared back. "Caine, this is—I do not understand."

"Your eyes told you no lies: I served her."

His head seemed to quiver. "So you are showing me that, if you choose, you can be less than she is?"

"No."

"Then why serve her?"

"To show you that I am no less than she is, but I am also not more. Human *women* have no less honor than males."

Yaargraukh's spine fur rose slightly. "This is what I find most alien in your race. As your Advocate, I worry how the Hkh'Rkh—particularly the Old Families--will assess you, were I to push them to believe this."

Caine smiled. "Yaargraukh, you are our Advocate. We leave it for you to decide what to tell them; we trust your judgment. But we needed to tell you this."

"Why?"

"Because sharing truths—particularly the dangerous ones—is how we will build a bridge of honor between us, and perhaps, a pathway of understanding between our peoples."

Yaargraukh's eyes disappeared for a moment, then bulged forth again. "Yes. This shall be how we make the bridge between us. We shall build it not merely by finding our easy similarities, but also by sharing—and accepting—our difficult differences. And I foresee that this could be a costly promise—for both of us."

Elena lowered her head slightly. "'Promises, like honor, are not washed away, but strengthened, by blood.'"

He stared at her. "You have already read the poet-sages."

Her nod was almost a shrug. "I encountered a few of their writings when reading your self-reference."

Yaargraukh slowly took his eyes from Elena, looked

at Caine and nodded. "Caine, you are lucky in your mate."

A split second of incomprehension was followed by a rush of heat in his face. "No—no, she's not my mate." Caine resolved to avoid looking at her, to remain unaware of her reaction.

Yaargraukh looked surprised. "No?"

"No."

Yaargraukh's tongue darted out, wiggled.

"What causes you to—smile?"

"Your answer. I saw her feed you, and you she: this was not merely honoring each other."

"I assure you: she is not my mate."

Yaargraukh's tongue swished once. "Not yet, perhaps. I must go; I will share much of our conversation with my delegation. They will be—interested—I am sure. I believe they will also agree to reciprocate this feast, perhaps as early as tomorrow."

Caine bowed. "They would do us much honor."

"They would not mean to, not precisely. But it would be a start." He turned to look for Elena; she was gone. "My words: did they—? Caine: I meant no insult to your fema—to the woman."

"I'm sure none was taken. Elena is very busy this evening; look, she left your plate and your drink."

Yaargraukh picked up the human dishware—like a child's in his massive hands—and focused on something over Caine's shoulder. "Another of your guests would speak with you. I shall withdraw. Until tomorrow." Caine nodded in response, turned—

—and found himself face to face with a water heater on wheels.

Chapter Forty-Seven

ODYSSEUS

Caine stared at the Ktoran environmental tank. *Wondered when they'd get around to chasing me down.* But he said: "Greetings. I am sorry, but since your tanks are identical, I have no way of knowing who you—"

"Of course. It is I, Wise-Speech-of-Pseudopodia. I thank you for your invitation to this gathering, Spokesperson Riordan: it is quite pleasant. And my thanks go to you as well, Ambassador."

Caine turned: Visser had approached from behind, with Wasserman and Durniak in tow. "Our pleasure, Wise-Speech-of-Pseudopodia. We are sorry that we had no way of knowing what foodstuffs you might enjoy."

"Do not be troubled. Ktoran biochemistry is radically different, so rather than share food this evening, we must take our pleasure in the sharing of ideas. And information."

A baited hook, trailed in deep water. Caine nodded: "Those are, after all, the lifeblood of diplomacy."

"Well put, Mr. Riordan. May I express my appreciation of your professionalism—all of you—during today's rather trying proceedings. It was not what you were expecting, I am sure."

Downing's voice arose from the other side of Wise-Speech. "I'll allow that it was a bit of a surprise."

"Yes. We—the Ktor delegation—feared that this might arise. Particularly when we perused your dossier: the question of whether your World Confederation ensures universal representation provided the Arat Kur with a serviceable point of disputation."

Visser folded her arms. "Apologies, Wise-Speech-of-Pseudopodia, but I was not under the impression that the Ktor were sympathetic to the objections of the Arat Kur."

"Indeed, we are not. Please: do not misconstrue my comments as suggesting that you are without grounds for claiming authority over your worlds. As you will come to know, Ktor can hardly be called a state or polity at all. We despair of the homogeneity of intent and action that seems to be the legitimizing desideratum for other races. Yet this does not stop us from claiming a practical authority over those systems in which we exert primary influence."

"I see—but then what is your point?"

"Merely this: when sovereign states insist upon deriving their authority from the consent of the governed, troubling inconsistencies inevitably arise. Indeed, the model of rulership through nation-states seems to be in disarray, and therefore in decline, everywhere—even on Earth."

Wasserman slipped into the group. "Just what do you mean by that?"

"Consider the difficulty your Confederation has in claiming that it is adequately representative. Even if the challenges recently presented by Indonesia's call for a sixth bloc are only half-hearted, other nations—particularly those of the Pan-Islamic sphere and Africa—have started entering into agreements that challenge the legal boundaries between national and corporate states. For instance, as we understand your laws, CoDevCo's recent land purchases now allow it to claim nationhood."

Caine did some fast current-events mathematics: how long ago had CoDevCo made those purchases? The answer came back quickly: the Ktor could not have gained that information through legal means.

Durniak was looking down her nose at the beaded sides of the life-support canister. "CoDevCo was ceded small wastelands in Namibia, Yemen, Uzbekistan and one island in Pacific Ocean, belonging to Borneo. This makes it a nation?"

"Ms. Durniak, what determines the right of statehood, of sovereignty? Does the right vest in ownership of terrain? If this is the primary criterion—and it does seem to be central to all Earth's legal definitions—then how is CoDevCo *not* a nation? Its lands—whatever you may think of the areas and the means whereby they were acquired—are not held through a lease, nor as a loan."

"And you're telling me that in your opinion—or that of the Ktor—this makes CoDevCo a national entity?"

The water tank rotated slightly in Wasserman's direction. "Please be calmed. I have not the temerity to attempt to tell you anything. It is time that will tell you and your people what all this means. But it is evident to us that this matter is already stimulating major debates over the definition of statehood."

"Perhaps, but a company can't simply buy itself

statehood, just by permanently acquiring a tract of land."

"If its employees elect to be its citizens, what is to prevent CoDevCo from claiming precisely this?"

"Well, those employees can't be said to be participating in their own governance. And even if we were to ignore that, how is a corporate board a government?"

"How is it not? The UN and World Court recognize monarchies and dictatorships as nations: why not a corporation? Furthermore, unlike autocracies, the corporation recognizes private property, and even has a representative dimension."

Visser frowned. "What kind of representation are you talking about?"

"Shareholder meetings—particularly if all employees are given the option to take part of their pay or benefits as company stock."

"Okay," conceded Wasserman, "but then the right to vote isn't inalienable: it's a commodity."

"According to our very limited observation, it seems that, for much of your world's population, this distinction would be a quibble at best, a sophistry at worst. A vote is a vote: its philosophical validation is of little importance to the overwhelming majority of those who are vested with that small share of political power."

Durniak's voice was decidedly hostile. "So you would urge us to recognize CoDevCo as a nation?"

"We are indifferent to the outcome. We merely note that the unanimity of will that you propose as the validation for your World Confederation is not so unanimous after all. And I am less than certain that CoDevCo is genuinely interested in being recognized as a nation-state. Indeed, I speculate that the megacorporations do not wish to become nations themselves; they merely wish to exert more influence over the international blocs."

"Or maybe control them."

Wise-Speech rotated back toward Caine. "Perhaps. I cannot comment on such a precise and detailed speculation."

Caine smiled slowly. "Strange, since you seem to be well-informed on the precise details of our other political issues."

"In addition to the Custodial report and the reference you provided yesterday, we have long been attentive to your omnidirectional broadcasts. They have provided us with a most stimulating perspective on your species—"

Nice dodge—and pure bullshit. Parthenon was only six months ago, but you're dozens of light-years away. However "stimulating" our news might be, it still doesn't travel faster than the speed of light...

"However, this is all tangential to the main issue that motivates the Arat Kur objections to your dossier. I doubt they are truly concerned with the legitimacy of your government."

"Oh? Then what are they concerned with?"

"Why, your expansion into 70 Ophiuchi, of course."

Of course. "Tell me, Wise-Speech-of-Pseudopodia, doesn't that last assertion of yours imply the location of another member state?"

"Surely, you have already deduced this yourselves. Consider: the Dornaani and the Hkh'Rkh have revealed their spheres of influence in their self-references. The Slaasriithi primer will no doubt do the same. And our seat of authority is quite distant, in the system you label 58 Eridani. Thus you know where all the races are—with the sole exception of the Arat Kur. So, when the matter of your entry into the 70 Ophiuchi system arises tomorrow, will you be surprised to find that it is the Arat Kur who raise the issue? Will you have any doubt whose border is threatened by that expansion?"

"You sound as though you are not very concerned by this issue."

"The specific violation? No: why should we be? It is not our border. But as a general principle, the Ktor feel that the dictatorial 'pathways of approved expansion' are in urgent need of revision. If not elimination."

Elimination? Here's the reason behind all the discord, rearing its ugly, Accord-splitting head at last.

Wasserman had shouldered into the front rank. "Why? Why eliminate the territorial restrictions?"

"I do not insist that they must be eliminated, but it is one possibility. At the very least, the process of adjudicating and adjusting the lists must be changed. The Arat Kur are also correct in insisting that the accords themselves must be revisited. We too often rely upon implicit understandings and vague precedents that only the Custodians may interpret or construe. This is unacceptable."

"And if the Custodians resist these appeals for change?"

"Then we will be compelled to take our own counsel and act as we will."

"You mean, ignore the permitted pathways of expansion?"

"Yes."

Visser looked sideways at Downing, who was already

staring at her. An unmistakable line was being drawn in the sand. Caine cleared his throat: "If you're right about the Arat Kur—that their concern is to remedy our 'unlawful' intrusion into 70 Ophiuchi—then wouldn't they *support* the accords? In short, wouldn't they insist on leaving the current constraints unchanged?"

"An astute observation. For sake of argument—and only that—let us project the endgame of a confrontation between the powers that desire change and those which do not. Among those powers that you reasonably believe will support the status quo—the Dornaani, the Slaasriithi, and the Arat Kur—the Slaasriithi can be made to stand aside quite easily. They find combat singularly aversive. We would of course provide our allies—particularly a technologically adept race such as yourselves—with improvements in space technology that you could quickly copy. With these improvements, and with the Hkh'Rkh as your eager foot soldiers, you could swiftly defeat the Arat Kur while we defeat the Dornaani."

"And what if the Slaasriithi—seeing the Arat Kur attacked and overrun—also take up arms in support of the current settlement limits of the Accord?"

"This should be of little worry to you. As you will learn soon enough, Arat Kur and Hkh'Rkh space completely separate your sphere from that of the Slaasriithi. So it would be the Hkh'Rkh alone who would be vulnerable to attacks from the Slaasriithi. In truth, the damage to them might well be considerable."

"Which doesn't seem to trouble you very much."

Wise-Speech paused. "Let us speak frankly. The Hkh'Rkh would prove excellent wartime allies, but they are largely ungovernable. If attacked by the Slaasriithi, they would be glad for your assistance. I also suspect—although they would never admit it—that they would eventually look to you for leadership. Already, there is great promise for friendship between you."

"Why do you say this?"

"Because I have observed your interactions this evening. And because you are both warlike species."

The mild bluntness of Wise-Speech's characterization of humanity was more unsettling than its content. Caine sought a contradiction: he felt a cool chill at the back of his skull when he realized that he wouldn't find one because Wise-Speech was right.

The Ktor did not pause. "The Arat Kur and Slaasriithi would lose this hypothetical war because they are not warlike races. The Dornaani would not be able to intervene, because they would be too late to help the Arat Kur, and because they are at great remove from the Slaasriithi. Most importantly, they would be compelled to guard their borders against us—and we are far more numerous than they. So the outcome of this unnecessary war would be identical to the outcome of the peaceful dissent we propose. Foreseeing what we have outlined here, the Dornaani will ultimately agree to the desired changes. The price of peace—either on the battlefield or in the council chambers—will be that the Accord shall be recast in a more practical mold, a mold which better fits our shared vision of energetic expansion."

"So you do not see war as inevitable?"

"We believe that the Arat Kur would withdraw their objections to human membership if they felt their borders were truly secure. Which would certainly be the case if the Arat Kur could be placated with assurances that you will expand away from their sphere. But that can only happen if the expansion limits are rescinded."

"And the Hkh'Rkh?"

"The Hkh'Rkh can be made to observe the Arat Kur boundaries if we provide them with the shift-drive technology they need to open up their expansion sphere in directions that are currently inaccessible to them. With each member state free to pursue unrestricted expansion, we will all have tranquility and prosperity."

"'Peace in our time,'" Caine muttered.

"My apologies: I did not hear your words."

"I did not mean them to be heard. My colleagues and I will need to discuss this."

"Of course." Wise-Speech began to wheel away, halted. "Naturally, we must have some indication of your interest before the Convocation resumes tomorrow. We will send a tight beam signal to you at the time you call midnight. If you return the signal, we shall know that you are interested in working with us to achieve a peaceful solution to these unfortunate frictions. I wish you a pleasant evening and thank you for your hospitality." He rolled to the door, where, joined by his three compatriots, he took his leave.

The last of the guests—the Hkh'Rkh—offered a farewell salute to Trevor and followed the Ktor. As Trevor came toward Caine, he grinned. "So, were you having fun with Mr. Water Heater?"

Caine grimaced. "Loads. And you?"

"The Hkh'Rkh sure don't have a lot of variety in their conversation. Honor. Conquest. Family. More honor. Treachery and punishment. Honor. Tactics. Still more honor. Oh, and did I mention that they like to talk about honor?"

"We get the picture. Sounds like bushido on steroids."

"Yup, just about. I'm heading back to the barn and relieving Opal. Try not to dance on the tables."

"We'll contain ourselves somehow."

Thandla emerged from the main alcove as Trevor ducked around the corner. Hwang stared down at the deck. "Wise-Speech certainly made an interesting—and damning—slip."

"What do you mean?"

"His reference to the sixth bloc initiative and Indonesia. The Ktor can't have known that yet—not legally."

Caine shook his head. "That was no slip."

"What do you mean?"

Downing sipped his glass of water. "Caine means that Wise-Speech wanted us to realize that the Ktor are not only aware of the state of affairs on Earth, but are determined to get what they want, even if they have to break a few rules—or a few necks—to get it."

"And what makes them think we won't report them to the Dornaani?"

"Frankly, I don't think they care if we tattle. They're trying to determine if we will support them, or if we will support the Dornaani. If we respond to their signal at midnight, they've got their answer. If we run and tell the Dornaani—again, they've got their answer."

Visser looked at Caine. "And what do you think of their proposition to us?"

"I think that Wise-Speech is Ribbentrop and we're getting to choose whether we're going to play the part of Neville Chamberlain or Winston Churchill."

Wasserman frowned. "Sorry; not up on my history."

"Long story made short: Britain's Chamberlain tried to appease Germany before World War Two, agreeing to look the other way while the Nazis gobbled up chunks of the continent. All to avoid war."

"Some great plan: look what happened."

"My point exactly—and I think that's the lesson we should remember right now."

"You mean, we should side with the Dornaani?"

"Yes."

"Who want to hem us in?"

"No, Lemuel. The accords set limits. And the Dornaani have given clear indications that the time may be ripe to redefine or even reduce those limits. But they are also trying to follow the law."

"You mean, they're being anal-retentive."

"Look: the Dornaani may be somewhat elusive, and they're not exactly the life of the party, but they've risked losing their official validation as Custodians over the principles—and integrity—of their duties. And if they lose that validation, what happens next? War? Or do the Ktor create a new Accord with new rules? And what do the Dornaani do if the Ktor's new Accord violates the limits set by the Dornaani Accord? Do the Dornaani go to war—start hostilities to enforce compliance to a set of restrictions that are no longer recognized by the majority of species? I think that the Dornaani, despite their technological edge, have become the underdogs—and the wronged party—in all of this."

Visser nodded. "And the Ktor smell like wolves."

"Actually, they smell like ammonia."

Caine, along with everyone else, turned to stare at Thandla. "What do you mean, Sanjay?"

"The Ktor must be native to a very cold environment: the heat exhausts of their cooling system were extremely obvious. From what I can gather, they must exist at less than minus eighty degrees centigrade."

"How can that be?"

Hwang shrugged. "It's theoretically possible. Goes along with the ammonia his chemical sniffers picked up: methane and hydrogen fluorine are two low-temperature alternatives to carbon as a potential basis for life."

Visser, arms folded, stared at the floor. "We are fortunate to have this information, but we do not have the time to consider its significance at length. For now, we must simply prepare ourselves for tomorrow, for the vote on whether we are to be offered membership or not."

"Sounds like we've got another choice to make before then." Lemuel stuck his hands in his pockets, looked around the informal council circle. "What do we do when Wise-Speech calls us at midnight? Because if we don't pick up the phone and make nice, I think it's pretty clear he's going to vote against us tomorrow."

Silence. Then Durniak shrugged. "I will propose ideas as—how do you say it?—as devil's advocate. So: if we show interest in the Ktor's proposition tonight, how does this benefit us?"

Hwang ticked off the benefits on his fingers. "We would be allied with the most aggressive species. They will place few or no limits on expansion, which means we can maximize our power and territorial reach. They are willing to give us access to advanced technology. We also seem to be their preferred partners: they are contemptuous of the Hkh'Rkh, dismissive of both the Slaasriithi and the Dornaani, and are willing to let the Arat Kur be overrun by us. So they seem to be suggesting that we would enjoy a special relationship with them."

Wasserman nodded. "Pretty compelling reasons."

Elena stared at him. "You *trust* them?"

"Christ, no; Wise-Speech is a lying sack of shit. And why would he be any less likely to sell us out than he would the Hkh'Rkh or the Arat Kur? But we're looking for the positives of joining him, right?"

Elena shuddered and nodded.

So did Durniak. "It may be a dangerous thing we would do if we choose not to side with the Ktor. The Custodians tried to keep us from having to make binding decisions—but it is happening otherwise to us." Tired, distracted, her facility for English was starting to erode.

"But it's the *wrong* choice. We all know that—don't we?" Elena looked around the group.

Thandla shrugged. "At least we would be choosing our own fate. And being friends with the most dangerous species means we have protected our world from them. Also, their preference for our cooperation might indicate that we have enough power that they will genuinely feel safer having us as their long-term allies. So, as long as we remain strong, we need not fear betrayal."

Caine shook his head. "Look, let's be realistic about what advantages we clearly *don't* have going into this showdown tomorrow. We are still utterly ignorant of the other star-faring races in this region of space, and even if we read and study all night, that will not have materially changed by tomorrow morning. Next, we have little to no idea of the real political interactions among them: just a few hints and innuendos that might be misinformation, and a few implied promises that might be just so much hot—or very cold—air. And we are, with the possible exception of the Hkh'Rkh, technologically inferior. So what assets can we really bring to any relationship with these other powers?

"If we choose the mercenary route—assuming the Ktor even mean what they say about allying with us—we become collaborators in an illegal attempt to subvert or destroy the Accord, either by war or political pressure. Either way, we wouldn't be doing that because we believe in it, but because we are scared."

"Yeah." Lemuel's voice was tired. "But what other options—or strengths—do we have?"

"We have the option to do the right thing, to follow the process as the Dornaani outlined it, which means, ultimately, supporting the Custodians and the rule of law. And I think that the strengths we bring to *that* relationship are greater, and ultimately offer greater protection, than the gutless sycophancy we'd bring to a partnership with the Ktor."

Downing frowned. "And what strengths would we bring to an alliance with the Dornaani?"

Caine looked him in the eye. "Courage. Versatility. Perspicacity. And, most important, integrity." *Half of which you seem to lack.*

"Let's hope you're right." Downing was looking at his watch. "Ten minutes to midnight."

Ten minutes later, Caine was sitting at the communications console in the hab module. The other nine members of the delegation were crowded into corners, in between banks of monitors, perched upon chairs that had been appropriated from other rooms. No one spoke.

On the console, a green light came on. Thandla,

sitting alongside Caine, checked his watch and nod-ded. "Incoming signal. Tight beam."

Caine raised his right index finger, looked around the room. "Are we all agreed?"

Stares became nods. Caine nodded in response, turned back to the console. He pressed a button well to the left side of the blinking green light. It—and all the monitors and gauges on the console—went dark.

"Powered down," announced Thandla.

Visser sighed, arms clutched tight against her chest. "It's done. Let us get to bed. We have an early day."

As everyone else headed to the exit—Elena was gone before Visser had finished speaking—Opal headed toward Caine. Her smile was wide, but a bit tentative. "Heavy day," she said.

"Yeah."

"But not *too* heavy?"

He looked down into the pecan-colored eyes, tried to chase away an after-image of wider, green ones that had been burned into the retina of his imagination. He leaned close, so he could concentrate on her, not the imaginary green eyes. "No: not too heavy," he answered.

He felt her arms go up either side of his back. "Good. No reason to lose tonight worrying about tomorrow."

Chapter Forty-Eight

ODYSSEUS

"So—are you worried?"

Caine glanced at Trevor. "Me? No," he lied.

The other galleries became transparent—except for the Arat Kur's and the Slaasriithi's. Alnduul's voice announced the outcome of the second day's first item of business: "The Accord is pleased to announce that its member states have unanimously elected to extend the Hkh'Rkh an offer of membership, and will expect a formal response at the next Convocation, to be held in one year's time."

First Voice rose, his spine-fur almost touching the ceiling of his gallery's canopy. "As First Voice of the First Family, I give my formal response now. The Hkh'Rkh accept this offer."

Alnduul made a waving gesture. "We acknowledge, but cannot recognize, your acceptance at this time. It must wait until the next Convocation. Now, we call for a vote on the membership of—"

The yellow quatrefoil winked on. "Uh oh," Trevor sat up. "Here it comes."

"The Arat Kur must insist that before the vote on the human candidacy may be called, a matter of territorial violation must be addressed."

Visser came to stand alongside Caine. "Just as the Ktor told us: 70 Ophiuchi."

Alnduul was pressing on. "We must remind the Arat Kur delegation that this matter is on our agenda for the afternoon—the agenda that was unanimously agreed to."

Zirsoo's voice sounded somewhat ragged. "The Arat Kur originally agreed to that agenda based on the presumption that there would be no vote, since the human dossier would surely be rejected on the first day. Since that did not occur, we are compelled to raise this issue now. The humans' violation of their permitted pathway of expansion is clear and unequivocal. They must agree to vacate the 70 Ophiuchi system before the Accord can justly vote on their candidacy."

Visser nodded at Caine, who stepped into the communications node. "We wish to extend our greetings and apologies to the Arat Kur delegation. However, we must point out that we entered 70 Ophiuchi before we were contacted, and thus had no knowledge that we were violating your space."

"We acknowledge this; the fault is not with you, but with the Custodians. However, we insist that the border correction is mandated before human candidacy is resolved."

Alnduul held out his arms. "This cannot be. I remind the Arat Kur delegation that neither the Accord nor the Custodians are empowered to discuss, much less mandate, Earth's territorial policies until it has been confirmed as a provisional member."

Zirsoo's voice was singularly flat. "Then the Arat

Kur member state must call for an immediate suspension of the proceedings of this Convocation, until the following three issues have been resolved.

"Firstly, the failure of the Custodians to convene the Accord to consider the question of human membership before the humans settled the system they designate 70 Ophiuchi.

"Secondly, the failure of the Custodians to suspend these proceedings pending an investigation into the failings and prevarications in the human government's legitimacy documentation.

"Thirdly, as a consequence of the preceding, an investigation into whether the Dornaani should be allowed to continue as the Accord's Custodians."

Alnduul rose to a fully erect posture. "These charges will be considered for inclusion on next year's Convocation agenda. However none of them are grounds for suspending the proceedings of this Convocation."

After a long pause, Zirsoo's voice announced, "It seems you refuse to hear us. Under these circumstances, we cannot participate in this stage of the Convocation's proceedings. Accordingly, we shall withdraw."

"With apologies, we must become involved." The voice came from Wise-Speech's image. "There is only one way to end these disagreements, because there is one common thread that binds them together. The fault does not lie with the Custodians, or with the humans, or with the Arat Kur. The culprit here is not a living creature but a document: the insufficiencies of the accords themselves.

"Consider how all these insufficiencies are brought into sharp relief by the current crisis concerning 70 Ophiuchi. The Custodians are empowered to censure member states that refuse to comply with the accords. However, there is no definition of the punitive dimensions of such censure. There is no legal mechanism whereby the Accord may address possible abuses of power by its Custodians. And there is no way to convene an unbiased commission to promulgate the necessary corrective emendations to the accords themselves, since the Custodians have the procedural right to ban such initiatives as groundless obstructions.

"That none of these quandaries have answers indicates that it is not the members of the Accord, but the accords themselves, which are flawed. Therefore, before further action can be undertaken, the accords must be subjected to thorough review and revision."

Alnduul's fingers flexed briefly. "There is wisdom in your words, but they fail to address the procedural precedents under which we operate. We must first complete the agenda we jointly agreed upon, and do so under the guidelines which were in place when today's agenda was passed. Accordingly, I must now call for the vote on human membership."

"The Ktor abstain. And we lodge a further protest over the illegal exclusion of the Hkh'Rkh member state."

"As do the Arat Kur: we, too, abstain."

"Vishnaaswii'ah of the Slaasriithi?"

"We are distressed by the disharmony of this Convocation. We see merits to both sides in the procedural debate. However, it seems to us that the human Confederation—while new and imperfect—has not substantively misrepresented itself. We feel that a call for an investigatory commission on the matter is overzealous."

"Hmmm," Downing muttered with a nod. "The Arat Kur won't like that."

Durniak matched his nod. "A gentle slap in face, but a slap in face, even so."

Vishnaaswii'ah was concluding. "Therefore, we find no reason to doubt the humans' self-representation, or their basic veracity. Consequently, we find no juridical basis for setting aside today's agenda. We vote to offer the humans membership in the Accord."

In the central half-dome, Glayaazh stood. "The Dornaani, also, vote in the affirmative."

Alnduul nodded as Glayaazh resumed her seat. "All votes have been recorded. This closes—"

First Voice's bellow drowned out Alnduul's attempt to close the proceedings. "The Hkh'Rkh abstain and we add our voices to those of the Arat Kur and Ktor in calling for a revision of Accord protocols and policies, particularly those which facilitate the dictatorial behavior of the Custodians."

"The statement is duly noted, but the Hkh'Rkh vote is ineligible at this time, and so, not recorded. The final vote is two affirmative, two abstentions—"

"Three!" roared First Voice of the Hkh'Rkh. "Three abstentions!" The thin veneer of his accommodation to pluralistic process was almost gone.

"The First Accord dictates that abstentions are to be construed as rejections. Therefore, the vote is tied."

"We object," intoned Wise-Speech calmly. "We hold that, given the acceptance of the Hkh'Rkh, the final vote is two-to-three and membership is, at this point, not offered to the humans."

Alnduul had not stopped speaking; he continued straight over the top of Wise-Speech. "Accordingly, until such time as a definitive outcome can be reached, the Custodians will outline the particulars of the interim status of the prospective human member state." He looked toward Caine and the delegation. "Although as Custodians, we could choose to break the tie with a directed decision, we cannot do so without exacerbating the frictions arising from our purported abuse of power. Instead, the question of your membership must be deemed to remain 'in process' until such time as all the member states agree to follow the extant voting protocols. At that time, another vote will be called. In the meantime, protections consistent with a provisional membership will be extended to the humans. You are thus protected against aggression and trespass as per the accords, so long as you also constrain your own actions to those permitted therein. We apologize for this unprecedented disruption of your membership process." He turned slightly. "We also address regrets to First Voice of the Hkh'Rkh."

Caine saw movement from the corner of his eye: the Hkh'Rkh were leaving, matching the long, angry strides that were already carrying First Voice over the threshold of the iris-valve.

Alnduul droned on. "Unfortunately, no delegate may be recognized as a voting member of the Accord until the membership status of their species is confirmed at a second Convocation."

Yaargraukh's eyes met Caine's; the expression was unreadable. Then the Advocate took one loping step to the exit and was gone.

"We hope that First Voice will not be offended by these procedural rules." Alnduul's hope was uttered to an empty gallery; the Hkh'Rkh's withdrawal was complete.

Alnduul paused for a long moment. "We solicit closing comments relevant to this morning's business."

The yellow quatrefoil winked out of existence. A moment later, the green of the Slaasriithi followed.

Wise-Speech rolled back slightly. "Those who can no longer lead effectively should remove themselves from leadership. It is sad, but true." The connection closed.

Alnduul looked straight at Caine and—with some difficulty—effected a somber nod. His image vanished.

Elena sighed and leaned her forehead on her hands. "How long do you think it's going to be?"

Visser frowned. "You mean, until we are officially part of the Accord?"

"No: until there's no Accord left to be a part of."

The session's afternoon business was effectively non-existent: given what had transpired and the boycotts that were now in place, almost every other agenda item had been stymied. Alnduul reached the end of the paralyzed "to do" list and then stood. "We must issue another directive to the Arat Kur before this Convocation may be officially closed."

Caine leaned forward. "Heads up; this could be serious." From behind, there was the clattering rustle of pens and palmtops being laid aside.

Zirsoo's voice was cautious. "There has been no procedural dereliction on our part."

"We beg to differ. Although you may decline answering the questions posed by a candidate for membership, you must at least identify your homeworld by system and planet. You have failed to do so. We understand that this may have been an oversight on your part."

"Like hell it was."

Caine shrugged at Lemuel's probably accurate

observation. "Alnduul had to add that. He's a diplomat and he had to play nice."

"Yeah? Well, that's no career for me, then."

Truer words were never spoken. Caine looked at the yellow quatrefoil, felt his stomach clench in response to a sudden, instinctual realization: *the Arat Kur have been silent too long. It's not just* tête-á-tête, *anymore: they're deciding upon a statement—*

—Which emanated from the yellow quatrefoil in the form of a different voice, proceeding at the slow, deliberate pace of a funeral march. "This is First Delegate Hu'urs's Khraam of the Arat Kur WholeNest. The Arat Kur member state categorically refuses to comply with this directive. It is in direct violation of the ruling which protects the informational privacy of all member states."

"With respect, First Delegate Khraam, the requirements of the Twenty-first Accord take precedence in this matter. As a probationary member state, the humans are subject to the full consequences if they violate this accord. They must therefore have the benefit of knowing which systems, if violated, would compel the Custodians to intervene."

"Your words dig tunnels in sand; they are meaningless sophistries, crafted to compromise our safety."

"We must disagree. This requirement—that each species has knowledge of the homeworlds of all other species—ensures that there can be no unwitting violations of the homeworld protections of the Twenty-first Accord. So we must direct the Arat Kur to reveal the location of their home system and world."

The Arat Kur did not respond. Alnduul's next gesture was peculiar: he stretched both arms high over his head. It looked awkward and uncomfortable, but was also very evocative. "We ask again: will the Arat Kur comply with the Custodial directive to reveal the location of their homeworld?"

"We will not."

"Then you compel us to impart this information to the humans without your approval."

"And I must warn you that your ultimatum leaves us no middle course: you force us to either scuttle back or shatter bedrock. Consequently, if the Dornaani Custodians reveal our homeworld, we maintain that they will have violated our privacy and the accords which ensure it, and must therefore be compelled to relinquish their Custodianship."

Alnduul did not pause. "We regret that the Arat Kur refuse to identify their homeworld, and so we must reveal it to be the third planet of the system known to humans as Sigma Draconis."

"Holy shit, the wheels just came off the bus." Wasserman stood as he said it, knocking over his chair.

Caine glanced over to check on the yellow quatrefoil— just in time to see it wink off.

Downing's comment was *sotto voce*, but the tone was similar to Lemuel's: "Bloody hell: Sigma Draconis. It means they're our closest neighbors. By far."

Elena nodded at no one. "Which is why our expansion made them so nervous."

Caine mentally reconstructed the starfield they had all studied in the holotank. "It also means they have systems from which they can strike several of ours, including our naval facilities at Barnard's Star. And that is only one shift away from Ross 154: Earth's only connection to its main colonies."

"And now they're pissed and won't talk." Wasserman grabbed his chair, threw it back upright. "Great. What happens next, I wonder?"

"More of the same." Elena pointed across at the Ktor delegation. "Look."

For the second time in one day, the water heaters were slowly but steadily rolling out of the gallery. Wise-Speech's image half-rotated, apparently preparing to join the rest of his colleagues. "We regret that we must join the Arat Kur in their protest. We are serving official notice of our departure from these proceedings. We furthermore feel that they may not be legitimately resumed until hearings have determined whether the actions of the Custodians are grounds for their dismissal. We wish all our colleagues good fortune and safe travels." He rolled away; the connection closed.

Caine looked over at the Hkh'Rkh; there seemed to be a rather heated debate in process, one which Yaargraukh was apparently losing, though not for lack of effort.

Durniak leaned her mouth on her steepled fingers. "What will come of all this?"

Visser shrugged. "Your guess is as good as mine. Maybe an unofficial summit where they will manage to bury this hatchet."

"Unlikely."

"I agree, Mr. Downing. But if not, then the Accord must either remain split, or be forcibly reunited."

"By which you mean—"

"War. Look."

Yaargraukh had reentered the communication node of the Hkh'Rkh gallery. "I bear the words of the First Voice of the First Family, and they are these: that the

Dornaani have dishonored him and the Hkh'Rkh by refusing to acknowledge his authority in this place, and have dishonored themselves by breaking the rules of the Accord. The Hkh'Rkh agree with the Arat Kur and the Ktor that redress is needed before further discussions are acceptable. Accordingly, we, too, turn our backs upon this Convocation." By the time he finished speaking, he was the last of his species in the gallery. He looked over at Caine, nodded, left.

Who in turn looked at Visser. "Well, now it's up to us: leave or stay. Fish or cut bait."

As Visser looked around the room, Caine followed her eyes from face to face: the outcome of the silent vote was obvious. Visser nodded at him.

Caine entered the communications node again. "Alnduul, the delegation from Earth stands ready to continue with the agenda, or informal discussion, at the pleasure of the Dornaani and the Slaasriithi delegations."

Alnduul bowed very low. "We note the continued participation of the Earth delegation and both commend and thank them for their decision to continue under these difficult circumstances."

Caine smiled, nodded, but felt a cold knot growing in his gut. *Unless I'm very wrong, the circumstances are going to get a lot more difficult before they get better.*

Chapter Forty-Nine

MENTOR

Downing looked up as Hwang came into the module's conference room and said, "Signal incoming. Holographic. I've sent pages to everyone else."

"Thank you, Ben." Richard checked his watch: two hours since the Convocation had ended, one since he had sent his requests to Alnduul. "Ben, please open the channel. And resend those pages, if necessary."

Hwang aimed his palmtop at the holotank and clicked a button—just as the rest of the delegation started filing in, scanning for seats.

Downing noted that Elena was not among the group: neither was Caine.

ODYSSEUS

"Just a moment, Elena."

She stopped, but did not turn toward him. "Yes?"

Christ: what the hell did I do now? He took the three steps needed to draw alongside her. "Look, I've been trying to find a moment to talk with you—"

"We're needed in the conference room. Now."

"I know. This will only take a second." And then Caine realized that while he knew what he wanted to say, he had no idea how to start. "About the other day, at the reception—"

Her eyes strained toward the conference room. "Don't worry about it. That was just a bit of nonsense. That sort of thing always happens when you're busy meeting a few new species over cocktails and canapés. Happens to me all the time." She turned and smiled—carefully—at him. "Don't give it another thought. I haven't."

He almost believed her. "Well . . . I'm glad you're not offended or—bothered." Now he wondered if he believed what *he* was saying. "I also wanted to say that I'm sorry if, on some other occasions, I have—that is, I find myself . . ." His mouth remained opened, but no words came out.

She closed her eyes and said, "Are you trying to apologize for staring at me?"

"Uh—well, yes. I mean, I really didn't realize I was doing it. Not most of the time, that is. I—it's just that—that—"

"Your eloquence renders me speechless." She smiled. "You too, apparently." She opened her eyes, but once again, they were aimed up the corridor toward the conference room. "I have to leave," she said. Without another word, she did.

Caine watched her walk quickly away, wondered how he had wanted the conversation to resolve, while simultaneously realizing that this outcome did not feel right. Not at all.

MENTOR

After days of becoming accustomed to Dornaani technology, their own holotank's image of Alnduul seemed grainy and crude. Downing spread his arms and fingers out. "Enlightenment unto you, Alnduul. Thank you for responding to my message."

"I am sorry I was not able to do so sooner. The events of this day have necessitated much discussion among our delegation."

"And with the other races, I'll warrant."

"Sadly, only the Slaasriithi—and of course yourselves—are responding to our messages, at this point."

"I am sorry to hear that." Downing cleared his throat. "Alnduul, besides changing the itinerary for our return to human space"—he ignored the surprised stares from various members of the delegation—"I would be grateful to learn, from both the Dornaani Collective and the Custodians, what kind of defensive assistance we can expect, if it becomes necessary."

Another Dornaani materialized next to Alnduul's image: it was Glayaazh.

Downing inclined his head. "Third Arbiter, we are honored that you have joined the conversation." *And dismayed that you were apparently eavesdropping.*

"I am honored to be welcomed into it. I may speak for the Collective. Ask what you wish."

Elena entered, flashed Downing a brittle smile, and sat.

Downing kept his focus on Glayaazh. "Third Arbiter, although we are under the protection of the Custodians, we do not know what shape that protection will take. Furthermore, knowing so little about our potential adversaries, we do not know how best to prepare our own defense. This leaves us uncertain as to our role in this situation."

Glayaazh seemed to wave at the walls. "Your role is whatever you decide it to be."

Visser stepped forward, her brow ruler-straight. "Third Arbiter Glayaazh, with respect, that is a most ingenuous comment. Just yesterday, you were waiting to see whether or not we would lie, or accuse the Arat Kur of having illegal access to information. You were hoping, very much, that we would do neither of these things. And knowing your hopes, we declined to do either. Now I ask you: given that our support of you has earned us the enmity of other members of the Accord, can you not at least give us some understanding of the potential foes we might face, and the deeper disputes that lie beneath today's friction?"

Glayaazh's mouth puckered tight. "I regret that I cannot do so, Ambassador Visser. Nor can we send an official delegation to Earth, as you requested earlier." Glayaazh waggled her fingers downward. "To do so could be interpreted as a de facto confirmation of your membership, which would only exacerbate the frictions in the Accord. And frankly, we fear more for the repercussions upon you, rather than any which we might face."

Downing saw Visser bristling, stepped in quickly. "Third Arbiter, allow us to remain on the topic of Earth's safety for one moment longer. As my delegation's security specialist, I must inquire: will you be monitoring our borders? If not, and if they are violated, how would we inform you?"

"As I stated in the last session, your status as a

provisional member puts us in a very awkward and unprecedented position. Since you are no longer a protected species, we are precluded from taking pre-emptive steps."

"We understand your dilemma, but we hope you will also understand ours. Not only do we lack the absolute security of a protected race, we also lack any useful knowledge regarding the Accord's other races. This places us in an extremely vulnerable position."

"Agreed." She looked toward Alnduul.

His inner eyelids flickered once and he nodded. "We will maintain limited contact with your leaders. In the event of a clear and imminent threat, we will provide compensatory assistance."

"Alnduul, this is hardly an—an optimal strategy," Downing sputtered, seeing Caine slip into the room.

Glayaazh's fingers were waving slowly. "Your words suggest that you presume war is impending. This is a hasty presumption, and to act upon it might convince others that you intend to wage war against *them*. We counsel you to be patient, and not to assume the worst."

Then you don't know much about the job and mind of a defense analyst, Glayaazh, old girl. "Your approach is ethically admirable, Third Arbiter, but still does not answer the question my superiors will—rightly—want answered: what will you do to aid us if we come under attack from other powers?"

Glayaazh folded her long-fingered hands. "Let us speak frankly, if hypothetically. Any attack on you would certainly trigger intervention by the Custodians. If that intervention is resisted, the ensuing conflict would probably follow the fracture lines of the Accord's present political impasse. The Dornaani Collective and Custodians would contend with the Ktor, the Slaasriithi with the Arat Kur, and yourselves with the Hkh'Rkh. In each pairing, the Accord forces enjoy a decisive technological advantage. Is this not sufficient reassurance against such an attack?"

"Perhaps," allowed Downing, "but your analysis is crucially dependent upon the pairings you've proposed. What if events unfold differently? For instance, it seems to me that the Slaasriithi tend to be diffident. If, in a true conflict, they failed to engage the Arat Kur vigorously, what would keep the Arat Kur from mounting a first attack on our worlds?"

Glayaazh blinked once and turned away. "Your words are wise. Such a course of events must not be allowed. This we resolve."

"So you might resolve, but what will you do?"

"For now, we will do nothing that could be construed as a military provocation. However, if any other state moves in a manner that could be interpreted as a prelude to hostilities, we shall so inform you and be prepared to intervene."

Wasserman tossed his stylus down on his dataslate. "So, in plain English, you're not going to do anything."

"If the only action you deem important is military, then you are right: at this time, we are currently disposed to do nothing."

Wasserman glared at the faces which were glaring at him. "Great allies you've picked, folks."

Glayaazh's image pointedly looked away from Wasserman and back to Downing and Visser. "Mr. Downing, Ambassador: we regret that we cannot offer concrete assurances at this time. But your behavior at these proceedings speaks well of your maturity and appreciation of rule of law, even under the most adverse circumstances. We shall not forget this.

"And now, this conversation must end: we will be recovering your module and intership coupler from the docking hub shortly. The transit to your new destination—Barnard's Star—will commence soon thereafter. Again, on behalf of both the Custodians and the Dornaani, we wish you fair travels, and hope that we shall meet soon again to resolve your candidacy."

"We hope the same."

Glayaazh vanished. Alnduul, who seemed vaguely troubled, remained behind a moment longer to offer a carefully practiced nod to the rest of the delegation, and then faded.

Hwang turned towards Downing. "Barnard's Star? Why there?"

Downing folded his hands. "After the results of this Convocation, it is now imperative that we return to Earth by that route."

Durniak's forehead was as furrowed as a washboard. "Why?"

Visser raised her chin. "We are returning via Barnard's Star because the combined fleets there must be placed on alert and receive a full briefing as soon as possible. Containing a potential invasion depends upon retaining control over the Barnard's Star system."

Opal frowned. "And why is that?"

Downing answered. "Because with the Arat Kur sphere somewhere in the vicinity of Sigma Draconis, Barnard's Star is on their most direct route of approach to Earth. Barnard's Star is also only one shift from Ross 154, which is the real gateway between Earth and all our colonies and outposts on the Green Mains.

If we lose the Ross 154 crossroads, our space will be cut into two halves. So, since the warning needs to be sounded in both directions, Barnard's Star is the best place to start it off."

Downing checked his watch. "According to the information Alnduul transmitted, we'll be leaving in less than two hours. If you have any last messages or tasks to attend to, this is the time."

ODYSSEUS

Caine and Yaargraukh looked out at the stars together, enjoying another long silence. Like the others, it was comfortable, companionable—but it was also heavy with the surety of ending. Caine nodded at the spacescape. "Looking at these stars is like looking out to sea when a storm is approaching. It's calm where you're standing, but you can see the edge of the tempest."

Yaargraukh pony-nodded. "It is the same on my planet, though we are not so fond of the water." He turned to face Caine. "You do me a very great honor inviting me into your module, Caine." He glanced at the flags of Earth's five blocs and the Confederation flanking the gallery window. "We have banners such as these, as well. It shames me that I am no longer able, or even allowed, to extend you an invitation to our module to see them. Or to have made a feast to repay your own."

Caine shook his head. "No surprise, there—and no fault of yours, Yaargraukh. Besides, your honesty and your openness is lavish recompense for our feast. What gifts could do us more honor?"

The top-heavy Hkh'Rkh turned his barrel-shaped

torso to face out into the sea of stars once again. "As we prepare to leave, the First's retinue already speaks of challenges and glory and new lands. I am not sure it matters to them which challenges or what glory or whose lands shall sate their appetites—but this day, they could feel the blood rising inside them. It sang to them and, in their hearts, they sang back. And so, now that the song has started, it must be finished. Yet, as I sit and listen, I cannot help but think that—had it been left to us, to you and I—the song might have been very different indeed, a better song."

"One with less blood in it?"

Yaargraukh's neck oscillated. "Perhaps. But, at the very least, one with more honor. The blood—that was ready to flow before any of us arrived here. I have sat at parley tables where the purpose was not to make peace, but to instigate war. So it was here, I think."

"I think you are right, Yaargraukh. Perhaps you can make First Voice hear that wisdom."

"Caine, understand: he knows this already. He is no fool. But he hungers for deeds of honor, and he believes that the Dornaani are weak and incapable of leading. He sees resolve in the Ktor."

"And the other races?"

"They are deemed akin to those they follow. I think he hoped that you would also turn your back upon the Convocation, but you did not, so he is satisfied that he now knows humanity."

"Knows that we are also weak and incapable of leadership?"

"So he thinks."

"And what do you think, Yaargraukh?"

The Hkh'Rkh let a long breath out though his nose;

there was a faint sound of warbling phlegm. "I think that First Voice of the First Family has much more to learn about humans. And I do not think he will like the lessons." He straightened, stepped back from the observation glass. "We end as we began—with truths that are the beginning of an enduring bridge between us."

This time, having skimmed the Hkh'Rkh self-reference, Caine knew the word to use. "Honor," he said in Hkh'i.

Yaargraukh nodded somberly. "Honor," he repeated. "It is sadness to me that we seem destined to fight before our bridge is built."

Risking one of the few phrases he had learned in Yaargraukh's language, Caine asserted, "If it is so, then it will be a waste of the blood of the brave." The axiom was more provocative in Hkh'i: a core proverb, Caine had determined that its closest human translation would be analogous to "It would be the desecration of heroes, even as they march to their deaths." It was an accusation of heinousness that bordered on atrocity.

Yaargraukh stopped nodding, stared a long time. Caine wondered if he had gone too far, but also felt that—for both his race, and himself—it had been the *right* thing to say. Because it was the simple truth.

Yaargraukh made a rumbling sound in his chest like he was clearing his throat somewhere near his lungs. "You are not the first to think it, Caine Riordan."

Together, they turned away from the stars and started the short walk back to the intership docking coupler that would lead Yaargraukh into the feature-less walkways of the Dornaani station, and ultimately, to his ship.

As they approached it, the lights in the coupler—a cubical node with hatches on all six sides—flickered once. The farthest door quivered as the explosive bolts ringing it detonated, blasting it away from the coupler and into open space—even as the door on their side of the node failed to close.

The sudden, outrushing cyclone gave Caine one fraction of a moment in which to think and act. He grabbed at one of the flagpoles before the vacuum sucked him straight towards space. But rather than fighting that outward plunge, Caine struggled to keep his body from tumbling, and to get the flagpole braced across his waist—

Which he managed a split second before he went through the wind-roaring hole into blackness. The ends of the flagpole caught on either side of the hatchway: the sudden, slamming stop against that life-saving cross-bar drove the air out of Caine, snapping his head and feet forward.

Dazed, he was aware of a heavy thump on the bar: Yaargraukh had caught it as well, crashing to a halt adjacent to the rim of the hatchway, where the lights of the door's control panel still shone brightly. Woozy, feeling the pressure soaring in his ears and eyes, Caine saw that the control lights were still illuminated normally: no red failure markers. Meaning that the failure was not in the local control console. Meaning that the malfunction was in a single circuit, somewhere beyond the door controls. Meaning that the safety override, which automatically sealed the hatch in the event of console damage, was still functioning. Meaning—

"Yaargraukh." Caine nodded at the Hkh'Rkh's ceremonial sword, then at the console. "Smash. Now."

The Hkh'Rkh didn't stop to signal understanding: he drew the blade and drove it half a foot into the panel, splitting the metal and spraying shattered buttons and broken switches, which were promptly sucked out into space.

Then the console's remaining lights went red—and with a shrill pneumatic scream, the automatic safety override slammed the hatch shut.

Chapter Fifty

MENTOR

Downing knew that standing stiffly with arms folded was not a receptive posture, but didn't much care as he traded stares with Alnduul. He glanced quickly at Riordan, who was still slumped against the far wall, dark maroon stains around his nose, his eyes fletched with the blood-red lightning streaks of burst capillaries. Downing determined that the time for well-mannered, soft-spoken diplomacy was long past. "Alnduul, we require an update: do you have any more news on the event?"

Alnduul's hands were folded and voice was tight. "The other delegations deny involvement of any kind. Except the Arat Kur: they still refuse to reply to any summons whatsoever. On the other hand, the Hkh'Rkh delegation has now accused your delegation of attempting to assassinate Yaargraukh."

Opal looked up sharply. "They *what*?"

Visser turned a withering stare upon Alnduul. "This is not only preposterous, but a transparent attempt to manufacture an incident in order to—"

Downing heard where Visser was going, derailed her by interrupting. "Alnduul, have your technicians determined why our coupler's doors failed?"

"No, but the chip that monitors the coupler's functions registered a brief pulse of power in the circuit that triggers the explosive bolts. This was what caused them to discharge."

"So there was an overload from some other system?"

Thandla answered before Alnduul could. "Mr. Downing, I do not think you understand the significance of what Alnduul has just told us. There is no way—there is no physical pathway—for a power surge to trigger the bolts. The bolts are physically isolated from all other systems until their arming switch is thrown. Furthermore, they are insulated from any other charge-bearing systems in order to prevent exactly this kind of failure."

Alnduul nodded. "My technicians confirm that the bridging switch to the explosive bolts has not been moved since it was last checked by your technicians on Earth."

"So an electric current just *appeared* in the circuits beyond the gap of the still-open bridging switch?"

"That is correct. And allow me to anticipate your next question: our station sensors would have detected any attempt to induce current in the line by projecting an electromagnetic or microwave flux at it. No such energy pulse was recorded."

Downing nodded, felt cold sweat on his palms. *There wasn't any power surge in Alexandria either, but it was the same species of mysterious failure there, too. And probably the same with Nolan's coronary controller . . .*

Alnduul was continuing. "Since we cannot identify a system failure of any kind, I have asked the Third

Arbiter to provisionally treat this event as an attempted assassination."

"Thank you. Does this mean that the Third Arbiter has approved my request that our delegation should now be returned as two separate groups?" Eyes turned toward Downing; he ignored them.

"Yes, although there was considerable discussion about the political wisdom of acceding to that request. However, your colloquial axiom that one should never put all their eggs in one basket decided the matter. However, I must ask that the party returning to Earth in your own module makes the journey in cryosleep."

"Of course, Alnduul. When will we be departing?"

"Twenty minutes: no more."

Stunned stares went back and forth between the other members of the delegation.

"We shall be ready," Downing promised.

"And we shall remain vigilant. I shall contact you soon again." Alnduul's image faded.

"Twenty minutes?" Hwang mused. "That's not a lot of time."

"That's the idea," replied Downing. "We don't want to give the assassins enough time to have another go at us."

Elena let out a long sigh. "A few hours ago, I wondered how long it would be before the Accord came apart."

Trevor looked over at her. "And now?"

"Now I wonder how long it will be before we're at war."

Visser shook her head. "*Nein*, Elena: we already are." She sent a sideways glance at Riordan. "What happened to Caine was the first shot, I think."

"Or just a warning, perhaps?" Durniak offered.

"More likely a promise of what is to come," Elena said grimly.

Visser nodded. "*Ja*, that is what I am afraid of." She closed her eyes. "Which means I have failed."

Wasserman waved dismissively. "Hey, you weren't alone here, Ambassador. We all blew it."

Caine cocked an eyebrow—which only called greater attention to his blood-streaked eyes. "No, *none* of us 'blew it.'"

Wasserman's chin jutted at Caine truculently. "Have you seen any *other* human delegations on this station? If not, then we're the bozos who screwed up."

"No, we didn't, Lemuel—because we never had a chance in hell of succeeding."

Thandla shook his head. "We could have allied ourselves with the Ktor."

"Yeah, but would they have allied themselves with *us*?"

Durniak shrugged. "They assured us of their support."

"Sure they did. But so what? I'll bet they offered their support to *every* race they thought might turn against the Dornaani." Caine spread his hands. "Let's assume for a moment that the Ktor wanted an alliance with us more than with any of the other races. A crucial question remains: an alliance against whom? The Dornaani? The Slaasriithi? The Arat Kur—who, if they make war on us alone, would get spanked and sent home by the Custodians? An alliance with the Ktor is meaningless because the only real danger to us *is* the Ktor. Which means we're not talking about an alliance at all: we're talking about extortion, a protection racket."

"Well," Thandla shrugged, "that still might have been to our advantage. It might have slowed down the avalanche of events which seem to be overtaking us now."

"No, Sanjay, buying ourselves time by masquerading as a Ktoran ally still won't enable us to close the tech gap between us and them quickly enough. And I doubt we could have conned them, anyway: trying to out-lie professional liars rarely works. Besides, if we were cowering in the Ktor's kennel, they'd probably turn right around and remove the only folks who might be able and willing to intervene if the Ktor *do* decide to eat us instead of keep us as pets: the Dornaani and the Slaasriithi."

"Who've done nothing to help us, so far," added Visser.

Caine shrugged. "I suspect it's in their nature to avoid conflict as long as possible."

"You mean, until it's too late to help," Wasserman sneered. "And I just love the way they've rewarded our fine, upstanding morals. Using your analogy from the other night, we took the higher road and played the part of Churchill: we stood up to the bad guys. Except it turns out that the Dornaani have happily taken on the role of Chamberlain and have hung us out to dry, trying to preserve 'peace in their time.'"

"That could be what happens," admitted Caine, "but I think the possibility that the Dornaani might fail us is a whole lot lower than the probability that the Ktor mean to consume us."

Visser's smile looked labored, broken. "You are trying to be kind, Caine, but we failed. The fault is ours."

"Failure and fault are two different things, Ambassador." Caine leaned toward her. "You came here expecting a tea party and found yourself in a diplo-matic death match. It was already half over, with the long-term pros jockeying for their final positions. We didn't even know the boundaries of the ring, much less the rules—and we didn't have the power or the knowledge to change the outcome."

Downing smiled. "So what you're saying is, there's no shame in losing a rigged game. True enough, I suppose. But did we have to lose by such a margin? From a security perspective, we have utterly failed our planet."

Caine looked up, spoke slowly. "That depends upon how you define 'security,' Richard: do you mean 'sur-vival at any cost'—including slavery—or 'living as a self-determining species'? If by security you mean nothing more than physical survival, then you're right: we failed. We had another option: we could probably have survived as slaves."

"Slaves?" Opal sounded horrified.

Caine shrugged. "If we had to fight off the Ktor alone, I'm pretty sure the endgame would be thralldom or extinction." He looked around the group. "But if by security you mean preserving our speciate right to what a bunch of guys in wigs once labeled life, liberty, and the pursuit of happiness, then you all made the best choice you could."

Visser shook her head, closed her eyes. "And so that is the report I'm to make to the world leaders: we didn't like the certainty of remaining alive on our knees, so we chose the possibility of being killed on our feet?"

Caine shrugged. "That's the report you have to make, because that's what we did. If they blame you for choosing that option, then they're not worthy to be our leaders. And then thank God we were here instead of them."

Downing checked his watch. "There are some last practical matters to address. The group that is going straight home in this module will not be going directly to Earth, but out to the Belt for debriefing. Your cryocells will be—"

Le Mule sat far back in his chair, arms folded. "No way," he snapped.

Richard curbed his annoyance. "I beg your pardon?"

"You heard me. But I'll say it again, with emphasis: no *fucking* way. When I came on this mission, I didn't agree to sell my body—or soul—to the guvmint, so they sure as hell can't keep shuttling me around from one windowless hole to the next. And now cold sleep, too? Why? The Dornaani brought us here without it, so why—?"

Downing rapped his knuckles on the table: Wasserman flinched, shut his mouth with a snap. "If you haven't noticed, Alnduul has intimated that he will help us in ways that exceed the comfort level of his superiors. And, possibly, exceed his own authority."

"And your point?"

"My point, Mr. Wasserman, is that putting the passengers in cryocells gives him a much freer hand to help us."

"Huh?"

"*Bozhemoi!*" exclaimed Durniak. "Truly you do not see? Alnduul has made it clear that he is on our side. So much so that he might do more than just ship us home."

"Like what?" asked Opal.

Downing steepled his fingers. "I suspect he intends to put a covert payload inside our own cargo containers in this module. He can't put it on the Dornaani ship that is taking the second group to Barnard's Star: too much chance that his own people will stumble across it."

Trevor looked eager. "So you're saying that he wants our people in cold cells so they won't see him load the 'special cargo'?"

Downing shrugged. "I'm saying that if Alnduul intends to do anything that exceeds his authority, he can't tell us openly. And if our passengers aren't awake to see what he does, then they can't leak any information about it—even to Alnduul's own people. Plausible deniability, and all that."

Visser nodded. "Mr. Downing is right. We shall go into cold sleep at once."

Wasserman threw down his dataslate. "Look, you all do what you like, but I'm still not climbing into a refrigerator bound for a grubby little rock in the Belt, where so-called experts will ask us the same questions over and over again. Hell, there's no reason we can't go straight to Earth, write our reports, and submit them when—"

Elena's voice was quiet. "You know that's no substitute for a live debrief, Lemuel. And you're not the only one who wants to go straight to Earth; I've got a thirteen-year-old son who hasn't seen me in almost two months, now. But remember what's at stake. We might be talking about the fate of our planet."

"Look, I don't have to—"

"Lemuel." It was Caine; although his face was still pale, his voice was firm. "The. Fate. Of. Our. Planet." Then he was staring at the wall again.

Le Mule looked like he was about to say something, then glowered at the floor.

Visser rose. "So who is traveling on the module to Earth, and who is going on to Barnard's Star, Mr. Downing?"

"Most of you will be going directly to the Belt, where Major Patrone will brief the military authorities. Trevor is one of the two people coming with me to brief the flag officers at Barnard's Star II C."

Visser stared at Downing, surprised. "Who is the other person accompanying you?"

Opal came erect. Downing was careful not to look in her direction. He looked at Riordan, instead. "I'm afraid that you're coming to Barney Deucy as well, Caine."

Caine closed his eyes. Then he nodded.

Downing barely concealed his surprise: although battered and dazed, Riordan's reaction should still have included some outcry against yet another violation of his personal freedom. But silence? Downing had a fleeting anxiety that Caine had been more seriously injured by the explosive decompression than anyone guessed...

But it was time for seven of them to enter their cold cells, and the other three to board the Dornaani craft that would take them to Barnard's Star. Downing turned off his dataslate. "Any more questions? If not, we should—"

Alnduul's image faded back into existence. "All is in readiness," he affirmed with the slightest inclination of his head.

Visser stood very straight. "We thank you, Alnduul."

"I have done nothing other than perform my duties to you."

"Okay, then," Opal said, after glancing quickly at Caine—a glance so brief that Downing was fairly sure he was the only one to notice it. "Since you've only been doing your job up until now, I'd like to impose by asking you just one personal question." Every member of the delegation stared at her.

Alnduul's inner eyelids blinked rapidly twice. "This is—uncommonly direct of you, Major Patrone."

"Yeah, well—I get that way when war looks imminent. Which Glayaazh says is not the case. But what do you think, Alnduul: is war imminent?"

"Major, although I cannot answer that question, I can give a relevant response to an earlier query. When Ambassador Visser asked about humanity's role in this tense situation, Third Arbiter Glayaazh told her that 'your role is whatever you decide it is.' I offer a different answer: 'You already know your role. You merely need to accept it.'"

Visser started. "We already know our role in this conflict?"

Alnduul nodded. "One of you has foreseen it, albeit indirectly."

"Who?"

"Mr. Riordan."

Caine looked up with blood-flecked eyes. "What? Me?"

"Yes. We have become quite familiar with the transcript of your statements at the Parthenon Dialogues. If I am not mistaken, you speculated that the earliest role of humans might have been akin to the earliest role of dogs. Do you recall the reason you gave for canines' original domestication?"

Caine frowned. "To hunt wolves."

"Exactly. Which is also a great irony: the most effective

protectors—the best wolfhounds, if you will—are often those which share many characteristics with the ravagers they have been bred to destroy. But that is hardly surprising, since—as you also pointed out at Parthenon, Mr. Riordan—one must often fight fire with fire."

Riordan shook his head. "Alnduul, I realize that you're limited in how much you may tell us directly, but are you implying that the Ktor are wolves and that we're—well, wolfhounds?"

Alnduul's mouth half-rotated in the Dornaani version of a smile. "No, Caine Riordan: it is *you* whose words have implied that. Both at Parthenon and here."

Caine looked no more edified than anyone else—possibly less so.

Alnduul gestured toward the exit with his tapering hand. "Now, I must wish you all safe travels. Mr. Downing, your party of three shall proceed to your embarkation point. The rest of you must enter your cold cells immediately." His image faded.

"Fine," spat Le Mule. "Let's get it over with." He was gone in a rush of resentful, gangly limbs.

Opal looked at Caine—whose eyes were unsteady, as if he still found it difficult to focus on distant objects. Although they hadn't yet engaged in public embraces, this was a logical moment for that breakthrough. But Downing saw that Caine's unsteadiness caused Opal to pause—and just that quickly, the moment slipped away: they waved awkwardly to each other, instead.

As Trevor helped Riordan into the corridor, Opal turned quickly to Downing. "I thought—"

"Orders change, Major Patrone. But in this case, the change is only temporary. Don't worry: Caine will be well guarded."

It was obvious from Opal's shiny, angry eyes, that her official duty to protect Caine was not the primary source of her distress.

Not at all.

ODYSSEUS

Trevor was the last to enter the podlike compartment in the same Dornaani ship that had fetched them from Earth, and Caine noticed a box under his arm. Seeing the look, Trevor explained: "Elena caught up with me and gave me this, along with the strangest—"

Alnduul's voice seemed to emanate from every surface in the chamber. "Please settle yourselves comfortably." The section of the pod they were facing—it seemed wrong to think of it as a bulkhead, somehow—slid aside, revealing the local starfield. "Forgive the malfunction, but your chamber seems to be defaulting into the external display mode. It is not safe to delay our departure long enough to correct it, but if the external view bothers you, we could easily—"

"No, no," Downing interrupted, "this is fine." And indeed it was: given the choice between looking at a blank wall or observing the operation of an exosapient starship, no intelligence officer would ever choose the former. And besides, Caine could tell that Downing wasn't buying Alnduul's excuse any more than he was: this wasn't a malfunction; it was a gift.

Trevor was looking around the peripheries of the featureless seats for straps, buckles, restraints. "Uh, Alnduul," he asked, "just how many gees of acceleration will we experien—?"

"Do not trouble yourself, Commander Corcoran. Just settle back. We are about to begin our journey."

Caine exchanged glances with the other two, leaned back as he had been told, found himself wondering what their sleeping accommodations would be like, and if the food would be varied enough to—

The hull vibrated faintly and Caine felt the equivalent of mental palpitations—as though his consciousness was shuddering, teetering at the edge of blackness. The next instant, the sensation and vibration were past. *Odd,* he thought, *what kind of preacceleration thrust system would—?*

Then he looked out the gallery window and saw that the starfield had changed. Not slightly; entirely. And it was motionless.

It was Trevor who spoke first. "Did we just—?"

Then the Dornaani ship came about—the new star field wheeling slowly past—and revealed the murky sphere that was Barnard's Star II's roiling hydrogen-and-ammonia atmosphere.

Caine heard Downing release his caught breath, heard Trevor gulp—a constricted sound—and found he could not put two thoughts together. The implications of what he had seen—instantaneous travel over a distance of sixteen light-years—were still rushing in at him.

It was Trevor who spoke first. "Well," he said hoarsely, "if Wasserman was here, he sure would feel better about our siding with the Dornaani."

Caine nodded, spoke to the ceiling. "Alnduul?"

"Yes, Mr. Riordan?"

"That was most impressive."

"We cannot do it often. It is very expensive and

requires us to overhaul what you would call our shift drive."

What we would call *your shift drive? Meaning that it isn't* actually *a shift drive? Hmmm . . .* but for now: "Even with that limitation, I find it puzzling that the Custodians or the Dornaani Collective feel that any other power poses a threat to them. With a fleet of ships capable of a sixteen-light-year shift from a standing start, and able to make a pinpoint transit to within—" Caine glanced at the gas giant, assessed, guessed "—five planetary diameters of a world, I would expect you to be invincible."

"Yes, one might readily infer that from our technological capabilities."

But if such vastly superior technology was still not decisive, then—"So the vulnerability of the Dornaani does not arise from a deficiency in equipment, but will?"

"I am, of course, not allowed to respond to that conjecture directly. However, it is a most elegant hypothesis."

"Elegant?" echoed Trevor. "Elegant how?"

Downing nodded. "It is elegant in that it resolves many apparent contradictions and also meshes with much of what we saw at the Convocation. The Dornaani do not lack power: they lack the commitment for decisive action." Downing looked up. "Except you, Alnduul. And, I am guessing, the Custodians in general?"

"Again, I cannot comment."

Caine frowned. "Maybe not, but given the duties of the Custodians, I would speculate that only the most—er, proactive members of your species would pursue such a career."

"Another highly stimulating conjecture on which I may offer no comment. However, I may mention this: we Custodians have had much occasion to monitor and learn of the peoples of Earth. And many of us were struck by the similarity between the oath of service that a new Custodian must take and a human axiom, attributed to the Irish philosopher Edmund Burke."

"And what is that axiom?"

"'All that is necessary for the triumph of evil is that good men do nothing.'"

Trevor smiled, Downing blew out a great sigh. Caine just nodded. "Thank you, Alnduul."

"Why do you thank me, Mr. Riordan?"

"For sharing that with us. And for being who you are."

After a pause, Alnduul responded, "And who else would I be?" The tone was wry, yet strangely serious, too. When he spoke again, it was with his customary inflection. "We have arrived unobserved, despite your automated surveillance satellites. And yes, Mr. Downing, I am including the small nonmetallic devices mixed in with the debris of the rings. You will experience a gee of acceleration now: we shall have you at your destination shortly."

Within the hour, their destination appeared just beyond the terminator of the gas giant: a small white disk that housed the naval base that humans called the Pearl. Wreathed in a thick, white, infamously noxious atmosphere, the world itself was the third satellite of its parent planet, and hence designated C, making it Barnard's Star 2 C. Or "Barney Deucy," in service slang. Angling up from it were several sleek silver slivers.

Trevor pitched his chin at them. "Welcoming committee. With weapons hot, I'll bet."

"That assumption is incorrect, Commander. We transmitted the codes Mr. Downing furnished to us when he boarded. I believe your craft will rendezvous with you in approximately thirty minutes."

Trevor frowned, looked askance at the ceiling. "Don't you mean, 'rendezvous with *us*'?"

"No, Commander, I do not." There was a distant rumble—and suddenly, the starfield seemed to shift a bit. "We have detached your pod for autonomous operations; it will now maneuver to the rendezvous. As soon as you have transferred to your own craft, and your pressurized cargo containers have been deployed for pick-up, this module will automatically return to our ship. It has been a pleasure meeting all of you."

Caine smiled at the ceiling. "I hope our paths cross soon again."

"It is difficult to foresee the circumstances which might permit that. And yet, stranger things have occurred." There was a long pause, so long that at first they thought Alnduul had departed without his customary salutation. "There is a datum I believe you should all have—but particularly you, Commander Corcoran."

Trevor started, looked up. "Me?"

"Yes. It concerns your father."

"Uh . . . yes?"

Caine heard the hesitation in Alnduul's voice: *he's breaking rules; he's not supposed to reveal this.*

Alnduul's voice was slow, deliberate. "The organism you found in your father's chest was not the cause of his death at Sounion."

Trevor gaped. "What? But—how do you know that?"

"Because we introduced the organism into his body to assist him. It did not malfunction."

"*You*—?"

"Enlightenment unto you all, gentlemen."

Trevor turned red. "Damn it, you had better enlighten me some more, you—"

But the almost inaudible carrier signal was gone: Alnduul had departed.

Chapter Fifty-One

MENTOR

Debarking from the Russlavic Federation shuttle inside one of the Pearl's subsurface hangars, Caine found himself mere meters away from military hardware he'd only read—and written—about. Downing impatiently gestured for him to catch up, leading them towards a bank of gray, yellow-stenciled elevators beyond the security scanning pad. "I am scheduled to brief and be debriefed in ten minutes," he tossed over his shoulder, "then back up here to catch a clipper to the outbound shift-carrier *Borodino*. If I miss it, I'll have a thirty-day wait."

Personnel in Federation gray-green and Commonwealth blue-black mobbed the three of them with scanners, sniffers, and snoopers, reprising a similar dance of detection that had swirled around the trio when they had first transferred to the shuttle just over an hour ago.

Downing went to the smallest elevator, ran his security fob over the sensor. The door opened and, hand extended, he urged Caine and Trevor to enter.

Caine stepped forward—and stopped. For the briefest moment, he felt—what? A profoundly sharpened awareness of his surroundings: edges seemed more crisp, sounds more clipped. Time itself seemed to narrow down into a tunnel of many rings, rather than a pervasive, shapeless flow. Yet it all felt more like a premonition than an experience, as if these sensations were important only because they presaged the moment to come—

Caine backed away from the open elevator. "No," he said.

Trevor blinked, then stared. "Caine, are you—are you okay? Problems from the decompression, again?"

"No. I—I think we should use the stairs."

Downing, still holding the elevator open, was studying him: Caine could feel the assessing gaze. "It's six flights down, you know."

"I didn't know. But the exercise will do us good."

"Caine, are you quite—?"

Caine, feeling foolish, shook his head and yanked open the door to the staircase. Maybe Trevor was right; maybe it was all some after-effect of having nearly been vacced a few hours ago.

But it sure hadn't felt that way.

He started down the stairs.

CIRCE

The tall man, who wore his sunglasses even in this dim room, made a gesture of annoyance and leaned back. To his left, a small cube with one open side emitted vapors and a pungent, musky stench. Near his right hand, a bowl of olives stood forgotten.

"This is most inconvenient," he murmured.

His assistant, unsure if the utterance had been meant for him, or was simply his superior thinking out loud, asked, "You mean, that Riordan chose not to enter the elevator?"

The man paused as if mildly surprised to rediscover that he was not alone in the room. "No. It is not his failure to enter that troubles me. It was his reason."

The assistant looked at the screen: the three men—Riordan, Downing, Corcoran—had disappeared into the staircase. "But how could you possibly know why he—?"

"I know," said the man sharply. "How I know does not concern you. But you should report to your superiors that, in Riordan's case, my abilities will be less efficacious now."

"Mr. Astor-Smath will want to know why."

The other man sneered. "And so the quizzical dog tasks his master to tutor him in cosmology. Very well, relate this: your employer has now had me exert my abilities many times in Riordan's immediate vicinity. Consequently, Riordan is starting to detect the onset of the Reifications."

"Reifications? What do you mean? Is that what you call your—?"

"You are familiar with the principle of quantum entanglement or—perhaps more suitable to your perception—Einstein's 'spooky action at a distance'?"

"Yes, of course." The assistant overcame the impulse to cross his fingers as he answered.

"Very well. Now imagine what might be achieved if it was possible to impose a limited amount of order on that statistically-predictable chaos for just one moment, and in a small volume of space."

"So you can focus—I mean, 'reify'—the phenomena of quantum entanglement to produce a desired outcome?"

"In a manner of speaking."

"But how—?"

"For now, all you need to understand is that when a person has been proximal to numerous Reifications, that person may begin to have the ability to detect their onset. A crude analogy would be how some animals know when they are approaching a magnetic field."

"Is that because the Reification manifests as a wave front, or a—?"

"Silence. You now know enough to explain why Riordan could be harder to kill."

"But surely, the occasional accommodations you have provided for Mr. Astor-Smath have not affected—"

"'Occasional,' you say? Let me remind you of just how 'occasional' the Reifications have been." The tall man flicked olive pits off the table with his long-nailed finger to punctuate each incident: "First there was the sustained influence required to ensure that the second engineer on board the *Tyne* would carry out his suicidal sabotage of its engines. Then there was the disabling of the enemy's security systems and independent power plant in Alexandria. And let us not forget the need to compel the attackers to wear the self-destruct vests provided by your employer. Then, in the space of three days, two Reifications were required to kill Nolan Corcoran and Arvid Tarasenko. I have also learned, within the hour, that my colleagues failed to assassinate Riordan with a technical malfunction at the Convocation Station. And now, he avoided the elevator which would have dropped him to his death—along with two other troublesome adversaries. You call this battery of requested accommodations occasional?"

The assistant shrugged. "Well, it was necessary: your success rate has not been as high as you guaranteed. But be assured that Mr. Astor-Smath has been happy to overlook that."

The man turned his shaded eyes upon his smaller assistant. "You are certainly not implying that these failures were in any way my fault."

"Oh no, no; I was just—"

"Your employer has involved me in actions that were routinely inelegant, rash, and unprofessional. Had your employer been less intemperate, he would have fared far better, and Riordan would not be sensing the Reifications. Indeed, he would be dead."

"Is there any way to distract Riordan during future attempts? To ensure that he misses the warning signs of—?"

"The only warning you should be interested in," said the tall man quietly, "is the one I am giving you now: cease your inquiries regarding the nature of Reification."

"My apologies," answered the assistant, whose anxiety compelled him to babble on. "I do not understand why Riordan is still important to us, anyway. He revealed all his crucial information at the Parthenon Dialogues: he is no longer worth killing."

The tall man smiled. "You could not be more wrong."

"Then what dangerous secrets does he still know?"

"Riordan knows things—or will—that he does not yet know he knows."

"What?" said the assistant.

But the tall man with the sunglasses had redis-
covered the olives and evidently, forgotten about the
presence—and possibly the existence—of his assistant.

MENTOR

Downing emerged from his debriefing and motioned
for Caine and Trevor to follow him into a nearby
conference room. Upon entering, he flipped on the
white-noise generators and ran his RF detector around
the room's perimeter.

"Clean?" asked Trevor, setting down the box he
had brought on board the Dornaani ship.

Downing nodded, motioned them to seats. *Well,
there's no use beating around the bush.* "Caine, I
have an Executive Order to induct you into the United
States Space Force."

"Induct me?" Riordan's smile was bemused rather
than sardonic. "I wasn't aware there was a draft in
effect."

"There isn't."

"Meaning that you don't actually have compulsory
powers in this matter."

"Caine, don't make me—"

"Richard, I'm going to save us all the embarrassment of letting you finish that sentence. My answer is
this: 'I serve at the pleasure of the President of the
United States of America.' Now, where do I sign?"

Just like that. Caine had agreed without a flinch
or a blink. *Just like that.* "Caine, I didn't expect—"

"Richard, our relationship—such as it is—has no
bearing on this moment. The threats to our world—to
our species—are no longer hypothetical, but real. And

when my country—in the person of the President, no less—asks me to serve, I say 'yes.' Without delay. Now, where are the papers?"

"I'll give them to you later. For now, let's go through what's going to happen once you sign them. Firstly, you will immediately commence twenty-nine days of combined Advanced Basic and OCS training."

Trevor smiled. "Are we making 'four-week wonders' now, Uncle Richard?"

"I'm not joking, Trev. He will complete the course in twenty-nine days—"

"Uncle Richard, I'm sorry, but not even you have that kind of clout. Basic qualification and commission cannot run concurrently, and are, by order of the Joint Chiefs, confirmed at a minimum of—"

"Commander." Richard hated doing it, but addressing Trevor by his rank rather than his first name stopped his godson in mid-word. "In time, or under immediate threat, of war, the concurrency limitation can be waived. Particularly when an Executive Order is involved. Furthermore, Mr. Riordan has already spent some time in the military—"

Caine raised an eyebrow. "I have?"

Downing consulted his notes. "You spent two weeks going through the first phases of BT with Army recruits back in 2098; it was research for your series in *Jane's Defense Weekly*. In 2102, book research led to a formal invitation to audit a course in strategy and tactics at Annapolis. Where, it seems, you received the highest mark in the class.

"President Liu has accepted the recommendation of the Joint Chiefs that these earlier participations in service-related training be recognized as counting towards both your basic and officer training. Hence, the wartime minimum of six weeks of training has been reduced to four. Questions?"

"Yes: why?"

"Why what, Caine?"

"Why induct me?"

"I trust you are not rethinking your commitment to serve?"

Caine shook his head. "That's not even an option, given the current situation. And since the Executive herself has signed off on everything, I'm as good as wearing blue already. I just want to know why."

"Fair enough. You are being inducted so that you have enough official clout to take command of conventional forces if you are in an intelligence-critical situation."

"Okay, but why the rush? And why do it here at the Pearl?"

"Firstly, I didn't want you arriving back on Earth with the rest of the delegation. The press would climb all over you: that spotlight would kill any future you might have as an intelligence asset for IRIS."

"Not sure I'd mind that outcome." Downing noted that Caine's tone was rueful rather than resentful. "But I see your point. Go on."

"Since your training will be swift and your promotion unorthodox, it will be easier to get it done on the sly out here."

"Just how is my promotion going to be unorthodox?"

"When you finish OCS, you will immediately be breveted up to commander, in recognition of your prior 'official service.' Five minutes later, you will be retired into the Reserves."

602 *Charles E. Gannon*

"I—?"

"He—?"

"Gentlemen, please. Let me finish. Trevor, you're going to be bumped up again, as well. For the same reason: the higher the rank you have, the more people to whom you can issue bigger orders—particularly in a crisis. Hopefully, you'll never need to play that rank card, but if you do, you'll have it up your sleeve. And in your case, Caine, it's best we keep that potential buried."

Caine smiled. "So I get retired into the reserves here at Pearl even before my commission papers begin their glacial movement through the system and into the endless reams of Earth-bound housekeeping dispatches. Which no reporter has ready access to or any interest in."

"Exactly. The rest of the delegation faces the paparazzi by returning first. You and Trevor slink back in after the furor has died down, with you wearing civvies. No fuss, no bother, no press. And I'm sorry to say that, from this point forward, keeping things from the press is going to be a routine necessity. For instance, only because you're both restricted to base until the end of Caine's training can I even reveal that I have just activated the final phase of an IRIS operation code-named Case Leo Gap, which initiates from Barnard's Star."

Caine leaned forward. "I heard you and Nolan mention Case Leo Gap once. What is it?"

Downing shook his head. "You don't need those details, yet; you only need to be familiar with the code name."

Trevor leaned back, frowning. "A damn odd name, too. 'Leo Gap'? What's it about, a lion's hole?"

"No, the pass that Leonidas defended against Xerxes: Thermopylae. Had that battle gone the other way, the

Hellenic world would have ended—and ours would never have arisen."

"Thanks, Uncle Richard, I get the resonances with our current situation: I just forgot the name of the Greek commander. Who had a hell of a fight on his hands, as I recall. How many of the Greeks actually survived?"

Downing hesitated. Into that silence, Caine inserted a recitation:

> *Tell them in Lacedaemon, passerby,*
> *That here, obedient to their word, we lie.*

Trevor looked at him. "That many, huh?"

Downing stood. "I've got about thirty minutes left before my clipper leaves. Any unfinished business?"

Trevor nodded. "Yes. Well, I mean, I think so." He picked up the box from the seat beside him. "As I was hustling to join you two on Alnduul's ship, Elena ran me down and gave me this. She says my father entrusted it to her about a year ago, and told her, 'Give it to Uncle Richard at the right time.'"

"'The right time'? What does that mean?"

"Elena asked Dad the same thing. He told her that the box would become very important if we were ever on the brink of 'fighting a war like no other.' She thought that the recent events probably satisfy that condition. I tend to agree with her."

"As do I." Downing received the box from Trevor: it was cumbersome, with something weighty thumping to and fro inside. Opening it, Downing discovered another, smaller box and momentarily suspected a monstrous practical joke. But then he saw the envelope on top, with "Richard" scrawled across it in Nolan's distinctive handwriting. He opened it and read:

Dear Richard:

If Caine Riordan is still alive, please give him the smaller, enclosed box. Except for one additional photograph, it holds the contents of the bag he was carrying when he was apprehended outside my suite in Perry City. Those contents should help him regain the one hundred hours he lost on Luna.

If Caine is dead, then you must open the box. Handle the contents as you see fit.

I wish I was there to help you with the coming troubles. I also apologize for not sharing all the secrets that I was privy to, but the photograph I added to Caine's box will provide adequate explanation, I think.

Your Friend,
Nolan

Downing stared at the card, felt grief, resentment, and confusion all at the same time. But mostly, he simply missed his oldest friend—even more than he felt curiosity.

He handed the inner box to Caine. "It's for you," he said.

ODYSSEUS

Caine opened the box cautiously.

And found himself staring down at an old bottle of red wine—Chateauneuf-du-pape, to be precise.

Alongside it was a desiccated rose and a photograph of a young woman who looked very familiar—because, he realized, it was Elena, when she was perhaps twenty-four or twenty—

The memories came unevenly, yet so quickly that he gasped. Luna. 2105. Buying a rose, a bottle of wine—Chateauneuf-du-pape—and porterhouse steaks: all outrageous extravagances on the Moon. All purchased because he had been surprised by joy in a place and at a time he could not have expected it.

The young lady he met while waiting in line for coffee only introduced herself as Elena, at first. She was not much older than a college kid, but she had an unwavering gaze, and a peculiar species of certainty, of intensity, that soon had him forgetting that this was a young woman with whom he should not become involved.

That prohibition against involvement arose not merely because she was eleven years his junior, but because, midway through their conversation, she shared her full name, thereby revealing that she was the daughter of the man he had come to Luna to interview: Nolan Corcoran.

Caine should have avoided her, but he couldn't. At their second chance encounter—which they both carefully engineered—Caine tried to adopt a casual demeanor, but instead she fixed him with her green green green eyes. He was not able to look away from them during the four-hour lunch that he had originally resolved to be the last forty-five minutes he would ever spend with her.

The memories were scattered, incomplete, ragged in places, but he did recall meeting her that night for a glass of wine. In the course of discovering that they had eerily similar tastes in most everything—from food to art to novels to films—Caine did the next thing that he promised himself he would not do: he gave her a poem he had written about her earlier that day. And in return, she gave him herself. Which led to mutual embarrassment over the speed with which they had become intimate. Which they resolved by becoming intimate again. And then again.

The next day, Caine found a note on his pillow suggesting dinner at her suite, that night. He could not have been happier, but wondered how she planned to evict her father, whom she was visiting on Luna.

The answer presented itself the next morning when Nolan Corcoran and Richard Downing began their interview by announcing that their time was limited: they were Far Side-bound. Then they turned the tables and asked the first question of the day: was Caine a writer or a patriot first? Caine had never thought about that before but was not long in doing so: as he told them, words gave birth to nations and held them to account, but writing itself never was, and never could be, the equal of lived hopes and ideals.

He could not recall all of their conversation, but they ultimately told him what he had come to learn, on the promise that he would only share select parts of it. They wondered at the ease with which he agreed to the secrecy. He wondered if, strange as it seemed, he might not be falling in love with Nolan Corcoran's daughter.

Which he cautiously intimated to Elena during a call later that day. Experience told him that a woman courted so quickly will back off, yet he was strangely certain she wouldn't. And she didn't.

So with wine and rose and steaks in hand, he arrived early to surprise her, to cook dinner for the young woman whose name—Elena Corcoran—had started to sound like music to him. But as he reached out to affix the rose to her door, the world went black.

"Caine? Caine?"

Richard's voice seemed very far away as Caine returned the bottle and the photograph, and mentally saw how the dominoes set in motion by both the romance and abduction had fallen. Elena's thirteen-year-old son was very likely Caine's child. And Nolan had undoubtedly known that, if not beforehand, then shortly after. It would have been simplicity itself for him to get a sample of the baby's DNA and compare it to Caine's.

But that still left the question of *why*: why would Nolan play such dire games with his own family? How could anything—even IRIS—be so important that he felt compelled to take these terrible steps?

Caine looked down into the box and saw that there was one last object in it; another photograph. But this image was not of a person: it was of the lunar surface. But no, it wasn't the Moon: on closer inspection, it was— *Oh. Of course.*

Next to him, Trevor was staring at the bottle and the old picture of his sister; he had obviously connected the dots and done the math. His voice was choked: "Why? Why would Dad choose to do all this?"

Caine shook his head. "He didn't choose to do it; he had to." He held out the last picture to Trevor. "Look."

Trevor stared, frowned. "What is this? A mining site on a planetoid?"

"Not exactly. Give the photo to your uncle. He'll know what it is."

"Why?"

"Because, except for the 'mining site,' I'll bet he's seen images of it before."

Richard took the picture, studied it, frowned. "You know, this does look familiar, rather like the images Nolan brought back from . . ." Then Downing went very pale. "Bollocks, this is the Doomsday Rock—the one that Nolan intercepted. Except—this one shows empty mooring points for a set of mass drivers."

Trevor was still frowning. "So what? Dad was mission commander; of course he would have kept a visual souvenir. Hell, they catalogued every meter of its surface before they—" And then the color bled out of Trevor's face, too.

Downing nodded. "Yes. They catalogued every meter of its surface before they used nuclear charges to bump it off course. And *only* nuclear charges. They didn't have a mass driver with them: there wasn't enough lead time to use it."

Trevor was hoarse. "Meaning that the missing mass drivers were used to push it *towards* us."

Downing nodded. "The Doomsday Rock was not a natural event: it was an attack. Some extraterrestrial power visited the Solar System and surreptitiously shifted the trajectory of a rock in the Kuiper Belt to swing in toward Earth and blast us back to the Bronze Age."

Caine suppressed a shiver: there was no other possible explanation. Even if a terrestrial nation had been suicidal enough to conceive of the plot, none of them could have carried it out: at that time, humanity hadn't had the ability to send major missions beyond

Saturn. "So *that's* what led to the creation of IRIS. It also explains how Nolan was so certain that an FTL drive could be built: the Doomsday Rock was proof that we had extrasolar neighbors who could get into and out of our system at will."

Downing nodded. "He also knew that the threat of an exosapient attack wasn't simply hypothetical: he had already fended one off, himself."

Caine rubbed his chin. "Yeah, which means that whoever weaponized a chunk of stone into the Doomsday Rock almost certainly learned that their attack had been foiled."

Downing kept nodding. "And so they would have to surreptitiously try to find out what had gone wrong. And who was responsible."

Trevor added the final piece. "Which they couldn't do by just by sitting at the edge of our space. And we all know who had legal access to our system besides the Dornaani."

Caine felt his skin grow very cold. "That would be our good friends the Ktor, in their role as Auxiliary Custodians."

Downing frowned. "Which makes it likely that they are somehow connected with the faceless adversaries that Nolan code-named 'Circe.'" He stared at the tabletop. "I wonder: do you think the Ktor might have had a direct hand in the deaths of Nolan and Tarasenko, and in some of the other 'odd events' we've been unable to explain?"

Caine shrugged. "Could be. But how would they recruit agents among us in the first place, or even establish contact? As Thandla discovered, they've got a radically different biology: hell, their natural environment is so cold that we can't even make use of the same planets. So how are we a threat to them? Why would they hate us so much?" Caine shook his head. "No: it still doesn't add up. Something's missing."

"I'll tell you what else is missing." Trevor's voice and eyes were hollow. "The reason why my dad never told any of us why Elena was clinically depressed after she returned from the Moon. Or who Connor's father was. Dad knew answers that could have saved all of us—but particularly Elena—a lot of grief."

Caine nodded. "Yes, Nolan knew—but he had to keep those facts to himself."

"Oh, c'mon. At least he could have told Elena."

Richard shook his head. "Trevor, Elena is the one person Nolan absolutely could *not* tell about Caine. We can predict the course of events if she had learned the truth: Elena would want Caine removed from cold sleep. Your father refuses. She asks him how he can expect his own grandson to grow up without a father—and why is it so important to keep Caine in cold sleep, anyway? What was Nolan to say then? That even if Caine was cooperative, he couldn't be released without a huge, smoke-screening story to throw the news jackals off his scent? That any detailed questions about Caine would have led back to, and unraveled, IRIS?"

Trevor frowned, ground his molars, and then turned sharply towards Caine. "So," he snapped, "are you going to marry my sister?"

Caine blinked—and became aware of the scent of Opal's shampoo on his shirt collar. At precisely the same moment, a memory—Elena moaning, sway-backed, hanging on to the bedposts as they moved together—tumbled newfound into his mind. "Hell," Caine rasped, trying to fight his way out of the conflicting sense-memories, "would Elena even *want* to marry me? Besides, I have to straighten things out with Opal first."

Trevor nodded. "Yeah. Okay. And given your—uh, situation—with Major Patrone, I don't envy you your lady problems right now."

"Me neither," sighed Caine. "But I'm thinking that maybe Elena got over me long ago. She didn't seem bothered by Opal—and she sure didn't seem interested in my company."

Now Trevor smiled. "Oh, brother—and I guess that's almost literally true, now—you don't know how to read my sister just yet. Yeah, she was dodging you, but probably because seeing the two of you post-corpsicle lovebirds together was making her crazy."

Downing took a very deep breath. "Which brings up a touchy subject. About Major Patrone, Caine. Your relationship with her is not exactly a chance event. She works for me."

"I know that."

"Caine, I mean she has *always* worked for me—every second of your time together."

Caine glared at Downing, felt his open hands becoming fists, and didn't really care what happened next. "So tell me, Richard: is there any part of my life that you *didn't* fuck with?"

MENTOR

Downing was beginning to worry that he might have to physically defend himself when Trevor intervened. "Hold on, Caine. Much as I hate saying so, this scheme with Opal sounds like it came from my dad. Am I right, Uncle Richard?"

Downing's first impulse—to defend Nolan, to take the heat as he always had—faded. *What is the use, here, in this moment, with these people?* He swallowed, nodded: "It was Nolan's plan. I didn't like it."

Trevor frowned. "I hate saying so, but Dad knew what he was doing recruiting a woman to be your guard, Caine. That would be the only way to control Elena once she learned you were back."

"Huh?" said Caine.

Downing nodded. "Yes, I see what you mean. Knowing Elena, if Caine had shown up again unattached, I suspect she would have read your father the riot act and become thoroughly—and quite vocally—unmanageable."

"Hell, she'd have called a press conference just to flip him a bird," drawled Trevor.

"Er...yes, probably so. But if she saw Caine already in the company of another lady, then—"

"Yeah," interrupted Trevor, "that's my point: Elena's a class act. She wouldn't go barging in under those circumstances. I'll bet that's just how Dad set it up." Trevor's certitude sounded suspiciously like a lament: these were hard—very hard—things to learn and hear about an idolized father.

Downing suppressed a sigh: he had known this side of Nolan for over twenty years, and even that didn't make today's revelations any easier to hear. But it all made sense now, particularly Nolan's understated pessimism about Caine and Opal's long-term prospects as a couple. He'd never wanted a permanent connection between them, because then Caine and Elena could not be reunited. Meaning he had used Opal miserably.

Trevor was apparently reflecting on the uneven ethics of his father, as well. "Given all the family secrets Dad kept from us, and all the shady crap he pulled, I guess I'm no longer so surprised that he had you sneak his body onto that government clipper for out-shift to another system."

Oh Christ; how did Trevor learn that? "Trevor, I—"

But Trevor wasn't listening. "I get the charade of the cremation and the memorial: an empty casket would have prompted a lot of questions. But why didn't Dad tell us he had found a way to be buried outsystem, Richard?"

Downing closed his eyes and hated each of the four words separately, ferociously, before he uttered them: "I cannot tell you."

Trevor frowned. "You mean, you don't know?"

"I mean I *cannot* tell you anything about it."

Trevor sat open-mouthed for three very long seconds. "Damn it, Uncle Richard, you are going to tell me where my own father's body is, and why it's there, or so help me, I'll—"

"Trev. Please. I can't tell you about how your father's body was ultimately handled because I don't know."

Trevor, who was half out of his seat, stopped. "You don't—?"

Downing looked away. "It was all arranged after his death. It wasn't his—or my—idea."

"Then whose idea was it?"

Might as well tell him. "The Dornaani."

"The—?" Trevor fell back in his seat. "What the— what the *fuck* do they want with Dad's body? And why the hell did you give it to them?"

"Trevor, I don't know what they want. But they—well, they seem to revere your father. And he wanted to be buried among the stars. And they made it clear that they would both see to that request, and also be—indebted—to us if we granted them the honor of doing so."

"So you traded away Dad's body for some alien goodwill? What are you, Richard, a fucking *monster*? He was your *friend*—your *closest* friend!"

Downing felt his eyes start to burn. "Yes, he was, Trevor. And this is what he'd have wanted. And you know it." Trevor's stare had gone from cold to arctic, and was dropping toward absolute zero. "Trev, please understand: I wanted to tell you about your father, but the President ordered it kept quiet."

Trevor's eyes did not change. His voice was emotionless. "Is there more on the day's agenda, sir, or are we done? Caine and I are due to report for our own debrief and then training."

Downing sighed. "Yes, we're done."

Trevor rose quickly; Caine took a moment longer. Downing made his way to the door, shook hands with Caine—who seemed, if not sympathetic, at least accepting—and then extended the same hand tentatively to Trevor. Who took it, but with even less warmth than Caine had.

"I'll miss you, Trev," Downing said lamely.

"Have a safe trip, sir."

Downing turned and tried to put Trevor's stony expression out of his mind.

And kept trying all the way to his ship.

Unsuccessfully.

ODYSSEUS

Caine and Trevor did not follow Downing back up into the subterranean hangar, but they had to pass through it on the way to their own debriefing. As they navigated the black-and-yellow-dashed safeways, they saw a familiar object amidst all the esoteric military hardware: a secure canister from the module they had inhabited during their time at the Convocation Station.

"What the hell is that doing here?" Trevor wondered aloud.

Caine considered its size, hermetic seals, and profuse marking labels: it was the container for the biological samples they had gathered at the party. It was also just large enough to be— "Maybe Alnduul is using it as his own personal Trojan Horse?"

Trevor turned to stare at the gray shipping module as it was loaded onto the same shuttle that Downing would soon board. "You mean, you think Alnduul's breaking the rules and going to Earth anyhow?"

"Somehow, I wouldn't be surprised."

As they watched the secure canister disappear into the shuttle's hold, Downing's spare, slump-shouldered silhouette appeared, moving steadily through the pre-boarding checkpoints.

Trevor became very quiet. "I guess I was pretty hard on Uncle Richard."

Caine knew to tread carefully. "Well, if you were, it's understandable. He dropped some pretty big family bombs back there."

"Yeah. Dropped a few on you, too."

Caine shrugged. "It's been a busy day."

Trevor's answering smile was a bit quizzical. "You know, Richard and I thought you'd make a fuss."

"About what?"

"About being impressed into service. He said you haven't exactly been an eager foot soldier for IRIS."

Caine shrugged. "When I'm hijacked or hoodwinked into service, I tend not to be happy about it. And it wasn't always clear that Richard's missions were, in fact, service to my country. More often, it seemed like they were serving his agenda. And although your uncle may have noble intentions, I don't equate his agenda with my country's needs."

"Fair enough. And I'm not sure I do, anymore, either." Trevor sighed. "But I have to hand it to him: he and Dad were right about the threats to us. God knows we got a nasty surprise at the Convocation."

Caine nodded. "Worse than nasty. After what happened there—well, now we're just living from one pivotal moment to the next."

"What do you mean?"

"I mean that we are on the crest of one of history's waves. Whatever happens next, it will change our lives—and our species—forever."

Trevor stared at him. "Huh. Sounds like you were already thinking about volunteering."

Caine nodded. "At a time like this, events trump individual wants, even needs. We just do what we have to do to protect those who depend on us."

Trevor nodded. "I remember reading about the Allies in World War Two; a lot of their soldiers felt that way, too."

"I think—I fear—there may be more than a few parallels, Trevor."

Who smiled down from his 6'2" height at his slightly shorter companion. "So, wordsmith, what's your advice for the times in which we live?"

"'Hope for peace, prepare for war.'"

"Whoa; now you're sounding like a career officer."

"Not my intent, I assure you. 'Going career' is a life choice. I'm just stepping forward to do my part."

"Well, career or not, you sure are starting to *sound* like a soldier." Trevor looked him up and down. "Now we just have to determine if you have what it takes to *be* a soldier."

Caine smiled. "Let's find out."

Appendix A

The Accords

1. The Accord is a democratic council comprised of politically equal member states. Membership is conferred through a process of mutual assessment and determination. Attendance at all Convocations of the Accord is mandatory; absences are treated as abstention and warrant the censure of the Accord. Accord policy and arbitration outcomes are determined by simple majority votes. However, changes in the accords themselves (additions, deletions, emendations) require unanimous approval (abstentions are construed as rejections). Issues addressed by the Accord include:

- accord policies and actions toward non-Accord powers, races, objects, or phenomena;

- interpretation and application of the accords;

- proper procedures for administering the Accord, including first contact, meeting, and communication protocols;

- reassessment and periodic alteration of the current pathways of allowed expansion for Accord member states.

2. A member state's membership in the Accord requires, and remains contingent upon, truthful self-representation in all disclosures of data or statements of intention: lies of omission or commission are expressly forbidden. If it is found that a member state misrepresented itself upon application for membership in the Accord, its membership is annulled.

3. One member state of the Accord is designated as the Custodian of the accords. The Custodians are charged with ensuring that all member states comply with the accords, that lack of compliance is corrected, and that disputes are resolved by arbitration commissions.

4. The Accord and its individual member states are expressly and absolutely forbidden from interfering in the internal affairs of any member state. The only exception to this is articulated in the Twenty-first Accord.

5. All entry into another member state's space must comply with territorial transit agreements negotiated between the member states in question. If no such agreements exist, a member state may declare any intrusion into its territory as illegal and may require the Accord to convene an arbitration commission to seek redress. The race designated as Custodians are excluded from these constraints when acting in their capacity *as* Custodians. However, they are expected and enjoined to use all possible restraint and to secure prior permission wherever and whenever possible.

6. No violence of any kind or on any scale is permitted between the races of the Accord.

7. No espionage is permitted between the races of the Accord, nor are other clandestine attempts to subvert or circumvent the autonomy, prerogatives, or secrecy constraints of another member state.

8. No agreement (legal or personal) made between individuals or collectives from two (or more) member states may ever explicitly or implicitly encumber or abridge the absolute indigenous autonomy of any of the parties to the agreement. Therefore, any member state (or inhabitant thereof) may terminate any agreement with any other member state (or inhabitant thereof) at any time for any reason, contractual obligations notwithstanding.

9. Disputes between member states and violations of these accords may only be resolved by a Custodian-appointed arbitration commission. Member states involved in a dispute may not serve on arbitration commissions convened after the commencement of their dispute until said dispute is resolved. All arbitration commissions are chaired by Custodians, and must follow the same determinative protocols as the Accord itself, as outlined in the First Accord.

10. Member states which are found to have violated an accord are instructed by the finding commission how to make amends for this violation. If the member state finds these instructions unacceptable, they may propose an alternate means of making amends, may request a reconsideration, or may

appeal for clemency or exoneration (if there are suitably extenuating circumstances).

11. Member states which flagrantly or willfully violate one or more accords forfeit their membership in the Accord. The same applies to member states which choose to ignore or reject the final determination of arbitration commissions. Former Accord member states may reapply for membership.

12. Members of the Accord must agree to restrict their use of interstellar-rated microwave and radio emissions to dire emergencies (such as distress calls, or in the event that all other communication systems have malfunctioned).

13. All Accord ships must be equipped with a transponder that, upon inquiry from any other Accord ship, will relay its member state of origin, its name or code, its master, and any special conditions under which it is operating.

14. All Accord ships must be furnished with multiple crewpersons who are conversant in the Code of Universal Signals and, if requested, must use this Code to initiate and respond to any and all communiqués.

15. All member states must maintain strict compliance with the Accord-prescribed pathways of allowed expansion. A single race may petition for a revision of its own expansion pathway: this is handled as an arbitration.

16. New races are contacted by the Accord *only* when they achieve routine interstellar travel, whether of a faster-than-light or slower-than-light variety.

17. The time and method of contacting a new race is determined by the Custodians of the Accord. Prior to contact, new races are designated as "protected races."

18. Monitoring of nonmember intelligent species is the responsibility of the Custodians. Routine supporting tasks may be assigned to one other member state that possesses sufficient technological and exploratory capabilities.

19. An outgoing Custodian member state selects the order in which member states are invited to succeed it. FTL travel is the prerequisite for Custodianship. The minimum duration of Custodianship is 24.6 Earth years. Minimum advance notice of resignation from Custodianship is 4.1 Earth years.

20. If no race is willing to accept Custodianship, the Accord is considered dissolved, as are all agreements previously made and enforced under its aegis.

21. Extraordinary circumstances: the Custodians are to intervene as soon as is practicable, and unilaterally if that is most expeditious, if:

- any member state's or protected race's homeworld is invaded or otherwise attacked;

- if any member state or protected race takes action that is deemed likely to result in the destruction of a planet's biosphere.

The Custodians may undertake this intervention without soliciting Accord consensus, and may, if necessary, violate other accords in order to ensure that the intervention is successful.

Appendix B

Worlds Permitted for Human Expansion by the Accord

Listed in ascending order of distance from Earth. Systems in **boldface** are those which humanity has occupied at the time of the Parthenon Dialogs. Those in *italics* are systems with "green" or "brown" worlds. The *70 Ophiuchi* system is omitted, since, although occupied by humans, it was not on the list of permitted worlds.

Proxima Centauri
Alpha Centauri
Barnard's Star
Wolf 359
Lalande 21185
Sirius
Luyten 726-8
Ross 154
Lacaille 9352
Ross 128
EZ Aquarii
Procyon
DX Cancri

Epsilon Indi
Tau Ceti
LHS 1565
YZ Ceti
Luyten's Star
Kapteyn's Star
Lacaille 8760
Ross 614
BD-12 4523
CD-25 10553
Wolf 424
Hipparcos 15689
Van Maanen's Star

Cincinnati
Hipparcos 72509
CD-46 11540
Ross 780
BD+44 2051
Groombridge 1618
Hipparcos 82725
CD-49 13515
CD-44 11909
Keid
AC+79 3888
Lalande 25372
Wolf 294
L 722-22
L 205-128

BD+01 4774
36 Ophiuchi
82 Eridani
HR 7703
Delta Pavonis
CD-45 13677
L 119-44
CD-34 11626
LHS 1070
BD+04 123
Beta Hydri
Rho Eridani
Zeta Tucanae
L 49-19
Gamma Pavonis

The following is an excerpt from:

CAULDRON OF GHOSTS

DAVID WEBER & ERIC FLINT

Available from Baen Books
April 2014
hardcover

CHAPTER 1

"So now what?" asked Yana Tretiakovna. She leaned back in her comfortable armchair, her arms crossed over her chest, and bestowed an impressive glower upon Anton Zilwicki and Victor Cachat. The first was perched on a seat as he scrutinized a comp screen; the other was slouched in an armchair and looking almost as disgruntled as Yana.

"I don't know," said Cachat, almost muttering the words. "I've been trying to get an answer to that very question from"—his finger pointed to the ceiling—"unnamable but no doubt exalted figures on high."

Taken literally, the gesture might have led to the conclusion that the hard-bitten atheist Victor Cachat had suddenly become a believer, since there was nothing beyond the ceiling other than the heavens. The large suite the three people were sharing was on the top floor of a former luxury hotel in Haven's capital that had been been sequestered for its own purposes decades earlier by the Legislaturalist secret police. After the revolution—the most recent one, that is—the new regime had tried but failed to find the rightful owners, since they'd all died or vanished. So, not knowing what else to do, they'd turned it into a combination safe house and luxury resort for guests of the government.

Clearly, though, Cachat was oblivious to the irony involved. Still half-muttering with disgust, he went on. "So far, I might as well have been putting the question to a streetlight. Except a lamp post would at least shed some light."

Anton's mouth quirked wryly. "I'm pretty sure the question you should be asking is 'where,' not 'what.'" He pointed to something on the screen. "See that?"

Ennui was shoved aside by interest, as Victor and Yana both rose from their chairs and came over to look at the screen.

"And what the hell is *that*?" demanded Tretiakovna. "It looks like scrambled eggs on steroids."

"It's an astrogational display showing traffic to and from the planet," said Cachat. "And that exhausts my knowledge of the matter. I can't really interpret it."

Yana stared at the screen again. The ex-Scrag looked rather alarmed.

"Do you mean to tell me that this is

how orbital controllers guide spacecraft to a supposedly—ha, ha, I'm dying of laughter here—safe orbit or landing? If so, I'm never flying again. Not even a kite."

"Relax, Yana," said Anton. "They don't use this sort of condensed display at all—leaving aside the fact that all orbital routes are selected and monitored by computers. No, I slapped this together just to see if my guess was right, which is that traffic is being shifted around to allow for some sudden and unscheduled departures."

He pointed to . . . this and that and the other, all of which looked like nothing much of anything to his two companions. "Think of these as boltholes, if you will."

Victor and Yana looked at each other, then down at Anton.

"So who's bolting?" asked Yana.

Zilwicki heaved his massive shoulders. For someone built along normal human rather than dwarf lord lines, that would have been a shrug.

"How should I know?" he said. "Victor will have to find out from his unnamable but no doubt exalted figures on high."

Yana said something in a Slavic-sounding language that was almost certainly unprintable. Victor, a bit of a prude when it came to coarse language, kept his response to: "Well, hell." And a second or two later: "Hell's bells."

❖   ❖   ❖

Luckily for the dispositions of Cachat and Tretiakovna, relief from uncertainty came a few minutes later, in the persons of Kevin Usher and Wilhelm Trajan. Usher was the head of the Federal Investigation Agency, Haven's top domestic police force; Trajan, the head of the Republic's foreign intelligence agency, the Federal Intelligence Service.

Yana let them into the room, in response to the buzzer. As soon as they entered, Cachat rose to his feet.

"Kevin," he said, in a neutral tone. Then, nodding to Trajan: "Boss."

"Not anymore," said Wilhelm. He glanced around, spotted an empty chair, and slid into it. Once seated, he molded himself into the chair's contours, as someone does who is finally able to relax after a long period of tension.

"You're being reassigned to the foreign office," he elaborated. "No longer part of the FIS."

He did not seem dismayed at losing the services of the man whom knowledgeable people, including himself, thought to be Haven's most brilliantly capable intelligence agent. When President Pritchard had notified him of her decision to transfer Cachat, Wilhelm's reaction had been: *You mean I can go back to running a spy outfit, instead of being a lion tamer?*

Usher took a seat some distance away from

Trajan. "It's one hell of a promotion, Victor. If you, ah, look at it in the right light."

Victor gave him a dark look. "Under very dim lighting, you mean."

Kevin's expression, in response, was exasperated. "Oh, for God's sake, Victor! No, I don't mean using night goggles. I mean bright—really, really, really bright—floodlights. Your days of creeping around in the shadows are over. *Over*— with a bang and a boom. O-V-E-R."

Trajan's tone was milder. "Be realistic, Victor. Your exploits in launching Torch almost blew your cover completely as it was. They left it pretty tattered. Now, after Mesa? You— and Anton, and Yana"—he nodded in their direction—"just brought back the biggest intelligence coup in galactic history for . . . oh, hell, who knows how many centuries? Do you really think there's any chance you can stay in your old line of work? Even using nanotech facial and body transformations won't help you, since they don't disguise DNA. Sure, that'd probably be enough for a modest, barely-known sort of spy. But you? Anybody who thinks you might be coming their way will have DNA swabs taken of anybody who might *remotely* be you."

"StateSec destroyed all my DNA records except theirs the day I graduated from the Academy," said Victor. "Those are still closely guarded and I've been very careful not to scatter my DNA traces about." His tone of voice was perhaps a bit peevish.

"True enough," said Anton. "You won't find Special Office Cachat carelessly discarding a cup after he's taken a drink from it, I will grant you that. But come on, Victor—you know the realities perfectly well. As long as you were obscure and nobody was *looking* for your DNA, those precautions were probably good enough. But *today?*"

"Exactly," said Trajan. He nodded toward the window overlooking Nouveau Paris. "Word's already leaked out to the press. Within a couple of days—a week, at the outside—your name and likeness will be known to every person on Haven above the age of five and with any interest at all in the news. As well as—more to the point—every intelligence service in the galaxy, each and every one of which will be trying to get their hands on your DNA traces. Sooner or later, at least some of them are bound to succeed. So give it up. And don't bother arguing with me or Kevin about it, either. President Pritchart made the decision. If you want it overturned, you'll have to figure out a way to get her out of office."

Usher wiped his face with a large hand. "Wilhelm, he gets enough ideas on his own without you making suggestions.

Trajan looked startled. "What? I wasn't—" Then, looked alarmed. "Officer Cachat..."

"I wasn't planning to organize a coup d'état," Victor said sarcastically. "I *am* a patriot, you know. Besides, I don't blame the president for the decision."

The dark look came back. "Clearly, she was misled by evil advisers."

Anton started laughing softly. "Ganny warned you, Victor. It'll be your turn now for the video treatment! I'd have some sympathy except I don't recall you ever showing any for me because *my* cover got blown."

Zilwicki looked over at Tretiakovna. "What's your guess, Yana? Ganny thought the news services would go for either 'Cachat, Slaver's Bane' or 'Black Victor.'"

"'Black Victor,'" she replied instantly. "Give Cachat his due, he isn't prone to histrionics. 'Slaver's Bane' is just too...too...not Victor. Besides, look at him."

Cachat's expression was now very dark indeed.

"'Black Victor,' it is," announced Zilwicki. "Victor, you need to buy some new clothes. All leather, neck to ankles. Black leather, it goes without saying."

For a moment, it looked as if Cachat might explode. At the very least, spout some heavy duty profanity. But...

He didn't. Anton wasn't surprised. Victor's deeds were so flamboyant that it was easy to forget that the man behind them was not flamboyant at all. In fact, he was rather modest—and extraordinarily self-disciplined.

So, all that finally came out, in a very even and flat tone of voice, was: "Where am I being assigned, then? I'll warn you, if it's someplace that has an active cocktail circuit, I won't be any good at it. I don't drink much. Ever."

"S'true," said Yana. "He's boring, boring, boring. Well, except when he's overturning regimes and stuff like that." She actually giggled, something Anton had never heard her do before. "Cocktail circuit! Diplomatic small talk! I can see it already!"

Victor now looked long-suffering. For his part, Usher looked exasperated again.

"We are not morons," he said. "Victor, you... and you and you"—his forefinger swiveled like a turret gun, coming to bear on Anton and Yana—"are all going to Manticore. Tomorrow, so get packed."

Anton had been planning to get to Manticore anyway, and as soon as possible. He hadn't seen his lover Cathy Montaigne in more than a year. He hadn't yet come up with a way to do so that the many and manifold powers-that-be were likely to approve, though, and now it had been unexpectedly dropped in his lap.

He saw Victor glance at him and smile. There was real warmth in that smile, too, something you didn't often get from the man. Not for the first time, Anton was struck by the unlikely friendship that had grown up between himself and the Havenite agent. Unlikely—yet all the stronger, perhaps, because of that very fact.

There were people in the world whom Anton liked more than he did Victor. But there were very, very few whom he trusted as much.

"And in what capacity am I going?" he asked Usher. "Somehow, even with all this newfound cordiality, I doubt that I've been assigned to Haven's foreign service."

Usher gave him a grin. "By all accounts—I was on Old Earth, remember, when the Manpower Incident went down—no star system in its right mind would assign you to its diplomatic corps."

"Yes, I remember."

It was hardly something Anton would forget. Nothing official had ever been said, and to this day Victor refused to cross any t's or dot any i's. Nonetheless, Anton was quite certain that Kevin Usher had engineered the entire episode. He'd stayed in the background, letting Cachat and the Audubon Ballroom do the rough work, but his had been the guiding hand.

Zilwicki's daughter Helen—no, all three of his children, since he'd adopted Berry and Lars afterward—were still alive because of Victor and Kevin. It was a reminder, if he needed one, that just because he didn't share someone's ideology didn't mean they didn't take it seriously themselves. Haven's political ideals were not Anton's—well, some of them were—but it had been those ideals that had shielded his family.

Suddenly, he was in a very good mood. The information he and Victor had brought back from Mesa had not only ended the galaxy's longest and most savagely fought war, it had turned two bitter enemies into allies. Uneasy and hesitant allies, perhaps, but allies nonetheless. That information had also turned a friendship right side up. All the wariness and reservations he'd had to maintain about Victor Cachat were now draining away. Rapidly, too.

Something in Victor's expression made it clear that he understood that also. But all he said was: "True enough. I may be a problem child for the diplomatically-inclined, but Anton gives them nightmares."

"You still haven't answered my question, Kevin," said Anton.

Usher shrugged. "How the hell should I know? All I was told by Eloise was to round up all three of you—and Herlander Simões, of course—and take you to Manticore. Victor, you're not exactly reassigned to the foreign service." He gave Trajan a reproving glance. "Wilhelm was overstating things a bit. For one thing, Leslie Montreau was in the room along with Tom Theisman when Eloise made the decision to yank you out of the FIS. She nodded quite vigorously when Tom said that maybe she didn't want—his words, not mine—'that lunatic bull in a china shop' in her department."

"What's a china shop?" asked Yana.

"It's an antique phrase," Anton explained. "'China' was a name for a fancy kind of what they called... porcelain, if I remember right."

"Lot of help that is. So what's porcelain?"

"Stuff that Victor could turn into splinters easily."

"Lot of help that is too. Victor can turn almost anything into splinters."

Victor waved them down impatiently. "So to whom *am* I assigned, then?"

Usher scratched his scalp. "Well... no one, really. Eloise just thinks having you on Manticore will be essential to firming up the new alliance."

"Why? Anton knows as much as I do—and he's Manticoran to begin with."

Usher was starting to look exasperated again. Zilwicki interjected himself into the discussion.

"That's sort of the whole point, Victor. I'm a known quantity, in the Star Kingdom. I've even had a personal audience with the empress. You, on the other hand, are a complete *un*known. Well, almost. I think Duchess Harrington has a good sense of you. But no one else does, in Manticore."

Cachat was staring at him, obviously in complete incomprehension. It was odd, the way such a supremely capable man could be so oblivious to his own stature. That was a feature of Victor that Anton found simultaneously attractive and rather scary. In the right (or wrong) circumstances, people with little in the way of egos—more precisely, little concern for their egos—could do...

Pretty much anything.

"Just take my word for it, will you? They'll want to see you, and talk to you, before they'll settle down with any information you bring to them."

"What he said." Usher rose from his chair. "Oh-seven-hundred, tomorrow morning. Be down in the lobby, packed and ready to go."

Trajan rose also, and went to the door. "Have a nice trip," was what he said. What he meant, of course, was "have a nice *long* trip." And there seemed to be a little spring in his step, as if a great weight had finally been lifted from his shoulders.

—end excerpt—

from *Cauldron of Ghosts*
available in hardcover,
April 2014, from Baen Books